WATCHER
OF THE DEAD

The eastern sky was beginning to lighten when he heard a second-story door swing shut. Heavy, measured footfalls sounded as someone descended the stairs. It was her, the woman. You could hear her age in the hesitation between steps. When she reached the ground floor, thick rugs muffled her movements. Minutes passed. No lamps were lit. Tin chinked against tin. Footsteps clacked against tile. A series of bolts retorted in quick succession—*Chunk. Chunk. Chunk*—and the rear door juddered into motion.

The watcher waited until he saw the woman's booted foot alight on the top step before launching himself forward. Free hand clamping the woman's forearm, he snapped the arm back and up, forcing it into a breakable V behind her back. His knife hand went straight for the throat.

"Scream and you will die," he murmured, aligning a foot of razor steel along the turkey skin that formed her jawline.

BY J. V. JONES

WATCHER
OF THE DEAD

Book Four of Sword of Shadows

J. V. Jones

www.orbitbooks.net

ORBIT

First published in Great Britain in 2010 by Orbit
This paperback edition published in 2011 by Orbit
Reprinted 2011

A CIP catalogue record for this book
is available from the British Library.

ISBN 978-1-84149-221-6

Typeset in Electra by M Rules
Printed and bound in Great Britain by
Clays Ltd, St Ives plc

Orbit
An imprint of
Little, Brown Book Group
100 Victoria Embankment
London EC4Y 0DY

An Hachette UK Company
www.hachette.co.uk

www.orbitbooks.net

To Jim Frenkel,
Who makes the books better

ACKNOWLEDGEMENTS

My thanks to Alan Rubsam, the good people at Tor who turned this manuscript into a book, cover and all, and to Paul for keeping the home fires burning.

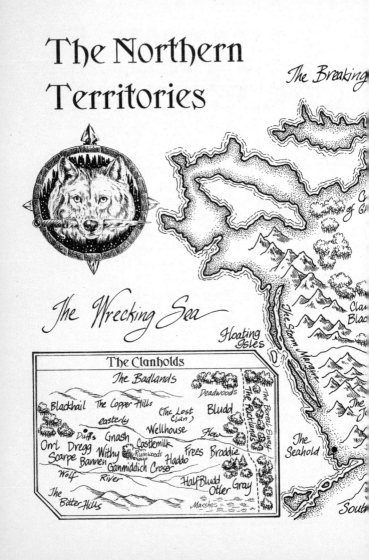

The Northern Territories

The Breaking

The Wrecking Sea

Floating Isles

The Storm Margin

The Boreal Sway

The Rucklands

Heart Fell
of G

Clan
Blac

Clan

The J

The Seahold

Sou

The Clanholds

The Badlands

Deadwoods

Blackhail   The Copper Hills   (The Lost Clan)   Bludd

easterly

Duffs   Gnash   Wellhouse   Flow

Orrl   Dregg   Castlemilk   Frees   Broddie

Scarpe   Withy   Ruinwoods   Haddo

Bannen   Ganmiddich   Croser

Wolf   River   HalfBludd   Gray

Otter

The Bitter Hills   Marshes

CONTENTS

The Story So Far

When he was seventeen, Raif Sevrance of Clan Blackhail developed the ability to heart-kill game. One morning while he was hunting in the Badlands with his brother Drey, his father and chief were slain back at camp. When he and his brother returned to Blackhail they found that Mace Blackhail, the chief's foster son, had declared himself head of the clan. Mace blamed the murders on Vaylo Bludd, chief of a rival clan. When Bludd sacked the Dhoonehouse of rival clan Dhoone a week later, Mace's story of Bludd aggression gained credibility. Raif found himself isolated. He alone believed that Mace Blackhail was a liar and a chief-killer.

War against clan Bludd followed, as Hailsmen sought to avenge their chief's death. When Mace received word that a caravan of Bluddsmen were on the road, heading west to occupy the Dhoonehouse, he ordered an attack. Raif rode with the ambush party. When he discovered the caravan contained women and children, not warriors, he refused to participate in the slaughter. For disobeying an order on the field and deserting his fellow clansmen in battle, Raif was branded a traitor to his clan. Four days later, Raif left Blackhail in the company of his uncle Angus Lok. His oath to protect Blackhail was now broken, even while he had sought to act with faith and loyalty.

The two men headed south. Upon arrival at Duff's stovehouse, they learned news of the massacre on the Bluddroad had preceded them. When challenged by a group of Bludd warriors, Raif admitted to being present during the slaughter. He told no one that he took no part in the massacre; loyalty to his clan prevented him from defending himself at their expense. With this admission, however, Raif forever damned himself in the eyes of Bluddsmen. He was the only Hailsmen they knew for a certainty who was present during the slaughter.

When Angus and Raif arrived at the city Spire Vanis they rescued a young woman named Ash March who was being hunted down by the city's Protector General, Marafice Eye. Angus had a strong reaction when he saw the girl and immediately put himself in danger to save her. Raif's skill with a bow proved invaluable. He single-handedly rescued the girl by shooting arrows through her pursuers' hearts.

As Raif, Ash and Angus headed north to the city of Ille Glaive, Raif learned that Ash was the foster daughter of the Surlord of Spire Vanis. She had run away when she learned that her foster father intended to imprison her in the city's citadel, the Inverted Spire. Heritas Cant, a friend of Angus Lok's, provided the explanation for the Surlord's behavior. Cant told Ash she was the first Reach to be born in a thousand years. She alone possessed the ability to unlock the Blind, the prison without a key that contained the destructive might of the immortal Endlords. Cant warned Ash she must discharge her Reach-power or die.

Raif and Angus agreed to accompany Ash to the Cavern of Black Ice, the one place where she could discharge her power without tearing a hole in the Blindwall that holds back the Endlords. As soon as their small party reentered the clanholds they were captured by Bluddsmen. The Bludd chief had lost seventeen grandchildren on the Bluddroad, and he was determined to make Raif Sevrance pay for those losses. After days of torture, Raif developed a fever and began to fail. Yet when Death came to take him she changed her mind. "Perhaps I won't take you yet," she told him. "You fight in my image and live in my shadow, and if I leave you where you are you'll provide much fresh meat for my children. Kill an army for me, Raif Sevrance. Any less and I just might call you back."

The next day Raif was saved by a group of Hailish warriors led by his brother Drey. "We part here. For always," Drey said as he let his younger brother, the traitor, slip away.

Later that day Raif met up with Ash, who had escaped from Marafice Eye by using her Reach-power. The Dog Lord had handed her over to Eye in repayment for a debt. Penthero Iss, the Surlord of Spire Vanis, had aided Vaylo's taking of the Dhoonehouse, and Vaylo had come to regret Iss' sorcerous help. Ash March was payment in full.

Ash's health deteriorated during the journey to the cavern. When she collapsed in the snow, Raif drew a guide circle and called on the Stone Gods for help. Two members of the ancient Sull people, Far Riders named Mal Naysayer and Ark Veinsplitter, heard this call, and rode to Ash's aid. Upon seeing her, they suspected that Ash was the Reach. They also suspected that Raif was *Mor Drakka*, Watcher of the Dead; the one predicted to destroy the Sull.

The Far Riders took Ash and Raif to a frozen river that led

to the Cavern of Black Ice and then departed. Ash discharged her power, but it was already too late. By blasting Marafice Eye's men in the Bitter Hills, she had caused a rent in the Blindwall. Back in her home city of Spire Vanis, a nameless sorcerer who had been enslaved by her foster father was already working to open the breach. "Push and we will give you your name," the Endlords promised him. Bound by chains, broken and tortured, the sorcerer accepted the deal. "Baralis," the Endlords named the sorcerer as he broke open the wall.

Meanwhile the clan wars were escalating. Blackhail waged war on Bludd to avenge the killing of the Hail chief; Bludd fought Blackhail for the slaying of its women and children; and Dhoone, dispossessed of its roundhouse by Bludd, fought to regain its territory. With the help of his half-brother Bram, Robbie Dun Dhoone claimed the Dhoone chiefship and retook Dhoone from the Dog Lord. Due to the desertion of his second son, Pengo, the Dog Lord had been holding the Dhoonehouse with a skeleton force. He, his remaining two grandchildren and his lady Nan escaped and headed north toward an old hillfort where his fostered son, Cluff Drybannock, was stationed with two hundred men.

In order to secure sufficient manpower to retake Dhoone, Robbie sold his brother to the Milk chief, Wrayan Castlemilk, forcing Bram to leave his clan. Bram was made welcome at Castlemilk, but his taste for intrigue—acquired in negotiations with Skinner Dhoone and the Dog Lord—made him break his oath and join the Phage, a shadowy brotherhood that aimed to defend the world against the Endlords.

Blackhail took possession of Ganmiddich, but lost it when an army led by Marafice Eye broke the Crab Gate that protected it. When news of Penthero Iss' death reached the battlefield, half of Eye's forces fled the field to rush back to Spire Vanis and vie for power, leaving Eye at the mercy of a newly-arrived army led by Pengo Bludd. Bludd took Ganmiddich. Marafice Eye led his injured army—plus four hostages taken from Blackhail—home to Spire Vanis where his father-in-law Roland Stornoway was holding power on his behalf. With Stornoway's support, Eye became surlord.

Back at Blackhail, the slain chief's widow, Raina Blackhail, struggled to come to terms with her new life. Like Raif, she suspected that Mace, her foster son, was responsible for her husband's murder, and she did not support his chiefship. After her husband's murder, Mace raped her in the Oldwood and then told clansmen it was consensual. Raina married him rather than risk her reputation and status, becoming chief's wife for the second time. While Mace was away at war with Bludd and Dhoone, Raina quietly began to claim power. When Stannig Beade arrived from Scarpe to replace Blackhail's guide who had been killed in the explosion of the Hailstone, Raina suspected he had been sent to watch her. Tension ran high as Beade began acting as chief. When Anwyn Bird, Raina's oldest friend, was assassinated in cold blood it was the final straw. Guessing that Anwyn had been murdered to silence dissension, and fearing for her own life, Raina Blackhail did the only thing she could to protect her clan. She entered the chief's chamber one night and killed Stannig Beade.

After departing Blackhail, Angus Lok returned to his home east of Ille Glaive. Upon arrival he found his worst nightmare had come to life: His house had been burned down. His three daughters and his wife were gone. Dead. Angus was a ranger, a member of the Phage. He blamed himself for leading evil to his door.

Ash and Raif, once they left the Cavern of Black Ice, headed north into Ice Trapper territory. Ash left Raif while he slept, departing in the company of Mal Naysayer and Ark Veinsplitter. She chose to have her blood drained, a ritual cleansing that would allow her to become Sull. When she and the Far Riders were attacked by Unmade forces at Floating Bridge, Veinsplitter was killed and Ash became separated from the Naysayer. As she traveled alone in Sull territory she met a stranger named Lan Fallstar who told her he would take her to the Heart of the Sull. They became lovers, but he betrayed her, leading her into a trap. Knowing that she was a Reach, Fallstar wanted only to harness the power of her body to kill the Unmade. The Naysayer found Ash just in time to save her from Fallstar's assassins, and together they headed south to the Heart of the Sull.

Raif joined the Maimed Men, an outlaw clan who lived in the cliffs above the Rift—the deep cleft in the earth's crust through which the Unmade sometimes escaped to attack mortal men. Traggis Mole, the leader of the Maimed Men, sent Raif to raid Blackhail as a test of Raif's loyalty to the Maimed Men. As the raid party left the mine known as Black Hole, Raif was challenged by his old friend and clansmen Bitty Shank. Raif killed Bitty to escape, and then fled into the Great Want, the waste at the center of the continent. He was lost for a time.

Meanwhile, Effie Sevrance, Raif's nine-year-old sister, had been forced to leave her clan. Effie had been born to the stone lore and was able to tell when bad things were about to happen. She was an unwitting witness when Raina was raped by Mace, and Raina feared this knowledge made Effie vulnerable. Seeking to remove the girl from Mace's sights, Raina sent Effie to Clan Dregg. Effie never made it. She was kidnapped by boatmen from cursed Clan Gray. On the journey to Clan Gray she met Chedd Limehouse, who had also been kidnapped, and fell into the Wolf River, where a pike snapped the stone lore from around her throat.

Raif was found in the Great Want by the lamb brothers, who were there searching for the souls of their undead. They told Raif about a battle thousands of years earlier where their people and many others had died. One warrior had turned the course of the battle, a man known only as Raven Lord, who wielded the sword named Loss. Legend held that after the battle, the field was flooded and all the dead, including Raven Lord, were frozen beneath the ice. When Traggis Mole was attacked by Unmade and lay dying, he forced Raif to speak an oath to protect the Maimed Men. Soon after, Raif left the Rift to search for the frozen battlefield and the sword. Strikes by the Unmade were becoming more frequent and powerful and there were some creatures in the Blind that could only be slain by the Raven Lord's sword.

Raif found the sword, and a moment later an old injury to his chest stopped his heart. His old friend, Addie Gunn, and the lamb brothers saved him. He awoke several days later to find himself in possession of the sword named Loss.

White Bear

Even though the temperature had not risen above freezing in nine months, the bear carcass was not frozen. When Sadaluk, the Listener of the Ice Trappers, poked it with the narwhal tusk he used as a walking stick, the flesh rippled beneath the coarse white pelt. It was a full-grown male, past its prime, with battle scars denting its snout and a ragged strip of cartilage in place of its left ear. *Dead for at least thirty days*, Sadaluk decided, squatting by the creature's head. The eyes and soft tissue around the muzzle had mummified in the dry air, and drift snow had compacted in the Y of its splayed rear legs.

You did not need to be a listener to know it for an ill omen.

It was Nolo who had found the bear. Nolo's dogs had sniffed out the carcass—most unluckily for Nolo as they were leashed to his sled at the time. In their excitement, the dogs capsized the sled and scattered Nolo's load of willow cords and blocks of frozen whale oil. Nolo was thrown from the runner, landing hard on the river ice. By the time he got to his feet, the dogs and the empty sled had reached the carcass a quarter league downstream. Straightaway Nolo knew something was wrong. Hungry dogs didn't stand three feet away from a potential meal and howl like half-crazed wolves. Hungry dogs ate. Nolo was young and still distracted by the pleasures of his new wife, but even he knew that.

Glancing at the rising sun, Sadaluk drew himself upright. His elbow joints creaked—a recent development that both bothered and delighted him. Age was his stock-in-trade, and it did not hurt a listener to have a body that snapped as it moved. Reminding the young of their youth was one of his tasks. Still, it did not mean that he liked lying within his sleeping skins every morning, waiting for his body to start acting like something that might actually take his weight.

Sadaluk drilled his stick into the snow, cleaning. Behind him he was aware that Nolo and the other five hunters were waiting for him to speak. As was proper, they stood in a half circle facing into the sun. All knew better than to cast a shadow on a dead bear.

When he was ready Sadaluk turned to look at them. The river's slipstream riffled their caribou pelts and auk feathers, and blew their exhaled breath against their faces. All were winter-lean and strong-bodied. Kill notches on their spears told of varying degrees of bravery and luck. Nolo was the youngest, but none of the six were over thirty. Their faces were still, but Sadaluk could see through the holes in their eyes to the fear that slid between their thoughts.

"Nolo. Retrieve your dog whip." Sadaluk pointed to the strip of salt-cured sealskin that lay curled in the hackled ice at the river shore. It had been left behind yesterday in the excitement of finding the bear.

Crouching to control the length of his shadow, Nolo shuffled upriver. For some reason he was wearing his formal dance coat, sewn from thin late-summer hides. Sadaluk could see the tooth marks around the cuffs where Nolo's wife had chewed the hide into softness. As the young hunter knelt to retrieve the dog whip, the Listener addressed the remaining five men.

With a backward flick of his stick, he said, "I name this bear Saddlebag. He was delivered by the gods. Inside him lies a message. Shura. Puncture the hide."

The Listener glared at the hunters. The bear scared them, and that meant he, Sadaluk, had to scare them more. When Shura hesitated to do his bidding, the Listener spider-jumped toward him. It was a small trick, and doubtless all gathered on the river this day had seen it before, yet five grown men stepped back in astonishment and fear. *Old man, eh?* Sadaluk thought with a small nod of satisfaction. *Old and bold. Sneaky and creaky.*

Scared and unprepared.

But he could not let them know it.

"Prick the belly," he commanded.

The morning sun washed the river channel with silver light. Snow, sucked dry of moisture by half a year of glacial winds, drifted in the air like goosedown. The village lay three hours by dogsled to the west. To the east loomed the towering mountains that clansmen named the Coastal Ranges, but Ice Trappers called by their real name, the Steps to God. Underfoot, the river ice was frozen to a depth of five feet. Water flowed darkly beneath the surface, fed by deep and unknowable springs. Tracks scored lightly into the surface ice told of dozens of journeys to and from the village. Winter was long, and sometimes a man or woman simply loaded a sled, harnessed their dogs, and took off. Sometimes the sledders never came back . . . but Sadaluk would not think about that now.

His thoughts must be with the bear.

Shura Broken Nose was the hunter with the most respect in the village. The kill notches on his spear stretched from the seal gut bindings that held the obsidian point in its socket all the way down to the bear foot grip. Normally at this time of year Shura and the other men would be out on the sea ice, hunting seal. Hunting had been bad this year, though, and the sea ice had formed early and grown as wide as a new country: the Land of Missing Seals.

Leveling the spear at shoulder height, Shura sprang toward the bear. Hoops of bone and mica charms suspended from the hem of his coat chinked like shells. One of the four remaining hunters inhaled sharply. Mananu, the eldest, pressed his thumb pads into his eyelids, sealing them closed in prayer. The spear shot forward. Air thucked as the point punctured the hide.

A sickening squelch was followed by the hiss of escaping gas. As Shura yanked back the spear, black liquid fountained from the wound. It stank like gangrene and fuel. Someone gagged. All save Sadaluk stepped back. Downriver, Nolo loosened his grip on the dog whip, letting the hard black leather spool onto the ice.

"Mananu," commanded the Listener. "Give me your horn cup."

The bear carcass deflated as Mananu raked beneath his caribou skins, locating his treasured drinking cup. Gusting wind failed to blow away the stench. Sadaluk imagined that if a man were to strike a flame at this moment the entire river trench would ignite. He watched as the black fluid rolled down matted fur and onto the river. It was steaming faintly, melting the top ice as it moved.

Mananu pulled out the fist-sized cup and handed it to the Listener without looking him in the eye. Age had yellowed the horn. Mananu's grandfather, Tunnu Fat Man, had spent three days belly-down on the sea ice, pushing himself forward with his toes to get close enough to slay the great tusked walrus whose horn the cup was carved from. King Walrus was the creature's name. It weighed over two tons and provided enough meat and blubber to feed the village during the last and hardest month of winter. The tusks were four feet long. As was fitting they were Tunnu's to claim and own. Tunnu had offered the right tusk to the Ice God, and a week later the sea ice had begun to break. The second tusk, the left one, he kept for himself. The cup in Sadaluk's hand was carved from its diamond-hard base.

Closing bare fingers around the horn, Sadaluk approached the carcass. He was a listener, and that meant he stayed still while others moved. You can hear what others cannot only when you make no noise yourself. Mostly he listened to his dreams as they whispered of the future and the past and the invisible fibers that bound both states into one. But on days like this he listened for the heartbeat of the being that created the world.

The Ice Trappers had many gods—gods of ice and sky, sea and seals, fire and rain, smoke and flies. They held power in their jurisdictions, but nowhere else. One force beyond the realm of nature held power in all states and territories. This force had birthed the gods. Whether it was a god itself or something else was a question Sadaluk had no time for. He was a man, and therefore unfit to probe the mysteries of creation.

He could, however, hear them.

Kneeling by the bear's sleek white head, Sadaluk let the sounds of the river drift from his mind. The squeak of ice beneath the hunters' boots, the tinkle of charms, and the shuss of the wind faded. All grew quiet. Black liquid trickled from the wound. This close, Sadaluk could smell its true nature.

Drink.

The Listener of the Ice Trappers leaned forward and pressed the cup into the bear's coarse underfur, just below the wound. With his free hand he massaged the belly. Liquid flowed. Oily green streaks flashed on its surface as it rolled into the cup. A gobbet of soft black blood plopped into the tusk, splashing Sadaluk's hand. The substance was warm. It tingled as its fluids evaporated.

It was alcohol, but it was not pure. The bear had died a month earlier, from what—starvation, disease, old age—Sadaluk did not know. Nothing had attacked it. Beneath its fur the black hide was intact. It had died whole; its torso sealed. Dense fur had insulated the internal organs from the cold, and soft tissue had not frozen. Heart muscle, kidney fat, lung tissue, sinew, offal, gristle had liquefied. And then fermented. It started in the stomach, in the curdled mix of bile and partially digested food that was known as chyme. Acids continued working after death, releasing heat. Usually the heat dissipated—most carcasses were too small or their pelts too thin to retain heat—but occasionally with caribou and white bears, the heat did not escape. It built.

Sadaluk had come across only two such carcasses before. The first was when he was apprenticed to Lootavek, the one who had listened before him. Lootavek had ordered hunters to drag the bloated caribou carcass onto the sea ice and thrust it through a seal hole. That way the two most powerful gods—the gods of ice and sea—might annul the bad omen. All, including Sadaluk, agreed the strategy worked, for a week later the tribe's second best hunter died after stepping on grease ice that was masquerading as shorefast ice with a covering of new snow. To lose one man, however valuable, to such an ill omen meant the tribe had escaped lightly.

The outcome with the second carcass had been less fortunate.

Two children had stumbled upon a dead she-bear while out sledding in the frost slags south of the Whale Gate. Just as today, when he had been roused in the dark hour before dawn, Sadaluk had been summoned to view the carcass. Unlike today, he had been young and untested, and still in possession of two fine earlobes. Lootavek had died the previous summer, and Sadaluk had been anxious not to make any mistakes.

So of course he had gone right ahead and made some. He had not listened, that was the thing. When faced with the dead bear—the mummified head and soft, bloated torso—he had let the sound of his own fear drown out any message from the gods. Foolishly, he had supposed that because Lootavek's solution had worked so well that the best course would be to duplicate his plan. Sadaluk too had ordered hunters to haul the bear onto the ice. And then stood by and watched as the seal hole was enlarged with picks. Only when the hunters began to wedge the carcass through the opening did the Listener feel his first thrill of apprehension.

The hunters had been lazy and the hole was barely wide enough to take the bear. Pressure had to be exerted. One of the men clamped his big meaty hand on the bear's snout and shoved down with all his might. Something tore. The hide split open like an overripe fruit and black oily liquid sprayed the hunters.

Sadaluk never forgot the smell. Forty-two years later and it still stank the same. If a god rotted it would give off fuel. And that fuel would smell like this.

"Nolo," the Listener snapped, adressing the young hunter who was still frozen in place upriver. "Close your mouth and use your feet. Join your brothers."

As Nolo tucked the dog whip into his belt and started down the ice, the Listener used his stick to lever himself to standing. Tremors passed through the liquid in the cup as he rose. Forty-two years ago he had made a mistake. *Drink*, the gods had whispered, and in the arrogance of youth he assumed he had misheard them.

A death occurred in the family of every man who came in contact with the black liquid that day. Not just the men who were sprayed, but those who stepped on the oil slick later and stamped black footprints around the hole. The deaths occurred over a single season. Newborns did not take the teat. Scrapes and knife nicks grew gangrene. Grandmothers hacked up blood. Hunters ran out of luck on treacherous spring ice. Seventeen died in all, and the Listener accepted responsibility for every one of them. The Ice Trappers had not blamed him. People who lived on the edge of the world, in a land that lay frozen for three out of four seasons, were not accustomed to laying blame. The expectation of death was always present. Trust had been lost, though. Enthusiasm for his ceremonies waned. Journeys were undertaken in spite of his warnings. Hunters went out on the sea ice without his talismans. When strangers appeared at the Whale Gate they were not automatically escorted into the Listener's presence for questioning.

Trust had eventually been regained, but Sadaluk did not fool himself over the reason for it. The accepted way of regaining trust with an Ice Trapper was to outlive him. Sadaluk No Ears had excelled at that. All the hunters who had helped haul the bear to the seal hole were now dead. Many of their sons and daughters were also dead. To those still living, the story of the bear had lost its sting. Sadaluk's youth had been emphasized. The dangers of not following the guidance of gods had been lost.

None of the hunters gathered here today had been alive back then. As Sadaluk raised the horn to his lips, he looked from man to man. Some were stoic, some wary, some afraid. Trust was the common thread, steadying each of them on the ice. The worst kind of luck lay on the frozen river at their feet, but their wise and crazy Listener would take care of it for them.

Fools, Sadaluk wanted to cry out. *Do you think I have the might to stop the world from ending?*

The Listener glanced at the bear. Its small eyes were sealed closed. *They used you*, he told it silently.

Just like they'll use me.

Sadaluk pushed the walrus cup against his lower lip and did not breathe. When he was ready he exhaled . . . and then inhaled. Fumes sucked up his nostrils by the contraction of his diaphragm entered his brain. It was as if a giant squid had injected him with ink. The blackness was instant. Dizzying. It killed all information entering his brain from his eyes. He had been prepared for something . . . but how could you prepare for a visitation from the gods?

Drink.

Opening his mouth, the Listener tilted the cup. As the liquid hit his tongue he had a sense that everything was tilting—his body, the river ice, the world as he knew it—sliding out of control and into free fall.

The Listener fell. He had lived a lifetime, and now he fell one.

His mind was a ball of mercury—heavier than his body and dropping at a greater rate. He experienced a small wrenching sensation as his thoughts broke away from his flesh. The blackness intensified. It was absolute and unbounded. Sadaluk perceived that time was its measure, not distance. No man with a notched stick could record its depth. It existed without end, cold and inert: the exhaled breath of creation.

The Listener fell through it with no expectation of landing. His senses fled from him in an order that seemed to make sense: sight, taste, touch, smell. Before his ears gave out he heard energy crackling as it jumped between states.

Sadaluk's thoughts came in broken spurts. *Did I drink poison? Am I dead?* The gods were not benign, he knew that. One man's fate was nothing to them. He could fall for an eternity and they would not blink an eye. Yet there was something turning in the darkness that was beyond them. Something infinitely old and massive. Sadaluk remembered a tale Lootavek had told him about the ships that sailed from the Fortress Isles. Their turning circles were so large that they would not stop if a man went overboard. By the time a ship completed a full circle, the man would be long dead. Sadaluk was struck with the idea that the presence in the darkness turned for no one. Not even a god.

Yet it was in motion. Sadaluk could feel the pressure building: a mountain bearing down on a square foot of earth. The presence had an absoluteness of purpose: it claimed. Space. Existence. Time. Its outriders might be evil, cunning, savage, but the thing that moved was implacable—merciless not because it was cruel but because it was beyond mercy. It existed outside of nature, on a plane Sadaluk perceived only as unknowable. He was an old man, possibly a dead one: it wasn't hard to accept that his mind was too small to comprehend all things.

So he listened instead. For thirty-five years he had listened without earlobes; how hard could it be to listen without hearing? The habit of stillness, the assembling of a quiet, habitable space in which to wait for the sounds to come, was deeply entrenched in him. All he had to do was exert his will: a relaxation of muscle, a suspension of thought and it was done.

And Sadaluk No Ears, son of Odo Many Fish, and Listener of the Ice Trappers, became the first man, dead or alive, to hear the end of existence. If he'd possessed ears it would have made them bleed. The sound was vast and deeply alien, punctured by world-shattering booms and explosive cracks. Everything was being ground up, sucked in and then destroyed so completely that nothing, not even the memory of its smallest part, remained.

Sadaluk feared for the Ice Trappers; for Nolo and the hunters, for their wives and children, the sled dogs, the ice bears. Himself. Images lied—you only had to walk half a league onto the sea ice to know that—but sound had never failed him. Sound was truth.

The Listener could speak three languages. None of them had words to describe what approached him. If pressed he would resort to Sull, for the Sull were the oldest race still living in the Known Lands and their language reflected their long association with darkness. They had a word, *mash'xa*, which could not be wholly translated. It described the state of cold oblivion that existed before Time; the force in perfect opposition to creation. The Sull believed that *mash'xa* was the one true state of being, and that all existence was nothing more than a struck flame that would burn until it was snuffed. Sadaluk did not disbelieve the idea of *mash'xa*, but he had long ago decided that it had no pertinence to his life. He existed in the world of seals and men. Ice formed and broke with the seasons. Gods were tricky, needy, seldom fair. Yet here, moving through the darkness, was something outside his experience as Ice Trapper and shaman, something that perhaps only the Sull could understand. A force of pure annihilation. *Mash'xa*.

The concussion grew louder. And closer. The presence, the thing that turned for no one, was moving on a tangent to intercept him. Not to meet or acknowledge him — Sadaluk knew better than to flatter himself with such claims — but simply because he, the Listener of the Ice Trappers, was falling in its path.

It was the gift of the white bear.

Or its curse.

Cold burns. The Listener fell and burned. He was stripped and scoured, smelted in the raw black furnace of extinction. A needle of ice punctured his left eardrum. A second needle raked across his cortex, erasing memories of winters spent on the sea ice as a boy. Down he plummeted, screaming without words, learning all the ways a paralyzed man feels pain.

As he drew closer to the presence he shrank and hardened. All thoughts were blasted away. His remaining eardrum imploded under pressure.

The quiet, habitable space began to fade.

Sadaluk listened as it diminished. He listened as the force that would bring down the world passed by on its slow and unstoppable march of oblivion. He listened. And learned.

When he woke a lifetime later, irrevocably changed and branded, the first words from his mouth were, "Nolo, round up the dogs. We have a journey to begin."

He could no longer hear himself speak.

CHAPTER 1

Departures

Raif Sevrance returned from the deerhunt to find the lamb brothers breaking up camp. A sharp wind cutting from the east pushed the men's dark robes against their longbones. The rising sun shone along the same path as the wind, creating shadows that blew from the brothers like sand off dunes.

Four of the five tents had already been reduced to skeletons. Hides and guideropes had been stowed. The corral was still standing, but the mules and the ewe had been strung on nooselines and led to graze. Frost had grown overnight on the tough winter rye, yet the lamb brothers' animals knew enough about hardship to take their meals where they found them. Warmer temperatures during the day had melted most of the surrounding ground snow, but lenses of ice were still fixed between the rocks.

Raif approached camp from the forested headland to the east. He'd opened and drained the deer carcass, but he could still smell its blood. It was a yearling. In a moonless hour past midnight he'd found her stealing milk from her dam. Her mother had just given birth and by rights the milk was for the newborn. The yearling had other ideas, and kept butting aside her younger brother to get to the udder and the rich green milk leaking from the teats. It had been a difficult kill. Three hearts beating in close proximity. Raif had known straight away which animal he wanted—the newborn and the dam were not for him—and he had been forced to wait under cover of a stand of hemlock until his target moved clear of the group. He had thought about taking the shot when the yearling stood directly in front of the dam. Part of him had wanted to test himself. See if he could skewer two hearts with one arrow. Yet if he killed the dam he'd have to kill the newborn—it wouldn't survive a day without milk or protection—and one man without horse or cart could not bring back three kills.

You kill it, you butcher it. Da's words concerning hunting were law.

What would Tem Sevrance make of his son now? What advice would he give to a man who could heart-kill any target he set in his sights? What laws governed Raif Twelve Kill, Watcher of the Dead?

Resettling the butterflied carcass on his shoulders, Raif entered the camp. Tents had been raised twenty days earlier on new-cleared softwood. The stumps were still oozing pitch. Circles of matted yellow pine needles marked the former positions of the tents, and potholes of blackened earth told of longfires, cook fires and smoke pits. One of the lamb brothers was filling in the latrine. Another was using a long pole to unhook a slab of bear fat from the safe tree.

Raif shivered. Waiting in the pines had chilled him. The air had been still in the early hours before dawn and the frost smoke had risen: white mist that switched between ice and vapor and then back again. Five hours later and he could still feel it cooling his burned skin. The damaged muscle in his chest had shrunk and stiffened, pulling on the sutures and creating tension between his ribs. The wound on his left shoulder, where the lamb brothers had drawn out the splinter of unmade horn, was healing in unexpected ways. The skin above the exit wound had knitted closed, but the wormhole underneath remained open. Raif doubted it would ever heal. He was not and would never be whole.

All of us are missing something. Yustaffa had said that four months ago in the Rift. He had been talking about the Maimed Men and their practice of taking a pound of flesh from anyone seeking to join them—Raif himself had lost half a finger in one of their initiation ceremonies. Yet he now understood Yustaffa's words went beyond physical damage. Maimed Men were outcasts, orphans, fugitives, runaways: they had a world of things to miss beyond flesh.

Drey. Effie.

Raif named his brother and sister in his head and then pushed all thoughts of them away. He had developed a sense about when it was safe to think of the people he loved, when it was possible to picture them in his mind without the pain of losing them. Today was not such a day.

"Got yourself a pretty doe," Addie Gunn called in greeting. The Maimed Man had led the ewe to the sole hardwood stump in the camp, and the creature was lipping the reservoir of hardened sap that had pooled on the flat surface. "Sheep like their sweeties," Addie said, scratching the back of the ewe's neck. "Milk'll be like honey tonight."

Raif made no reply. Bending at the waist, he shucked off the yearling and let it fall to the ground. Her fawn spots were nearly gone and the white mating blaze on her rump was beginning to come in. She'd fallen with her eyes open—a steel arrowhead piercing the right ventricle of the heart rarely gave a creature time to do anything save die—and her gaze rested on a fixed point in the distance. Raif wondered if the point marked his position as he lifted his finger from the bowstring. Had she heard the soft twang of the recoil as the arrow shot toward her heart?

Reaching down, he closed her eyelids. "We leave at noon."

Addie's hand stilled on the ewe's neck. He looked carefully at Raif before nodding. "Aye."

Raif Sevrance and Addie Gunn had traveled hundreds of leagues east together through crippling cold and hostile terrain. There was no need to say more between them. They were Maimed Men and failed clansmen: both knew the dangers of becoming too attached to people or places. Addie had been a cragsman at Wellhouse and consumption had lost him his herd and clan. His fellow cragsman had carted his failing body north to the Rift and given him a choice. Jump into the deepest crack in the earth and die an honorable death, or cross it and join the Maimed Men. Addie had chosen to live.

Most clansmen would have jumped. Raif had been born into Blackhail, the oldest and hardest of clans, and of all the Hailsmen he knew he could not imagine one of them leaving Blackhail to become a Maimed Man. Clansmen were proud. They had few good words to say about people who weren't clan, and nothing but curses for Maimed Men. They were robbers, murderers, freaks. No oaths or code of conduct bound them. They tilled no fields nor practiced any professions. Their living was made from raids, robbery, extortion, kidnapping for ransom.

And he, Raif Sevrance, would be king of them.

Raif glanced at the position of the sun. A lone bird of prey soared across its swollen face. Two hours until noon. He had known for the past twenty days that he would have to leave this place, this hillside south of the Lake of Red Ice, and return to the Rift and the Maimed Men who lived there, but he had imagined the decision of when to leave would be his. Now the lamb brothers had made it for him. They were departing, and they had not informed him they had planned to go. Raif told himself it was their privilege to do so, but he still meant to move out before they did.

Leaving the doe carcass at the camp perimeter, he made his way to the only standing tent. As he hiked between the stumps he was aware that one of the lamb brothers—Tallal, judging by his height and the color of the cloth panel covering his lower face—was attempting to catch his eye. Raif ignored him. The lamb brothers would have to wait to collect their remaining tent. Raif needed to sleep. Addie would make what preparations were needed; quarter and parcel the yearling, fill waterskins, wax leathers, barter with the lamb brothers for tea herbs and salt. The Maimed Man enjoyed sound relations with the lamb brothers: tea and sheep were powerful forces for goodwill.

As soon as he'd slipped through the tent flap, Raif bent forward to lessen the pressure on his chest. Ignoring the pain during the hunt had been easy enough, but he was paying for it now. Twenty days ago his heart had stopped. Dead. There'd been a length of time when he, Raif Sevrance, ceased to exist. He'd been just another corpse on the ice. Blood had stopped moving and pooled in his veins, muscles had locked, his lungs had slumped to a close as poisons flooded his liver and kidneys. How long he'd lain there, empty and decomposing, was something he never wanted to know. Time served among the dead was something he hoped to forget. He couldn't avoid the sudden weaknesses and failings, though: his body enjoyed reminding him it had died.

Inside the tent all was dim and still. The safety lamp had burned out, but the wick was still smoking. Its pitchy scent smelled like wound dressing, and mixed uneasily with the stink of old animal skins. The tent walls, the ground canvas and the bedding were all made from pierced hides. Expertly clarified skins formed the walls. Raif did not recognize what animal they came from, but he appreciated the work that had gone into fatting and leaching the skins until they lost all natural pigment and let through light. The longbones that formed the support struts were another thing alien to him. He had handled one a few days back and was surprised to discover it was as light as a bird bone. The lamb brothers were not from the North. Home was the shifting sands and baked earth of the Scorpion Desert. Perhaps they had birds the size of horses there; Raif did not know.

Lying on the heaped skins, he tried to sleep. Closing his eyes might have helped. Instead he stared at the parasite holes in the ceiling hides. Needles of sunlight punctured them as the sun moved overhead. When his eyes began to sting, he dropped his gaze to the six-foot-long package that rested close to the tent's rear wall. The package was raised off the ground by a crude plinth of stripped timber. Ten days back Addie had judged its content vulnerable to damp.

"It's damaged goods," Raif had said in response, as the Maimed Man chiseled wood curls from the plinth. "Cankered, blackened. Why bother?"

Addie had shaken his head impatiently. He wasn't a natural woodworker and the wood curls grew thicker as he spoke. "We bother because this sword deserves respect. It was made for kings. The last man who wielded it died out on that ice, trying to hold back evil so potent that even the gods fear it. Yes, the sword is damaged, but what if underneath the rust the edge is still true? We *owe* this sword, Raif. The clanholds, the Sull, the Maimed Men. You saw the bodies under the ice—we weren't winning. We were being hacked and decapitated. Cut in two. I've been on fields after battle's end—Mare's Rock, Falling Bridge. I've seen what close combat with live steel can do to an army. It's seldom pretty. The guts. The shit. The blood. Never seen anything like the Red Ice, though. Thirty thousand bodies reduced to parts. *Parts.* And maybe, just maybe, this sword and the man who wielded it turned certain annihilation into a draw."

Raif swung his feet onto the ground canvas. Thinking about Addie's words stirred him. *The gods fear it,* he had said. Not feared.

Fear.

Abruptly, Raif rose to standing. He would not sleep. It had been foolish to even try. And bloody-minded to force the lamb brothers into delaying their departure by sleeping in their tent. They had shown respect. They had not broken up the tent in his absence, exposing his possessions to the cold spring sun. Raif gathered those possessions now. The recurve longbow, horn arrow case, bedroll, waterskin, gear belt with all its attendant hooks and weapon-care pouches, shammies, hand knife, tin spoon, wood cup, small linens, leather traces, buckskin mitts, Orrl cloak. Stormglass.

Sliding the finger of glass from its rawhide pouch, Raif

tried to sort through his thoughts. *Once in a very long while when lightning touches sand it turns to glass.* The stormglass felt good and heavy in his hand. Light tumbled within its chambers even when he held it still. It was rarer than diamonds, a gift from the lamb brothers. And it had endangered and then saved his life.

Tht.

Raif glanced up at the sound of gravel hitting the tent wall. No sand here, in the far north of the clanholds. The lamb brothers were reduced to throwing stones to request entree into another's tent.

Raif returned the stormglass to its pouch. "Come."

Brown hands, oiled and meticulously trimmed, parted the tent flap. Tallal entered. Custom dictated that host speak before guest, so the lamb brother waited, head low, gaze down, face panel swinging to vertical. With a small thrill of unease Raif realized there were now five black dots tattooed in the space between Tallal's eyebrows. Yesterday there had been three.

"Sit," Raif said, indicating the piled hides. Aware at this point he was expected to offer refreshment to his guest, Raif struggled to come up with something—*anything*—that could be drunk or eaten in fellowship. As Tallal knelt effortlessly on the hides, Raif frowned at the deflated waterskin. It had been on the deerhunt with him. Ten hours of resting against his rump. This wasn't going to be pleasant.

An awkward moment passed where Raif assumed Tallal would untie his face panel and reveal his lower face, yet the lamb brother was still. The two new dots on his forehead looked raw. Clear liquid oozed from the one closest to his left eye. Finally understanding that Tallal meant to retain the formality of the veil, Raif pulled the waterskin from the floor. Uncorked it and squeezed the last shot of water into a cup. He offered the cup to the lamb brother without a word.

And without a word it was accepted. Tallal slipped the cup under his face panel, drank, and then swallowed. Handing back the cup, he said, "Do not consider returning the storm-glass. I will not accept it."

Raif blinked. How had he known? Until three minutes ago, Raif had barely known himself. It was the unlowered face panel that had decided it for him.

The lamb brother's brown eyes with their strange bluish whites assessed Raif. "Drink," he said, "and we will speak."

Raif drank. The water tasted exactly as he imagined: stale, meaty, warm. Returning the cup to his pack he noticed dried deer blood wedged beneath his fingernails. Outside, the wind had strengthened and gusts were *whumpfing* against the tent. Raif sat by one of the struts. Spine against bone.

Tallal waited for a lull in the wind before speaking, his eyes were focused on a distance beyond the tent canvas, and the face panel sucked against his lips with each inhaled breath. "In my land there are three seasons. Summer, Rain, and Scourge. If we are blessed the Scourge lasts sixty days. The winds blow and do not stop and the air becomes desert as the sand is torn off the dunes. A man exposed overnight will be skinned. The sand is sharp. It moves faster than an arrow shot from a bow and strips all hides in its path. We dig ourselves deep into the earth and pray. We speak the Petition For Good Fortune, which is a cycle of eight prayers. The prayers ask for grace, forgiveness, deliverance from the Scourge, water for our animals, milk and dates for our chil-dren, patience for ourselves. The final prayer in the cycle asks for something more. It is the Prayer of the Fortunate Stranger. *Please God*, we ask, *bring us new friends in our time of need."*

Tallal paused. The face panel hung still as he delayed his next breath.

"My people have a saying, *Mul'ah ri ashanna.* We must meet prayer halfway. One of the ways we do this is by giving gifts. We believe it is not enough to hope that a stranger will dig us out if our cave beneath the sand collapses, so we increase the odds. Turn strangers into friends. We offer food and shelter and what small tokens we can. It is the custom of the dunes.

"That is why you received the stormglass. Not because we knew you would lead us to the Red Ice, but because we thought: Here is a stranger who could dig us from a cave."

Raif thought and did not speak. Somewhere in the heavy rawhide packs being loaded onto the mules by the two other lamb brothers were thousands of leather pouches. Each pouch represented the reclaimed soul of one of their dead. The battlefield beneath the Red Ice had rendered tens of thousand of frozen corpses, many of them belonging to the people of the Scorpion Desert. By recovering the sword named Loss, Raif had also recovered the long lost remains of their ancestors. He'd helped the lamb brothers plenty. Question was, had they helped him?

The sword was now his. There it lay, wrapped in deer velvet, sitting on a throne of wood. Names came at a price, Raif knew that. How much was Loss going to cost him to bear?

He glanced at Tallal. The lamb brother waited, his head perfectly level and his long fingers resting on the sable wool bridging his lap. He had appealed for an amicable parting.

Raif searched for a way to give him one.

I am two now, he realized. Raif Sevrance, son of Tem, brother to Effie and Drey. And *Mor Drakka*, Twelve Kill. The lamb brothers had not helped Raif Sevrance—they had sent him on a journey that had ended with him dead on the ice—but they had helped *Mor Drakka*, Watcher of the Dead.

They had armed him.

Who had armed Raven Lord? Raif wondered. The last man to wield Loss must have been someone's son, brother, friend. Had he felt the same way that Raif did now: that the sword's first cut would be to himself?

"Tallal," he said, "you and your brothers saved my life. For that I thank you."

Tallal was no fool. His response to the carefully framed thanks was to let his gaze alight on the plinth.

Raif blinked and saw Raven Lord's headless body beneath the ice; the black and spiny armor entombing the frozen torso, three gray and bloated fingers still clasping Loss' hilt. "Ask me in ten years if I thank you for the sword."

If I live that long.

The lamb brother shrugged, not lightly. "When the Sand Men head north I will remind them to ask you."

A gust of wind shook the tent, rattling its bones. Raif heard air whistling in cavities once filled with marrow. "Why will the Sand Men head north?"

Tallal smiled: Raif could see it in the crease of the face panel. But not the eyes. "Sand Men will head north when they hear what this lamb brother has to tell them."

"And that is?"

"That lightning has struck twice. First to create the storm-glass and second to anoint it." Tallal paused, letting silence do his work for him. Here was something dipped in the deep and biding stillness of prophecy. Men had been waiting for this moment. Raif waited right along with them.

When he was sure his point had been made, Tallal nodded at Raif's hand. "That is a piece of my homeland. Dunes burned into glass. Only once in ten thousand strikes will lightning fuse sand. This lamb brother has not studied with the mathematicians of Hanatta and so cannot reckon the odds of lightning striking those same grains of sand once more."

Raif squeezed his fist around the stormglass. He could feel it straining to pop out of its pouch like seeds in a pressed grape. His uncle Angus Lok had explained the laws of chance to him two springs back as they'd tracked and then cornered a rare white moose in the stink bogs north of Cold Lake.

"Have you seen one before?" Raif remembered asking, excitement making his voice high.

Angus had shaken his head. "Nay, lad. A wee beastie like this is a once in a lifetimer. Take it down and skin it and you'll have yourself the only white moose pelt in Blackhail, and only the second of two in the entire clanholds."

Raif had been quiet for a while, thinking. As always with his uncle there was a lot of information packed between the words. *You'll have.* Not we. You. Angus had ceded killing rights to Raif. And also, Raif realized gradually, the decision whether or not to make the kill.

"If I let him go will he mate and make more white moose?" Raif had asked as they stood, ankle deep in tannic-brown seep water.

"Nay. Odds are against him winning a rut. He's an aberration, poor little bugger. He won't smell right, his eyesight's dodgy, he's liable to get burned in the sun. Parasites'll love him. Decrepit one-eyed wolves will be able to track him. He'd be lucky to get a whiff of a cow. He's already beaten a mess of odds by reaching maturity. You'd have to times those odds by themselves to reckon the likelihood of him mating and producing another little ghostie like himself."

As he resettled his spine against the tent strut, Raif considered the odds of lightning striking the stormglass twice. It was some kind of big number, one bigger than the odds of the white moose reproducing.

"The Sand Men are singular amongst our people," Tallal said. "They live apart. They ready themselves for battle. They wait."

Raif met gazes with the lamb brother and Tallal nodded imperceptibly. He didn't need to. Raif understood what they waited for. It made him afraid; afraid of losing himself, of becoming something brighter and less human than Raif Sevrance, something that men and armies would follow. A battle standard. A war cry. A myth.

He recalled the moment when his broadhead punctured the white moose's hide. It was a good shot, for a boy of fifteen. Hitting high on the neck, just below the roof of the jaw, the arrow had carried sufficient force to travel through an inch of dense, skull-supporting muscle before slicing open the jugular. Blood shot out at force, spraying the sedge mats and willow tangles and cratering the bog water. The blood had been a shock. It was warm and red and stinking, and it had made him feel sick about the kill. Stupidly he had thought that the ghostly white pelt and the high and fancy odds added up to the creature not being real. A ghost. A myth.

Raif stood. The lamb brother had more to say to him but Raif decided he didn't want to hear it. If he and Addie headed out now they had a chance of reaching the Bludd forests before nightfall. Good cover there. Cover suddenly seemed important. The white moose should have stayed above the snowline or amongst stands of silver birches. Damn creature had just made itself a target in the bog.

Tallal rose a moment after Raif. His robe pitched like water finding its level in a glass. Two darkening ovals on his face panel showed the damp weight of his breath.

"You have the wrong man," Raif warned him before he had a chance to speak. "If the Sand Men find me I will send them back."

Tallal said nothing. Raif had the sense that the lamb brother was controlling the impulse to call him a self-deluding fool. Time passed as they faced each other. Raif saw himself inverted—a speck in Tallal's eye.

"I wish you water to weep," the lamb brother said finally.

The double-edged blessing of the Scorpion Desert. Raif accepted it like a blow. Already the lamb brother was withdrawing his attention: His gaze slid to the tent flap and his long brown fingers formed the hooks required to lift the canvas.

As he stepped away, Raif said to him, "The bodies that were under the ice. What happened to them?"

Tallal did not turn as he answered. "We laid their remains to rest."

"All of them? The northern armies? The city men? The Sull?"

The back of the lamb brother's head shook as he raised the tent flap. "We ministered solely to the people of the desert."

And then he was gone.

Raif stared at the tent flap as it smacked back into place.

They had left them to rot. The lamb brothers, with all their talk of God and holy purpose, had rummaged through the bodies, hauled away their own and ignored the rest. Raven Lord's headless corpse was still out there, rotting as quickly as only thawed meat could, teeming with maggots and coffin flies, unregarded and unblessed.

Raif thought about that, did what he needed to do, and then left the tent.

"Addie, we're off," he called as he pulled on his sealskin mitts and squinted into the shrunken noonday sun. A bird of prey gliding parallel to the northern horizon was the only thing moving in the greenly blue sky.

Addie was kneeling on one of the yellow tent circles wrapping severed deer hooves in waxed linen. The little curly-haired ewe did not like the smell of fresh blood, but she did like Addie and was nervously cropping weeds a few feet upwind of him. At the camp's southern perimeter the three lamb brothers were packing the mules. Girdle straps and neck harnesses were padded and adjusted.

Twisting the last of the packages closed, Addie stood upright. He was a small man, bowlegged and, as he was fond of telling everyone, bow-eared. Raif could not guess his age. Addie's entire life had been lived outdoors. His skin was baked against his bones. He'd heard enough in Raif's voice to spur him to swift action and he scooped up his packs and bedroll and slung them across his back. He glanced toward the lamb brothers and then Raif, who told him everything he needed to know by starting west.

I'm done here.

Addie spat thoughtfully, patted the ewe's delicate head and then followed Raif out of the camp.

The descent was easy. A deer trail wound through low-growing pines and blackthorns, edging creeks that were wet but barely running and looping around gnawed yews and dog-woods. The ground cover was thawing, and weeds and leaf litter squelched greasily underfoot.

The lamb brothers watched them leave. Raif didn't turn around to confirm it but he knew they did. He also knew that as soon as he and Addie descended sufficient distance to pass out of sight, they would collapse the remaining tent. In their eagerness to be gone from a land they had no love for, the brothers would work in haste: rolling two or more skins at once, balling the ground canvas and binding it tightly with rope. Chances were they would miss it. Chances were it would get bounced into a crease and lie there, undetected, until the tent was next unpacked. And the tent wouldn't be unpacked until the lamb brothers returned to the Scorpion Desert. It was the fifth tent, the spare. Four other tents existed—one for each brother and one for God—they wouldn't need it on the journey home. Only when they reached their destination and all their official duties had been discharged would they turn their attention to the business of checking and repairing their gear. That was when they would find it: the stormglass in its dun-colored leather pouch, tucked away in the folds of the fifth tent canvas, a message received months after it was sent. Raif Sevrance would wear no beacon for the Sand Men. No amount of lightning would reveal his whereabouts in a storm. He was dead to the people of the Scorpion Desert, as dead as Raven Lord's headless corpse.

Addie seemed to understand much about Raif's parting with the lamb brothers. The Maimed Man was silent for the first hour, quietly and efficiently steering them from trail to trail. When he unrolled a pat of sheep's cheese to eat afoot, he did not offer any to Raif. A few minutes later when he moved on to deer jerky, he tapped Raif on the arm and passed him a stick of the black and leathery meat. No words passed between them but Raif understood that while the cheese had come from the lamb brothers the jerky had been cured by Addie himself.

They chewed in silence, their jaw muscles aching as they worked long cycles on each bite. After Addie swallowed his final mouthful, he nodded at the northern sky. "Hawk's been up there since noon. You'd think it would have bagged itself a squirrel by now."

Raif frowned at the last of his jerky—Addie must have cured it with cement. Tucking it into his gear belt, he said, "It's a gyrfalcon and it's been aloft since dawn."

Addie mulled over this information for the better part of an hour. As they reached the valley floor and started south through the red pines toward the Bludd border, the eweman said, "It's hers then; Yiselle No Knife's."

Raif nodded as he moved ahead of Addie to take the lead. He was being watched by the Sull and there was nothing he could do about it. The lamb brothers would send the Sand Men north even after they discovered the stormglass, and there was nothing he could do about that either. The sword named Loss bounced against Raif's back as he leapt across a shallow creek. He was known now, marked, judged.

Followed.

CHAPTER 2

A House in the City

Snow fell on Ille Glaive on the night known as Gallows Eve. Warmed by the spring sun during the day, the black mass of the city melted the snow on contact. Paved streets were slick with grease. Dirt roads were sodden and stinking, slowly disintegrating into rivers of animal waste and mud. The rats were out. Thousands of rodents scuttled along ledges and drain ditches, up crumbling walls, armless statues, soot-blackened trees and lead roofs. The explosive snap of traps being sprung was the only noise that broke the silence before dawn.

The watcher crouching in the shadows heard but did not heed it. His cloak of boiled wool was topped with a second layer of waxed pony skin so he felt neither the cold nor damp. The pony skin had been purchased at Tanners Market seventeen hours earlier, and the watcher had sat and waited in a nearby alehouse while the vendor had dyed the skin to his specifications. "Matte black?" the vendor had cried upon hearing the watcher's requirements. "A fine blond hide like this and you want to ruin it with cutter's ink?" It mattered little to the watcher whether the vendor's protestations were a result of genuine indignation or a plot to drive up the price. The watcher had haggled because a person buying an expensive waterproof cloak and requesting that it be rendered worthless by cheap dye was unusual enough. A person refusing to haggle for such a cloak would be the talk of the market within an hour. Vendors loved to crow about their takings. This particular horse-and-donkey skin vendor would never crow again however. Once the watcher had picked up the cloak he'd had a change of mind. Despite its growing population and the continual redrawing of its walls, Ille Glaive acted like a small town. People knew people. Word got round. And the watcher crouching in the shadows could not risk word of his arrival entering the wrong ears. He knew the game. He had lived it. Better to kill a man quietly and bloodlessly by snapping the small bones in his neck than risk alerting enemies to one's presence.

The watcher had felt some tension in the minutes leading up to the kill and then nothing after it. His thoughts had not returned to the vendor since. He was different now, burned. All that was combustible had gone up in flames and only case-hardened iron remained.

Rocking onto the balls of his feet he kept his leg muscles limber. Out of habit he read the wind. It blustered south to north and then east to west as if it were trapped within the city walls. Not a good night to loose arrows or hunt deer. If the people in the house he was watching had kept dogs they would be alerted to his scent by now. There was no blind spot, no downwind to conceal oneself from animals with exceptional senses of smell. The watcher knew this house and its two occupants though, knew they kept no dogs and set no watch. Despite this he would take no chances. Circumstances may have changed.

It was the watcher's one wish in life that they had changed in his favor.

Two lamps were burning in the house. The brighter one was set close to the lower rear window on the left. Thick oak shutters had been closed against the darkness but the house was old and damp, its owner had no interest in spending money on repairs and the shutters were warped and poorly fitted. Light poured through knotholes and around the frames. The second lamp burned in an interior room, showing itself as a faint glow around the windows on the east side of the building. Like many dwellings in Ille Glaive the house was narrow but deep. It was built from amber sandstone that had aged badly. The bricks were soft and porous. A heavy rainstorm would strip them, leaving milky orange puddles around the foundation. It was a problem with entire generations of buildings in the city, resulting in the strangely rounded skyline of Ille Glaive.

Silently the watcher rose to standing. Time to get a closer look.

The three-story house was unusual in that it commanded an acre of walled land in the rear. The property had once belonged to some minor lordling who had used the grounds closest to the house as his pleasure garden, equipping it with a copper-roofed folly, a fountain carved to resemble a lake trout and a courtyard laid with alternating black and white stones. The lower half of the land had once been a working kitchen garden, complete with boxed vegetable beds, a stock pond and caves for storing ice. All of it was overgrown, tumbled-down and streaked with bird lime. A litter of rat droppings and poisoned rat carcasses had killed the lawn. Weeds had grown to man-height in beds once raised for artichokes, and a thick crud of algae now booby-trapped the pond. The entire property—both the house and grounds—looked as if no one had tended it in thirty years.

The watcher knew this to be untrue. To tend meant to care, and the owner of the house very much cared about its setting. Over the three decades he had occupied the building he had cultivated the shambled, run-down appearance it presented to the city of Ille Glaive. Despite its well-regarded address, this house did not appear to be lived in by people with money or consequence. Thieves gave it the once-over before moving on to richer prospects, fishmongers and milkmaids seldom bothered to solicit for business, passersby rarely gave it a passing thought.

If they'd looked more carefully they would have seen the locks and bolts. Vor-forged iron, the finest in the North, had been hammered at high heat to form the door hinges. The locks themselves had once secured cell doors on the infamous Confessor's Walk in the Lake Keep. The house's owner had received them in exchange for a favor—he specialized in turning a blind eye into hard goods. The Lake stamp could still be seen on the lock plates if you knelt very close and studied the mark below the keyhole. It was the same with the rickety shutters: put your eye to a knothole and the truth was there to see.

Wrought-iron grillwork, posts sunk deep into the sandstone and fortified with cement, barred entry to the house through its windows. This did not worry the watcher. He knew these people and their routines.

And he was prepared to wait.

Dropping to a crouch he approached the lamplit window. Broken glass had been spread on the ground beneath the lintel. The man toed away the debris as he moved. Although he'd been taught stealth a quarter century earlier, entire years had passed where he'd had no reason to use it. In many ways his life had been arranged like the checkerboard pattern of the courtyard: black and white, black and white. Stealth, weapons-training, secrets and surveillance were part of the black, part of the life that he'd once believed was his calling. His missions and travels were all in the black. The white . . .

The white was gone. Over. Even a child knew that if you burned something to a cinder the only thing left was black.

The watcher took up position beneath the window. He had been observing the house from a distance since nightfall and had seen nothing out of the ordinary in the sequence of lamps lit and snuffed. No one had arrived or left—also ordinary—and the footprints stamped in the mud on the front and back paths revealed little. During the eight hours of darkness, the watcher had kept his speculation to a minimum. Too early to draw con-clusions. Too little information to rule anything out. Now, though, as he rose level with the knothole and took his first look into the house's interior, his breathing pattern changed. It slowed with readiness.

And anticipation.

The coin-sized knothole was partially obscured by the underlying grillwork so his view of the room was restricted to a narrow wedge. The watcher could see a closed door. A worn but exceptionally fine silk rug covered the floor beyond the entrance. Its colors had faded to drab rusts and grays and its design of fully fanned peacocks' tails and halved figs was barely legible. Bookcases stained a color close to black lined the walls. Folded manuscripts, rolled scrolls, chained psalters, loose papers, glazed and lidded pots, specimen jars, wood boxes and books, hundreds of books, had been jammed at force into the space between shelves. The house's owner spoke seven languages and could read more than twenty. His body had been wheel-broken thirty-one years earlier by an enemy shared by both him and his watcher, and he could not rise from a chair unaided nor walk without the aid of sticks. Yet he possessed one of the finest minds in the North.

The watcher respected the mind. He knew enough to accept that he could *not* comprehend all the powers that the mind possessed. He had been careful with his actions and thoughts. Mental restraint had been taught to him along with stealth, but it had never been a discipline he had mastered. He knew enough to approach the house long after midnight, when its owner's mental capacities were likely impaired by fatigue and red wine or stalled by sleep. He knew enough also to avoid strong spikes in his thoughts, and he did not name what he hoped to find.

The owner was slouched in a padded, high-backed chair in the center of the lamplit space. The chair was angled away from the window and the watcher could view only a sliver of its side profile. He saw a hand extending beyond the heavily cushioned armrest; the wrist slender, the fingers crowded so close they looked fused, the nails as yellow as dog fangs. The hand trembled but executed no voluntary movement.

The watcher settled in to observe the hand. It was likely its owner was asleep, but nothing was certain.

Darkness endured. Snow stopped falling and the temperature dropped. Ice skinned puddles and formed a crust around the watcher's boots. He listened and did not move. The house was quiet, undisturbed by footfalls and opening doors. When the second, interior lamp went out he guessed its fuel was spent as no noise accompanied the sudden darkness.

Neither of the two known occupants of this house was capable of quiet movement. Still. If there was a third occupant, a newcomer . . .

If.

The owner's hand jumped off its padded perch. The watcher reined his thoughts. The hand hovered, suspended in space, and the watcher held his breath as he waited for its tendons to relax. As seconds passed he imagined its owner *questing*, taking stock of his surroundings, assessing change. The watcher doubted whether the strong emotion in his thoughts had roused the owner, but he could not rule it out. Coincidence as a concept left him cold.

Finally the hand relaxed. It moved inward and then disappeared as the owner brought it to his lap. Cushions stuffed with horsehair creaked, and the watcher caught a glimpse of the owner's head as the owner tilted forward in the chair. The skull was close shorn and the small white crater behind the left ear was clearly visible. Their mutual enemy had not been wholly satisfied with the results of the wheel-breaking and had ordered the drill. He, too, had been aware of the fineness of the owner's mind and had sought to limit it. The watcher suspected that their enemy had miscalculated, for when the drill bit emerged from the skull, globs of gray matter clinging to the bore, the owner had entered a fugue-like state that lasted a year. He awoke the next spring to find the hole in his skull patched with a plate of hip bone and his mental abilities expanded in ways that no one could have anticipated and very few people alive could comprehend.

The watcher pushed his lips into a hard line. *A hole in the head. Worse things could—*would—*happen.*

He remained still as the owner angled his torso sideways

and attended something on the opposite side of the chair. Pottery clinked. Refracted light streaked along the bookcases as the owner raised a glass to his lips and drank. Done, he resettled his weight against the backrest. The watcher waited for the owner to reach for one of his canes and beat it against the floor in summons, but the man remained still. After a time his breaths grew shallow, and the number of seconds between exhalations became constant. The watcher knew this because he counted them.

So the owner would not take to his bed for the final hour of night. To do so he would have had to rouse the second occupant to help him from the chair. When he was satisfied the owner was asleep, the watcher backed away.

An owl growled as he slipped through the shadows toward the rear door. The call sent a shiver of expectation down his spine. Old habits died hard. Raven and owl. Both birds— neither of them natural homers—were used by the Sull to bear messages over distance. It was an owl that had marked the beginning of his calling, and a raven call that had ended it. The last journey, that final absence, had begun with a raven perched in a tree.

Aware that he was entering dangerous territory, the watcher closed down his thoughts. His choices were made. They could not be undone.

Sliding into position against the rear wall, the watcher listened for signs of stirring. The first cock was crowing in the east, and that meant the house's second occupant would be on the move. Like many who were tower-trained, she was a creature of routine. Up before dawn, fire to be lit, water to be boiled for the pot. The watcher glanced at the covered woodstack that lay on the opposite side of the door and drew his knife.

The eastern sky was beginning to lighten when he heard a second-story door swing shut. Heavy, measured footfalls sounded as someone descended the stairs. It was her, the woman. You could hear her age in the hesitation between steps. When she reached the ground floor, thick rugs muffled her movements. Minutes passed. No lamps were lit. Tin chinked against tin. Footsteps clacked against tile. A series of bolts retorted in quick succession—*Chunk. Chunk. Chunk*—and the rear door juddered into motion.

The watcher waited until he saw the woman's booted foot alight on the top step before launching himself forward. Free hand clamping the woman's forearm, he snapped the arm back and up, forcing it into a breakable V behind her back. His knife hand went straight for the throat.

"Scream and you will die," he murmured, aligning a foot of razor steel along the turkey skin that formed her jawline.

The woman did not scream. She whispered two words.

"Angus Lok."

His name. He did not acknowledge it. His mind was on the door—open and letting in cool drafts—and the exact placement of the knife. Before asking his first question he twisted her forearm into her back.

She gave a little cry of fear and shock as the powerful reflex to step forward drove the blade against her throat.

"No screaming," he reminder her, his lips kissing her ear. She smelled old and sexless. A dried-up hag who stank of the meals she cooked and the bedpans she emptied. The half-filled sack that was her right buttock was pressing against his right thigh. Mary Gagg was her given name, though she preferred to be called Mistress Gannet, and she kept house for the man in the chair.

"Where is my daughter?"

The woman hesitated.

Mistake. He drove the forearm into her back. This time he did not relax the pressure and the knife blade opened flesh.

"None of your daughters are here. They're all dead."

Her voice was surprisingly defiant for someone who was bleeding at the throat. She always had been a tough old bird. He remained calm as he repeated the question. "Where is my daughter?"

"Which one? They're all buried behind your house."

Angus Lok glanced at the door and then along the rear wall to the study window. No change in the lamplight, but that didn't mean anything. "When did she come here?"

The woman blew air through her nostrils with force. Blood sheeted across the blade. "She hasn't come. No one has come. Search the house—you won't find anything. They're all dead."

Another twist of the forearm into the back. The blade was in her throat now, resting against the ribbed membrane of the trachea. "One more time. Where is she?"

The woman measured her breaths; one for each word. "I. Don't. Know."

He moved the knife inward. Distributed evenly, the force on the blade pressed but did not cut. "Last chance. Where is she?"

She was scared now. He could feel the tension in her muscles and ligaments: a woman made of wire. Mentally, he relaxed. Here it was, the moment all torturers waited for, the instant when their subject perceived they weren't getting out unhurt.

There's a world of hurt out there, Angus Lok thought as he maintained pressure on her throat. He'd seen it, he'd inflicted it, now he lived it. The woman didn't know her luck. Live or die, it barely mattered. She still wouldn't know her own luck.

Even before she drew a breath to speak, Angus Lok expected the truth. This interrogation was done. He knew it, the woman knew it, and now the only question in her mind would be: *Will I live?* She hoped to—that's where the truth came in—but she wasn't a fool and knew she no longer dealt with reason.

She inhaled at some cost to her throat tissue. "She never came here. Cant received a message ten days back—it concerned her."

He waited, but she had nothing else to tell him. He killed her swiftly and soundlessly and laid her body on the ground below the step. Dawn had broken. The world had broken. Light neither warmed nor illuminated Angus Lok as he turned his back on the corpse and entered the house.

These rooms and hallways were known to him. This had been his waypoint, the first stop on his travels. Information, equipment and hard currency had always been available to him at this house. Its hospitality had been taken for granted. Three years ago, for a period of nineteen days, he had lived here, recovering from injuries he'd judged too revealing to be viewed by his family. Deceit laid upon deceit. He had thought of Heritas Cant, the house's owner, as his friend. Now he knew differently. They weren't friends, they were co-conspirators. They conspired, he and Cant. Masters of the North, collectors of secrets, keepers of mysteries, instigators, saviors, judges, executioners, liars. The Brotherhood of the Long Watch, the Phage. Cant hadn't been his friend, he'd been his *source*. That brilliant mind filtered information into perfectly separated particles. It doled out only what you needed, no more. *This must be done. This must be watched. A threat is rising in the South.*

So where had been the warning? *Your family is in danger.*

Five words that would have changed everything, yet Cant had never spoken them. He, who never missed anything, who had spies spying on spies, who possessed foreknowledge of every assassination and failed assassination in the Lake Keep, and who monitored every gate, tunnel, break in the wall and fortuitously placed ladder that offered entry into the city of Ille Glaive.

Your family is in danger.

He had known it—as sure as the gods were dead he had known it. Assassins the caliber of the Crouching Maiden were routinely monitored by the Phage. Kings and ruling houses had been brought down by the Maiden's hand. She should never have been allowed within a hundred leagues of the farmhouse. Yet she had been allowed, and Darra Lok, Bess Lok and Maribel Lok had died by her hand.

Wife. Daughters.

Angus Lok breathed and did not think.

He acted, because that was what the Phage had trained him to do.

The rattle of a pot filled with water on the boil masked the sound of his footsteps down the darkened hall. The walls had been painted with lime and the soft porous finish had trapped a decade of smoke. An oblong-shaped paleness marked the absence of a framed painting. Angus Lok tried to recall the painting's subject, but failed.

When he reached the entrance to the study, he tensed his thigh muscles and kicked down the door.

Surprise had been lost the instant he crossed the threshold

into the house—you learned early in the Phage that sorcerers always warded their doors. Over the years he'd learned a few things for himself, though. One of them was: *Violence creates its own surprise.*

The door smashed against the floor. Splinters shot across the room like darts. Dust ballooned from the rug. A screw dropped from one of the hinges, bounced across the room, and came to rest at the foot of the chair.

Heritas Cant leaned forward and studied it. A pair of bulb-headed walking sticks were propped against the side of his chair and he tapped the closest one lightly as he contemplated the screw and then the door it had anchored. "Half inch longer and the door would have held," he said.

Seen head-on, he was not a lovely sight. Muscle had withered. Tendons shortened by disuse had drawn in his limbs making him look like a man about to shiver or pray. There was a ball of bone behind his neck: collarbone, rib cage or spine? Angus did not know. Live through a wheel-breaking and you became a puzzle of bones. Spurs, bunions, extra knuckles, serrated ridges: anyone who looked long enough gave up trying to name the pieces. There were too many for a start. Put the puzzle back together again and you'd be left with spare parts. Beside, there was the greater puzzle of Heritas Cant: How did he manage to live?

Angus slapped a heavily booted foot on the door and entered the room. He had detected a decline in Cant—an additional hollowing around the eyes, a thinning of the skin across the bridge of his nose—and it freed him of fear. Coming to rest in front of Cant's chair, he looked down at the man he had known for thirty years.

"Where is Cassy?" His voice was low and controlled. It was

the first time he had spoken his eldest daughter's name in twelve days. The sound of it filled him with something too reckless to be called hope.

Heritas Cant's head palsied in a chicken-pecking motion, yet his gaze remained level. His eyes were a deep bloody brown, and you could see the reckoning in them. When he spoke his voice was sharp. "No pleasantries, eh? Will you murder me in my chair, or drag me outside like Mistress Gannet?"

It was bait and Angus knew better than to bite it. "You received a message ten days ago. Where is she?"

Cant sighed thinly. He was dressed in a loose blue robe of goat wool belted with a strip of black silk. Underneath he wore a floor-length linen nightshirt that was slip-tied at the neck. His feet were shod in the kind of boiled wool slippers that were slipped on babies' feet and called booties. They swung weightlessly as he pulled himself into an upright position in the chair. "Casilyn Lok, or someone matching her description, was seen selling a pendant at the thrice-day market in Salt Creek."

Salt Creek was southeast of the farm. Cassy had no knowledge of the terrain or the roads to the east and no reason to head anywhere but west to Ille Glaive. "It wasn't her," Angus said. "She would come here." Both his wife and eldest daughter knew what to do in an emergency. *Take the old sheep road to Ille Glaive. Enter the city at night by the northern gate and head straight for Cant. He will protect you from harm.*

The man they loved had lied to them.

Cant slid his right hand beneath the silk belt. Arm muscles moved beneath his skin in a complex series of pulleys as he closed his fist around an object. With a gleam of triumph he tossed something shiny onto the floor.

Angus knew several things then. First, that Heritas Cant was tracking his daughter—that was Cassy's gold pendant on the floor—and second, that despite all stealth and precaution, Cant had been aware of his presence all along, probably from the very moment he had entered the city. The pendant had been ready inside his belt through the night.

Squatting, Angus scooped up the chain and its strawberry-shaped pendant. A pretty fancy bought for a daughter on her sixteenth birthday. The metal was too brightly yellow to be named pure gold, but that had never bothered Cassy. *I love it, Father. It's beautiful. What do the words say on the back?*

Angus pushed the necklace into his weapon pouch. Standing, he appraised Cant. The broken man watched him from from the padded coffin of his chair. With difficulty he retied the silk belt as his waist. As always it was a shock to see him use the dead hand. Cant's left had been shattered and rebuilt. It looked like a hand, but did not function as a hand. All the small finger bones had fused, and the right hand had to do the fine work of forming and cinching the bow. The left was reduced to weight work; pinning the silk as the task was done. It had not always been that way. Cant, like most sorcerers, had been born severely left-handed. The drilling had altered him. As the bit corkscrewed his brain, severing connections and subducting gray matter, it had cleared a space for change. His orientation had shifted instantly, left to right. Colorblindness had been corrected; for the first time in his life he had been able to differentiate between red and green. An echo chamber, Cant called the hole dug by the drill. A place where thoughts could repeat infinitely, where tissue could expand in ways not normally permitted in nature, and where ideas might travel to destinations unintended by their original spark.

Angus wondered what was moving in that brain now. What was coiling in readiness to repulse an attack? He said, "You knew they were in danger."

It was not a question. You could not interrogate a sorcerer.

Cant executed a one-shouldered shrug. "*Knew* would be too strong a word."

There was no end to how much a man could despise himself, Angus decided. He should have kicked in Cant's face for that remark. Even knowing what he did about sorcerers he should have tried. So what if Cant had whiplashed the strike right back at him, accelerating it with such fury that when it touched flesh it burned? Angus knew of no living person who could attack with sorcery, but was aware of a very small number who could protect themselves with it, spinning whatever was used against them into the mother-of-all-defenses. Cant was one such man. And he, Angus Lok, hesitated to try his chances against him. Much had been lost to him, yet the instinct for self-preservation was still there.

Cant bowed his palsying head, acknowledging Angus' thoughts as if they were spoken words. *Yes, go ahead. Despise yourself.*

The broken man said, "The Maiden is subtle. We were aware she headed north to Ille Glaive, yet when she failed to enter the city we believed her business must lie farther north. With the clans."

Lies and truth always sounded identical leaving Cant's mouth: interchangeable, a left and right hand. "You sent Darra no warning."

"Your wife was ever headstrong. I sent her a similar warning three years ago—which she ignored."

Crack. Angus kicked out the closest front leg of the chair.

The leg exploded backward, and for a brief moment the seat base hung suspended in the air. Cant inhaled, and the minute shift in weight and pressure was enough to tip the corner of the seat and send it thudding against the floor.

The chair cushions and their occupant slid forward. Cant flung out a wedge-shaped foot and jammed it into the rug. At the same time his right hand scooped up one of sticks that had fallen along with the chair. Using the stick as a lever he attempted to push himself back in the seat. Blood flushed his neck as he labored.

Angus watched and felt nothing. So breaking a sorcerer's chair did not count as an attack on a sorcerer. Or maybe it did, and Cant was playing possum. It didn't matter either way. He was done here. More questions would just means more evasions. More lies. It might suit Cant to have Darra and the girls gone. More likely he fancied the Maiden's head—and who better to take it than a Phage-trained manhunter with a personal grievance? One thing was certain, you could not outthink him: that empty space in his brain was lined with traps.

The stench of hot metal drifted into the room. In the kitchen, the unattended water vessel had boiled dry. Briefly Angus wondered if it was a lidded kettle or a pot. A kettle might explode. Fire might start.

As Cant cleared his throat to speak, Angus Lok turned his back and walked to the door. He knew Cant—there'd be a carefully constructed expression that would have nothing to do with how he really felt. Fear was what would fill him now. A broken man, abandoned. An empty house.

He would not call for help. The answer to the question *How did he manage to live* was simple. Pride.

Angus left him to it. He had an assassin to hunt and kill. Death would not come swiftly for the Maiden. When the damned killed the damned the only language they understood was pain.

As he stepped from the house into the gray light of day, Cant's voice pushed against the small bones of his ears. It was a cheap trick, performed at sideshows and spring fairs by anyone with half a claim on the old skills, yet it never failed to please the crowd. That voice in your ear, a whisper for you alone from a man standing fifty feet away on the opposite side of a screen.

Cant's whisper was a warning.

"Descend too deeply, Angus Lok, and I will not be able to pull you back."

Angus Lok did not break a stride as he headed east.

CHAPTER 3

Do and Be Damned

Stannig Beade left the Hailhold in the same cart he'd arrived in, a six-axle wheelhouse with walls of poison pine. He was dressed in the same narrow-shouldered robe of polished pigskin collared with mink and shod in the same nailhead boots. His hair and beard had been freshly dyed, his nails clipped, and his skin unctioned with resin harvested from thousand-year pines that grew in Scarpe's Armored Grove. His ceremonial chisel was mounted in his right fist, and it was a testament to Blackhail's wire-pullers that you had to look very closely to see the steel thread holding the fingers in place. No such subtlety marked the stitching of his wounds. Thick black sutures tracked the length of his throat, disappearing beneath the glossy mink collar, cinching hardened crusts of skin.

Raina Blackhail was relieved to see the last of them. As she stood on the paved court at the front of Blackhail's round-house and watched the team of horses pull the wheelhouse south, she prayed they wouldn't stop.

Go, she wished.

All the days of living with fear.

Go.

Sunlight flickered in and out of existence as bands of clouds passed overhead. It was close to midday; two hours later than planned. There'd been a problem with the wheelhouse—one of the rear axles had required remounting—and repair had caused delay. Raina had not known what to do with herself during those hours. She could not sit and wait. Walk? Ride? How could you go about your life when you feared being discovered for a murderer? In the end she had worked, taking herself off to the cattle shed to assist the spring calving. It was hard, bloody work and it had helped. A distressed cow in labor required one's full attention. Two calves had been born, but only one had stood and suckled. Raina and the head dairyman, Vern Satchell, had been been lifting the second calf to encourage it to stand when the call had come from court.

"All ready with the wheelhouse."

Raina had left the sick calf to Vern Satchell and now she was here, outside the Hailhouse, watching the wagon lurch into motion. Orwin Shank, Corbie Meese, Gat Murdock, Merritt Ganlow, Sheela Cobbin and other senior clansmen and clanswomen formed a silent company at her back. Scarpes were out in force. The dead man, Stannig Beade, had been their guide for seven years and respect was due. Scarpes in full mourning were a strange and unlovely sight. Over three hundred men, women and children had dyed their left hands black. Arranging themselves in single file around the great paved court of Blackhail they swayed from side to side as they named the Stone Gods out of order.

It was chilling to hear Behathmus, the god of darkness, named first.

They have not finished harming us, Raina realized as she watched them. All, even children, were armed with knives and lean-bladed swords. Their roundhouse had burned to the ground. Their chief had plundered her own clanhold, seizing livestock and grain from tied clansmen and distributing the spoils amongst her favorites. Now their guide was dead— killed, rumor had it, by a Hailsman.

Or Hailswoman.

Raina forced herself not to react. She was getting good at that. Harder. Cooler. Less like herself. More like a chief.

Rumors had infested the roundhouse like mice; squeaks here, a trail of droppings there. Ten days ago at dawn Stannig Beade had been found dead in the chief's chamber. That was fact. Everything else was up for grabs. Mutilated, the rumors went, drained of blood, decapitated, his heart carved clean from his chest. *Cowlmen,* Hailsfolk said. Anwyn Bird and Jani Gaylo had already been taken by them. In this very house. It had to be a trained assassin from an enemy clan. Who else?

One of your own, countered the Scarpes. Beade kept his chamber door bolted while he slept. He opened it only for those he knew and trusted. And then there were the bloody footprints leading up the stairs from Beade's chamber. The killer had been barefooted, and small if he were indeed a man.

Raina had kept her mouth shut and her eyes averted. She found manual labor during the day and kept company with the widows by night. Even bone tired she could not sleep. Leaving the chief's chamber that night, after killing him, she had been filled with a sense of her own power. It hadn't been enough to take Beade's life, she was going to destroy the monstrosity of a guidestone he'd hauled here in that very wheelhouse from Scarpe.

Something had happened to her as she climbed the stairs from the chief's chamber, though, and her thoughts had turned to self-preservation. She could feel Beade's blood drying to a sticky paste against her legs. Footsteps sounded as she reached the top of the stairs, and her heart jumped. Light was filtering into the entrance hall and she could hear the clan awakening. Soon warriors would come and push back the door, luntmen would begin snuffing lamps, kitchen boys would fuel the bread ovens and children would run down the halls.

Scarpes would stir right along with them. One of the many silly girls who worshipped Beade would bring the guide a breakfast of warm milk and fried bread. In all likelihood she would be the one who'd find him dead, and if Raina wasn't careful the girl would also find the person who killed him standing at the top of the stairs with bloody feet. Raina hurried. Slipping through the roundhouse's shadows, she made her way to her chamber beneath the kitchens. Once there she had stripped and cleaned herself with a wet rag, and then slept until she was awakened two hours later with the word of Beade's death. Orwin Shank broke the news and quietly returned the knife.

Raina regretted leaving the guidestone intact. From her position on the court she could view it; the halved monolith that had once belonged to Scarpe. Thick seams of bitumen made it weak, and its newly exposed face was already eroding. When Beade was alive he'd directed it to be covered when it rained and snowed. No one bothered now. Birds shit on it and bitumen leached from the granite, staining it black. As Raina watched, a raven landed on its west corner and goose-stepped along the top. The guidestone was a worthless hunk of earth, and Hailsmen knew it. In the cold spring sunlight it looked like an abandoned shack.

Raina returned her attention to the departing wheelhouse. The wagon had cleared the court and was now on the dirt road heading south. Dust smoking from beneath the wheels soon obscured it from view. Raina took a deep breath and then another one. It was foolish she knew, but she had convinced herself that once Beade's body was gone from the Hailhold she would she be safe. Out of sight, out of mind.

We are Scarpe. Our tongues cut as deeply as our swords. Wrong us and you will feel the swift lash of both. The Scarpe boast. Raina had always thought it a nasty set of words.

Raina studied the Scarpemen and women. They stared back with dislike. It was no secret that the chief's wife barely tolerated their presence in the Hailhouse, and with Beade, their biggest champion, gone, they were vulnerable. Scarpes had made themselves cozy in the Hailhouse. They were well fed by Hail farmers and cooks, and protected from the cold by the roundhouse's nine-foot-thick walls. Return to the Scarpehold and they would be forced to find food and shelter for themselves. Yelma Scarpe, the Scarpe chief, ran a lean clan. She offered little incentive for refugees to return home.

And she's coming here, Raina reminded herself. What had Longhead said? She will travel when the snow clears? Raina looked from the dry pavestones at her feet to the increasingly blue sky. *A woman can always hope.*

"Warriors returning!"

The cry came from lookouts stationed on the great domed roof of the roundhouse. Everyone who heard it looked to the southern horizon. The Scarpe mourners continued wailing and swaying, but their postures became alert.

"Five," said the hammerman, Corbie Meese. At over six feet tall he saw farther than most. "I think Ballic's among them."

Unable to help herself, Raina asked, "And Mace?"

It was a long three second before Corbie said, "No."

Raina exhaled. Quite suddenly her nerves could no longer stand the sound of wailing Scarpes. "Empty the court!" she cried. "All inside."

For a wonder they actually shut up. Unarmed Hailsfolk began to make their way indoors. They knew and respected the custom of warriors greeting warriors. At first the Scarpes hesitated to follow them—they were keen to see who was arriving—but the Hailsfolk left them little choice. *Herded* was the word for it. Hailsfolk herded Scarpefolk into the house.

No one, not Corbie or Orwin Shank, made a move to herd Raina Blackhail. Glancing over one shoulder and then the other at the remaining warriors, Raina realized they were arranging themselves in formal ranking around her. Orwin, acting chief of the roundhouse and senior warrior, did not shift from his position at her right hand. Orwin's brother-in-law Mads Basko, hero of the River Wars, took up position on her left.

Raina took a breath, raised her chin. It was possible, she realized, to feel relief and apprehension at exactly the same time.

The returning warriors rode through dust raised by the wheelhouse. As Corbie had promised, one of the five was the head bowman Ballic the Red. Grim Shank, Orwin's eldest, was also in the party, together with the young swordsman Jessie Mure, who had been apprenticed under Shor Gormalin, and the young hammerman Pog Bramwell. The fifth rider was a woman. Bareheaded with gleaming chestnut hair fanned out across her shoulders, she attracted the gazes of the men. Her mount was a full-grown stallion, dock-tailed, and discreetly trapped in gray suede. As she drew closer, her facial features came into view. *Pretty* was not a word you could use for her. Her cheekbones stopped sunlight from reaching her lower face and her chin was strong like a man's.

Raina could not tell if she was clan. Certainly the woman knew how to hold herself in the saddle, knew also her formal place in a party of four sworn clansmen: middle rear. Raina could feel the warriors' interest. Glorious hair, skill at horse: Here was a woman Hailsmen could admire.

"Welcome," Raina called, as the party slowed to a halt on the court.

Ballic the Red bowed his small neat head and dismounted. As was proper, the remaining three clansmen followed his lead. The woman regarded Raina boldly, with interest. Dismounting a beat later than the men, she demonstrated her recognition of Raina's status as chief's wife by meeting her afoot.

Clan then, Raina decided. Such subtlety of custom was seldom understood outside the holds.

"Lady," Ballic said, coming forward and grasping her forearms. Hazel eyes accustomed to spotting and tracking prey over distance inspected Raina. The bowman's grip tightened. "I am at your service, always."

So he found her changed. In need of service. Raina nodded a response. Accepting the greeting of the remaining three warriors she kept her face still. In the distance, the wheelhouse turned west onto the old clan road, a black phantom trailing dust.

One Scarpe down. A thousand more to go.

"Lady. Da." Grim Shank broke into her thoughts. The huge fair-haired hammerman had caught the strange woman's hand in his own and was bringing her forward. The woman's cloak was heavy and very fine. Gray velvet gleamed like pewter as she moved.

"This is Chella Gloyal of Clan Croser." Like all the Shanks, Grim had a ruddy complexion that burned easily in sun and wind. As he spoke, his color was so high across his cheeks it looked as if his face might explode. "My wife."

Raina glanced at Orwin. From the expression on the old hatchetman's face she guessed this was news for him too. He rallied himself well, though, stepping forward and catching the woman in his arms. "Daughter," he murmured when his mouth was close to her ear. "Welcome."

Beaming with relief, Grim clamped his father and his new wife together in a giant bear hug. Chella smiled serenely. Her eyes were gray-green and as cool as a forest lake. As she disentangled herself from the hug, her gaze found Raina.

"You have surprised us," Raina told her.

Chella took the coolness in her stride. Bowing at the neck, she set her auburn hair in motion. "Love marches quickly in times of war."

"Aye," Grim agreed, slipping his hand around his wife's waist. "Wait and your chance may be lost."

All the warriors gathered on the court felt the truth of this statement. Silence fell. Looking at the bowed heads and ax-bitten hands of her fellow clansmen, Raina felt a welling of love and respect. *My clan. And I must protect them.*

It was easy then to be gracious to the self-composed stranger from Croser. She was a clanswoman, after all. And it made sense that Hailish warriors, working in alliance with Croser against Bludd, would come into contact with Croser maids. Dagro had been a firm believer in the benefits of unions between clans. "Every marriage is a length of string," he had told her once. "Enough of them and we tie a rival to our side."

Raina said to Chella, "Today you are a Hailswoman."

Sometimes she forgot her own power. Five words spoken by the chief's wife were enough to change the mood from somber to celebratory.

"Aye!" called the warriors in agreement. Bullhammer came forward and clasped Grim's arms in celebration. One-armed Gat Murdock hollered to the roundhouse for beer. Orwin gave Raina a sweet and noisy kiss on the cheek. Even the sun stayed out.

Chella smiled and nodded appropriately, but in no way seemed relieved. Why should she? Raina thought. Chella had not been worried in the first place.

As they waited for the beer to come, Bullhammer began the questioning and the mood shifted once more.

"Who holds Ganmiddich?"

"Pengo Bludd," Ballic replied. "He repaired the gate and is staying right behind it. We've charged twice and he won't ride out and meet us."

Scathing curses followed this pronouncement. Sitting tight against a charge was considered cowardly by men who worshiped the Stone Gods.

"We didn'a do it," Mads Basko said softly, referring to the strike against Ganmiddich by Spire Vanis. Even outnumbered three to one, Blackhail had ridden from the Crab Gate to engage the army led by Marafice Eye.

"It's worse," Ballic said. "When Bludd reached the Crab

Gate, the Spire army withdrew so quickly they left their equipment on the field. Pengo went prospecting and got himself some siege fire and a thrower."

Raina felt out of her depth. She had never heard of siege fire, though she knew by the men's reactions that it was something serious. *How can I lead clan when I know nothing of war?*

Learn was the only answer. "What happened?"

"They didn't know what they were doing during the first charge," Ballic said, loosening the cloak ties around his throat. "Had the thrower up on the wall, spewing out black oil. No flames—at least not till some damn fool set a torch to it. Entire wall goes up. The Bluddsmen manning the thrower get scorched. A handful of hammermen down below take harm, then the wind switches and the flames get blown back into the roundhouse. Charge breaks on the wall and we laugh our way back to Bannen. Pengo's no Dog Lord. He's not the brightest lamp in the hall.

"Six days later we mount a second attack, thinking that if we're lucky the Bluddsmen will burn down their own gate. Someone there knows what's he's doing though. Had the thrower up and working. Waited until we were right on top of them—even cracked open the gate to goad us—and then blasted the van with fire. It was hell. Burning hell. Men. Horses." Ballic shuddered. "Gods save them."

Grim, Jessie Mure and others touched their horns of powdered guidestone. Chella Gloyal observed this before touching her own guidestone that was held in a pouch of orange silk at her waist.

"Who took harm?" Raina asked.

"Banmen formed the van. The honor was due—Hail led the first charge."

Raina nodded softly. The clouds had returned, and a

sharp wind gusted around the court, rattling the hammermen's chains. To the south, the wheelhouse had passed
beyond view. Good riddance to it.

"How many were lost?"

"Three hundred and their horses." Ballic paused. His short
stubby fingers with their bowman's calluses twitched when
he added, "They were screaming to be killed."

Burned and still alive. Raina pictured the horror of it and
fixed the images into place in her memory. Bannen had been
Blackhail's ally for a thousand years; their losses and suffering
counted as her own.

Orwin said, "Bludd be cursed for its cowardice."

"Aye," seconded his son. "Siege fire is city evil. It has no
place in the clans."

"Where do our armies stand now?"

Grim turned to address Raina. Not one of these men, she
realized, questioned her right to be here.

"We're camped a day's ride northwest of the Crabhouse, on
Bannen Field."

Raina made herself think about this. "So Mace plans to re-
attack?"

"Aye."

At either side of her warriors stamped their feet and
nodded. Corbie Meese reached over his shoulder, uncradled
his great war hammer and sent the lead and iron head thumping against his left palm. Cheered, that was how he appeared.
Raina did not share the feeling. Dark half-formed thoughts
drifted through her head. Eight months ago Mace had given
the order to slay women and children on the Bluddroad. Now
Bludd was blasting Blackhail with liquid fire. Both actions
were unworthy of clan. What next?

With Mace you could not be sure.

"Any news of Dun Dhoone?" Orwin asked.

And there it was, the final distasteful piece in the puzzle: Robbie Dun Dhoone, the man who had tricked his fellow clansmen into a fatal attack on Withy as a diversion while he retook the Dhoonehouse. Dhoone had betrayed Dhoone. There was no greater wrong in the clanholds than a chief selling out his own clan.

"He's expected to move on Withy any day now," Ballic said. "Last thirty days he's been laying siege. Hanro and Thrago Bludd have been sitting tight, but supplies'll be running low. Dun Dhoone has the roundhouse surrounded—and rumor has it he's salted the wells. Both sides'll be getting jumpy. That means one of two things is likely. Either Thrago will order a charge from the gate, or Dun Dhoone will go right ahead and force one."

The dark thoughts began to coalesce in Raina's mind. It was surprisingly easy to anticipate disaster ahead. Dun Dhoone would take Withy. A house cut off and surrounded was dead meat—even a chief's wife knew that. Bludd would be routed. Then killed. Robbie Dhoone was famous for taking no prisoners; the only Bluddsmen to live through the retaking of Dhoone were those who had found a secret tunnel and escaped right under his nose. So Robbie would take possession of Withy, crown himself a king, and then?

"He'll come looking for Crab."

She was hardly aware she spoke.

Looking into the faces of the warriors she was surprised to see that none of them were ahead of her. Ballic, Orwin and others nodded quickly enough but she could tell that they were following her thoughts, playing out in their minds a future where the three northern giants met in battle over the small but exquisitely placed clanhold of Ganmiddich. Dhoone. Blackhail. Bludd.

"Robbie knows Ganmiddich like the back of his hand," Chella Gloyal said, surprising everyone by speaking. Her sage gray eyes looked straight at Raina, and Raina found herself wondering if the Croserwoman hadn't been ahead of everyone.

"How so?" Ballic asked. Raina knew the master bowman well, and could hear the challenge and impatience in his voice. What business did a Croserwoman have speaking up at a Blackhail warrior's parley?

If Chella heard it too, it had no effect upon her. Calmly, she pushed her hair behind her ears before answering. "He lived there for three seasons when he was fourteen."

This was news. Orwin raised his eyebrows at Raina. Ballic frowned. Grim frowned too, but he obviously knew some things about his new wife that others did not, for his frown was one of agreement, not disbelief.

Chella touched his arm. The wind was pressing her cloak against her body, outlining her slender waist and full hips. "His father Mabb Cormac sent him away after he killed his horse. Robbie rode the old mare from the Stonefly to the Dhoonehouse without stopping to let her rest. She collapsed on the banks of Blue Dhoone Lake and he left her there to die. Mabb was furious and beat his son with a birch switch. When the beating was done Mabb still wasn't satisfied and sent his son to Ganmiddich for two hundred and fifty days. Best part of a year later, Robbie returned riding a stallion he'd won in a race from the Crab's nephew Addo Ganhanlin."

Men nodded. Now things were beginning to make sense.

After being ousted from Ganmiddich, Addo Ganhanlin and others had taken refuge at Croser. It was possible Chella had heard Addo's story firsthand.

Raina fastened the ties on her cloak to give herself time to think. *Listen first to what people say, and then second to how they say it.* Dagro's words, spoken fifteen years earlier to his young, inexperienced wife, echoed in her mind. Chella Gloyal had told a story and issued a warning: Robbie Dhoone knew more about Ganmiddich and its defenses than anyone could have guessed. The second thing was more subtle. She spoke with authority, assuming equal status with sworn clansmen, and she spoke in an accent that wasn't wholly clan. This woman had spent time in the Mountain Cities.

Glancing over her shoulder, she saw that anxious clansfolk were beginning to gather by the door. The meeting was going on longer than anticipated and Hailsmen were assuming the worst. Addressing the young swordsman Jessie Mure, she said, "Pass the word inside—no Hailsmen have been lost."

She was not prepared for the bow the lean, dark-haired young man delivered to her, touching the hem of her cloak in courtly respect. "It is done, lady," he said, turning to make his way to the house.

He'd learned that from the master swordsman, Shor Gormalin. Shor had been dead for half a year now, killed by crossbolt to the back of the head. Mace Blackhail had ordered the killing; Shor had been his rival for the chiefship. And for herself.

Heart be strong, she told it.

"Mace is unaware of Robbie's knowledge of the Crabhouse?" she asked Ballic.

"Aye."

"Then a message must be sent."

"I'll see to it."

"Good. Chella. I would have you think on what other intelligence you possess that may benefit your new clan."

The Croserwoman finally had the grace to look surprised. She took a breath, considering her answer, but Raina halted her.

"Do not speak now. You are weary from the road. If something occurs to you later visit me. You will find me in the chief's chamber."

Gods do not send a bolt of lightning to strike me. Chief's chamber? Where had that come from? Until the very moment the words left her mouth she had no inkling she would say them. Heat flushed her cheeks, and there didn't seem much option other than to stand there and wait for the condemnation to come.

It didn't.

The warriors seemed careless, as if she had said nothing out of order. Ballic was unclipping his bowcase from its shoulder harness. Grim had stepped back to steady his horse. Others were getting impatient to get inside the house and greet their kin. Only Orwin and Chella regarded Raina. Orwin had been present that day in the game room, when Raina had declared her intention of becoming chief. He knew her purpose . . . but perhaps this was the first time he'd heard her claim it publicly. After a long moment of appraising her, he said, "Come on, lads. Let's get some food and ale in your bellies."

Raina watched as the group broke up and began heading toward the roundhouse. As Chella Gloyal passed alongside Raina, the woman murmured, "In the chief's chamber. I won't forget."

Raina stared ahead. Her chest was tight. Word would get around. It would get back to Mace. *Raina Blackhail issues commands from the chief's chamber.*

The wind blew across the open ground of the graze and the court, cooling Raina's hands and face. During the meeting the only thing that had seemed important was Blackhail's security. Over two thousand Hailsmen were camped northwest of Ganmiddich, and if Robbie Dun Dhoone succeeded at seizing the Withyhouse then Dhoone would march south to retake Ganmiddich. Dhoone, Blackhail, Bludd: The three giants would meet on the shores of the Wolf. That was what seemed important—not who took action or said what.

Do and be damned, that was what Dagro always said about being a chief. Mostly he said it with defiant joy—*I'm chief, to hell with my critics*—yet there had been times when he'd spoken it softly with fear, when he'd ridden into battle out-manned and outpositioned. To lead one had to *do,* Raina realized. That was the message of Dagro's words. Inaction did not make a chief.

Risk did.

Settling that thought into her mind, Raina made her way to the house.

As she passed into the dim lamplit space of the entrance hall, she spied a group of Scarpes building a fire in an iron brazier. Bristling, she gathered herself to engage them. Smoke would choke the ground floor. Yesterday, when they had dragged the brazier indoors she had done nothing. Not today though. That was the thing about declaring yourself chief-in-absentia: Once you did it you had to act like one.

As she opened her mouth to issue a command, she realized she hadn't thought about Stannig Beade in hours.

CHAPTER 4

Marafice Eye

Marafice Eye spooned the jellied eel into his mouth and swallowed. Twice. Sweet mother of all beasts, how did these grangelords do it? Sitting around in their stiff silks and itchy collars, sipping wine as tart as acid and chewing fish parts? Any beggar in Hell's Town could eat better than this: beer and sausage, beer and pork pie—and they could slouch in loose linens as they did it. Frowning in disgust, Marafice pushed away his plate and leaned back in his chair.

The throne.

"Is my lordship displeased with the food?" The question came from Marilla Theron, Lady of the Salt Mine Granges. Her husband, Philip, was hosting this feast in the newly cleared space of the quad. Red and gold canopies had been erected overhead and long oak tables had been laid out in a giant U. Marafice sat at the head of this construction, elevated a foot above everyone else on a dais of gilded wood. There was no room underneath the table for his knees and he sat with his thighs and weaponry exposed, on level with the tabletop and its unappetizing array of food. Some fool had made a three-foot-tall killhound out of cherries and turkey feathers, and there was a smoking dragon formed from salmon that was beginning to attract the flies.

It was not pleasant being here, with the sun losing power in the west and sharp mountain winds blowing through the two-hundred-foot gap in the wall. The Splinter, the tallest tower in the North, was gone, fallen, and it had taken part of the south ward and curtain wall with it. For the first time in two thousand years the city of Spire Vanis was not securely walled. And here were five dozen of the most powerful grangelords in Spire Vanis, making merry by the timber scaffolding and rubble heaps, as carpenters hammered nails and raised joists and laborers wheeled away carts loaded with granite and dust.

Bizarre did not begin to describe it. High atop one of the hills of fallen stone, a group of masons were sitting on tarps, gnawing on chicken bones and gawking at the spectacle below them. Marafice imagined he could feel their scorn. It made him hot and grumpy.

"The food, my lord?" persisted the unlovely boniness that was Marilla Theron. "Is it not to your liking?"

"Yes," Marafice growled. And then, just to make sure, "No."

He always found himself flustered around highborn women. He suspected they were looking down on him, and if the glance Marilla Theron shared with her long-nosed sister Margo was anything to go by, he was right. These women had nothing to do all day, save dress themselves in staggering amounts of jewels and silk and gossip about the shortcomings of men. At least working women worked.

Laughter drifting down from the masons was suddenly too much for Marafice and he flung down his handcloth and stood. He'd been surlord for twenty days now and he still wasn't used to it: stand and everyone else followed suit.

So much gold glittered as the grangelords and their wives rose, Marafice was temporarily blinded. When his eye cleared he saw his handcloth had landed on the table, in a bowl of gravy and . . . something. The cloth turned brown as it soaked up the sauce.

Marafice frowned harder. "Sit. Eat," he commanded the party, hearing the rise in his voice but powerless to stop it. "I thank our friend the Lord of the Salt Mine Granges for this fine supper. Feast," he corrected himself. Suspecting a compliment was called for, he cast his mind for one and then corrected himself again. "Eye-boggling feast." People tittered. Marafice stepped back. His left heel struck his chair leg and it toppled from the dais with a loud crack. Heat rushed to his face.

"I'm off."

Snickering followed him as he walked across the open ground of the quad. *I'm off.* Where was his brain? Surlords didn't say I'm off. Surlords said farewell and good tidings and blessings to you and your sons.

I'm off.

Truer words had not been said. Marafice Eye, Surlord of Spire Vanis, Rive Watch Keeper of Mask Fortress, and Master of the Four Gates was seriously off. His surlording skills were wanting and his patience was worn as thin as those fancy wafers that dowagers ate instead of bread. How had Iss managed to do it? Put up with all the cronying and flattery? The hours of ceremony, the feasts, banquets, balls, parades?

Reaching the entrance to the east ward, Marafice accepted the salutes of the sentries stationed by the gate. "I see you made ten years," he said to Flukey Brown, the older of the two brothers-in-the-watch. Flukey's bloodred cloak was fastened with a killhound brooch mounted with chips of jet to represent eyes. The jet chips were the mark of ten-year service. Another ten and they would be replaced with rubies.

Flukey did not raise his gaze to his surlord as he pushed back the door. "Aye, sir."

Marafice studied him. He and Flukey had ridden side by side during the Hound's Mire campaign. At the end of the daylong pitched battle, it had been he and Flukey who had ridden through the killing field dealing mercy to fatally wounded brothers-in-the-watch. Now the man wouldn't look at him.

Get used to it.

Ducking under Flukey's arm, Marafice entered Mask Fortress.

No matter how often the servants swept they couldn't get rid of the dust. A shear of white powder had settled on the polished granite floor in the places where men and servants rarely stepped. The corridor leading to the Red Forge was clean, and not for the first time Marafice had to resist the urge to take it. That was his old stalking ground—the Rive Watch barracks—and the desire to head there for ale and the silent camaraderie of fighting men was strong. There'd be a big fire, overcooked ham and beans and small coin gambling. Old-timers would be passed out on the rear benches and new recruits would be heaping their plates high, unaccustomed to the luxury of free mess. God, he missed it. Now it was impossible for him to go there without upsetting the peace. Overnight he'd gone from being a fellow brother-in-the-watch, to an intruder. When a surlord entered a room soldiers stood.

And kept standing until you left.

Turning a sharp right he headed across the dust field to the Cask. It was the principal fortified structure in the fortress—and therefore the entire city of Spire Vanis—and it housed the surlord's official and private quarters. The walls were twenty feet thick at the base. Inside it was as cool and quiet as a mountain cave. The Splinter's collapse had damaged the two other standing towers, cracking masonry, collapsing roofs and destroying struts, but the Cask had remained untouched. It was where Roland Stornoway had holed up during the first ten days of his regency as he claimed power in his son-in-law's name.

Marafice pressed a fist into his empty eye socket. Thinking about his father-in-law was not good for his sanity, yet he couldn't figure out how to avoid it. The man was always there for one thing, wheezing and tap-tapping around the fortress on his canes. One look at the floor and you could see that he'd been here. The cane tips left tiny holes in the dust. Spying them, Marafice comprehended that Stornoway was ahead of him. The Lord of the High Granges had taken the Walk of Bastard Lords toward the surlord's chambers, and had not returned. Marafice touched the grip of his sword and then slid his hand along the gear belt to the hand knife mounted in the small of his back. If pushed he could draw it left-handed.

The Impaled Beasts of Spire Vanis, grotesquely cast in black iron, flickered in the torchlight as Marafice rounded the hall. Dragons, basilisks, werewolves, serpents, saber-tooth cats, moon snakes and dozens of nameless monsters had been rendered thrashing on sharpened poles. Legend held that the Founding Quarterlords had rid the Spire Valley of fearsome beasts before building the city at its head. Marafice didn't know about that, but he understood well enough the message of the poles. Spire Vanis was a violent city. Rule it, and be prepared to put on a show. It wasn't enough that your enemies died. They had to die in agony, in public, screaming your name.

"My lord."

Caydis Zerbina, Iss' former hand servant, stepped out of the surlord's chambers and held open the door. Zerbina had continued his duties since Iss' death, and Marafice wasn't quite sure what to make of it. Certainly it was good to have someone care for the fancy chains and silks of office, and discreetly bring food and drink and women when necessary, but it was a new and not entirely comfortable experience to have someone serve and anticipate your needs. In the past if he wanted a whore he'd walk to Cunt's Street and buy one. If his kit needed cleaning he'd clean it. Now he couldn't leave the fortress without an armed escort, and he had so many ceremonial robes and gewgaws that caring for them would take half of every day. At least Zerbina spared him that.

He was a queer bird though, a brother of the Bone Temple, and you could never tell what he was thinking. His dark brown face with its striking features and high cheekbones remained still as Marafice approached. Long fingers pushed against the ironwood door.

"Is Stornoway in there?" Marafice asked.

Zerbina bowed his head. Mink oil in his hair flashed green.

"How long?"

Twenty, Zerbina mouthed.

"Anyone else?"

No.

Marafice nodded. "Bring me ale . . . and a fresh cup."

The servant understood the urgency of this request and

departed. It was, Marafice supposed, one of the benefits of inheriting Zerbina. He'd served one surlord; he knew the drill. If Stornoway had spent time alone in the chambers there was no telling what mischief had been done. Food and drink were not the only thing that could be spiked with poison. The vessels that bore them could be tainted too.

Bracing himself for impact, Marafice entered the room.

The first thing to hit him was the scent of burning amber. The fumes made his eye sting and set off tingles of pain in the cavities behind his nose. Knee-high smoke rippled ahead of him as he moved toward the fire. White coal burning in the grate released small, tooth-shaped flames. Roland Stornoway stood in front of them, poking the embers with one of his sticks.

"Has Theron hit you up for cash yet?"

Stornoway did not turn around as he spoke, and Marafice was forced to address the back of his bald head.

"Theron gave a feast. He said nothing about cash."

The Lord of the High Granges cackled with delight. His small bent back huffed up and down and he had to work to stabilize himself with his canes. "Chair," he commanded as he wobbled out of control.

Fall and die, old man. Marafice couldn't explain why he brought the chair anyway. Or maybe he could but it made him feel shame. After a lifetime obeying grangelords the habit was hard to kick. "Here. Sit," he said, pushing the chair seat into the back of Stornoway's knees and forcing the man down.

"Not so close to the fire," Stornoway cried, lashing out with his right cane. The tip was smoking from the fire. It missed Marafice's shin by half an inch.

Grabbing hold of the seatback, Marafice dragged Stornoway and the chair away from the fireplace. The man weighed less than a bunch of twigs. Roland Stornoway had to be eighty years old. He might have shrunk in size and weight but what remained was so hard and sharp that it seemed far more dangerous than bulk. Marafice was quick to release him.

Father-in-law. Marafice tested the phrase, hoping to find some sense in it. He was married to this man's daughter. By seizing control of the fortress after Iss' death, Stornoway had made it possible for Marafice to name himself surlord on his return from the clanholds. Trouble was Stornoway fancied that title himself. It hardly seemed possible—the man was hobbling into his ninth decade—but the truth was in his eyes. A gaze as shrewd and flat as a raptor's pinned Marafice Eye.

"When a grangelord feasts a surlord it means he wants something. In Philip Theron's case he's after cash. He's broke. He'd been banking on the clanholds campaign to fill his coffers but we all know that ended duck's arse up."

Marafice felt at a loss. Stornoway had that effect upon him. The man knew things—personal information about the grangelords that Marafice hadn't figured out how to discover for himself. "Why didn't Theron come out and ask me?"

Stornoway answered this with a withering look that said everything about how the grangelords viewed their new surlord, the butcher's son. "He'll send a request to your Master of Purse."

"I won't allow it. That bastard left us for dead in Ganmiddich, rode right off the field with the rest of them."

"Yet you managed to swallow his food without choking."

Thrusting away the words with his fist, Marafice stalked to the far side of the room. High-backed chairs carved from ebony and zebrawood sat on a rug the size of a bull ring. Behind them a series of tapestries embroidered in red and gold depicted the military triumphs of Spire Vanis. Unframed and crudely nailed to the wall, their edges were curled and fraying. The hind legs of Callan Pengaron's horse were gone, reduced to dangling thread. Marafice gave its rider another decade at most.

Surlord of Spire Vanis: What did anyone have to show for it? Iss, Horgo, Hews, Pengaron: All had suffered early deaths.

Marafice turned to face his father-in-law. "I know I must make alliances, but I'll be damned if I'm going to pay for them."

Stornoway laughed; it sounded like he was choking. Dressed in an ancient black half cape with a molting beaver collar, he didn't look like a man who controlled the most lucrative mountain pass in Spire Vanis. The Lord of the High Granges collected tolls on goods entering the city from the south. Bolts of silk, baskets of strawberries, pots of myrrh, alabaster lamps, glass beads, pigments for dyeing cloth and illuminating manuscripts, and dozens upon dozens of spices: saffron, nutmeg, black and white pepper, cloves, cumin, turmeric, cinnamon, cardamon, galangal, fennel, star anise, paprika. In theory Stornoway surrendered half of all tariffs to the city but his accounts hadn't been audited in decades. Substantial bribes paid to Horgo and Iss had taken care of that.

"You need friends," Stornoway said. "It's time to buy some. Philip Theron's as good a place as any to start. Where Salt leads the Far West follows. As compass points go it's a minor one, but as you're so intent on fostering enemies in the east and north it doesn't leave you much choice."

Marafice scowled at his father-in-law. Garric Hews, the Lord of the Eastern Granges, hardly required fostering—the man had refused to acknowledge Marafice's surlordship and had vowed to storm the fortress. To the North lay the lords of the Spillway, the Wheatfield, the Mercury, the Black Soil and Black River Granges. None of them were friends to Surlord Eye and some were in open collusion with Hews. Most of them had withdrawn forces during the strike on Ganmiddich.

Thinking of that moment of desertion made Marafice see red. "What's it to you if I make enemies, old man? All the more people to murder me." As he spoke he knew it was a mistake, yet he couldn't seem to stop himself. "Explain the difference between yourself and Garric Hews. From where I stand I see two vicious bastards who wish me dead."

Stornoway's cold gray eyes flashed in triumph. He'd been waiting twenty days for this. "When they punctured your eyeball did part of your brain go with it?" The Lord of the High Granges did not pause for an answer. "Time is everything here. Yes, mayhap you and I will duel later, but for the immediate future it serves us both to consolidate your position and secure the city. Poison you tonight in your sleep and I give the keys of the fortress to whichever grangelord is bold enough to mount the first offensive. Right now your sole strength is the Rive Watch. Lose you and I lose them."

Mother of God the man was bold. A snake revealing himself to be a snake and not the slightest bit ashamed of it. Marafice glanced at the door. Where was Zerbina with the ale?

Forcing himself to think, Marafice paced the room. There were no windows at ground level, so he moved between blank walls. Coming to a halt directly in front of Stornoway, he murmured, "Remind me why I shouldn't kill you for what you just said."

The old man rested his canes on his lap. This close you could see the moth holes in his cape. "When the Splinter fell it took the fortress's and the city's southern walls with it. As we sit today the High Granges and its allies are the only things preventing Hews from launching an attack through the gap."

"I have the Watch and the Cloud Fort."

"The Cloud Fort stands off my southern border. I know exactly how much rain gets through that roof and many men stand beneath it getting a soaking. As for the Watch . . . well I think we all understand they're best used as a last line of defense. The glory days of riding out and engaging the enemy are twenty years in the past."

Marafice sucked air into his lungs to object, but by the time he was ready to speak he realized he didn't have anything to say. At best he could remind his father-in-law that the Hound's Mire campaign had taken place fifteen—not twenty—years ago. Certainly the strike on Ganmiddich had proved disastrous. There was no getting around that. Stornoway was right: The Watch was best for defense, not offense.

"How many hideclads are stationed at your grange?"

"Two thousand pensioned. I can call out double that number if needs must."

"Do it."

Again there was that flash of triumph in the raptor's eyes. "A dozen companies will need to be stationed in sight of the walls."

On land owned by the city, not a grangelord.

A soft knock on the door announced the arrival of Caydis Zerbina with the ale. The servant moved across the room without a sound. Depositing a tray with a pewter jug and two cups on a footstool close to the fire, he looked to his surlord for direction. Marafice raised a finger. *Leave us*, it said. *I will pour the ale myself.*

You had to give it to Zerbina: He understood nuance better than anyone. *Mayhap, I'll keep him*, Marafice decided, feeling comforted by the sight of yellow foam on top of the jug.

"Ale?" he asked Stornoway as Zerbina withdrew.

"Might as well."

It was the closest Stornoway came to courtesy and Marafice obliged by pouring him the first cup.

Stornoway rested his ale against his bony thigh. "So do we drink to our alliance?"

Marafice stretched the time it took him to pour his own ale and stand upright. Hideclads patrolling city land—that was what his father-in-law was proposing. Spire Vanis owned all land within a quarter league of the city's southern wall. Most of it formed the skirts and lower slopes of Mount Slain, but to the southeast the land opened into valleys. Stornoway's grange lay there, incorporating high and low valleys and the lucrative Eagle Kill Pass. It was his right to patrol all roads and passes in his territory. It wasn't his right to patrol city land. That took special decree by the surlord.

And only a fool of a surlord would allow it.

Or a desperate one.

Truth was he needed Stornoway and Stornoway needed him. The old goat was right when he said that if he, Marafice, died tomorrow it would be unlikely that Stornoway could hold the fortress. The Rive Watch were still suspicious of him and there was no telling who they might follow in wake of their surlord's death. A handful of grangelords had served in the Watch—the Lord of the Black River Granges and Lord of Almsgate sprang to mind—and if any of them declared themselves as surlord they had a fighting chance of carrying the Watch. Stornoway needed time to ingratiate himself. Favors needed to be bought, and a custom of command and obedience established. Plus he needed Marafice to make a public show of acknowledging his grandchild, Marafice's newborn son.

God help me to stay sane. Son indeed. Liona Stornoway had been visibly pregnant when he'd married her. The squalling, red-faced brat she'd produced was spawn of another man, some dirt-poor student at the Great Library whom she'd met while out taking the cure at Scalding Springs. Marafice flicked a speck of foam from his fist. There wasn't enough hot water in the entire city to cure all that ailed his wife. The woman wasn't right in the head.

Most days he managed to avoid her. Besides, he'd known what he was getting into. It was his price of entry into the grangelords: none of their sound-minded females would have had him.

Both of them, Liona and Stornoway, were eager to have Marafice acknowledge the baby as his own. Liona because her reputation was at stake; Stornoway because a surlord's son could be useful to him. Marafice could hear him now, addressing the Rive Watch. "I don't claim power for myself but as a steward for Eye's son."

Jon Marafice was his proposed name. Blond and tiny with psoriasis on his arms and buttocks and a mild clubbing of his left foot, he was awaiting Purification. During the ceremony a full name had to be given, complete with surname. As of today, Marafice had refused to grant him the use of Eye. The whole thing was a mess. Whatever the baby was named— Stornoway or Eye—his so-called father, the Surlord, would be the laughingstock of the city.

Marafice inhaled sharply. He could smell the hops in the beer.

Truth was it might be to his benefit to claim the boy. Stornoway owned one of the richest and oldest granges in Spire Vanis. The old goat couldn't live forever, and Roland Stornoway the younger, his son, wasn't a well man. Jon Marafice would likely inherit his grandfather's wealth, and that meant Marafice could control it until the boy reached his majority. Thirty years in the Rive Watch did not make one a wealthy man.

Nor did it make one popular. The grangelords did not love him: he was a butcher's son, an upstart, and he'd drawn swords on them countless times. The watch controlled the city; access through its gates, access to Mask Fortress and the sur-lord. It stuck in the grangelords' craws. They held vast estates outside the city but were reduced to supplicants within its walls. Now the man who had held this over them for seventeen years was surlord.

He wasn't one of them, and his only ally in their ranks was sitting in that chair, canes drawn up on his lap, ale going flat as he waited upon a response.

I wanted this, Marafice reminded himself, raising his cup in toast.

"To an unholy alliance," he told his father-in-law.

"Aye," replied Stornoway, smiling his brown-toothed smile. "And as a show of good faith I'll even drink first."

CHAPTER 5

North of Bludd

"We go the long way," Raif reminded Addie Gunn.

The small fair-haired cragsman frowned, said nothing, thought about it some more and spoke. "Most people given the choice between traveling through the clanholds or the Sull Racklands would pick the clanholds."

"I'm not most people."

"They're after you."

Raif considered this, decided it didn't matter if Addie meant Sull or clan. "I know."

Not long after that the sleet started. The clouds had been dropping all day and the temperature had hovered above freezing. An unsettled wind sent the sleet spiraling around rocks and brushcone pines. No soil softened the headland, and crevasses between boulders were the only places for trees to seed. The pines were gnarled and dry. Their needles had the color and texture of rusted nails.

The air smelled of gas. Earth had moved in the night, and Raif found it easy to believe that matter trapped beneath the surface was leaking out. He and Addie had been woken in their tentless camp at midnight. A low rumble had been followed by a series of concussions as unstable boulders crashed to lower ground and dead and diseased trees fell. The quiet that followed had lasted until dawn. Neither wolves nor owls wanted to be first to let their presence be known in the darkness.

Addie had brewed tea, and he and Raif watched the moon set and stars turn. There didn't seem any point in pretending to sleep. When dawn came it was a relief to hear the birds. Ptarmigan, ravens, woodpeckers and longspurs called from cover as the sun rose. The world looked the same, but didn't feel it. Addie and Raif were on the trail within the hour.

It was midafternoon now and Raif was beginning to flag. The wound in his chest was pulling tight and a looseness in his knees forced him to concentrate on every step. Addie too was weary. Fighting the wind and sleet on three hours sleep was draining and his shoulders and head were low. One hand cinched his cloak at the throat while the other white-knuckled his walking staff. The fact that he had brought up the subject of heading south into the easier terrain of the clanholds was telling. It was the closest Addie Gunn came to complaint.

Raif said to him, "We should start looking for a place to camp."

Addie poked his stick into a pile of scree, testing for firmness. "Might as well stop here and sleep on the boulders. Ain't getting any cozier."

"You know this land?"

"Know. What's to know? I've eyes. I can see."

Raif scrambled up a shoulder of granite and looked north and east. Addie was right. There was nothing to see but more of the same landscape of stunted trees and granite bluffs. They were north of Bludd and ten days east of the Maimed Men. Since they'd left the lamb brothers' camp three days back the going had been slow. Bad weather had hampered the pace. Raif's desire not to set foot in the Bluddhold hadn't helped either. The borderland was a breaking ground of rocks.

"At least the bird won't be out."

Addie's statement took Raif a moment to understand. Easing himself down from the ledge, he said, "When was the last time you saw it?"

Addie hadn't shaved in four days, and sleet caught in his bristles. A cap he'd stitched together from strips of black lambskin rested too low above his eyes. *Wait and see,* he'd told Raif a few days back. *A week of rain and it'll shrink up just right.*

Wagging his chin, Addie said, "Bird was out this morning afore the wind kicked up."

He was speaking about the hawk they'd seen every day since leaving the Lake of Red Ice. The bird was not wild. It had silver jesses tied to its legs. Neither he nor Addie had spoken the name of who they believed had fastened them there. Raif did not want to think about the hour he'd spent in Yiselle No Knife's tent. She was Sull and her people believed that he, *Mor Drakka,* would end their existence. The hawk belonged to her.

Raif met Addie's gaze and Raif could see the question in the cragsman's eyes. *We're in danger here: how could stepping into the clanholds be worse?*

"Find us some cover," Raif said.

Addie nodded slowly, thinking. "An hour back we passed that creekbed running north. Be undercuts there if we're willing to turn east."

"Let's do it."

Both men were silent as they made their way deeper into the Racklands. Addie Gunn was a smart man, Raif reckoned. Smart and good. The hawk wouldn't fly in the wind and sleet. Now was as good a time as any to hide from it. Once the weather cleared, the bird's owner would send it west. She would not imagine that Raif and Addie had backtracked east. If they spent the night under cover and raised no smoke they might be able to evade further surveillance. It meant a longer journey and more time spent in Sull territory, but Raif found nothing within him that was eager to return to the Maimed Men. As long as the journey lasted he had no responsibilities to anyone save Addie and himself. Later he would become King of the Rift, but for now he had a kind of freedom. And Addie guessed he wasn't in any hurry to give it up.

The wind streamlined as they made their way northeast. It blew from the south, pressing their cloaks against the small of their backs and carrying the scent of copper and red pines. As they climbed higher the great dark mass of the Boreal Sway became visible in the far east.

"Largest forest in the Known Lands," Addie said softly as they stopped for a moment to comprehend it. "A man could wander for a lifetime and never see the sun."

Raif tracked the black mass until it disappeared into mist . . . and warned himself not to think about Ash. She was gone. The Sull had claimed her. It did not matter to him if she was somewhere down there. Swigging water from his flask, he turned away.

Behind the clouds, the sun descended. As he and Addie worked their way down into a draw the wind died and temperature dropped. By the time they reached the creek, sleet had turned to snow. Dogwood canes and winter-killed thistles choked the banks. A trickle of water darkened the rocks. Something dead—a fox or a fisher—lay eviscerated and partly eaten midstream.

"Wolf-kill," Addie said, turning the carcass's head with his stick. "It'll be as much about territory as meat."

Raif nodded, and headed upstream. There didn't seem any place to rest his thoughts. Ash, the Maimed Men, the lamb brothers, even the wolf kill: everything seemed like a warning.

Pushing forward, he opened up a space between him and Addie Gunn. Last night's tremor had felled shallow-rooted pines along the bank and Raif clambered over them. The sword cross-harnessed against his back kept striking his left shoulder and right hip. Its weight didn't bother him, but its length was becoming a problem. Sull warriors had special harnesses for their weapons, ones that mounted swords higher on the shoulder so their crosshilts were parallel to the shoulder blade. Raif guessed he would need a similar rig. Clan blades were rarely over four and a half feet in length and most were carried at the waist.

That was another thing: He'd have to learn how to use it. The sword was a full two-hander. Hailsmen armed themselves with hatchets and one-handed blades. Wielding Loss would require skills rarely practiced by clan. Grinding and refitting it would also take skills unknown at Blackhail. Someone would have to take a chisel to the rusticles that had grown from the crosshilts and grind the jagged metal left behind. Raif couldn't imagine the repairs would make for a pretty sight. A grinding that deep would scar the blade. Still, there was something in him that wanted to see what lay beneath the canker. This sword that had belonged to a friend of his, Raven Lord, the man without a name.

Spying the black shadow of an undercut, Raif slowed to investigate. Water had flowed with force here and a broad seam of sandstone had been carved into a hollow. Crouching, he edged his way into the opening. The cave was shallow and smelled of muskrat. Iridescent bird feathers were half-buried in the gravel floor. An abandoned nest still contained pieces of eggshell and puffs of down. Except for a small mosquito pool at the rear, the cave was dry. Deciding there was enough space for him and Addie to spend the night, Raif backed out.

While he waited for the cragsman, he dragged one of the fallen pines downstream and jammed it against the cave entrance.

"Won't stop the wolves," Addie warned as he approached.

With no fire to build, camp preparations were sparse. Unable to forgo the habit of tea, Addie filled his pot with cold water, crushed some herbs into it and prepared for a long wait. Raif untied his bedroll and laid it parallel to the cave entrance, leaving the low-ceilinged rear to Addie. The cragsman argued the point, but Raif shook his head. If anything came for them in the night, it would have to deal with Raif Sevrance first.

Not all the people he cared about were far away.

Addie grumbled. Frowning at the cold-brewed tea, he settled himself on the fallen pine and said, "My father was a Fontsman at Wellhouse, companion to the chief. Back in the days when he hoped his son would would become a warrior like himself he told me something I never forgot." Pausing, he patted down his waistcoat, locating his stash of smoked meat. After brushing off a piece of lint from a stick of jerky he took a bite and began to chew.

Raif waited. He knew that jerky. This was going to take a while.

It was getting dark and Addie was soon nothing more than a profile against the northern sky. He swallowed with force and then spoke. "My da told me that information protects a man better than any sword. It gives him an extra edge. And right now, as I see it, I'm not sufficiently armed. On a night like this, in wolf country, in land claimed by the Sull and within kissing distance of the Want, a man needs all the protection he can get. I need something to fight with. So start talking. Why are we keeping clear of the clanholds?"

Raif hunkered by the shore. He'd been expecting this. Addie knew why the Sull feared him—some of it—but little else. It was hardly surprising he was growing impatient. Unable to think of a good way to start, Raif said, "I'm wanted by Bludd."

Addie's profile registered no surprise.

"You've heard of the massacre on the Bluddroad?"

"Aye."

"The Dog Lord's grandchildren and the wives of his sons were slaughtered in cold blood by Hailsmen. I was there." Raif waited for a reaction, but Addie held himself still. "Seven days later I defended Blackhail's actions at Duff's stovehouse. Four Bluddsmen died."

There was no need to add, *By my hand*. Addie understood.

The trickle of water in the creek was the only noise in the darkness. Seconds passed. Addie said, "So you declared your part in the slaughter?"

"I'm the only the Hailsman Bludd knows for a certainty was there."

"Sweet gods." Addie sucked in breath. "I wouldn't want the Dog Lord and all seven of his sons after me."

Raif waited a beat. "I am condemned in Blackhail too."

"Stillborn said you killed a sworn clansman at Black Hole."

Suddenly Raif did not trust himself to speak. He moved a hand.

Addie was clan. It wouldn't be difficult for him to imagine the horror of killing one of his own. The cragsman's silence was knowing. He left it awhile and then changed the subject.

"What about the sword?"

Raif had not imagined he would ever be grateful to talk about Loss. "You saw me kill the . . . thing on the ledgerock the night Traggis Mole died?"

"Aye."

"It took two swords to do it. The first one bent. The second went in only because it used the entry wound made by the first. There's a limit to what normal weapons can kill, Addie. The creature was on the edge of that limit. And it's not the worst. The worst's to come."

A fisher screeched a warning in the east. *Wolf.*

"The sword will make a difference?"

Raif shrugged. "It did thousands of years ago, the night before the lake was flooded. The man wielding it changed the course of the battle."

"Will the Sull try and take it?"

Unable to contemplate the answer and sit still, Raif stood. "No," he said quietly. "They will try and take me before I learn how to use it."

"They track you?"

"I believe so."

There had not been powdered guidestone at Addie's waist in ten years, yet he touched the place where it had once hung from his belt. "Days darker than night lie ahead."

The old words, spoken by storytellers around the hearth and clan chiefs in time of war, had weight to them. They didn't blow away, and it wasn't easy to speak into the silence as they sank. Addie made the effort. Upturning the cooking pot he said, "No fire, cold tea. I'm off to sleep. As Giddie Wellhouse used to say, may our enemies appear in nightmare, not flesh."

Raif hiked upstream as Addie kicked together a mattress of pine needles. Giddie Wellhouse had borrowed those words from the Sull; Raif had heard Ark Veinsplitter say them to Ash. Addie had changed *your* to *our*.

The stars would not come out tonight, Raif decided. Clouds smothered the north. The world felt unsettled. It had moved once, it could move again. Out of habit, he tracked heartbeats in the darkness. The wolf trotted east, deep into Sull territory. A pair of ground owls with eggs in the nest waited for it to be gone before hunting. To the west an injured stag nosed milkweed from between rocks. Its heart was beating too quickly: it feared wolves and rivals were drawing close.

Raif knew how it felt. Briefly, he considered stringing his bow and stalking it. He didn't need meat though, and he was wary of the impulse to heart-kill. Was it stronger now? Had he always felt that spike of anticipation in his gut?

He headed back, tired but sure he would not sleep. The camp was dark and he edged his way around the fallen pine and into the undercut. Once he'd placed Traggis Mole's longknife and the Sull bow within arm's reach, Raif closed his eyes and tried to stop his thoughts. The pain in his chest felt like heartache, and it was difficult not to think of Effie and Drey and Ash. He must have dreamed, for he felt Ash put her lips to his ear and whisper the words she'd said to him before she'd left to join the Sull.

Guard yourself.

In an instant he was awake. The darkness spun as he oriented himself within it. Usually he had a sense of how much time had passed while he slept, but that instinct failed him in the moonless, starless night. His raven lore was pressed against his throat; it felt as if it were taking a bite. Thumbing its cord, he pulled it loose. With his other hand he reached for the Sull bow. The arrows were still suspended across his chest in their suede case; they rose as he did.

In the quiet of absolute blackness every noise was amplified. As he scooped up Traggis Mole's longknife, the crunch of his fingertips pushing sand sounded like footsteps. Addie did not wake. Raif left him there and ducked out of the cave.

Something moved to the south. Raif perceived it as a ripple in the darkness. The air it displaced touched his cheek. It smelled like smoking ice. Raif turned his head before inhaling. He did not want to breathe it in. What had been made in this world, had fed and grown and felt sunlight upon its back, had been unmade by the Endlords. Flesh and blood had been replaced with something *other*. The Sull called it *maer dan*—shadowflesh—but Raif did not think the word sufficient. It was as if the blackness between stars had been condensed and forced into human and inhuman remains. It had weight and density and purpose. And just like living flesh it required a pumping heart to sustain it.

Raif tracked the heart as it swung across the creek downstream. Experience warned him not to let it settle too long in his sights. It would suck him in. His own heart was racing, pushing blood at pressure through the arteries close to his skin. His fingers jumped against the belly of the bow.

The night's frost had killed the creek. Raif stepped into the dry bed, brought an arrow to the plate, and waited. Anything that came at him would have to clear the rocky banks. Seconds passed. All was still. Raif's eyes grew accustomed to the gloom. He had lost track of the unmade being, and resisted the temptation to focus on its last position. From the brief glimpse he'd had, its form was subhuman. No telling how fast it could move

Wind trilled the pines. Raif smelled something, and before he could put a name to it the earth moved. A wave of sound rolled along the creek. The ground shuddered into motion. Rock buckled and popped. A tree cracked. Stones bounced down the bank. Raif braced himself. Something hit him in the back and he swung around. Nothing. Probably a stone. The earth jerked wildly, throwing his weight forward. Sheets of scree rolled into the creek. Raif could not track all the movement.

By the time he sensed the heart the creature was nearly upon him. Its black form poured down the bank. Big and massively broad, it was missing some essential proportion that was common to all humans. Voided steel purred in its grip.

Possible actions flashed across Raif's sights. It was too late to draw and aim the bow. Turn and run to get some distance and he risked being impaled. Traggis Mole's longknife was only two feet long from pommel to tip, but it was sharp and it would have to do.

Springing to his left he flung the Sull bow in the opposite direction. The creature's head whipped around as the bow skidded to a halt on the far side of the creek, providing a fraction of a moment for Raif to use. Feinting backward he slid the arrowcase from around his shoulder and launched it straight at the thing's chest. As the creature raised its free hand to its rib cage, Raif sprang forward. Moving inside the edge of voided steel, he stabbed the creature's hand, ramming the blade toward the heart. Thick iron armor chewed up the knife and Raif had to use the heel of his left hand to punch in the point.

Shrieking, the creature swung its sword. Raif yanked out the knife and leapt sideways. The point had touched the heart but hadn't homed and the black insubstance of unmade flesh smoked through the hole. The creature rippled, re-formed, and struck with inhuman speed. Raif had time only to raise the crudest block—a diagonal across his chest—and the creature's downstroke drove right through it. As the voided steel slid downblade it sheared the edge from the longknife. Curls of live steel were sucked into the void.

Raif danced back, ducked. Voided steel ripped down his side, slicing the Orrl cloak and his deerhide pants. If skin opened he didn't feel it.

He didn't even know if the earth had stopped shaking.

The thing was fast and it was watching his eyes. When Raif moved to the left it moved right along with him, cracking its sword into air barely cleared by Raif's leg.

If you are killed by voided steel you are taken. Unmade. If you die later from your wounds you are also unmade. Angus Lok's words kept running through Raif's head. They didn't help. With sword and arm length combined the creature's reach was nearly twice his own. That wasn't what worried him the most, though. It was the ways in which the creature was different from other Unmade that chilled him: calculating, intelligent, prepared to wait. The others struck with no thought for self-preservation. This thing intended to survive.

Even injured, it was ferociously fast. It forced Raif back along the creek. Stones slick with ice provided no traction and Raif had to dig in with his heels. Traggis Mole's longknife took a beating as he blocked blows; the only thing it would be good for later was staking a tent. He snatched glimpses of the creature's heart, but couldn't move quickly enough to act on them. That was the thing about heart-killing at distance with a longbow—you had the luxury of time.

"*Argh.*"

Raif sucked in breath as voided steel opened his knife arm from elbow to wrist. Hot blood welled to the surface.

The creature hissed. It lowered its strange, streamlined head and launched itself straight at the weak spot. Raif circled the longknife counterclockwise, protecting his arm as he edged backward. Blows forced him down onto the bank. Rolling downstream, he tried to move clear of the creature's range. Stones crunched against his back. Voided steel slid into his shoulder muscle. Pain whitened his vision. He lost a second. The creature rippled above him, an armored shadow with holes for eyes. Raif saw the absence that was voided steel arc toward his heart.

In that instant he knew what his victims felt: the loosening of gut as panic gave way to a single word.

No.

His heart contracted. He saw Da.

Hailsmen do not close our eyes when we die.

Raif opened his eyes, saw something his mind could not immediately translate. Two figures stood where there had been one. The shadow had a shadow . . . and they were connected by something. A bright silver ribbon spooled from the hand of the second shadow and seemed to float through the chest of the Unmade. The ribbon glowed with moonlight— yet where was the moon?

Raif blinked. He felt pleasantly tired. It was good to be lying down.

Suddenly the second shadow pulled back the ribbon and the Unmade stumbled. Its high-pitched scream made Raif's neck hair stand on end. Crumpling to its knees it seemed to shrink. It rocked for a long moment and then collapsed. The voided steel made a queer buzzing sound as it hit the creekbed and Raif watched as it began to sink through the loosely piled stones. The sharp, grassy odor of burning rock made him retch.

"Take my hand. You must stand."

The remaining shadow spoke and Raif obeyed, clasping the hand that was thrust at his face.

All kinds of pain had to be endured as he was yanked to his feet. *Hold steady*, he reminded himself as the shadow withdrew support. Soaked in his own blood, Raif felt shivery and sick. Wanting to put some distance between himself and the voided steel, he took a few steps. These took him to the opposite bank where he was faced with the task of climbing out of the creek. It was too much and he picked a rock and sat on it.

"Drink."

Again something was thrust in his face. This time he realized that the words that accompanied the gesture were not Common. He had translated them. They were Sull.

Fear woke his brain. A Sull warrior stood above him, holding out a flask wrapped in snakeskin. Raif recognized him as Ilya Spinebreaker, one of Yiselle No Knife's men. All became clear. No Knife had tracked them to the creek and sent out a warrior to slay the Unmade that Raif Sevrance, *Mor Drakka*, could not slay himself. The silver ribbon was Spinebreaker's six-foot longsword.

Spinebreaker acknowledged the realization on Raif's face with a cold bow of his head. "Drink," he repeated.

Raif pushed away the flask. Blood sheeted down his arm. "Where is Addie?"

"He is ours."

The words, spoken in Common, chilled Raif. He stood and immediately his knees buckled. Rings of green light floated across his vision as he slumped back down on the rock.

Spinebreaker's nostrils flared in contempt. He was uncloaked and armored in iridescent hornmail that reflected the colors of deep water at night. His sword and knife holsters were made from leather that had been silvered and then burnished so they glinted like iron bars. A series of opal clasps cinched his waist-long braid and pulled back the hair from his face. Small tattoos of the moon in all its phases ringed his hairline.

"Take me to Addie," Raif said. His voice seemed to come from a distance. Weak echoes repeated in his head. *Take me. Take. Take.*

"You are being unmade, Clansman. I would make no demands of this Sull if I were you."

Smoke slithered across Raif's forearm as Spinebreaker sheathed his sword and headed upstream. Raif tried to brush away the smoke, but his fingers passed right through it and it would not disperse. It joined with a second curl and pooled above the open wound. Raif imagined it tapping a weakened vein and being sucked toward his heart.

"Help me," he cried.

The Sull warrior was already too far away to hear him and the only answer came from the echoes in his head.

Take. Take.

Taken.

CHAPTER 6
Wolf Dog

"Nan, you've done enough. Leave him." The Dog Lord knew he sounded hard, but he could not think of any way to soften his words. Nan was nursing a sick clansman when she should be readying herself and the bairns for the journey. "We depart within the hour."

Nodding, Nan turned back to her patient, the young swordsman Yuan Bryce who had been injured during the battle with the Unmade. He was lying on a matress raised off the floor by a wooden pallet. Cluff Drybannock had built the pallet and four more like it. Only Yuan's was now in use. The four other men wounded on the Field of Graves and Swords were dead.

He, Vaylo Bludd, had killed them.

The Dog Lord crossed to the pallet and laid his hand on Yuan's shoulder. The skin was cool. Blood of poppy glazed his eyes. He was a boy, Vaylo reckoned. Nineteen. He'd spoken three yearman's oaths. Next winter he would have taken his full oath, swearing himself to Bludd for life. His back was broken though, and he could not move his legs. For twenty days Nan had nursed him, hoping that function would return. It had not. Cluff Drybannock had built a wheeled cart and furnished it with a padded seat. It stood on the far side of the sickroom door, out of sight. The one time Yuan had seen it he had become so agitated Nan and Cluff had been forced to restrain him. You could still see the bruise on Nan's face.

"Gods watch over you," Vaylo said quietly.

"They do not."

Vaylo had not expected the boy to reply. Nan caught Vaylo's gaze.

Careful, she warned.

The boy's pupils were so large Vaylo could not tell the color of his eyes. They watched him though, waiting upon a response. Vaylo did not have one. You could not tell a warrior "be glad you are alive" when he could no longer wield a sword. Could one say "be glad your injuries came from being thrown from your horse and not from voided steel"? Five men had been carried from the battlefield on stretchers that night. If Vaylo had been a betting man he would have named Yuan most likely to die. The boy's injuries had seemed the worst— not enough to invite mercy killing, but sufficient to make a favorable outcome unlikely. The other men had various hurts; cuts, slashes, piercing, tears. Nothing, Vaylo judged, that would not heal if the wounds were cleaned and properly tended.

Nan Culldayis and Jud Meeks had stitched and tended those wounds, and Vaylo did not think any two people could have done a better job. Washed with alcohol, poulticed with mud and herbs, stitched with cat gut, painted with silver, monitored day and night: the wounds should have healed. Yet they didn't. Infection had set in. Tissue had not swollen, pus had not formed, yet bodies had been eaten alive. Something had leaked between the stitches. Something black and smoky that smelled like frozen earth.

When it became apparent the men were not recovering, Cluff Drybannock, Vaylo's fostered son, broke open his horn of powdered guidestone and drew a guide circle around the sickroom. "*Xha vul*," he murmured. "They are being taken."

Hearing the words Vaylo had both known and not known what they meant. *We are chosen by the Stone Gods to guard their borders.* For some reason the Bludd boast sounded in his head. It struck him that the injured men were crossing a border, and he, Bludd chief, could not allow that to happen. Malice bided on the other side. How he knew this he could not say. Perhaps it was the faint, empty scent of the smoke, or the look of solemn expectation in Drybone's eyes.

What Vaylo had failed to realize straightaway was what those words would cost. Even Drybone had not fully understood. He had drawn a circle in powdered guidestone, passing the men's fates into the hands of the Stone Gods. For twelve hours the sickroom became hallowed ground. Bluddsmen came, spoke prayers, left. The injured men slept restlessly, tossing and moaning. Each time they awakened there was less life in their eyes than when they'd fallen asleep. Fear made them clutch at Nan as she tended them. One, the swordsman Boyce Willard, had begged Nan to open his stitches and let "the filth out." She had done just that, taking her maiden's helper and slitting the cat gut.

It was then, seeing the smoke vent along Boyce's leg, that Vaylo knew what he had to. Nothing could save these men— no nursing, prayers or guide circles—and it was his duty as chief to kill them before they could be consumed by the smoke. Cross that border and they were lost. The Stone Gods could not claim them in that blasted land. Drybone had told him that men who were killed by *Kil Ji*, voided steel, were unmade. And right now, as he watched the smoke of annihilation cumulate in the hollow of Boyce's belly and pelvis, Vaylo realized that the only way to prevent them from being destroyed by voided steel was to slay them with live steel instead.

You could not call it a mercy killing if one of your motives was protecting yourself. *"Once a man or woman is unmade they join the ranks of the Endlords. They too will wield* Kil Ji *and unlike those who are imprisoned in the Blind, they have no need to force their way out. They are here, amongst us, and they walk by night."* Cluff Drybannock's words, spoken a month earlier in the broken tower, came back and haunted Vaylo.

Arno and Gormalin: They were the only Bluddsmen he had not killed as a mercy. Perhaps he had killed them in self-defense. Perhaps rage. Either way he did not regret it. His brothers had deserved to die.

Not these men, though. Not Boyce, not Mad Malky, not Hector nor Jon. These were men who had volunteered to ride out from the fort with their lord and chief. Unlike others, they had survived the Field of Graves and Swords.

Unlike Yuan, they had not been able to live with their wounds.

Vaylo looked at the paralyzed boy, and thought about the morning he'd taken the lives of the four injured men. He'd ordered screens to be raised around the pallets and then visited each man in order of rank. Boyce, as the senior clansmen, had been taken last. Vaylo knew he had done a poor job of honoring him. Boyce had heard the gasps and soft cries of his fellow patients and when his chief appeared before him he said softly, "I see you've cleaned your sword."

No words existed to describe the pain Vaylo felt at that moment. They had damaged muscle in his heart. Inhaling, he waited out the memory.

When he exhaled he spoke to Yuan Bryce. "You have two arms. Be glad of them. Get well and learn to load and fire a crossbow from your seat. You have taken an oath to guard Bludd borders. Guard them."

Nan shot him a stern glance, but Vaylo did not care.

The lone window in the room was covered with a horse blanket. Light shone through the strap holes in the wool. Yuan's skin was pale. Sweat greased his forehead and throat. He blinked.

"Aye, chief."

Vaylo nodded brusquely. "When you're ready come see me at Bludd."

He left without looking back.

You'll have an advantage when it comes to being chief. You're a born bastard. Ockish Bull had said those words to him in the dark hours after he'd slain Arno and Gormalin. Vaylo had not thought himself capable of laughter that night, yet somehow Ockish had forced it out of him. They were both bloody, he remembered. Ockish had dealt with the bodies, and then broke the news to clan. They had a new chief.

Gods I miss him. Only Ockish had been able to lift his mood when he was at his lowest, when chiefing made him do terrible things.

The wolf dog had made itself comfortable in the padded cart outside the sickroom door, and Vaylo beckoned it impatiently.

It was looking older, he reckoned. So was he. Together they made their way through the hillfort and out the southern gate.

The wind was lively, pushing clouds. Overnight the brown winter grasses of the Copper Hills had greened. Heather was sprouting. Streams were running on distant hillsides, flashing silver when sunlight caught them just right. Vaylo let the sun and wind work on him, resting his eyes and breathing deeply. The Copper Hills represented something essential to clan—the call of open space—and the Dog Lord found some part of himself wanting to ride out and never come back.

Already the party had started to congregate on the dirt court. There would be forty-five in all, including Nan and the bairns, and mounts would be in short supply. Horses were being strapped and saddled and supplies hauled from the fort. Hammie Faa was in charge of logistics and he appeared to be doing a thorough job. The chubby armsman only looked slightly flummoxed as he packed the spare horse with blankets, fire irons and oil-soaked millet. The horses would need to graze enroute as grain was short. Meat was in short supply too, and Bluddsmen would need to hunt.

Again, there was that pang of anticipation. To be ahorse, traveling through the Copper Hills, hunting for one's supper and camping under the stars, was not a bad way to live. Clansmen dreamed of such pursuits. In spring and autumn they would mount longhunts, exchanging the comforts of hearth and kin for the joy of the wild north.

"Granda. Are we going yet?" The excited call came from Vaylo's nine-year-old granddaughter Pasha. She was sitting astride his horse, a rangy black stallion with a white starburst on its nose. With horses short, it had been agreed that Pasha and Aaron would take turns riding with Nan, Hammie, Mogo Salt and their grandfather.

Just as well I no longer have Dog Horse, Vaylo thought. *As the gods-ugly beast wouldn't let anyone ride him save me.* Dog Horse had been lost during the assault on the Dhoonehouse. Robbie Dun Dhoone had torched the stables, and the only way to save the horses was to fling back the doors and let them run free. Vaylo had a bolt-shaped burn scar on his right palm as a souvenir of that night. He had not felt the burn of hot metal at the time. His mind had been on his horse.

So much lost. So little gained.

"Granda," Pasha cried. "When are we *going*?"

"Get down," Vaylo said. "Go and find your brother and help Nan with her things."

The girl's smile collapsed and she slid awkwardly from the horse.

"Today is not child's play," he told her. "We leave behind a hundred clansmen. Conduct yourself accordingly."

Pasha ran toward the hillfort with a little whimper of distress. Vaylo watched her slip beneath the gate. He could not seem to keep his temper today.

Whistling for the wolf dog to follow him, he went to talk to Hammie. The armsman had some last-minute questions and Vaylo was glad of the opportunity to tell someone—who appreciated it—what to do. By the time they'd finished conferring, the court was packed with men and horses. Vaylo looked for Drybone, but could not spot his fostered son in the crowd. When Nan came out with the bairns, men began mounting their horses. Hammie helped Nan with her packs. Little Aaron insisted on bearing his own bedroll and training hammer, and stoutly shook away all help.

Everyone fell quiet as Big Borro brought out the swords. Nine in all, five belonging to the warriors who had died or suffered mercy killings on the Field of Graves and Swords and four belonging to the injured whose wounds had not healed. Big Borro carried the swords in a flat oval basket. Collectively they had to weigh close to fifty pounds, yet Borro bore them at arm's length, held out from his body, in ceremonial display. The Dog Lord did not know who had cleaned the swords, but whoever it was had polished them so fiercely the sun bounced back to the sky.

Nine blades to be returned to widows, mothers, fathers and children at Bludd. Of all the trials that lay ahead, it was this that disturbed Vaylo the most. *Your child is dead.* No four words in all the universe cut as deeply as those.

Mogo Salt put his lips to his sackpipe and blew the stark and plaintive notes of the Cragsman's Farewell. Bluddsmen touched their measures of powdered guidestone. Some clenched their fists. None wept. As prearranged, Vaylo stepped forward and accepted the swords. The basket had been lined with soft suede and Vaylo saw that Nan had embroidered it with the War Dogs of Bludd. Where did she get the time, this lady of his?

Nan had the bairns in hand. Their packs had been set on the ground and their heads lowered in respect. Vaylo passed them as he brought the swords to the stallion that would bear them home. The horse had been trapped and blinkered in maroon leather. In place of a saddle, a buckskin cradle had been strapped to its back. The swords would be transported in the cradle, and no man, woman or child would mount the stallion until the swords had been brought home to Bludd.

Hammie and others helped lash the basket in place. Vaylo

checked the cinches twice. He'd be damned if this package was coming loose. While he worked, the wolf dog bellied in the dirt and waited. When its ears angled toward the hillfort, Vaylo glanced up to see Drybone standing in the shadows behind the gate.

Cluff Drybannock had dressed and armed himself in full Bludd regalia. A crimson collar overlaid his greatcloak and his waist-length hair had been braided into a warrior's queue and bound in a knot at the back of his neck. Copper wire had been wrapped around the grip of his longsword, and his hand knife was suspended at his waist in a dog tail sheath. Vaylo counted the details and resumed his task.

Drybone meant to honor his chief and clan with his dress, yet he did not look like clan. He looked like Sull: the red skin with its metallic tinge, the cheekbones cut like diamonds, the eyes that took in light and then gave it out.

When had he changed? Vaylo wondered. Dry's mother had been a Trenchlander whore, his father a Bluddsman. Surely there had been a time when Dry looked more like clan?

At Vaylo's feet, the wolf dog let out a single, high-pitched whine. Every night the dog accompanied Cluff Drybannock as he walked the hill-wall, keeping watch.

"Go," Vaylo told it.

The black and orange dog sprang up and raced toward Drybone. Dry put out a hand to still it and the creature dropped to its haunches ahead of the the gate.

"Hammie," Vaylo said. "Call the column to order. You and Nan in the front with me."

"Aye."

Vaylo walked wide of the court to give men and horses

space to maneuver. He waited. Drybone did not move from his position by the gate.

"*Come with me,*" Vaylo had said to him in the dark hours after the Field of Graves and Swords.

"*I cannot, my father. I am Bludd and I am Sull. This is where I choose to make my stand.*"

Vaylo glanced at the old Dhoonewall fort. Damp had rotted the masonry. Chunks of fallen stone lay embedded in the courtyard. One of the chunks had a crisp crater surrounding it. Vaylo wouldn't have been surprised if it had fallen in the night. Even so, the fort was still defensible. Its broken watchtower was still high enough to provide early warning of an attack. The copper roof would resist fire and the exterior, although damaged, was double-walled. There were worse places a man could call his own. Vaylo just wished Dry had picked one closer to Bludd.

Buckling his cloak, Vaylo crossed to his horse. Most of the men were mounted now and the horses were lively, shaking their heads and kicking. Odwin Two Bear's gelding reared and Odwin had to pull back the reins and ride the animal off the court. The bairns were already mounted. Pasha was sitting behind Nan on Nan's white gelding, and Aaron was trotting Mogo's short-necked stallion in rings. Hammie was holding Vaylo's horse.

Dust kicked up by the horses blurred the air. Vaylo could taste the copper in it. It tasted of Dhoone. The dust at Bludd had tasted of baser metals, of iron and nickel and lead. He recalled the time his father had beaten him on the redcourt in front of a dozen sworn clansmen. "Swallow," Gullit had roared as he pushed his booted foot into the back of Vaylo's head. "No bastard talks back to the chief."

Vaylo thought he might have been ten at the time. Gullit had been preparing for a boar hunt in the Tick Woods. As he walked from the stable with his saddle, Gullit had caught sight of his youngest son. "Boy. Run in the house and fetch my weapon." Vaylo remembered bolting into the Bluddhouse, pleased that his lord and father had set him an important task and anxious to perform it swiftly. When he opened Gullit's weapon case in the chief's chamber he'd been dazzled by the rows of honed steel. No one opened Gullit's case without his sanction and to look upon the armaments amassed by Bludd chiefs was a privilege. Longswords, broadswords, short swords, swan necks, scimitars, knives and more knives hung by their hilts in individual slots. The throwing spears were less carefully arrayed and had been dumped into the door box like sticks in a jar. Vaylo picked the last spear he'd seen his father use, closed and latched the case and sprinted onto the court.

His first indication that something was wrong was when his father did not extend his hand to accept the spear. "What's this, boy?" he'd demanded from the saddle. "I said bring my sword."

Even at ten Vaylo knew not to contradict his father. His mistake had been more damning than that. "But you'll need a spear for the boar."

The Dog Lord winced to think of it. There had been twelve men within earshot. Some had laughed.

"Boy thinks you can't make a kill with a sword," Dinny Hawks, Gullit's favored drinking companion, had quipped.

"You are getting slower, Chief," Roland Ingo had added. "Best put some distance between you and the wild pigs."

The comments were typical warrior talk, the kind of jests men made before hunts to relieve tension. Yet Gullit Bludd had not laughed. His mouth had narrowed and he'd slid from his horse.

"You think me incompetent, boy?"

"No, sir."

That was the moment when Vaylo realized the beating would be a bad one. His father had appraised the contrition in his eyes and found it wanting.

"Get down on the ground." Gullit pointed to the dirt with his riding crop. "I'll grind that smirk off your face."

Vaylo vividly recalled the sting of false accusation—he had not smirked—but could not recall speaking up to defend himself. Instead he had fought back and that had only made the beating worse. Already he knew how these things worked, yet his anger always overruled his sense. He wasn't that different from Gullit when it came down to it.

He'd beaten his own sons.

Vaylo put his foot in the stirrup and mounted the stallion. Bludd was a hard clan and Bluddsmen were hard men. Its dirt was hard and black—even in summer when it was bone dry— but it had never killed anyone to swallow it.

After the beating, he'd pulled himself off the ground and watched as Gullit and his best men had ridden south into the woods. Spitting out blood and dust, he'd made his way back to the roundhouse. He was a Bluddsman and this was home. There was nowhere else for him to go.

Vaylo looked east toward the black hills and forests of Bludd. He'd been away too long. Dhoone, Ganmiddich, the Dhoonewall: between them he hadn't stood on Bludd dirt for close to a year. Now he and forty men were heading home, and the only thing he expected for a certainty was trouble. His eldest son, Quarro, had chiefed the clanhold through three seasons and it wasn't likely that he would welcome back his father with open arms. Bludd didn't have a fancy throne like Dhoone and no kings had ever ruled there, yet it had things a man could grow possessive over; silent forests of cedar and hemlock, creaking forests of ancient oak and ash, the best boar hunting in the clanholds, the Pipe Rapids on the Snarewater, the Garnet Room at the heart of the Bluddhold. Vaylo knew how it felt to lord over them. It was not likely his firstborn would relinquish them without a fight.

It would be bloody. Quarro would need to be beaten and turfed. The Dog Lord didn't much like the thought of it. All dealings with his natural sons left him cold.

Shortening the reins, Vaylo turned his horse to look back at the gate and Cluff Drybannock, his eighth and fostered son. The only one he had never beaten. The only one he had ever loved.

Dry's gaze met his through the dust. Pride burned in Dry's methane blue eyes. Seeing it, Vaylo realized that they would not bid one another farewell. Dry would not move from the gate and he, Vaylo, would not cross the thirty feet to Dry's position.

They understood each other. In this.

Vaylo did not think he would ever understand what it meant to be Sull.

Dry's gaze was level, his face still. Vaylo acknowledged him with the smallest possible movement of his head. Twenty days ago an offer had been extended and refused. The Dog Lord respected Dry's choice, but a chief did not speak words of comfort to a man who had opted not to follow him. Banking the stallion, Vaylo whistled for his dogs.

"East to Bludd!" he bellowed to the forming line.

One by one the dogs fell in behind him as he took up his position in the fore. The wolf dog came last, tail down. Every few steps it halted and looked back at Drybone. Vaylo ignored it. Nan was trying to catch his eye to give him one of her gentle smiles. He ignored her also.

Best to focus on the journey. Forty men now depended upon him for their welfare. All had volunteered to make the journey home to Bludd. They were Cluff Drybannock's men and that meant they used swords, not hatchets. Some carried hammers and axes out of custom and a handful were proficient at wielding them, but Vaylo knew he stood alone as an avowed hammerman. It made him feel like a killhound or an aurochs: creatures that had once thrived in the north and were now dying out.

"Charge to the first hill!" he bellowed, kicking heels into horseflesh. He needed to put some space between himself and his thoughts. "Last man gets latrine duty."

Hammie, Gods love him, knew the jig so well by now that he got the best start of the lot of them. The others caught on quickly enough but not before Vaylo and his armsman had pulled ahead. The dogs howled in excitement and sprinted after the horses. Well, three of them did. The wolf dog was subdued and when Vaylo glanced over his shoulder he saw the creature falling behind. It moved through the space between the column and the fort, a lone wolf padding through the dust.

Vaylo filled his lungs with air and concentrated on reaching the hill. Hammie had passed him and he could hear others at his heels. The topsoil was finally dry after the thaw and the horses threw powder as they charged. Big Borro was riding one of Ockish Bull's stallions and the creature was a wonder to watch. It almost didn't hurt to have it pass you. When he got back to Bludd, Vaylo reckoned he'd buy himself a horse from the Bull stables. Something that wouldn't beat his tailbone black and blue.

As the land began to rise, Vaylo's stallion slowed and no amount of thigh squeezing would cajole it. A handful of men with superior mounts passed Vaylo, and he found himself struggling to keep ahead of the pack. He felt out of sorts, bothered by his visit with the injured boy, regretful of not having spoken farewell to Dry.

It was a relief to reach the hill. A rocky bluff provided a natural finish line and Vaylo counted seven men assembled ahead of him. From the way he was joking and preening, Big Borro looked to be the winner. The men cheered when their chief made it. Vaylo acknowledged their goodwill with a grunt. He was sore and out of breath. Then his stallion went and embarrassed him by lowering its head and pulling up a thicket of grass.

"Some racehorse you have there, Chief," Big Borro said. "Five minutes from home and it's ready to feed."

Men laughed, and suddenly Vaylo understood how Gullit must have felt that day on the redcourt. His father would have been getting old by then. Over fifty, and that famous Bludd vigor would have been in decline. Perhaps he'd just discovered he could no longer stay ahead of his men. Perhaps the incident with the spear had touched a nerve.

Vaylo patted the stallion's neck and forced himself into good humor. "He's a soldier's horse. Stuffs himself whenever he can."

The joke was an old one, but the men needed it. *He* needed it. Gullit Bludd's ghost had to be exorcised, lest the son end up as bitter as the father. Spying Nan and Pasha bringing up the rear with the sword horse, Vaylo found a genuine smile.

"You said last *man*," Nan told him calmly. "That wouldn't be me."

The warriors laughed again, this time with genuine warmth. Nan Culldayis was their lady. For the past two months she had cooked and cared for them, listened to their private fears about absent loved ones and worrying ailments, and given sensible advice on everything from the best way to clean brass belt buckles to the wording of messages sent by bird. They loved her, Vaylo realized with pride. And that was something his father had never possessed: a woman as fine as Nan.

"Who," Vaylo bellowed above the stamping and panting of horses, "in this sorry crew of warriors came last?"

"Wull did," cried Odwin Two Bear.

"No, I didn't," replied the lanky, tattooed former Castleman. "It was Midge."

Midge Pool's eyebrows disappeared beneath his thatch of red hair. "Not me. I got here ahead of Wull."

"You blind, boy," countered Wull Rudge, who at twenty-eight was a good ten years older than Midge. "I had time to groom my horse, dismount and take a piss afore you got here."

"But I—"

"*Silence!*" Vaylo roared at the lot of them. "Bluddsmen don't squabble like little girls. If no one is prepared to come forward and admit the rear then all will be on half rations tonight."

Shamed, the warriors hung their heads. They were whelps, Vaylo decided. He had twenty-five years on the eldest, Marcus Borro. How was he going to take back the Bluddhouse with a crew of forty boys?

"I was last," Midge Pool murmured, gaze on the ground.

"No. It was me," Odwin Two Bear corrected him. "In all the dust I failed to see I was bringing up the rear."

Big dark-haired Wull Rudge gulped. "Chief, it was me. I was last."

Vaylo glowered at them as he waited to see if anyone else would claim the rear. When no one else spoke, he said, "All three of you, latrine duty—and no rations tonight. When I ask a question I expect it answered promptly and with truth."

Turning the stallion smartly, he headed east along the bluff. Nan and Hammie fell in behind him and others followed. Wind sent the heather rippling. Vaylo smelled stag musk. The dogs were ahead of him, following a scent trail uphill. Uncharacteristically, the wolf dog lagged behind. A whiff of deer was usually enough to drive it wild.

Vaylo made himself look ahead. Behind him the column was quiet. Forty men had just realized that they were no longer under the command of Cluff Drybannock. Six months back they had headed north from Dhoone with Dry as their leader. Now here they were, riding east to Bludd, under direct command of their chief. Vaylo knew he had to be hard on them. Dry had commanded quietly, by example. But Dry had never had to set Bluddsmen against Bluddsmen. By the end of the fifteen-day journey the forty had to be ready to obey him without thought, as a reflex. Fifteen days was not nearly enough.

Vaylo rode in silence. Clouds marched the length of the sky. A goshawk spied a grouse and made a dive. The horses lathered as they climbed the steep slopes. At midday, the column rested and took a cold mess of bread and cheese. Midge, Odwin and Wull did not eat. And although he had not specifically forbidden them a daytime meal, Vaylo was satisfied.

"Form up!" he cried when he judged the horses restored. "We ride until dark."

They did just that. The ground was good, so they maintained a fair pace. After a couple of hours Aaron was handed off from Mogo Salt to Hammie, and Vaylo received possession of Pasha. The girl insisted on taking the reins and after a few minutes of supervision he left her to it. Her hair smelled nice. He liked the way she didn't look over her shoulder for guidance when faced with problem terrain. She had the sense not to speak much either, though Nan may have primed her on that.

The height of the hills made for a short day. The sun disappeared behind a knife-edge ridge leaving a metallic sheen in the sky. Vaylo sent scouts ahead to check for a suitable campsite, and they returned after the light failed. As they led the way south to a high moor, Vaylo questioned them quietly about Dhoone.

"No sign of Dhoonesmen in the hills," Rufus Black, the eldest scout, answered.

Vaylo nodded. This part of the clanholds was windblown and remote and the only folk who who used it regularly were cragsmen. Even so, Vaylo found himself cautious and ordered watches in all quadrants. Suspecting he would not sleep he elected to take the southern watch himself. Rufus volunteered to second him, but Vaylo turned him down. "I have the dogs," he replied.

In truth he was glad to be alone. Hiking south as the camp was raised, he ate a dry supper of trail meat and pickled quail eggs. Nan had snuck him one of her fancy honeycakes but he fed it to the nearest dog. His mind wouldn't settle. He'd volunteered to take the most likely watch himself, but now he wondered if he should be looking north, not south.

Like Dry.

It was the boast, the damned boast. *Chosen by the Stone Gods to guard their borders.* What borders? Bludd borders? Or those encircling the entire clanholds? And guard them from what?

Vaylo sunk to his haunches and whistled for the dogs. They'd been ranging back and forth in search of game and they did not heel immediately. Settling down to wait, Vaylo tried to push aside his unease. He had men to lead and a roundhouse to retake, and it didn't do much good to dwell on Dry and his hundred men guarding the Dhoonewall. Did even less good to imagine that it was Dry, not he, the Bludd chief, who was upholding the promise of the boast.

Chief first. Boast later. Once he'd taken possession of the Bluddhouse, he'd have all the time in the world to figure out mystery of the boast.

Plucking a wad of chewing curd from his belt pouch, Vaylo made himself comfortable for the watch. The stars were out, some of them, and a half-moon was shining through thinning clouds. Vaylo sat and did not think for a while.

The dogs came to him in their own good time. At first he didn't realize that the wolf dog hadn't homed. It could be willful at times and reluctant to obey a summons if it was closing on a kill. Vaylo whistled again, waited. Oddly enough, it had been Gullit who had given him his first pup. It was a sight hound, the runt of the litter. With irregular vertebrae in its tail and an infection in its right eye Gullit had judged it unworthy to be reared for the hunt. "Take it," his father had said to him, "but you'll to have to wean it yourself as I won't waste a teat." Vaylo had done just that, dipping a shammy in pig's milk so the pup could suckle on the hour. After a week he'd taken her to Mogo Salt's grandfather, the field surgeon Roagie Salt. Roagie had been the one who'd tended him after the worst of Gullit's beatings; the dislocated arm, the broken collarbone, the punctured spleen. Roagie had given Vaylo drops for the pup's eye and advised him to grind bonemeal into her milk to make her strong.

"She'll never run straight with that kettle tail," Roagie had said, "but she'll sure sprint a fast curve."

Moya, Vaylo had called her, after the legendary chief's wife who defended the Bluddhouse from Dhoone's armies while her husband was away.

Moya, the dog, turned out to be a brawler. Vaylo grinned thinking about her. Fierce and scrappy, she would lunge at anyone who looked at him the wrong way. He'd never been without a dog since. They had made him who he was. A boy with a dog at his heels was no longer alone. He had someone to back him up in a fight, an extra set of eyes and ears to keep watch, and something warm—and smelly—to sleep next to through the long winter nights. Vaylo had lost count of all the dogs he had owned. Hundreds, certainly. At some point he had stopped giving them names. It didn't seem necessary. They were part of him like an arm or a leg. Might as well have called them Vaylo.

The wolf dog had been different though. Its dam had gone missing four summers back and Vaylo thought he'd never see her again. Fifty days later she'd turned up, fat and pleased with herself, trotting in from the north. When she'd given birth a month later it became apparent she had mated with a wolf. Right from the start, the wolf dog held itself apart from its siblings. More wolf than dog, it was the largest of the litter and suckled the hardest. It sucked its dam dry, depriving its brothers of milk. Its sisters lived, but there was never any doubt over who was top dog. Vaylo had taken the wolf dog in hand, but he realized early on that it could not be wholly tamed. Part of its soul lived in the north beyond the clanholds. On icy nights lit by stars no latch or tether could hold it . . . but it had always returned.

Until now.

The old pain in Vaylo's chest knifed him. Ignoring it, he stood and headed south. He had a watch to keep. Three dogs ghosted at his side, serious and alert. To the north, Cluff Drybannock would be mounting his own watch, looking not to the clanholds but to the Rift. Vaylo wondered how long it would take the wolf dog to reach him.

The dog had chosen a new master. It would not be coming back.

CHAPTER 7

Captive

The buzzing grew louder and more complicated as individual threads dropped in and out of hearing. He ignored it. The sound came from a place he didn't want to be. The place was trouble, and he didn't want trouble. He wanted to drift on the warm sea a while longer. Reason cast a dim light here, memory an even dimmer one. Drifting was safe. Drifting was good.

Or so he'd thought. Things began to gather on the horizon, in the shadows where salt water smoked into gas. The things had necks humped with rotator muscle and the fortified jaws of wolves. They waited for him to drift within striking distance. He was whole and they wanted to tear him into parts.

Watcher, they hissed. *Over here. We'll show you how to use that sword.*

The words were a puzzle, but not a pressing one. Other things pressed harder. Drift and you were at the mercy of currents and undercurrents, prevailing winds and tides. For the longest time he had assumed he was drifting in circles. Harmless and unharmed. He was aware of the tow now. It was dragging him toward the hump-necked things, forcing him to make a choice. Do or be done to. Take action or let action be taken to you.

Raif Sevrance opened his eyes. Looked. Blinked. Failed to understand. Closed his eyes. It required an exertion of will not to return to the warm sea. He concentrated on receiving reports from his senses to hold himself alert.

The buzzing sound had the particular resonance of mosquitoes in flight. Anyone who had camped in the badlands in spring and summer knew the noise. *Music of a thousand bites,* Da called it. *"While you're out hunting in the Badlands, the Badlands is busy hunting you."*

The words were truer than Da had known. Tem Sevrance had died on a longhunt in the Badlands, split open from solar plexus to groin by a sword that cauterized blood vessels as it severed them. He'd been tracked down and hunted like prey.

Muscles clenched in Raif's chest. His weight shifted and the room began to rock. A sawing noise sounded directly above him. Creaking and rustling followed. As the rocking motion subsided Raif smelled trees. Cedar and bloodwood scents were so strong he wondered why he hadn't registered them sooner. And then there was the strange tingly odor of icewood. The smell of a full moon.

He opened his eyes, looked right, left, overhead. He saw the deep greens and blues of pine forest canopy and the gray of an overcast sky. Things were beginning to make sense. And at the same time no sense at all.

The base of his spine was pressed against a hard ridge. Judging from the numbness in his left foot and left buttock, it had been pressed there a while. Hot points of pressure underlay his entire body, creating alternating welts of pain and numbness. Realizing that his left ear was bearing the weight of his skull, he turned his head. Tears sprang in his eyes as blood rushed into the freed earlobe. It hurt like hell. Irritated, he sat up.

The movement set his prison in motion. He was caged, suspended from the limb of a bloodwood by two ankle-thick ropes that twined in a sheet knot three feet above the cage and were rigged to a pulley. The bloodwood's trunk was five feet away. Raif judged that if he rocked the cage hard enough he could smash into it. He hadn't looked down yet, but he was beginning to understand things. Smashing into the trunk might break open the cage—it was constructed from hardwood lashed to a steel frame—but it wouldn't free him, unless you counted a drop to the death as freedom. The bloodwood was massive. Its trunk had to be at least twenty feet round—too wide to grip in a descent. Below the pulley limb, the tree had been expertly delimbed. All potential footholds had been planed smooth. Raif was on eyelevel with one of the scars left behind by the delimbing. It was as smooth as a tabletop. Some kind of shiny sealant had been painted on the exposed wood. Raif looked at the workmanship for a long time. The people who'd hauled him up here knew exactly what they were doing.

When he was ready, he rolled onto his stomach. The mosquitoes that had been feeding on his neck and forearms buzzed into flight. Raif ignored them. It was harder to ignore the flares of pain sent up by his numb flesh. A lattice pattern was stamped into the meat of his palm.

Concerns about his body fell away as he looked down at an eighty foot drop. Bloodwoods were the tallest trees in the north. Raif had seen stripped logs two hundred feet long. The trees themselves could be double that. He supposed his captors could have hauled him higher, but then they'd have to put more effort into raising and lowering the cage. Eighty feet was plenty high enough to discourage a prisoner from attempting escape.

Wire cut into Raif's thighs and chest. As he shifted to relieve the pressure, the cage fishtailed on its horizontal axis and seesawed on its vertical axis. Ropes ticked as they managed the tension. Raif bellied closer to the middle of the cage. He decided the best way to minimize the rocking was to keep his weight centered. The cage was a six-by-five oblong, four feet high. Raif wondered who had made it. Not clansmen, that was for sure. Clansmen would never hold a prisoner in a contraption that held his feet above the earth. All men, even the condemned, were allowed congress with the Stone Gods.

This was city-built. Their god floated in air. Raif imagined that an elevated cage might even bring a city-prisoner and his city-god closer. So what was a city-built contraption doing in possession of the Sull? The cage was too ugly and heavily welded to be Sull-wrought. And judging from stories told by Angus Lok, the Sull weren't known for taking prisoners. Warn once, then kill: that was their policy on trespass. Yet they had taken a prisoner. Him.

That was a Sull settlement below.

Raif's gaze tracked the details through the forest. The settlement was like nothing he had ever seen. It stood in a partial clearing of pines. Perhaps one tree in ten had been left standing. The standing trees had been decrowned, delimbed and honed to points. The pointed stumps formed gray-white spears, each a hundred feet high. Raif wondered if it was possible for standing timber to fossilize, for that's what the trunks looked like: trees made of stone. The closest of the trunks formed the points of a perfect square. Canvas had been suspended between them at a height of about twelve feet creating a large open-walled shelter. Light shimmering off the top of the canvas formed a crosshatch pattern Raif recognized: ray skin. Orwin Shank owned a dagger with a ray skin grip. "Grip alone's worth more than ten blades," Orwin was fond of telling people. "Removes the need for violence—I draw it handle up and hypnotize my foe."

Raif calculated that Orwin's dagger had possessed about half a square foot of skin. Right now he was looking at over six hundred square feet, carefully—invisibly—seamed. The canvas rippled in the breeze, rolling waves of blue and silver light. If clansmen had owned such a thing of wonder and wealth, they would not have turned its decorative surface toward the sky. They would have pitched it face down for all to see.

Raif paused on that thought. It told him something fundamental about the Sull. They were not clan. They were not even human. The possessions humans coveted held no value for them. It occurred to Raif that to understand a people you had to know what they valued . . . and in that regard clan knew less than nothing about Sull.

His best chance for survival here would be to watch and learn.

Not that a man in a cage had much choice. It hurt to grin. It hurt to breathe. His unconscious body had not been treated kindly. Shifting position, he rested his knees. The cage bobbed like a cork in water. Pine needles that had settled on the top of the cage fell through the gaps and rained on him. They smelled like soap.

As he brushed them away, movement below caught his

eye. A figure emerged from beneath the canopy. Even seen from above at eighty feet, the figure was unmistakably Sull. Muscle in Raif's gut loosened. He couldn't control it. It was what all clansmen felt upon spotting the race who reigned in the East: fear of the unknown.

The figure, an unarmored male with hair notched into a battle ridge that ran from the center of his forehead to the base of his neck, strode with purpose across the clearing. He did not look up. Raif tracked him as far as a stone platform ringed with a barrier wall before losing him from sight.

A wind gust rocked the cage as Raif tried to get a better look at the platform. Branches from surrounding trees limited his view. He could see the area directly below the cage, but densely needled bloodwood limbs cut into his line of sight in all directions except north across the ray skin canopy. As far as he could tell, the platform and ringwall were falling to ruin. Chunks of stone were partially embedded in the platform, as if they had fallen from a great height. Saplings and staghorn ferns had rooted in the cracks. Raif pumped the cage, forcing a sharp upswing. At the upswing's zenith he caught a brief glimpse of the platform's far wall and what looked to be more ruins stretching back into the forest. He swung again. Dozens of canvas shelters had been erected amid the ruins, utilizing standing walls, stone piers and decrowned trees as anchor points. Lean figures wove through the maze, shadowy, silent, armed for war.

Rolling onto his back, Raif let the cage fall still. Directly overhead, his view of the sky was partially blocked by the dense mass of the bloodwood. Needles ran along its branches like oars on a longboat. The longer Raif looked at them the more they seemed to move. To row.

Shortening his focus, he concentrated on the cage. A water-skin was hooked halfway down the wall that faced the tree trunk. Besides that, there was nothing in the cage, only him. Raif took inventory of his body and clothes. The Orrl cloak was gone. He tried not to let it bother him. His sealskin was stiff with dried mud and blood. So were his pants. Resin oozing from the bloodwood had stained both fabrics with dark, sticky spots. A flattened mosquito was glued to one of them.

He would get cold, that was his first assessment. If he was held here overnight he'd get chilblains, possibly frostbite. Bending at the waist, he reached for the waterskin and weighed the water. About a gallon. No food. Judging from the light, it was close to midday. Raif lay down, went back to watching the needles. This had to be a temporary holding place. If the Sull wanted him dead they would have killed him. If they wanted him to die in the cage they would have withheld water.

Unless they intended to let him waste away—die without staining their hands with blood. Raif twitched. The move-ment dislodged something at the base of his throat. Raven lore, the hard black piece of bird ivory that had been given to him at birth, jerked against its twine. So it was still here. He and the Sull had something in common. *Neither of us wants the raven.*

Raif closed his eyes, shifted his position to relieve pressure on his shoulders and buttocks. He listened to the mosquitoes swarm him. Tomorrow they'd all be dead.

"*Addie,*" Raif bellowed at the top of his lungs. "*ADDIE.*"

The only reply was the drill of mosquitoes.

It took a while for his heart to calm down. Where was Addie? What had they done to him? Raif couldn't imagine a worse fate for a cragsman than to be hung in a cage. Cragsman lived their entire lives in the open spaces of the clanholds, following their herds. They hated confinement. "Even the largest roundhouse in the clanholds," Addie liked to point out, "is just so many walls."

Raif forced himself to think. No sign of Addie might be good. Perhaps the Sull only caged those they feared. Yiselle No Knife and Ilya Spinebreaker had barely spared a glance for the cragsman during that meeting thirty days ago at their camp. Raif recalled the cold glitter in No Knife's eyes as she figured out his identity. He was lucky she'd let him go. So why pick him up now? What had changed?

Loss, he realized. The sword had been under ice when he'd met Yiselle No Knife in her tent north of the Rift. She had helped him find it, though Raif seriously doubted that had been her intent. *"They will never find Mish'al Nij,"* she had murmured as he and Addie left. Until that moment he'd had no idea where to look for the sword. *Mish'al Nij* was the answer. The Place with No Clouds.

Raif grabbed the water sack from the cage wall and drank deeply. The water tasted green and sharp. Acquiring the sword made him more of a threat. He considered this for a while. The Sull were now in possession of Loss. If that's what they wanted why not kill him or let him go? Why imprison him? Clansmen took prisoners on the battlefield so they could ransom them later for goods. Blackhail would pay nothing to retrieve Raif Sevrance, and the Maimed Men had nothing to pay. Ransom couldn't be the reason. It made no sense. The Sull didn't play that game. Was it punishment then? Or were they awaiting word from He Who Leads? Perhaps No Knife didn't have the authority to decide Watcher of the Dead's fate.

The temperature was dropping. Raif rolled onto his knees to check for activity below the cage. Two horses, both saddled, were cropping grass alongside the canopy. He hadn't heard them arrive. One of the horses had hard-sided panniers leveled across its rump. Supplies? Food? Raif's gut clenched. His stomach was empty except for the water. When had he eaten last? How long had he been here?

He watched and waited. The canopy rolled in the breeze. Someone, one of the horses' riders, strayed close to the edge of the shelter. Raif saw an arm, a hip, a weapons belt. Female.

It didn't make him feel any better. He shunted into a squat, head brushing the top of the cage. It was a relief not to be pressed against the mesh, let the soles of his boots take the punishment. Relief didn't last long. His thigh muscles started to ache and the cage wouldn't still. Dropping to a sit, he steadied the motion of the cage. He tried, but couldn't steady his thoughts.

Why hadn't they acknowledged him? What were they doing under the canopy? The horse with the panniers pricked back its ears to listen to a command. It turned and walked under the canopy. A moment later, the second horse followed. Raif strained to hear something. Dimly he was aware of four hearts beating below the canopy. Two large and relaxed: the horses. And two faint and alien and more difficult to read: Sull.

He drank more water. Waited. In the quadrant of the sky that was visible from the cage, clouds were moving. He watched them until the snap of metal buckles caught his ear. The Sull were mounting their horses. Minutes passed and then two riders emerged from the canopy, trotting their mounts south toward the settlement. The first rider was a woman warrior decked in a cloak of clarified hide and armed at the waist and shin with chained knives. Her hair was as dark and glossy as a river at night. A quarter-moon section above her left ear had been shaved to the scalp. The second rider was Spinebreaker.

Raif grabbed the cage and shook it. "Where's Addie?" he screamed at him. "What have you done with him?"

The riders held their spines steady, muscles taut. They did not look up. The horses' ears twitched but their legs didn't break stride. Raif watched as they passed beneath the forest canopy and disappeared from sight. He was breathing hard. A new kind of fear lit his chest. It was so unknown to him that he couldn't have defined what it was. It existed in the space between words. Unseen. Alone. Disregarded.

Raif recalled the story of Rangor Bannen, the Echo Chief. Rangor's son Poadie usurped the chiefship in all but name. Out of loyalty and cruelty, Poadie did not kill his father and did not take the title chief. Instead he imprisoned Rangor in a pigpen, chaining his father to the seven-foot wall. Poadie and his men would come by every day and taunt him. They grunted like pigs and asked if he had any pronouncements to make from the mud. At first Rangor was bitter and would rattle his chains and demand to be released. "You are not my son," he would shout at Poadie. "You're a spineless disgrace of a man." After a while the taunting lost its novelty and Poadie and his men ceased to visit the chief-in-name-only. Bannen slid into a war with Scarpe and Harkness, and the old chief went disregarded. A kitchen girl would bring slops once a day, and there came a time when Rangor no longer bothered to pick up the carrot stumps and chicken bones with his hands and gobbled them from the mud like a dog.

Raif had heard the story told many times. In some tellings

Rangor was left alone and disregarded for years, in others it was just two seasons: summer and fall. All stories agreed on what became of Rangor Bannen. He went insane. Alone and disregarded, his mind turned in on itself, went as soft and rotten as the carrot stumps left in the mud. No one spoke to him anymore. Mothers feared to let their children close to the stinking old man who lived in his own filth. Warriors did not acknowledge his existence. He shamed them and they shamed him. If anyone spoke of the old chief at all it was when mood was darkened by strong malt. "Poadie should have killed him," they muttered. "What purpose is served by letting him live?"

Poadie was struck down at the Battle of Barrel Hill by a Harkness sharpshooter positioned deep behind the treeline. In the chaos that followed, five hundred Banmen lost their lives. No one with sufficient jaw to be chief survived. That was when the elder warriors made the decision to release Rangor from the pen. "He never stopped being chief," they told themselves. "And he's led us before in hard times."

They freed him and scrubbed him, shaved his beard and clipped his hair, and dressed him in the fine gray lamb fleeces of chief. Yet even as they tended him, they knew something was wrong. When he was asked a question—which sword, which robe, which boots—his answer was to repeat the question. "Wool or linen?" he recited back to his attendant, face slack, eyes focused on the space between objects. "Wool or linen? Wool or linen?"

Rangor became known as the Echo Chief. Raif supposed someone must have assumed the role of clan chief, but that part of the story was seldom told. A man could lose his mind, that was the point of the story. A man alone and disregarded could float so far away from his body that there was no coming back.

Raif pulled open his pant laces and pissed through the cage wire. He thought of Rangor gobbling food from the mud, and then closed his eyes and didn't think at all.

Sleep took him to all the old places: the Blackhail round-house, Da's tent in the Badlands, the greatcourt on the day he swore his yearman's oath. The past was so close he could touch it. He could feel the rough texture of the swearstone beneath his tongue, taste its mineral coldness, hear Inigar Stoop cry, "Swear it."

Raif woke. The past slid back into its place and the illusion that it might be changed evaporated.

It was growing dark. The sun had descended below the canopy and the pines were black. Raif sat up, bringing his knees to his chest to conserve heat. Stars appeared as the cage rocked. After a while he grabbed the waterskin and drank. He could smell Sull cookery; charring fruit and spices. Lamps had been lit in the settlement, blue and violet specks in the distance. Some moved and Raif imagined Sull carrying torches as they walked between tents.

At first he didn't realize that his expectation was that one of the lights would break away and move through the forest toward him. At first he thought he was just watching. Not waiting. Minutes passed and then hours, and night chills shook his body. No one approached. They would come tomorrow, he told himself. They had to. The waterskin would be flat by morning.

He slept again. Wires cut into his flesh as he dreamed. Da stood before him, his opened torso bluing as it froze. "Son," he said. "Why does the man who killed me still live?"

Pain bolted through Raif's left shoulder. He awoke, or thought he did. But no, he was mistaken, for dreamlike forms moved through the darkness. Teeth flashed. Hands that did not love him touched his bare flesh. A night heron shrieked a warning, and then the dreams withdrew. He slept like the dead.

He awoke to a world of mist. Gray cloud pressed against all six planes of the cage. It was dawn, and the temperature balanced above freezing. Raif took stock of his body. Some pounding in his head, an ache in his shoulder, but surprisingly no numbness in his fingers and other extremities. Sitting up, he reached for the waterskin.

It was full. The deer hide was taut and round, jutting out from the cage wall like a ripe fruit. Last night it had been slack, barely a cup of water left inside. Raif unhooked it, needing to feel its weight. Every hunter knew that gas could bloat an unopened carcass, but he didn't think this was gas. The skin was heavy. A beat of fear passed through his heart. He uncorked the skin and sniffed. Same water as yesterday. Sharp, colder than the air that surrounded it. Sull.

He had no choice but to drink. Even suspecting what he did, he had to drink. He knew what thirst looked like when it killed. It looked like a weary, shivering horse.

"Bear," he said softly, letting the memory of the little hill pony who had guided him through the Want turn in his thoughts before shutting it down.

He needed to think. Mist pushing against the wires was sliced into cubes as it entered the cage. Raif watched the cubes dissolve as he pieced together what had happened. A quick investigation of his right shoulder revealed a small red hole in the skin. The surrounding flesh was tender but clean. Some kind of shiny ointment had been spread over the wound. Raif sniffed it. Nothing.

They had put him to sleep. Fired a tipped dart through the wire, waited until he was unconscious and then lowered the cage. Once he was on the ground, they'd plucked out the dart, tended the puncture wound, refilled the waterskin. What else? Raif did not want to replay last night's dreams in his head. If the answer was in them let it stay there. Instead he looked hard at the cage. Condensed mist slickened the steel. One small drop in temperature and the water would turn to ice. Had they given him something to prevent frostbite? Did such a thing exist?

The mist began to drain and giant bloodwoods emerged like sunken ships. Dull sounds carried across the forest. Someone below and not far to the east was honing metal. Someone else was hammering stakes. Camp sounds. Raif forced himself to resist their familiarity.

These people had drugged him. Strange, but all the times Angus Lok had talked of the Sull he had never mentioned their cruelty. Proud, lethal, swift to act: those were the qualities Angus' stories emphasized. If you crossed the Sull you ended up dead, not strung up a tree and drugged.

Hooves drumming below signaled the approach of several riders. Raif did not look down to track them. He understood the game now. They would ride to the canopy, stay awhile and then return to camp. Their purpose was to ignore him. The Sull, the oldest race in the North, were trying to break him. They had almost certainly drugged his drinking water. He could feel it; a loosening of muscle around the heart. When required, they would fire a dart and send him to sleep while they cleaned out the cage and replenished his water. Their intention was to deprive him of contact, to isolate and weaken him.

Raif settled himself in the cage and stared at the pine needles as he tried to figure out how to keep his mind.

CHAPTER 8

Stovehouse

"The choice is yours. Stealth or candor: take your pick."

"I—"

Hew Mallin blinked like other men wielded knives. Warning lived in the lean edges of lidded flesh. "Do not reveal your choice to me."

Bram Cormac, half-brother to the Dhoone chief Robbie Dhoone and deserter of his adopted clan, Castlemilk, closed his mouth, canceled his reply and considered the anarchy in Mallin's words.

Mallin was a ranger in the Brotherhood of the Long Watch, the Phage. He and Bram were sitting in an illegal stovehouse, four leagues southeast of Dhoone. The building had been newly raised but the stove had seen better days. Creosote oozed from the chimney neck and smoke leaked from an out-of-sight crack in the underbelly. All the smells of timber—freshly cut, cured and burned—gave the house a tinderbox feel. Lighting was dim. A handful of men leaned against the walls. Two women shared a bench, drinking steadily. The older one wore a dress cut so low her large brown nipples were exposed. A storm had just passed and cloaks were steaming. When a patron tried to dry his Dhoone-blue cloak over the stove, the stovemaster growled.

"No colors in my house." Thickset with a broken nose and brown teeth, he stared the Dhoonesman into compliance. Stovemasters were respected throughout the clanholds. They were hard men. They had to be.

Mallin did his trick of watching this exchange yet not seeming to. A piece of tack leather rested on the table before him. He was working wax into it with his thumbs. His gaze never left the leather, but a certain stillness in his face revealed to Bram that his attention was on the stovemaster. When the Dhoonesman removed his cloak from the stove and draped it over the nearest bench, the stillness in Mallin's face relaxed. No fight tonight, not over this.

Mallin took a mouthful of malt and Bram did likewise. The alcohol was fiery and Bram felt it going down. He'd never been allowed to drink hard liquor before, and when Mallin had bought him a dram he had secretly disapproved. A clansman would not buy strong malt for a boy of sixteen. A sense of responsibility would stop him. Mallin had no such sense.

"I am not your father," the ranger had warned early on. "Do not expect me to rule you."

Bram had nodded, though he had not fully understood what the ranger was telling him. He wasn't sure he understood now, but he was learning. Rangers were not clan. They did not function as caretakers for one another. You were allowed freedoms and the right to hang yourself with them. It was a new concept to Bram, this lawlessness. He felt as if he'd been plunged into deep water with no place to rest his feet.

He had traveled with Mallin for twenty days now, entering

a world of margins and shadow. Bram thought he had known the clanholds. He was wrong. He knew the well-traveled paths, the long-standing stovehouses, the clan-maintained bridges and crossings. Hew Mallin knew the ways through the darkest woods, the secret entrances to sealed mines, the natural bridges across waterways and the caves beneath the hills. Mallin's world was peopled with men and women who lived on the ragged edge of clan: illegal settlers, bear trappers, fugitives, malcontents, prospectors, prostitutes and wild men. They lived in shanties, reed villages, clearings in the woods, abandoned buildings, mineshafts and wells: everywhere, if you knew where to look.

Hew Mallin knew where to look.

"Take it."

Mallin spoke quietly but with force. With his right hand, he pushed his half-finished malt toward Bram. With his left he slid a slim package under the table. Bram accepted both simultaneously. To cover himself while he concealed the package, he slugged the malt. Pleased with his own quick thinking, he glanced to Mallin for approval.

Hew Mallin wasn't looking his way. After a few seconds the ranger nodded and Bram nodded back, relieved. At first he didn't realize that Mallin's signal wasn't intended for him. It was directed toward the younger of the two women across the room. The woman turned her head slowly in response, appraising the ranger. Her dress was more modest than her companion's and to Bram's mind less interesting because of it. She was pretty though, with patches of high color on her cheeks and dozens of tiny copper hooks in her ears.

"I'll catch up with you on the south road," Mallin said to Bram rising, "in the morning."

Bram stared at the back of his head.

Reaching the women, Mallin introduced himself and began a softly spoken conversation. Within seconds, he was invited to sit down. Within a minute his hand was resting on the younger woman's thigh.

It took a while for Bram to understand the ranger wasn't coming back. That was it? No help? No warning? A package to be delivered—a letter, by the feel of it—and no instruction on how to get it done.

Stealth or candor: take your pick.

Bram sat and blinked. Smoke leaking from the stove burned his eyes. Or perhaps it was the malt. The sun had set an hour back and outside it would be full dark. And wet. Bram was warm and dry and comfortably hazy-in-the-head and the thought of trekking through damp fields in the darkness held absolutely no appeal.

Nor did delivering the letter.

Soft laughter tinkled from Hew Mallin and the women. Bram stood. His hip banged against the table and knocked over the two thumb cups. The sound wasn't especially loud, but the room was small and men were armed and wary. All turned to look at him. Hew Mallin touched his lips to the older woman's ear and whispered a single word. She gasped and slapped him across the face. Instantly the attention of the room shifted, and much though Bram would have liked to watch what happened next he recognized his cue to slip away.

He was careful as he slid between the benches. For some reason his body was overresponding. His steps had more kick than they needed and his hands applied unnecessary force to the door, making it ricochet against its hinges. He was relieved when he was finally outside. For a few moments he leaned against the exterior wall and breathed. It was hard to not to think that leaving Castlemilk had been a mistake.

The air smelled ripe and rainy, and the tail end of the storm pushed wind gusts against Bram's face. *First things first,* he told himself. Ride or walk? *Walk, definitely walk.* If it all went horribly wrong he didn't want Guy Morloch reclaiming his horse.

Despite everything Bram grinned. Two months ago Guy Morloch had abandoned him on a hillside east of Dhoone. Guy's stallion had done a runner, and as the horse's chances of coming back seemed low, Guy had commandeered Bram's mount as a replacement. For a wonder Guy's stallion, Gabbie, had returned the next morning. A few weeks later Wrayan Castlemilk had gifted Gabbie to Bram, which meant that Gabbie was now the property of Bram Cormac. Still. Bram wouldn't bet good money on either Wrayan Castlemilk or Guy Morloch honoring the settlement.

The thought of Wrayan Castlemilk heated Bram's face. The Milk chief had welcomed him to her clan, seconding his yearman's oath, and just like Robbie, he'd betrayed her. Dhoone was no good for Milk.

Bram thrust himself off from the stovehouse wall and sprinted west. Who was he fooling? He wasn't Dhoone. *"You can't claim my name, Bram,"* Robbie had always been fond of pointing out. *"We may share the same father, but my mother was a descendant of kings. Yours was a rabbit trapper from Gnash."*

Reaching the road, Bram cut north toward the woods. The sky was a dark ceiling barely tall enough to contain the trees. Rain had stopped falling but the groundcover was wet. Sword ferns soaked Bram's pant legs and boots. His cloak was goat wool, dark brown and closely spun. Its slippery lining repelled damp. Hew Mallin had given him the cloak on the night they left Castlemilk as they camped on the banks of the White. The following morning Bram had decided to burn his old cloak, yet when he crossed to the fire with the Dhoone-blue garment, the ranger halted him.

"Keep it," Mallin had said quietly. "It might prove useful."

Bram could not outrun the chill of those words. He was Phage now. Old loyalties no longer existed, but tokens of those loyalties were fair game. They might come in handy for disguise or defense. The cloak was in the stovehouse lean-to, a closely rolled cylinder claiming space in the bottom of his pack. Bram wondered if Mallin had intended him to wear it tonight.

With the ranger you could not be sure. He was lawless in ways Bram was still discovering. Mallin had walked right up to Wrayan Castlemilk's door and stolen one of her sworn men in broad daylight. Later he'd had the nerve to enter the Castlemilk stables and order the stablemaster to saddle Bram's horse. Mallin did not care how things were done, just that they were done.

Stealth or candor: take your pick.

Bram slowed to a walk. He was sweating heavily. His head was banging and he thought he might be sick. *Shouldn't have finished the malt.* He tugged a fern from the ground and mashed it into his face. It seemed to help. Now how was he going to get the letter to Rob?

"What I give you must be delivered to Dun Dhoone tonight," Mallin had said an hour earlier as they entered the stovehouse. *"He leaves for Withy at dawn."*

Bram dropped the fern. Tiny hooks in the stem had

pierced his palm and his hand stung as air and nerve endings met. He had not imagined he would return to Dhoone. He had assumed that walking away from Castlemilk was the same as walking away from Robbie and clan.

The woods were quiet as he headed west. Cover thinned as hemlock and blackstone pine gave way to oak and ironwood. Something had been trapped just beyond the path. Bram smelled fresh urine and fear. He knew this area. His mother had set traps here. Wires mostly. Sometimes drop cages. Her secret was to acid-burn the metal so no telltale gleam of light could give away a tripwire. Bram was careful where he put his feet.

When he passed the Stagpost, a tree trunk carved in the shape of antlers marking the end of trapping territory and the beginning of hunting grounds, he turned north again. His hand was still stinging so he slipped it under his cloak. The package blocked his way, preventing his fingers from reaching the heat of his chest. Inside lay a message from the Phage to the Dhoone chief. Bram wondered what it said.

He wondered a long time.

An hour passed as he ghosted through woods. When the moon slid across a break in the clouds, he received his first glimpse of the Dhoonehouse. Viewed from south, the largest roundhouse in the clanholds was a blind hill of stone. Dozens of recessed chimneys punctured the vast arch of the dome, making the roundhouse smoke like a coal kicked from the fire. At its southern apex, the twin Thistle Towers stood lean and still. Men stationed there lit no lamps nor set fires, under direct order from Robbie Dun Dhoone. Bram could not say with certainty the reason behind the order, but he knew his brother. He could guess.

Bram drifted west along the treeline, delaying the time when he crossed open ground. He had spent hours in the Thistle Towers as a boy, playing defend the fortress and then later keeping watch. The stairs were slippery and cut strangely high and the air stank of mice. Even before Robbie's chiefship, guards were allowed few comforts. Some ancient, hard-nosed chief had ordered chairs carved from stone to be placed in the uppermost chamber. "Wood's too soft," he was supposed to have said. "Once a man's arse goes to sleep his head's not far behind."

Bram didn't think discomfort was the reason Robbie allowed no fires, though. Robbie Dun Dhoone liked to catch his intruders unaware. Light from fires and lamps acted as a deterrent: Guards here, keep away. Robbie preferred to let his enemies approach and pick them off one by one.

Bram suspected the effects of the malt were wearing off. It was becoming easier to sustain panic. Rob would kill him. He'd see him and kill him. Bram Cormac was a traitor to his clan. He'd forsaken his oath to Castlemilk and broken the bargain struck between the Dhoone chief and the Milk chief. Even worse, he'd brought shame upon his brother, the man who wanted to be king.

Oh gods. What was Mallin thinking? Why couldn't the ranger deliver the letter himself? The least he could have done was trained his helper.

Right now training would be good.

Bram ducked from the trees into open ground. The timing was right. Light swinging in a narrow arc at the base of the east tower meant the door had just opened and closed. The watch was changing. Attention would be diverted. A sixteen-year-old boy with good eyes might slip by undetected.

Rain had turned the graze to sludge. Mud rivers oozed toward Blue Dhoone Lake, carrying frost-split seeds to the water and sucking at Bram's boots. Trees that no longer existed were on his mind. As long as he could remember, a stand of ornamental willows had grown at the lake's north shore. The willows were gone. As he moved closer he corrected himself: the willows' crowns had gone, but their stumps remained. Someone had done a brutal job with the felling. Decapitation was a word that sprung to Bram's mind.

And stuck there.

Bram made himself move forward. He would use the stumps anyway, crouch down and wait until he had some kind of plan. He knew every entrance to the Dhoonehouse and rated his chances of sneaking in as low. The stables would have been his best bet for stealth, but they'd been torched in the retaking. There was a secret entrance in the Tomb of the Dhoone Princes—the Dog Lord had used it during his escape—but Rob had ordered the entrance sealed with roof nails. Bram supposed that a man with a sledgehammer could rip open the door. He didn't have a sledgehammer though, and even if he did, it would hardly be stealthy. Or healthy. A sledgehammer could tear off a man's head.

Bram tried to stay calm as he shadowed the lake. This close you could see the water rippling. Glass eels skimmed below the surface, hunting prey. They were trapped, Bram reckoned. Unable to leave the Dhoonehold without skipping over leagues of mud. They needed a way out. He needed one in.

Reaching the willow stumps, he squatted for cover. An impulse he wasn't proud of made him reach for the package. Ideas were suddenly there in his head and he acted before he could outthink them. A small tug was all it took to break the seal. A single sheet of vellum, folded in two, lay inside. Bram centered the letter on his kneecap and ran a fist down the crease, flattening the page. Moonlight filtering through rain-clouds made the animal hide glow. Its message was short and unsigned. Bram read.

You could stop your lungs from racing but not your heart, Bram realized as he threw the outer package in the lake. It floated, seal up, on the surface until an eel snatched it from sight.

Bram stood. He could smell the sweet scent of burning alder drifting from the house. *We both know you were never cut out to be a Dhoone.* Robbie's words, spoken three months ago, repeated in Bram's head. They had a different shape to them now, like a new tooth that had punched through a gum. Robbie might as well have said clan. Never cut out to be clan.

The walk toward the west Thistle Tower took seconds. Bram's arm was already in motion as he closed distance toward the door. Rain had soaked the wood. Thumping it with the heel of his hand produced a dull rumble. Almost immediately, light and noise touched off within the tower.

"Who goes there?" came the shouted challenge from the other side of the door.

"Bram Cormac to see his brother."

The door did not open; Bram had not expected it to. Tower guards were no fools. Moments passed as he was inspected through a series of finger holes drilled at eye height. Bram kept himself still. Chances were high that his inspector knew him.

"Tell Robbie I await him by the lake."

Hearing a grunt of acknowledgment, Bram turned and headed back to the shore.

The temperature was dropping and the lake began to steam. Something close to self-destruction kept Bram's mind still as he waited. Right here, on the north bank of Blue Dhoone, things were changing for him. Think and he might stop them. Think and it might be possible to hold on to the Bram Cormac who was just a bad Dhoonesman and bad clansman.

And not yet a bad man.

It didn't take long for Robbie Dun Dhoone to emerge from his house. Bram recognized his brother's silhouette. Rob carried muscle high in his shoulders as all hammermen did, but there was balance in his legs and hips, a perfection of proportion that singled him out. Hammer strokes that other men strove to execute were effortless to him, so he didn't need extra bulk in his upper body. Early exposure to swordcraft had helped him devise new ways to wield blunt and heavy blades.

He was dressed in a Dhoone-blue wool cloak edged with fisher fur, gray moleskin pants and tunic, and thick-soled leather boots. He was armed but not armored. Da's longsword, the horse-stopper forged from mirror steel, dissected the lines of his back. It had to weigh over a stone, but Robbie moved lightly, without burden, as he crossed the hard standing of the bluecourt.

Bram picked his moment and then made the small adjustment that angled his body toward the light. He experienced a stab of satisfaction as his brother jerked in surprise. Until then, Robbie Dhoone had not realized how close his half-brother stood to him.

He covered it well. "Bram," he said smoothly, asserting force with the word.

"Rob."

Robbie waited. So did Bram. He watched as Robbie

appraised him. The golden charm, which Rob worked like a muscle, relaxed. No point in expending energy here.

"What do you have for me?"

"Information if you want it."

Robbie's eyes glittered. "Wrayan Castlemilk said you'd joined them."

The Milk chief's name was all it took for Bram to lose hold of his calm. Pinpricks from the fern became hot stabs of pain as blood pumped at force through his face and palms.

Robbie nodded, satisfied by evidence of Bram's shame. "Say what you came to and leave."

"Strike the Withyhouse tomorrow and you'll fail."

"Unless."

The instinct was swift and unmistakable: *Bargain here. Tit for tat.* Bram considered what he wanted. His hastily assembled plan had been to bargain for safe passage from the Dhoonehold—*I give you information and you allow me to leave, unharmed*—but the same instinct that told him to bargain told him he was selling himself short. The information was worth more. It would make Robbie Dun Dhoone a king—and that's what he'd wanted for twenty years, ever since his mother had told him he could trace his ancestry back to the warrior queen, Weeping Moira. So what did he, Bram Cormac, want from his brother? Mallin had ordered him to deliver the letter, not profit from it. Yet hadn't Mallin allowed him free rein? *Stealth or candor: take your pick?* Wasn't that the same as saying, *Do anything you see fit?* Bram decided it was. He also decided what he wanted.

"Two things."

Robbie Dun Dhoone was no one's fool. His smile was knowing. "And they would be?"

"Your guarantee of safe passage from the Dhoonehold."

"You have it."

Bram hesitated. Water plinked as an eel broke the surface of the lake.

"And?"

"Da's sword."

Two words and the air cooled. All was known now. Resentment. Jealousy. Anger. That sword, one of the two their father Mabb Cormac had owned, meant everything between them. The day Da died, Robbie had taken possession of both swords. His plan had been to trade the lesser of the two to Wrayan Castlemilk in return for manpower to help retake Dhoone. Guilt had halted Robbie's hand though. *Traded your brother instead. Gave him the sword to soften the blow.* Bram held Robbie's gaze. This man had sold him to Castlemilk. He, Bram Cormac, deserved that second sword.

Rob looked away first. When he spoke his voice was soft with contempt. "You're too small. You'll never be able to wield it."

"Maybe I'll grow."

"Maybe I'll order your killing. Go back on my word." *Like you.*

Bram heard what hadn't been said. Maybe he was going insane, but it didn't hurt. *Decapitation unnecessary. Already lost my head.*

"If anyone's going to hunt me down and kill me it should be Wrayan Castlemilk. It was her oath I broke. Not yours." Bram didn't know where the words came from—couldn't even be sure if they were true—but they sounded right. His voice was strong and he'd caught some of Robbie's contempt and given it back to him. "A king doesn't do a chief's work."

Seconds passed and then Robbie snapped open his sword holster. "Here," he said, handing the sheathed sword, blade out, to Bram. "Careful how you wear it—it might knife you in the back."

Bram took the sword. Its weight was shocking. Seizing the grip in both hands, he let the point rest on the ground. The tooled leather of the scabbard blackened as it soaked up rainwater.

The detail did not go unregarded by Robbie. "Speak and get the hell off my land."

Time slowed. Bram inhaled mist from the lake, held it, held it, and then used it to become someone else. He told his half-brother how to take the Withyhouse, how it was weakest where it appeared strongest, how a portion of turf abutting its infamous northern wall disguised the underground doors that were an escape hatch for horses and livestock in the event of invasion or fire. Bram felt a sense of expansion as he spoke. Right here on the Banks of Blue Dhoone Lake, the future of the clanholds was changing. He, Bram Cormac, was changing it.

With information.

You didn't have to be strong or skilled or a leader of men to be powerful. You just had to acquire knowledge: trade it and deal it out. It was a revelation. Clan valued force. Clan chiefs ruled by force of law. Cleverness was not praised or rewarded. At Wellhouse, Withy and Castlemilk you could learn the histories and warriors might say, "Let's ask Bram about the last time we attacked the Scarpehouse—he knows his stuff." That was the most you could hope for, the occasional request for advice. You couldn't make a name for yourself out of it— unless you were a fearsome warrior first. One-Armed Gregor was famous for being clever, but he was just as famous for wielding the great war hammer Wallbreaker one-handed. Clever with might could be celebrated. Clever without might was sneaky and unclannish.

That was, Bram realized, the difference between him and Robbie. Robbie was not opposed to lies and double-crossing, but because he was a fine hammerman it didn't hurt his reputation. That was what allowed him to stand there, looking at his brother with disgust.

Bram suddenly felt tired. The air that had puffed up his lungs slipped out. He had one more thing to say and he thought he'd better get it done. "Make sure the tower watch doesn't shoot me as I leave."

Robbie stroked his chin. "It's hard to tell friend from foe in the dark. People get shot by mistake every day."

"Tell them to make a special effort. Their chief might need me again."

Robbie recognized the promise of further information when he heard it. "Brother." The word was an acknowledgment and a barb.

Bram pumped the handle of the sword with both hands. With a single, unlovely swing, he raised the point off the ground and rested it flat against his shoulder. At his right hip, both his wrists were straining under the pressure of being fully flexed. Bram fought the urge to make the adjustment necessary for comfort. He didn't want Robbie to see him fumbling.

Caving his chest forward to balance the weight of the sword, Bram nodded his farewell.

Robbie eyed him coolly and turned away. The weighted fabric of his cloak snapped as he walked toward his house. You could still see the imprint of the sword on his back.

Bram tucked his head down and left.

CHAPTER 9

Sinking into the Swamp

"You'll explode if you eat one more of those."

"If you wrinkle your nose any harder it'll stick," Chedd Limehouse replied to Effie Sevrance. "And I'd rather be exploded any day than pig ugly."

Effie Sevrance unwrinkled her nose instantly. Chedd was right. Exploded was better than ugly. "Hand me one," she ordered, pointing to the apple pastries. "Quick."

Chedd's hand circled above the platter like a bird of prey. The pastries, embedded with hazelnuts and shiny with honey, all looked the same to Effie, but not to Chedd. Chedd's eye could discern infinitely small differences in size, weight and toppings. He seized one and handed it to Effie.

"More nuts," he said tersely.

Effie raised the pastry in toast. "To Clan Gray. Where the living is good."

Chedd motioned to the unshuttered window high above Effie's head. "So's the dying."

It was hard to eat her pastry after that. Chedd took another one—his fourth—and folded it whole into his mouth. He chewed methodically without pleasure, getting the job done.

They were sitting in one of Clan Gray's cave-like pump rooms. Thick clouds made afternoon as dark as sunset. The frogs were already croaking. She and Chedd were on pump duty, but the man who was supposed to be watching them wasn't watching—he'd left, returned with pastries and left again—so that meant they were doing nothing at all. They were seated on high iron stools that were half a foot deep in water. Four paddles looking very much like giant wooden spoons jutted from the exterior walls at chest height. They were the pump shafts. She and Chedd were meant to be working them. According to Tull Buckler—the clansman who had left them unsupervised—the pumps needed to be manned day and night "else the entire roundhouse'll sink into the Stink." The Stink was the marsh that surrounded Clan Gray for thirty leagues in all directions. Hell's Moat was another name for it. "The devil's sucking us down," Tull had informed them earlier. "We have to work to stay put."

Effie shivered. "We'd best get pumping," she said to Chedd.

Chedd slid from the stool and plonked into the water. "Right then."

"Gloves on," Effie warned him, nodding at the iron table where two pairs of boarshide gloves lay beside the pastry platter. "Blisters kill, remember."

Chedd groaned but obeyed. At eleven he was two years older than she was but in matters of safety Effie Sevrance was the boss.

The gloves were as stiff as planks and about a hundred sizes too big. "Bear claws," Effie cried, seizing the pump handle.

"Udder hands," Chedd shot back, making her laugh.

Within five minutes they were sweating. Effie had to swing her entire weight onto the pump handle to force it into motion. The sluice gate opened as the handle depressed and water spurted into the swamp.

"Seeps back in as quick as we pump it," Chedd said. "Walls might as well be sponge."

It was true enough. After an hour of pumping, the water level was no lower. Rings of black crud circled the pump room wall, marking past flood levels. The highest ring fell just an inch below the ceiling and a foot above the window. How had they managed to pump that one out?

"It's smells bad," Chedd said mildly. "Like cabbage poached in fart water."

Effie nodded. You had to hand it to Chedd Limehouse: He had a way with words.

"How long are we supposed to do this for?" Chedd asked.

"Don't know." Effie was breathless. Pumping was a lot easier for Chedd. "I suppose Buckler will come and get us sometime soon."

"Nah, Eff. With all that's going on he's likely forgot."

Halting the pump, handle down, Effie glanced at the window. "Should we sneak up and take a look?"

"No."

"But—"

"No." Chedd frowned so hard cheek fat and forehead fat met in front of his eyes. "Nothing to see. Just some weird clannish death rites. No reason for us to look."

Effie released the pump, sending thick, oily water rushing over the top of her boots. A horn sounded in the distance, its lone note blowing south from the Isle of Grass. Yesterday there had been a death in the clan and today they were disposing of the body. Every clan had their own way of dealing with their dead. At Blackhail they rubbed corpses with milk of mercury and laid them on open ground. At Castlemilk corpses were cut in two and sunk in grave pools, and at Scarpe they were doused in alcohol and set alight. She'd heard the ashes were fed to the poison pines.

"What do they do at Bannen?"

Chedd pumped and didn't answer. Bannen was his home clan. He'd been abducted from the north bank of the Greenwater while out turtling. Effie had been taken a few days later on the Wolf. Waker Stone had kidnapped both of them and floated them upstream to Clan Gray. They'd been here twenty days now and Effie guessed that it bothered Chedd more than it did her. Chedd had been a warrior-in-training at Bannen. When warriors were captured they were supposed to escape.

Understanding that Chedd didn't want to talk about Bannen, Effie nodded at the window. "Why do you think so many of them die?"

Chedd shrugged. "It's Gray. They're cursed."

Effie continued nodding. "Two died last week. A baby and a three-year-old."

"It's a newborn they're sending off tonight."

"Oh." Effie stopped nodding and pumping and began thinking. Swamp water cooled her feet. "Perhaps the babies are born sickly."

"Or they *get* sickly."

Effie examined Chedd's face. The pillowy cheeks and folded-blanket jawline caught your attention straightaway, but if you looked longer you noticed the eyes. They were deep brown and all sorts of smarts lived behind them.

"Stop pumping," Effie ordered.

Chedd complied, halting the paddle midstroke. He was breathing heavily. Big oval stains had spread from his armpits to his blue linen shirt.

"Do you think that's the curse?" Effie asked him. "That Gray's children get sickly and die?"

Chedd shrugged. The motion squirted a gallon of water into the swamp. "That's what I'd been thinking."

Effie squinted at him. When Chedd came up with a theory before she did something was very wrong with the world. "We have to find out for sure."

"How?" Chedd raised the paddle to its resting position and then waded over to the table. He took a pastry, bit deeply and said, "Why?"

"Because—" Effie followed him, abandoning her paddle midstroke and allowing water to flood back into the pump room. "Because there's never been a curse laid that couldn't be lifted."

Chedd stopped chewing. "Huh?" he mumbled through a mouthful of pastry.

"Yes," Effie said with growing conviction. She'd sort of made it up, but now that she was giving it some thought it sounded feasible. "Remember the tale of the chief's wife, Maudelyn Dhoone?"

"No."

"Maudelyn was married to Hoggie Dhoone, but she wasn't Hoggie's first choice. Hoggie was betrothed to the beauteous Beatrice, but Beatrice took a fall while out riding." Effie ran a thumb across her throat. "Broke her neck. They carted her back to the roundhouse but it was too late. She was already on her deathbed. *'Bring me Maudelyn,'* she commands.

Maudelyn arrives and Beatrice beckons her real close. '*I know you loosened the catch on my saddle strap so you could steal my husband from me. So in return I give you this curse. Though your womb will quicken as swift as any maid you will never give birth to a live bairn. I swear this on the names of eight gods and only the ninth can forsake it.*'"

Effie paused to appreciate the stricken expression on Chedd's face. "Yes," she confirmed. "A terrible curse. Beatrice dropped dead as the last word was spoken, binding the magic in place. Maudelyn wailed a ghastly cry and fell upon the corpse. '*Which of the gods can forsake the curse?*' she screamed. '*For I did not loose the strap, I swear it.*'"

Chedd whistled. "Mother-of-Bludd. What happened?"

Effie picked a hazelnut off the top of the remaining pastry and popped it in her mouth. "Maudelyn married Hoggie within the month. She'd been giving him the eye all along—which explains why Beatrice got all cursey. So of course Maudelyn gets pregnant and her belly swells. And all the time she's worried but still hopeful. Perhaps the curse won't take. Perhaps by swearing on eight of the Stone Gods not nine, Beatrice made a crucial error. Anyway, nine months go by and Maudelyn gives birth and two dead babies are delivered. Twins." Effie held out two fingers. "A girl and a boy, perfectly formed and perfectly dead. Poor Beatrice is beside herself with grief. She goes a bit loony and spends the next twenty years getting pregnant, giving birth to dead babies, and trying to lift the curse."

"She had to find which of the gods could lift it?"

"Exactly. One in nine. She tried the women first—and that was a mistake."

Chedd was quick to nod. "Should have started with Behathmus and worked her way back."

Effie nodded right along with him. They were master strategists now, working out the rules of the game. "But Maudelyn didn't think like that. Behathmus being the god of death and all, you can't really blame her. He seemed most likely to seal the curse, not lift it."

"But he's also the god of judgment. At Bannen we've a carving of him with a pair of scales. She should have asked him to judge her first."

Effie kicked water toward Chedd in her excitement. "Yes. But by the time Maudelyn gets around to pleading her case to Behathmus she's getting on. She'd been slow on the uptake, and we all know Behathmus doesn't suffer fools. And even if Maudelyn hadn't loosened Beatrice's strap she'd doubtless thought about it. So Behathmus passes judgment and decides to reverse the curse. He allows Maudelyn to give birth to a healthy baby boy but takes her life in the process."

"Damn," Chedd said with satisfaction.

"You two," came a harsh voice from the stairs above the doorway. "Back to work."

Effie and Chedd scrambled to the pumps as Tull Buckler entered the room. Buckler had the pale-skinned clammy look of someone who had not spent enough time in the sun. He had changed out of his work clothes, and was now dressed in richly oiled beaverskins trimmed with teal feathers and the gray, tooth-shaped stones that were known as swamp pearls. Like all Graymen he wore knee-high leather boots proofed with tar.

As Effie swung the paddle into motion, Buckler used a flint and striker to light one of the oil lamps chained to the wall. Shadows shivered into existence, making the pump room seem darker than before. Flames burned differently in Gray, Effie noticed. They flared unexpectedly, sheeting and hissing, powered by invisible bursts of fuel.

"Is the funeral over?" she asked Buckler.

Not wanting any part of this impertinence, Chedd ducked his head low and put extra effort into pumping. Effie thought he may have edged away from her, but as his feet were underwater it was difficult to tell.

Buckler put a finger to his lips and exhaled. Knuckle rings glittered his reply.

Effie resumed pumping. She knew the question showed disrespect, but surely being kidnapped and held against your will was disrespectful to her and Chedd? She considered speaking again, but Buckler's gaze defeated her. It was as cold and murky as the swamp.

"Go," he said when the better part of an hour had passed. "Return to your cells. Do not tarry."

Chedd helped Effie rest her pump. Sweat sheened his face and neck. He'd lost some of his ruddy color in the past twenty days, she realized. Perhaps they both had.

As they waded across the room, Chedd cleared his throat. Effie turned to look at him, but Chedd wasn't looking at her. His gaze was on Buckler.

The Grayman waited. A small movement of his hand brought his knuckle rings into the light.

Chedd pulled off his gloves. Effie continued toward the doorway, expecting him to follow her. Chedd stood his ground. "You mean go back to our cells *after* we've had supper?" he said to Buckler.

Buckler's mouth twitched. It wasn't a good twitch, like it might lead to a smile. It looked more closely related to a snarl. "Go," he breathed.

Chedd went, racing up the stairs after Effie. By the third step he was clear of the standing water. The switch from swamp to air made him stumble. Effie had felt it too—you had to put more effort into wading through water and when it suddenly disappeared you got unbalanced—but she managed to stay upright. Chedd toppled. His chin made contact with the stone step, driving his teeth together.

"Come on," Effie said, pulling him up and away. "Let's go."

The Grayhouse stood on an island that had been sinking before there was such a thing as clan. The current roundhouse had been built atop the ruins of the previous roundhouse and that one built atop another one, a cycle that Effie had learned had been going on for nearly a thousand years. Gray periodically flattened the roundhouse and used the remnants to build up the remaining land. As far as Effie could tell Gray was due another rebuild. Even above water level, on the roundhouse's first floor, the walls were deteriorating. Moss was breaking apart the stone. Expanding into crevices and forcing out the mortar, it channeled water through the roundhouse like a system of pipes. The smell was everywhere. Green. Dank. Decaying.

Effie poked one of sandstone blocks as she hurried up the stairs. It gave like rotten wood.

"Eff," Chedd asked, brushing his chin, "am I bleeding?"

"No," she lied.

Gray's upper levels were quiet. Sworn clansmen had taken to the Salamander Hearth, and the Flood Door that spanned its entrance was closed. A handful of women were chewing mallow and weaving baskets by the foot of the second-story stair. Three goats blocked the way above them. Effie shooed them away.

"They're having supper," Chedd said, kicking a mound of oats that had been spread across the stairs.

"So can you." Effie patted the neckline of her dress. "Always supposing you agree to my terms."

Chedd slowed. "You took the last pastry?"

Reaching the top of the stairs, Effie did not look round. "Possibly."

"How?"

"We are Blackhail and we are the first amongst clans," she said breezily. "That's makes us first among pastries as well."

Chedd hurried to catch up. "Don't joke with me, Eff."

"Your cell or mine?" she asked.

"Yours. It's rained this morning. It'll be drier."

Effie cut across the hallway, heading for the north ward. This section of the Grayhouse was part collapsed. Chunks of roof had caved in and makeshift repairs woven from bulrushes were jammed in place. Effie and Chedd moved easily across the buckled floors. Sometimes Effie skipped just for the fun of it.

It was odd, really. Even though she was kidnapped and held prisoner in a foreign clan a thousand leagues from home, she didn't mind very much. She didn't feel in any danger. Mostly the clansmen and women ignored her, and apart from goat pat duty and pump duty she wasn't obliged to do very much. And it *was* very interesting, being in a Bludd-sworn, water-logged, cursed and enemy clan.

And of course there was Chedd, who made everything that bit much better just by being here and being his own Chedd-like self.

"Bring the torch." Effie said as she ducked into her cell.

The room was tiny and perfectly dark. Chedd lit the lamp

with the torch but it didn't have much effect. The lamp's slender wick was damp and the flame produced was as small as a child's fingernail. As Chedd returned the torch to its coupling in the hallway, Effie prized off her boots. Underneath her toes were swollen. Water had got into her boots and the skin felt fragile and loose. Quickly she dried her feet with the bedclothes. When Chedd returned he did the same, and then sat next to Effie on the room's only furnishing: a wooden cot topped with the worst mattress in the clanholds.

Effie smoothed out a square of mattress as best she could, reached down into the bodice of her dress, pulled out the pastry and centered it on the smooth part of the mattress. The pastry looked like it had been chewed on by a dog. Most of its honey and all of its nuts were gone—Effie did think her armpit felt a bit sticky. "Food of the gods," she said with confidence. She knew Chedd. That pastry was looking a lot better to him than it was to her.

Chedd looked it over. "Terms?"

Effie thought about Dagro Blackhail, the old Blackhail chief. He had a way of disguising his negotiations as conversation. He'd talk in his plain and homely way, get people nodding and before anyone knew it they'd agreed to his terms.

"You need to help me lift the curse." Not Dagro quality exactly, but then she was only nine. She had thirty years to catch up with him.

Chedd didn't blink. He looked from her to the pastry, weighing his options. He was better at this than she was, she realized. He was cool and she was hot.

"As a Banman my primary responsibility is to escape. So any tasks I undertake must be secondary to that mission."

"How can you escape?" Effie blurted. "Thirty leagues of

reeds and bulrushes on all sides. It's a maze. That's why they let us go wherever we want in the roundhouse, because even if we could get a boat we'd be lost the moment we took to the water. Graymen spend years learning the Reed Ways. We'd be lucky to get to the Isle of Grass."

"There's a quick way out of here somehow. They have to keep their horses somewhere."

"The Watermen keep their horses at Clan Hill," Effie said, balling her fists. "If you'd bothered to learn any history you'd know that."

"Oh." Chedd fell into silence so Effie sized her chance.

"Very well. You—we—have a duty to escape the clanhold. As long as lifting the curse does not interfere or slow that purpose are you willing to help me, in return for this pastry?"

"Yes."

"Spit and clasp on it?"

"Spit and clasp."

Chedd excelled at the spitting part, depositing a fat gobbet in the palm of his right hand. Effie did what he called "a fly's piss" and they clamped palms to seal the deal.

"Sweaty," Chedd said, working the entire pastry into his mouth. "But good."

Effie reached down for the water bucket and drank. That was one of the fine things about living in Clan Gray; you never had to haul up water from the well. A bucket left under a crack in the ceiling would be full in half a day. "So," she said, passing the bucket to Chedd. "Since we've been here at least three young 'uns have died. Any adults?"

Chedd shrugged. "Either no, or there's no official song-and-dance when they do."

Effie and Chedd exchanged a thoughtful look. They shook

their heads at the same time in agreement. It didn't need to be said. Wherever you were in the clanholds death counted. If a man or woman died, clan reacted. Hearts were carved from guidestones, wrists slit, special fires lit, twenty-year malt cracked open and drunk, ceremonial robes charred, messages sent, songs sung, a body cleaned and arrayed: death was always marked.

"Newborns are always dodgy," Chedd said. "At Bannen we'd lose one about every ten or twenty days."

"There's a lot more people at Bannen than Gray." This quieted them for a while.

Eventually Chedd said, "If you're a clan and your babies keep dying then eventually you'll die too."

"Slowly." Effie stood, replaced the bucket under the drip, and walked a circuit of the cell. This took exactly eight steps. "It'd be a really bad curse, to be doomed to watch your clan die off with each generation."

Chedd ran a hand along his chin, picking up a couple of crumbs and a streak of blood.

"It wasn't bleeding much," Effie said, heading him off. "And it's stopped now."

For a wonder Chedd ignored her. "Yet Gray hasn't died out. And there are children—we've seen them."

"Not many though."

"Doesn't matter. How long since the curse was laid?"

"A long time, I think."

"Hundreds of years?"

Effie saw Chedd's point. All newborns and children couldn't die, else the clan would be wiped out in sixty years.

Chedd picked off and ate the crumbs from his hand. Eating helped his brain work. "They were mourning someone the day we arrived, remember? The swamp lights were burning, the cages were up."

"Yes," Effie said, getting excited. "There was a girl—she was crying for her brother."

"The girl with the red hair and freckles. She's always on the dock, mooning and looking east."

Effie crossed to the door. "Let's go see her."

"No, Eff." Chedd shook his head. "It can wait until tomorrow. Buckler told us to go straight to our cells."

"You've already disobeyed him," Effie said, "by coming here. A second trespass hardly counts."

This logic engaged Chedd. He thought for a moment. "Second trespass has already taken place—the pastry. Buckler told us not to get supper."

Effie considered her options. If you were going to be nit-picky, Chedd was incorrect: Buckler's order had been "Do not tarry" not "Do not eat supper." As Chedd had acquired the pastry without tarrying he was in the clear. Clear was not a place Effie wanted him to be though. "That's settled then, we're going. Third trespass doesn't count."

Chedd hung his head in defeat and followed her from the room.

It was full dark now and the roundhouse was sparsely lit. Goats and a couple of drunks were asleep in the halls. Wall torches buzzed as they burned; Effie didn't know why. She and Chedd crept past the Flood Doors, holding their breath. It was a policy that seemed to work. Reaching ground level, they headed across the Salamander Hall to the entrance doors. The hall's ceiling and two-story-high walls were tiled with turtle shells. About a third of them had fallen off, and what once may have filled visitors with a sense of awe now looked shabby and diseased. Frogs were taking over, laying milky eggs in puddles and calling to each other from cracks.

Chedd wasn't happy walking toward the warriors who policed the door. Seeing him hunch his shoulders and slow his pace, Effie decided countermeasures were called for and began speaking loudly about playing dice. "Everyone knows double six beats triple two unless you're playing on a soft surface like . . . cushions. Then triples win every time."

Chedd looked at her as if she'd grown a second head.

Effie's mind was on the Graymen who were armed with paired knives and six-foot spears and armored with the darkly beautiful chainmail Gray was renowned for. Effie knew from experience they weren't interested in the comings and goings of children but she was starting to get worried. The great double doors that were rotting from the base up were closed for the night. And that meant the warriors would have to open them, and from the looks on their faces that didn't seem likely.

"I like to spit on them," Effie continued, approaching the door, "but Drey always said if you want the really best luck you have to snot them instead."

Chedd looked genuinely afraid now. The younger of the warriors, a yearman with a four-toed salamander tattooed along his left cheek and jaw, raised his chin in inquiry.

"Open, please," Effie said. It was tempting to say more, come up with some wild-goose reason why she and Chedd needed to be outside, but she didn't. A half-understood idea about less being more stopped her.

"Only warriors with oaths cross the Salamander Door this night." It was the younger guard who spoke, so Effie addressed her reply to him.

"What if someone without an oath needs entry, say a bairn who missed curfew?"

The young warrior opened his mouth to reply, but his older companion beat him to it.

"Sod off." The words were spoken calmly, without malice. He was a veteran as old as Da, and he wasn't about to play games.

"C'mon, Chedd," Effie said, turning from the door. "Let's go catch some indoor frogs instead."

Chedd's color wasn't good. For the first time Effie found herself worrying about the cut on his chin. Buckler had warned them several times about the danger of open sores. "Wounds don't heal well here. If you get a cut go to the healer to have it doused and stitched."

"I don't want to catch frogs, Eff."

She took his arm, directing him toward the ramp that led to the east ward. "We're going to the kitchen."

"No. I've had enough trouble. If Buckler sees us we'll get a beating."

"No we won't because I'll tell him we're getting your cut malted."

The death rites had subdued the clan and only the baker, a couple of kitchen girls and an old-timer asleep on a bench were in the kitchen. Skinned muskrats were roasting on a spit above the cookfire and their charred pork-like scent filled the room. Effie stepped inside, carefully avoiding the dozen or so fish that were dying in a wire cage near the door.

"Excuse me," she said when it became obvious that no one was going to attend her. "My friend here needs some alcohol for his cut." And then to Chedd: "Chin up. Show them some blood."

The baker and the girl cranking the muskrats ignored them, but the second kitchen girl waved them to the nearest bench. "Have some bread and smoked fish and I'll be with you in a minute." Her voice was soft but weary. She returned to the business of chopping leeks while Effie and Chedd helped themselves from the platter of food laid out for hungry clansmen.

The fish was salty and the bread was fresh and full of air. Chedd regained his spirits as he ate, though he didn't relax his watch on the door. Effie felt her own good spirits draining. Saying Drey's name out loud in the Salamander Hall made her miss him. "Raif," she said softly, to herself, so that she missed both brothers equally.

"Let's take a look at it." Done with leek chopping, the kitchen girl had located a jar of spirits and a soft cloth and now approached Chedd. She was sixteen or seventeen and pretty in a fragile way. Gray was one of the few clans where women wore tattoos and a delicate shape etched in tones of green and orange was visible on the curve of her left breast above the neckline of her dress.

She dealt with Chedd competently, cleaning his cut and then protecting it with paste. "Can't be too careful," she said. "The swamp gets into everything."

She smelled of leeks and water lilies. Effie stood and asked her about the tattoo.

"Oh," she said, surprised, pulling up her dress. "It's nothing. Just some old thing that's faded next to naught."

The more she spoke, the more Effie heard in her voice. Glancing at the baker, who was busy covering dough balls with wet cloth, Effie said, "Orange is the color of Clan Croser."

"Hush now," the girl said, following Effie's gaze. "They've pulled salamanders covered with orange spots from the Stillwater."

"Really?" said Chedd, getting interested. "I'd like to see one of those."

Effie and the girl shared a glance over his head.

"Best get back to work." The girl picked up the jug of spirits and held it to her chest. "You should run along now. Buckler doesn't like his charges up so late."

Reacting to the girl's discomfort, Chedd rose and crossed to the door. "C'mon, Eff."

Effie looked at the girl a moment longer, taking in the details of her hazel eyes and blond hair, and then turned and followed Chedd from the room.

It was late and Chedd had probably had enough excitement for one night, so Effie didn't tell him what was on her mind as they returned to their cells. Frogs wailed from the darkness. The noises of the roundhouse, the dripping water and straining wood and hollow echoes, spoke the truth. Clan Gray was failing. Buckler knew it, the warriors sealed in the Salamander Hearth knew it, and Waker Stone and his da knew it too.

That's why she and Chedd had been taken. It was why the girl in the kitchen had been taken. They were like the bulrushes covering the broken bits of roof: a stopgap jammed in place. The kitchen girl was from Croser, not Gray. Effie had seen Crosermen at the Hailhouse: their tattoos had the same orange and green coloring. Effie recalled Raina telling her that Croser girls whose fathers were killed in battle were allowed the privilege of transposing their father's tattoos.

Gray was losing people. Its halls were empty, its hearths black and cold. Waker had kidnapped her and Chedd to replace what had been lost, and now she was beginning to understand that she and Chedd weren't the first. Perhaps Waker and his da had been doing it for years—decades even. Children went missing along the riverways all the time. Drowned, fallen through ice, dragged downstream by high or fast water. Croser lay on the Wolf: easy pickings for Waker and his da. Bannen was on the Greenwater. On a quick accounting of clans, only Blackhail, being land bound for leagues on all sides, seemed safe.

So was Gray forced to kidnap children because of its curse? And what was stopping the kitchen girl from returning to Croser? Effie guessed that she had been here for years. Wouldn't she know the Reed Way by now?

The scratchy and uneven mattress helped keep Effie awake. The unease that had awakened in the kitchen wouldn't go away. What if the curse took children as well as newborns? What if she and Chedd weren't immune?

CHAPTER 10

The Treasure Hall

*T*ake it, Raina. By rights this is yours to do.

Raina Blackhail recalled Orwin Shank's words, spoken last night in the privacy of the chief's chamber, as she entered the Great Hearth. Noon was the best time to find Blackhail's principal chamber, domain of its sworn warriors, empty. Hailsmen were out riding patrol, practicing on the weapons court, and hunting in the Northern woods. Raina had hoped that its great curved benches would be empty, thereby saving her the trouble of making her business public.

She was out of luck. Gat Murdock and a couple of old-timers were playing some dusty old game with pieces on a board. A pair of sworn Scarpemen were building up the fire, and Corbie Meese was oiling the chains on his war hammer. The old-timers, who looked half bored to death to begin with, regarded Raina with interest. Here was something to lively their game: the chief's wife, without cleaning crew or kitchen crew, entering the Great Hearth with purpose. Women were not disallowed in the hearth, but custom did not favor it. Raina girded herself, there was no other word for it. She drew air into her chest, squared her shoulders and sucked in her gut. Gods, this would be all over the clan by sundown. What was Orwin thinking?

"Lady." It was Corbie Meese, offering a greeting and a question. *Can I aid you?*

She couldn't trust herself to reply. What would she say? The act would speak for itself. Nodding briefly, she passed the hammerman and entered the cleared central space. The Scarpemen attending the fire paused in their efforts to watch her. As a rule, sworn Scarpemen were more mannerly than the great unsworn masses of their clan. That wasn't saying much. These two had the slender stature of bowmen, and now that Raina drew closer she could see they were proofing arrowheads: exposing the steel blades to flames until they turned black. Neither man addressed her, but their opinions were clear enough.

Raina allowed something—she could barely say what—to enter her thoughts. Tissue-thin muscles controlling her eyes and mouth reacted. Her left hand was occupied with a lamp, but the fingers of her right hand twitched. The Scarpemen inhaled, sucking in information.

Beware, she realized she'd warned them later. *Your guide is dead. You may be next.*

If there had not been Hailsmen in the room, the Scarpemen would have blocked her. They detested being threatened. The older of the two thrust a log into the fire. His small, greasy-haired friend kept his gaze on Raina as he released his grip on his arrows, letting them clatter noisily to the floor.

Raina sent her mind elsewhere, directing her hand to reach for the key hooked to her belt. Sharp-faced liver-spotted Gat

Murdock was the first to realize what was happening. His occluded and watery gaze jumped from the key to Raina's face.

Yes, old man. I have the chief's key. Watch me use it.

Walking past the hearth and the Scarpemen and turning her back on Gat Murdock and the old-timers, Raina approached the small snakewood door set deep into the Great Hearth's west-facing interior wall. It was the only door made from snakewood in the entire roundhouse. The wood had been hauled on a cart from the Far South, chosen for its hardness and its resistance to flames. Fire and axes could break the door: but they would need more heat, more force. More time.

Raina slid the key in the lock and turned it. If it were possible to feel gazes on one's back, she felt them now. The lock barrel tumbled and she pushed her palm against the door. Holding the lamp ahead of her, she entered the absolute center of the roundhouse, the securest chamber in the clan-hold, accessible only through the Great Hearth: Blackhail's strongroom.

Dust and stale air stirred as she turned and closed the door. Chiefs had died here, in this circular domed space that looked like a tomb. It had no windows; Raina had not expected it to. She was surprised to see its walls were painted, though. Blackhail seldom dressed its stone. Centuries of ash and dust had dulled the paint, but there were sections where objects had been removed, exposing patches of the original color. The walls of the strongroom had once been black as night. The thought gave Raina a chill.

Would she ever understand this hard and dour clan?

Bending, she set the safe lamp down on the floor and

wondered where to start. *"Mace needs gold and coin,"* Orwin Shank had told her earlier. *"He's running out of supplies."*

A messenger had arrived before dawn and demanded private parley with Orwin Shank. Raina had made herself busy at the stables, but she could not say she had made herself calm. Jebb Onnacre had brought in the messenger's horse and from its trappings and saddle, it was easily identified as belonging to Scarpe. After the meeting was done, the rider himself arrived to collect his saddlebags. Muscles in Raina's heart stiffened. It was Wracker Fox, one of Mace's trusted companions. He looked right through her, as if she didn't exist. After leaving instructions with the groom for his horse's care, he took himself back to the roundhouse, where he gathered Scarpe warriors about him in the Great Hearth.

Raina was not proud to admit she listened to the gossip surrounding Wracker and his message. It was known he had come from Bannen Field, and she was desperate to learn whether or not Mace would be returning to Blackhail. By the time Orwin sought her out in the kitchen, she was living on nerves. Mace had to know by now about Stannig Beade's death. What rumors had flown south with the facts?

Orwin had bid Raina walk with him to view the repairs to the east wall. Outside, beyond the hearing and watch of the repair crew, he had handed Raina the chief's key. "Wracker has been charged with returning with sufficient coin to hold the army on the field for thirty days. Go to the strongroom and portion what to send."

Raina had been so relieved to discover Mace had no immediate plans to return to the roundhouse, she took the key from Orwin without question. The fact that Orwin had possession of the key in Mace's absence had not surprised her—

Blackhail's treasure had to be managed in its chief's absence—but now that she was here in the strongroom she wondered at Orwin's motives. Had the aging hatchetman intended to signal the entire roundhouse that Raina Blackhail was now in charge of its wealth? Or had he simply not wanted to be bothered with the task? With four sons dead within a year who could blame him?

Turning a full circle, Raina tried to take it all in. Light from the safe lamp glinted on stacks of silver ingots piled three feet deep and five feet high against the wall. A smaller stack of gold began where the silver ended. An attempt had been made to cover the gold ingots with an aurochs hide, but the chiefs of Blackhail did not make good housekeepers and the moldy and maggot-eaten skin had fallen to one side. Crates and coffers were piled on top of each other. Some were laid open, exposing dusty armor, metal cups, hammer chains, jeweled horns, sheathed daggers and swords: the spoils of war. Containers of every sort lay in heaps; cloth bags, saddlebags, arms cases, embroidered purses, jeweled boxes, horns and baskets. A Dhoone Queen's breastplate was filled with coins like a bowl. No order ruled here. Chiefs had not been gentle as they searched for what was needed. There were more boxes open and overturned than sealed. Carpets, rare skins and bolts of rich fabric had been left to molder on the floor.

Part of Raina wanted to roll up her sleeves and send for a broom, but she resisted. That was her old life, her old self. Only chiefs and their trusted deputies ever set foot here. A deputy would not dare alter anything. And a chief would not care.

Raina Blackhail made herself not care.

How many hundreds of years of wars, raids, confiscations,

ransoms and tributes did this room represent? A portion of all spoils, inheritances and gains was demanded by the clan. Once a year, tied clansman, those who made their living within the clanhold and were defended by its warriors and roundhouse, paid tribute to the chief. Wealth accrued over the centuries, and was depleted only in times of hardship and war. One glance around the room was enough to know that Blackhail had been fortunate in recent times. More wars had been won than lost, and harvests, lambing, calving and hunts had been plentiful as far back as anyone could remember.

It changes.

Raina dragged a finger through the dust on one of the tabletops. The lambing was not going well. The ground was still hard, and bitter frosts cracked down every night. No longhunts in months meant that the clan had missed the annual migration of caribou and elk. Shorthunts were still bringing in boar and deer but numbers were down, and rumor had it that wolves were competing for kills. Raina had seen for herself how low grain stocks were. In her twenty years at Blackhail she had never known the wheat level to dip below the quarter mark. Canna Hadley, the head grain wife, said that if you removed the moldy bottom layer from the reckoning there was only three months supply remaining.

It was the Scarpes, the damn Scarpes. For every Hailsman in the roundhouse there was a Scarpe. Blackhail's resources were being consumed at twice the normal rate. And Scarpes were doing naught to pay for their keep. Newcomers had dropped even the pretense of gifts. Two families had arrived this morning with nothing. Not one bale of hay or skinny sow between the ten of them, and the first thing they did was head to the kitchen for bread and meat.

Wiping her finger on her skirt, Raina moved around the room. Railing against the Scarpes was not going to help get the job done. Where to start? So many containers, so much jeweled and gilded junk. On impulse she pulled down a felt bag that had been thrown atop the heap. It was heavy and she stepped back as it thudded to the floor. Kneeling, she loosened the cinch rope and pried it open.

I've broken it.

A bowl made of some rich and heavy stone lay in two pieces, split nearly down the middle. Alabaster? Jade? Annoyed with herself, Raina pushed away the bag and its contents. What if it was something Dagro had received as a gift?

The possessions of a chief and its clan were one and the same.

Dagro had not come here often. He had cared little for wealth and the show of it, and the clan he raised around him felt the same. Yet Mace had been here too. Looking around, Raina realized that no one would ever know what her new husband had taken. No catalogue of Blackhail's treasure existed. Such a thing would be considered petty and unclanlike.

It did not make management easy, that was certain.

Raina thought awhile and then went to fetch Corbie Meese.

Within an hour her task was done. By the time she and Corbie emerged from the strongroom, the Great Hearth had more than tripled its occupancy. Raina calculated a good half of her spectators were Scarpes—as if they had any right to question a Hailswoman in her own house. Corbie, gods love him, was a rock. It took two trips to carry out the items she'd selected and he never by as much as a word or a look questioned her authority. That meant something. Where

Corbie led hammermen followed, and in Clan Blackhail hammermen were king.

Descending the stair to the entrance hall, Raina saw that her audience wasn't limited to sworn warriors. Women, children and tied clansmen had arranged themselves to get the best view of the chief's wife carrying booty from the strongroom. Raina recalled some bit of wisdom about dealing with potentially hostile crowds: Imagine them naked. She found it worked better to imagine the Scarpes had imbibed fatal poison and would all be dead within the day. She smiled serenely after that.

She and Corbie had packed the treasure in burlap sacks, which only seemed to heighten interest. Mace must have taken treasure to Bannen Field, but Raina had no memory of him carrying it through the roundhouse. Stealth was one of his tricks. Yet . . . yet. She could see this was a mistake. Blackhail's chief was absent, its warriors awar, its guide dead and its guidestone replaced by a lump of foreign granite: Hailsfolk did not need one more thing to worry them. Watching Blackhail treasure being hauled from the roundhouse was not good for morale.

Gods, but Dagro had made it look easy. He'd hunt in the morning, take parleys in the afternoon, drink beer with the warriors at sunset and then sleep like a dog at night. She hadn't known, hadn't thought to pay attention, had lived with one of the greatest chiefs in the clanholds and hadn't learned a thing.

Well start learning now, Raina Blackhail. Make a list.

"Call Wracker Fox," she ordered Jessie Mure as she and Corbie reached the stables. Then, to Jebb Onnachre, "Shut the doors. Allow no one but those summoned in."

The stables were housed in the old cowshed while a new structure was being built so the effect of closing the smaller cattle doors was not the same as closing the great iron-and-wood double doors that had once secured Blackhail's horses. Still. Seeing the grooms swing the simple plank doors into motion as thirty or so people watched from the cattle court was chilling. Stable doors were opened before dawn and not closed until two hours past sunset. Yet here they were being closed.

Raina stood in the dim stillness and waited. Grooms moved around her, lighting safe lamps. Horses whickered. Jebb walked the rows of boxes, closing stalls. When he and the other grooms were done with their tasks, Raina dismissed them and they withdrew to the tack room at the far end of the stable and sealed themselves in. Corbie attended to the calls and knocks at the door, granting entry to the handful of people Raina had sent for. Taking his cue from Raina, he was silent and grave.

Orwin and Grim Shank and Orwin's nephew Drew were first to arrive, followed by the swordsman Stellan Satchell, who was the head dairyman's son and had apprenticed under Shor Gormalin. Wracker Fox, called for last, arrived last. He did not come alone. When Corbie rolled back the door, Uriah Scarpe stood at Wracker's side. Corbie did not need to look at Raina to know what to do. Taking a step to the side, he barred Uriah Scarpe from entering the stable.

Uriah was nephew to the Scarpe chief, Yelma Scarpe, and that meant he was some kind of cousin to Mace. Raina saw it all on his sharp clean-shaven face: the sense of entitlement, surprise at being barred from the parley quickly followed by the understanding that it was she, Raina Blackhail, who was doing the barring.

Whore, Uriah mouthed for her eyes alone as Corbie closed the door.

Raina absorbed the insult. The word did not bother her, but its malice chilled her. He had been one of the men responsible for burning a Shankshound alive. She said to Wracker, "You will leave in the morning for Bannen Field. The three sacks contain silver bars. Some gold. They will be transported directly to my husband, Mace Blackhail." As she spoke she indicated three of the four sacks that she and Corbie had borne from the strongroom. On her instructions, Corbie had set one aside.

Wracker had the lean muscle and ready stance of a swordsman. His hair was raven-wing black and he wore it part-shaved and braided. His pants and coat were simple black suede. Two weasel heads attached at the coat's lapels were the only decoration. Toeing the closest of the sacks, he tested its weight.

"The silver needs to be replaced with gold," he said to Orwin. "It's too heavy for my horse."

Orwin's gaze shot to Raina.

"You will not be riding alone," Raina said to Wracker. *I'm not trusting a Scarpe with Blackhail's fortune.*

Again, he ignored her. Addressing Orwin, he said, "Mace said I was to return with the loot."

"I can't see as a small crew disavows that order," Orwin said reasonably.

Wracker weighed his options. He was not a stupid man, and had to rate as high his chances of looking foolish to five sworn clansmen. He couldn't win here; Raina had seen to that.

Reaching a decision, he said, "Very well, I'll form a party." Then, addressing Drew Shank, who was the youngest present. "Fetch back Uriah. He rides with me."

Drew Shank, all of twenty-one and two months into his full

oath, hesitated. He looked to his uncle for guidance. And his uncle looked right back at Raina.

She might have laughed if she wasn't terrified. Quite suddenly she remembered that Wracker Fox had been in the forge too, the night Effie was tried as a witch and a Shankshound was sent to the fire. This was no game. And a win here would bring Mace's eye upon her more certainly than any half-baked rumor about Stannig Beade's death.

Do and be damned. If I were a clan those words would be my boast.

Putting a hand out to stay Drew Shank, she addressed Wracker Fox. "I have chosen the party who will accompany the treasure to Bannen Field." She inclined her head, indicating Grim Shank, Drew Shank, Stellan Satchell and Corbie Meese. All knew—she had bid Corbie and Orwin to arrange it beforehand—and they gave her the gift of their solemn silence. It was into this still and proud hush, where men who had sworn to defend their clan faced the certainty of going to war, that Raina knew she must speak.

She had to finish off her enemy.

Looking Wracker directly in the eye, she said, "It will be your honor to be the sole Scarpe who accompanies Blackhail's treasure south."

Wracker's sword hand flexed and she realized that if he could he would have slain her right then. She had thwarted his plans, taken charge of his mission and bested him in a room of sworn men. Little matter that he was the interloper here, the foreigner from the poison pine clan. He did not understand the wrongness of a Scarpe sending a Scarpe to collect Blackhail treasure—for that was what Mace Blackhail was. A weasel dressed in Wolf clothing.

A rapist. A murderer. A Scarpe.

"Go," she told Wracker. "Make what preparations you must." Before he could react, she turned her back on him. She did not need further evidence of his ill will.

When she finally heard him move toward the stable door, she allowed herself a deep breath. Corbie moved close, put out a hand, but did not touch her. She felt its contact all the same. "Go," she repeated more softly, swinging about to address Grim, Drew and Stellan as well as Corbie. "Spend time with your wives and families. Blackhail does you honor this night."

The young warriors took their leave. All paused or made effort in some way to show her respect. Stellan bowed deeply, touching the hem of her dress. He was half in love with her, she guessed. Perhaps they all were.

It made her feel old and sad; gave knowledge to all she had lost.

"A word," she said quietly to Orwin Shank.

The hatchetman sealed the door and they were alone. Winter had aged him. Liver spots had spread across his hands and neck, and cataracts bounced light from his eyes. Raina counted her own losses as nothing compared to his. She had lost a husband and a dream of what the future could be. Orwin Shank had lost sons.

And she had just sent one of his remaining three sons back to war.

Apologies, explanations, sympathy: none would do. Words were too small. Lightly, she touched his swollen arthritic ax hand and just as lightly moved away.

"The fourth sack," she said, nodding toward the water pail where Corbie had set it down, "contains gold. I would have you ride east to Dregg and use it as barter for grain and what other supplies you see fit."

Orwin Shank had been head clansman under two chiefs. He was the one both Mace and Dagro went to when they needed aid or counsel. Without his approval, Mace could not have claimed the chiefship. More than anyone else, Orwin understood what she did here. Blackhail's wealth and its chief's wealth were one and the same. The gold and silver in the other three sacks traveled to Bannen Field on Mace's command. Mace did not command the gold in the fourth, smaller sack; Raina Blackhail did.

In this she had made herself chief.

Horses shuffled and nickered in their stalls. One of the safe lamps smoked as it burned dregs. Raina spared a thought for the grooms, holed up inside the tack room. Feed to be spread, coats to be groomed, horses to be exercised: she was preventing them from doing their work.

Orwin would not be rushed, though. The hatchetman shook at low frequency as he stood and looked at her. Hay beneath his feet crackled as he spoke. "I will leave in the morning—an hour after the Bannen Field party."

She nodded and did not thank him. A moment passed where they regarded each other and understood each other. She saw his desire to caution her and the decision to keep his peace. It was too late.

Finally he turned for the door.

"Orwin," she said, stopping him. She had one more power to claim. "While you're there seek out Walvis Harding, the Dregg guide. Ask him to send his best apprentice to us. It's time Blackhail had a new guide."

It did not surpise him. "As you wish. Anything more?"

"Arrange a watch outside the stable."

Orwin glanced at the burlap sacks. "And inside?"

"Blackhail's grooms guard its treasure tonight."

She had surprised him . . . but not displeased him. He twinkled a smile at her. "'Tis well done, Raina."

She basked in those words for a whole minute after he left. She'd pulled it off. Everything she'd decided in the strongroom was done. That was what being a chief meant—having a plan and seeing it through. Smiling, she walked the row of stalls. The grooms needed to be informed of their charge.

"Lady."

Raina halted in her tracks at the word. As she spun to track the position of its speaker, the door of the stall just behind her swung open. Chella Gloyal stood in the box, abreast of her fine gray stallion. Both she and her horse looked remarkably composed.

"I ask your pardon," the Croserwoman said, stepping into the horse walk. "I was brushing down Rumor and was caught unawares and did not think to make my presence known . . ." A brief shrug, "at first. By the time I realized I should have alerted you and withdrawn it was too late."

I bet it was. To cover her surprise, Raina inspected Chella. The Croserwoman was dressed in a dove gray riding coat and blue silk skirt. The coat was expertly cut to show off her small waist and full breasts, and its color provided the perfect contrast to her chestnut hair. She was the sort of woman who could make you believe she was beautiful. Judging by how swiftly Grim Shank had married her, she probably made men believe a lot of things.

Raina said, "It appears I must rely on your discretion."

"You have it."

Chella Gloyal knew how to give her word with conviction. Her gaze was steady and knowing. She had heard everything then, including the command that would send her husband back to war and the treasonous order to spend Blackhail gold. Trouble was hers if she wished it, yet Raina did not think she would break her word.

"Chella." The word was a dismissal. Raina Blackhail was done here.

Chella spoke to halt her. "If I may offer some advice?"

"You are bold."

Chella Gloyal did not deny it. Stepping closer, she said in a low voice, "You made two mistakes."

Gods help me not to slap her. Raina headed toward the tack room. She would not listen to this.

"You should have sent an archer in Stellan's place," Chella murmured, keeping pace. "A party made up solely of sword-and-hammermen cannot protect their cargo at distance."

Raina halted. She was keenly aware that only twenty paces separated her and Chella from the tack room door. "Quiet yourself," she commanded.

Chella raised her eyebrows. Her voice had barely risen above a whisper and they both knew it. Who was this clever and self-possessed woman? Raina wondered. Were the differences between Croser and Blackhail so great they could explain her?

"When I require your counsel I shall ask for it," Raina said coldly. She did not trust this woman. "Leave me now."

Chella bowed lightly and immediately stepped back. Holding Raina's gaze she said, "I pray ask soon, for you have just placed yourself at great risk."

Raina watched her walk away, and then went to inform the grooms of their task. Fear had pierced her heart.

CHAPTER 11
The Sull

We are Blackhail, the first amongst clans. We do not cower and we do not hide and we will have our revenge.

Raif's lips moved in time with the clan boast, but he could not tell if he spoke the words or thought them. Differences like that were getting harder to separate. Whole days had passed where he could not be certain if he was asleep or awake.

He was pretty sure he was awake now. Mosquitoes were feeding. A couple of hours of sunlight and they would hatch from pools in the snow and rise in a cloud to torment him. He made an easy target. A sitting duck. Throwing his weight forward, Raif forced the cage into motion. The mosquitoes took flight and he had a minute of peace as the insects scrambled to match trajectories with the cage.

We do not cower, Raif thought with satisfaction. Maybe he said it.

A hunger cramp sliced through his gut and he pulled up his legs and chest to wait it out. His body hardly seemed to belong to him anymore. He could not keep track of all its weaknesses. His back and shoulders were a landscape of pressure sores raised by the ridges of the cage. At night he used the waterskin as a pillow for his head but there was nothing to cushion the rest of him. He was beginning to understand it didn't matter. The worst sores, the ones that were leaking and beginning to ulcerate, were tended.

And they took good care of his hands.

Raif shivered. He did not want to think about his body in their possession. Taking a shot of water, he focused his gaze on the rising mass of the Boreal Sway. The sun had come and gone and snow clouds were closing in from the north. The first stirrings of wind moved the forest canopy and Raif watched as the wave it created rolled toward him. His sole unobstructed view was to the north. This was it. Wake in the morning and wonder if he'd been darted and drugged overnight, piss and shit through the cage, drink, sleep.

Patrol.

He had a place to go to now. The line between days was dissolving, and although he could look at the record of his days spent in the cage—eleven horizontal scratches on the northeast corner post—he could no longer recall when he'd added to it. Time moved differently in the other place. Shifts in light, wind and gradient were what mattered. Raif licked his lips and scanned the forest. The light was changing now, decreasing. Hearts were on the move, hunting, evading, feeding.

It was an easy thing to loose his sights, to send his mind's eye out of the cage and into another living thing. A shock of heat, a switch in rhythm, a seasickness moment where movement and mind did not match, and then he was inside, in the heart. Elk. The index finger on his right hand twitched. The reflex to release the bowstring was strong. Enter, mark the target, loose the arrow: that was how he hunted. Yet there were no arrows anymore, no heart-kills, just Watcher of the Dead and beating hearts.

The elk heart raced with fear. She was young, a yearling separated from her dam and herd. She'd lost their scent and was heading southeast through the forest. Blood was rushing through her arteries at force. Raif felt her terrible alertness. Any movement in the trees could be her death. Nothing large enough to take her down was close, but she did not know it. She saw shadows beneath the bloodwoods and smelled wolf scat. Raif stayed with her as it grew colder and darker, living her fear and exhaustion. As she moved further east his connection began to fade and he strained to keep it intact. Slowly, she drifted from him and he found himself back in the cage.

It was dark and the mosquitoes were gone, killed by the cold. His body was shivering and his fingers were numb. Tucking his hands under his arms, he shifted his position to ease the pressure on his butt. The motion rocked the cage, driving it against the canopy. Raif spotted pale fires to the east. He had to search his mind for their meaning. *Sull*, the word came to him.

His knee-jerk reaction was to escape and he refocused his attention on the forest, searching for something to carry him away. Night brought out the predators. A gray owl was circling above the ridge, silent as the dead. Raif touched it briefly, felt the surprising heft and unfamiliar geography of its heart. Again there was the reflex to release the string. He moved away, descending beneath the canopy, questing for another heart.

Fox. A female in her prime with a strong and steady heartbeat. She was still, listening intently. The instant she located her prey the great veins descending from her lungs to her heart expanded, fueling the muscles in her haunch. Within a second she pounced. Saliva jetted into Raif's mouth as she muzzled through the snow to reach the stunned mouse. As her jaws sprung to snap its neck, she heard something. Releasing the carcass, she listened. Raif could not understand what she heard but he understood her reaction. Abruptly she took off, abandoning her kill and fleeing north.

Raif withdrew his sights and scanned for the source of her fear.

The Sway at night was studded with hearts: voles, skunk, mink, winged squirrels, deer, lynx, bears. Raif saw them as small fires in the darkness. The fox had headed north so he patrolled south.

Something large was on the move. Raif's fingers hooked the walls of the cage as he perceived the creature's heart. Muscular, cool and alien, it had a rhythm he did not recognize. Pushing away his misgivings, he entered.

An inkling of awareness, like the partial opening of an eye, acknowledged his presence. It knew he was there. As quickly as Raif received the sensation it was gone, and he was left with the strange tows and suctions of a reptilian heart. Three chambers instead of four pumped blood around the body, and there was a place where fresh blood and stale blood mixed, a delta of dark currents that flowed both ways. The creature was moving at speed across old, hackled groundsnow, sidewinding in perfect silence, white upon the white.

Moon snake. Its name cast a spell, conjuring dread in its purest form, smoking with old myths. Generations of hunters had murmured its name around campfires. At night—always at night—after long bloody days spent butchering their kills, with the stench of organ meat weighing their shirtsleeves and malt liquor concentrating in their veins, hunters spoke in hushed voices about moon snakes. Someone in the party would know someone who had lost a sheep, a calf, a mare. The stories, like elk, migrated east. Raif had listened to Dagro Blackhail's account of the time his father, Burdo Blackhail, had parleyed with the new-minted Dog Lord at Bludd. No Hail chief had ever set foot in the Bluddhouse and Burdo had camped to the north with a company of twelve men. Right from the start the horses were spooked and Burdo ordered the corral to be raised to a height of eight feet. Afterward, he realized it made no difference. The moon snake slid under the barricade and tore off a stallion's leg. Within seconds the screams of the horses brought clansmen from their tents. When torches were lit, a bloody trail leading east into the forest was clearly visible. Burdo gave the order: *Do not follow*. As Dagro told the story, it was the only time his father's jaw failed him. *It was the marks the thing left behind*, Dagro had whispered, *like whip cracks in the snow*.

Back in the cage, Raif's body shivered. In the forest, at ground level, he cast off the memories like snakeskin.

The night was a revelation, a wholly new world of taste and heat. Animals were silver forms against the black. The owl overhead, the fox, the dead but still warm mouse, the elk: the moon snake saw them all, knew them all. Feared none. Licking the taste of their exhaled breath from the air, she tracked and calculated, applying the sure mathematics of death. Distance, direction, size, state of health: they were her parameters. Her heart beat smoothly as she muscled across the snow, choosing her prey.

In all the years he had entered hearts, Raif had never

experienced anything like it. Snagcats, bears, wolves: predators, but they lived with fear. The moon snake was beyond emotion. She tracked the possibilities, figured the odds. Killed.

Raif settled into her primitive heart and moved with her as she tracked the elk yearling east. Later, he would understand that his connection with the moon snake was stronger than the ones he'd formed with other creatures. He traveled farther with her, far beyond the point where he'd lost contact in the past.

The night was at its coldest and the snow began to steam as the moon snake closed distance on the elk. Reading the exhaustion in its breath, she moved downwind and picked up speed. Back in the cage, a blow dart pierced Raif's neck. The impact did not register. Within seconds his body was limp. Raif felt the familiar pull to return to the cage as his mind dimmed along with his breaths. He fought it, holding fast to the moon snake's heart. She flicked her consciousness toward Raif, touched him, and then returned to the hunt.

Raif felt it as an act of kinship. He had been allowed to maintain his hold.

As the Sull lowered the cage containing Raif's unconscious body, Raif's mind ran with the snake. Moving on a tangent to intercept the trotting elk, she accelerated like a bolt shot from a crossbow. Ice mist dampened the sound of her belly whipping against the snow. The elk's form brightened and clarified, its details rendered in silver and white. The moon snake observed the motion of its forelegs and hindlegs, calculated the pattern, switched a valve in her heart like a trap so only fresh red blood pumped through her arteries, and then struck.

There was an instant when the elk understood everything.

Veins in its eyes ruptured. Its bladder failed and the musk of fear seeded the air. Quarter of a second later, the moonsnake closed her jaws around her front hoof. With perfect violence, she wrenched off the leg at the shoulder. Blood jetted onto the snow. The elk moaned, a terrible low wail that Raif would remember for the rest of his life. Briefly, he had a glimpse of its heart: the rhythm he had become familiar with earlier that night was gone. In its place was a fluttering, fading pulse.

Raif discarded the elk and refocused on the moon snake. Flinging aside the severed limb, she set upon the fallen elk. No heart-kills for the moonsnake, she tore her live prey into parts. Raif felt a cool flicker of satisfaction as she began to feed.

She took the limbs whole, disconnecting her jaw and gorging. Her heart slid back and to the side to make way. Her senses tracked the nearing of pack wolves, drawn by the smell of carrion. She was alert but unafraid. After swallowing two limbs she nosed through the torso and detached the elk heart. Sending a single glint of awareness to Raif she devoured it.

Raif shivered.

Kill an army for me, Raif Sevrance. Death's words echoed in his head. Somehow they were now connected to his father. Da was dead. He, Raif Sevrance, was the only person who knew the killer. And that made him the only person who could avenge Tem Sevrance's death. Why hadn't he done it? He had slain four Bluddsmen at Duff's for less. He had slain Bitty Shank at Black Hole for less. Death promised him he would kill an army: wasn't the only death that mattered Mace Blackhail's?

Raif fed on this thought as the muscles in the moon snake's abdomen pushed the elk heart into her gut. She was still for a moment, tasting the air. Picking up a whiff of dawn, she withdrew from the elk carcass. She was heavy now, swaying like a pregnant mare. The pack wolves danced nervously as she cut into the territory. The top dog howled as if he'd caught sight of the moon. Ignoring him, the snake homed. A deep languor was setting in. She needed to sleep and rest. Hunting did not strain her heart, digestion did.

Sidewinding north, she began to shut down. Her movements and responses slowed. Her heart engorged, sending enriched blood to her gut. Raif experienced her lassitude as his own. Even now, she possessed no fear. She inhabited a world where nothing could challenge her.

That thought stayed with Raif long after she burrowed through the snow to her den and slept.

"Wake."

Raif snapped into consciousness but did not show it. He was immediately on alert and on his guard. It was the first word spoken by another person he had heard in days. With eyes closed, he inhaled deeply. He could smell them. The Sull. They smelled like the full moon on cold nights. Just as swiftly he was aware that he was on solid ground. Deep inhalation shifted weight in his body, and that shift always stirred the cage. Nothing stirred. Furtively he flexed muscles in his feet, pressing his toes against stone.

"Open your eyes. Your friend is here."

Raif recognized the voice. It belonged to Yiselle No Knife.

He opened his eyes and looked up. She stood above him, tall and slender, dressed in supple hides that had been molded to her breasts and waist, and a skirt armored with leather panels. Her hair was drawn back from her face, displaying the sharp bones of her cheeks and jaw. She smiled coldly.

"To your left is a sword. Pick it up and use it."

Raif blinked. He was lying on his side on a stone clearing surrounded by bloodwoods. Flakes of snow were drifting in the air. He could not tell what time of day it was, just that it was light.

"The sword," repeated No Knife. "Take it and defend yourself." She stepped out of his line of vision, revealing four figures on the far side of the clearing. Addie Gunn, hobbled at the ankles, his hands tied behind his back and a gag in his mouth, was in the custody of two Sull swordsmen. Raif was shocked by Addie's appearance. The cragsman had lost weight and his eyes were dull. A wound on his neck was black and dry.

As Raif looked at him, Addie nodded. Raif understood the gesture as if it were words. *I'm all right. Take care of yourself.*

"Stand up." No Knife's voice was as bright as steel. "If you won't defend yourself, defend your friend."

The snick of steel being drawn from leather followed her words and the fourth figure, the towering form of the Sull warrior Ilya Spinebreaker stepped forward, a six-foot longsword balanced perfectly in his hand.

Automatically, Raif rolled onto his knees. All sorts of pains and weaknesses shot through him and he stumbled as he attempted to lever his weight onto his legs. His right knee shook, and he had the strange sensation of wanting to right himself against the movement of the cage. Frustrated, he pivoted to the side and grabbed the sword.

Ilya Spinebreaker's weapon scribed a perfect arc in the air and falling snow as it descended on Raif. Raif raised his sword in a two-handed T-block above his chest and braced for the blow. It dazed him. The force buckled his shoulders and sent his lower teeth driving against his upper jaw. Spinebreaker's dark alien eyes looked straight into his as swordblade scissored against swordblade. A moment of relief followed as the Spinebreaker drew back his blade for a second blow. Raif represented his T-block. It was all he had time for.

The force of Spinebreaker's second strike was crushing. His blade slammed Raif's sword into Raif's face. Raif felt the hot sting of metal on his nose, lip and chin and immediately smelled blood. The Spinebreaker had a choice; fall to one knee and drive Raif's own blade further into his skull or withdraw for a third blow. Raif guessed what he would do even before he saw it in the Sull's eyes. The Spinebreaker would finish this ugly little dance with the elegance of a final blow. Thrusting a man's blade into his face was pure tavern brawl and Ilya Spinebreaker thought himself better than that.

Raif had perhaps a second to prepare himself as the Sull warrior positioned both hands on his blade and moved through a form Raif didn't recognize. Raif's gaze flicked to Addie and he noticed for the first time that the cragsman wasn't standing freely; one of the Sull warriors was holding him up. *They've been treating him worse than me.* This was madness. These people weren't the Sull Angus Lok spoke of with respect.

Anger focused Raif more swiftly than fear. Ilya Spinebreaker had a beating heart and that meant Raif Sevrance had a chance.

Raif sent out a line to the swordsman's heart. It filled his sights like a glance at the midday sun. And it wasn't human.

Not even close.

Fear touched Raif then. He was a clansman far from home and here he would die, at the hands of people he could never hope to understand. Would word ever get back to Drey and

Effie? How would they know their brother had loved them until the end?

Finally, as the Spinebreaker's great sword descended and Raif pivoted his blade from a block to a strike, Raif recalled the moon-snake. She had no fear. It was all calculation: What could she take down and how? Her assumption was that she could kill anything. He was *Mor Drakka*, Watcher of the Dead. Spinebreaker should fear *him*.

Raif made the calculation and adjusted the sword as six feet of steel descended above his head. He saw the opening and thrust into it, and then a massive shearing force slammed the sword from his grip. As Raif's fingers sprang apart his entire body moved sideways with the blow, driving him against the ground. The Spinebreaker's longsword was still completing the motion—a beautiful form like the letter C. Raif could barely understand what had happened. Blood from his face wounds pooled in his left eye.

"Enough." Yiselle No Knife spoke to halt the Spinebreaker's next blow.

The warrior halted his blade on the upswing. He was breathing fiercely, nostrils flaring. In a perfectly executed motion, he recouched the sword. His gaze never left Raif.

It was an indictment.

Raif rolled to a sitting position. He was shaking. Two knuckles on his right hand had begun to swell. He still couldn't understand how the Spinebreaker had shifted from one form to another so swiftly, but he did understand he had underestimated the speed and intelligence of his opponent.

"He attempted the heart-kill?" No Knife's voice was almost soft.

The Spinebreaker nodded in response. He did not speak.

Raif received the impression that the Sull warrior believed the exchange that had just occurred was beneath him. He was probably right.

Yiselle No Knife perhaps understood this too. "Go," she told Spinebreaker. "Ask Sora and Gloran to attend me."

The warrior bowed. "A man who has been kept in a cage for twenty days cannot be expected to fight."

"Go." No Knife repeated quietly. "Prepare for the quarter moon."

Twenty, Raif repeated to himself as the Spinebreaker crossed the clearing. It seemed important to remember the true number of days.

Yiselle No Knife approached him. The snow had stopped and the increase in light made her skin shine like metal. She appraised him, her gaze alighting on the newly opened wounds on his face, the muscles beneath his coat sleeves, his eyes. No one spoke. Within minutes, two warriors, male and female, emerged from the forest. Raif was beginning to get his bearings. He was in the stone ring he could see from the cage. The Sull settlement lay directly to the east.

"Take him to the stone chamber," No Knife said to the two warriors. "He will be able to stand there."

Hands yanked Raif from the ground. His knees wouldn't lock and the Sull had to support his weight on their shoulders.

"You will fight every day now," Yiselle told him once they were eye-to-eye. "If you refuse your friend will die."

Raif hissed at her.

She stepped back in fright, reappraised him, then smiled.

As the two warriors led him east, he was struck with the idea that she had won some sort of victory from him.

CHAPTER 12

A Maiden's Head

The town of White Kiln was located six days' foot travel east of Ille Glaive. Pottery made from a composite of local clay and ground dog bones weighed the banquet tables of lords and merchants across the North. The kilns fired day and night, reaching temperatures so hot they melted rock. Giant plinths of basalt had been floated upriver from the west as bases for the kilns. The native sandstone buckled under the relentless heat.

You could tell the kiln workers from the burns on their hands and faces. Angus Lok walked the market square and watched them, strong men dressed in their God's Day best, bearing the scars of their work with something like pride.

Unremarkable in a brown deerhide coat, squirrel skin hat and scuffed boots, Angus drew little attention in return. His weaponry was smaller now. Leaner. He no longer had use for the implied threat of a sword. The hat was the one item that had become indispensable. Brimmed with a wedge of squirrel fur, it prevented casual observers from seeing the hell in his eyes.

As he approached a glovemaker's stand Angus made

himself smile. The midmorning sun did the glovemaker no favors, sending light into the interior of his mouth, illuminating the rotten stumps and black absences that resulted from a poor diet over a long life.

"Day, sir."

Angus nodded in return. In preparation for his approach, he had stripped off his gloves and tucked them into his gear belt under his coat. They were old and worn but made of the kind of pieced swanskin favored by master bladesmen for its articulation. The glovemaker was probably the only person in town who could correctly identify their purpose.

"Looking for anything particular?"

Angus shrugged. The stand consisted of two handcarts with a plywood board balanced between them. A three-foot square of orange silk covered half the board, unequivocally dividing the glovemaker's wares into two camps: fine goods on the silk, serviceable on the wood. Angus reached for the serviceable.

The glovemaker had been doing this too long to show disappointment. "Nice thick boarshide. Good for farm work. They'll soften if you oil them."

Angus turned over the gloves to inspect the stitching. Not bad for work wear. "How long does it take to make them?"

"Pair like that, quarter of a day."

"And those?" Angus indicated an especially fine-looking pair of lamb's leather gloves, pin-tucked at the top for a snug fit.

"If the leather's in my shop, a full day."

"Did you receive a commission six weeks back for a pair of small, fine gloves from a woman passing through town?"

The glovemaker's head was shaking even before Angus finished speaking. "No."

"Did she purchase a pair of ready-made gloves?"

Again the glovemaker's head shook. "No. Yes. How would I know? Women stop and buy my gloves all the time." He was getting agitated, which was just fine with Angus Lok.

Agitation was counter to deceit. "If you met this woman you would remember her voice, sweet and gold like honey."

The glovemaker threw his hands in the air. "No such woman stopped by here."

Angus took a good long look at him. Honest work was not always done by honest men. "Who is the best surgeon in town?"

This question did not surprise the glovemaker as much as relieve him. "Walther Crane. He has rooms above the inn."

Angus slid a hand inside his coat, gaze steady upon the glovemaker.

The glovemaker's eyes widened. "I told the truth. I swear it. I sold no gloves to an out-of-towner. I swear it."

Angus drew his hand from his coat and placed something on the table, on the square of orange silk.

"For the gloves," he said, turning and walking away.

If the glovemaker was surprised by the silver piece or by the fact that his interrogator had kept the boarside gloves, Angus Lok would never know it. He did not look back. Pulling on his new gloves, he wound through the crowd in the general direction of the inn.

The glovemaker had been a longshot. If the Crouching Maiden *had* been in this town and *had* needed gloves she would have likely sent a boy to make the purchase. Still. Old habits died hard. Information was the lifeblood of the Phage and procuring it became a reflex. *Move from the outside in.* That had been one of the first lessons Hew Mallin had ever taught him. You never arrived in a town and made a beeline for your mark. You sauntered, spoke with fruit sellers, old women and drunks, got a feel for the rhythms of the place, listened to local gossip, calculated the geography of the streets.

White Kiln was prospering. The God's Day market was large and stocked with all manner of items from the mountain cities and clanholds. Gravel had been spread between the stands to firm the mud, and a roofed arcade with tie posts provided all-weather shelter for the horses. The Wheel was located across the street from the arcade, a whitewashed freestanding building three stories high. Its doors were open and the sunshine had encouraged a handful of patrons to drink on the stoop. As Angus drew closer he heard music—pipe and fiddle playing a bawdied-up version of an old spiritual—and caught the scent of roasting game bird.

He walked to the end of the street before crossing. From the side, the inn's horse court and stable block were clearly visible. A groom was sloshing water over the cobbles. Angus took a detour to speak with him.

"Fine day," Angus said.

The groom looked up. He was young and soft-lipped like a girl. The hand that held the bucket appeared remarkably free of blisters.

Good.

Wagging his chin toward the stables, Angus said, "Is Walther's horse playing up again?"

The groom looked from Angus to the stable. "He's quiet now but he was giving me grief at feeding."

Angus nodded with understanding. Spend a lifetime with horses and you learned many things. The important one for interrogators was the fact that they were always playing up.

You could count on any given horse on any given day causing some sort of trouble to its caretaker. The groom was too new at his job to know it.

"Walther's in his room?"

The groom set down his bucket. "Aye. He should be finished with his meal by now."

Glancing at the upper stories of the inn, Angus executed a self-deprecating smile. "Last time I was here I . . . er . . . was a little too deep in my cups if you know what I mean."

The groom did and nodded.

"I've clean forgot which room's Walth's." Angus squinted. "Is it to the right of the stairs?"

"No. Straight ahead, at the top. You can't miss it. We put a bench outside so those too sick to stand can sit as they wait."

Angus was all smiles. "Appreciate your help."

When he turned away from the groom the smile stopped so abruptly anyone looking would have thought tendons in his jaw had been cut. Although there was a door connecting the inn to the horse court, Angus opted for the more public front entrance. After this long practicing stealth, he was acting on pure instinct. The kitchen noises coming from the back door meant the cook was in residence, and cooks the world over were aggressive about their territory.

Angus briefly appraised the two prostitutes at the front door. One was younger than Cassie, a plump and spotty girl of fifteen dressed in her God's Day best. *Go home*, he wanted to tell her. *Evil is everywhere. I am proof.*

The interior of the Wheel was lit by the block of sunlight streaming through the door. It smelled of stale ale, woodsmoke and roast pheasant. A handful of kiln workers were eating their midday meal at a trestle table covered with a passably clean cloth. Three old women were embroidering silk panels and sipping hot wine by the fire, and in the far corner a Bone Priest sat alone with neither food nor drink to occupy his hands. Angus tucked his head low to avoid inspection. He was surprised at the presence of a Bone Priest, but did not consider it a problem. They had their own world of secrets to protect.

The stairs were to the left of the beer counter and as neither alewife nor innkeep stood guard, Angus felt free to head upstairs. The groom had made it clear that the surgeon's rooms were on the third story but Angus stopped at the second to take a look. He'd seen better and worse run places. The floorboards were parched from lack of wax but they were free of dust. As he passed one closed door he heard rhythmic knocking, wood against plaster. A couple having sex.

Angus headed up the second flight of stairs. A quick reconnoissance of the third floor revealed four closed doors, and one open door. The open door led to a tiny room with a sloped roof and a north facing window furnished with a basic straw-filled mattress and a pine chest. Angus ghosted past, coming to rest at the surgeon's door. No one sat waiting on the newly installed hickory bench. A floorboard creaked on the far side of the door. A voice spoke and a second replied. Male and female. Angus relaxed the tension in his shoulders and lowered his weight back onto the heels of his feet as he prepared to wait. He didn't speculate on the relationship between the man and the woman nor did he listen at the door. His entry was guaranteed now—at some point in the future the door would open to allow the woman to exit—so he let the stillness take him.

The stillness wasn't calm and it wasn't peace, but it was the closest a damned man could get to them. It would do.

Minutes passed and the cadence of the voices changed. A floorboard creaked sharply and footsteps tapped toward the door. Angus moved into position. The interior latch was raised with a *click*.

"Thank you, sir. Thank you. I'll send Jess round with the ham." The door opened and a woman with gray hair and ruddy cheeks stepped out. Angus immediately stepped toward her, entering the space once occupied by the door and preventing it from being closed on him.

The woman stepped back. "Sweet God!" she said to Angus. "You gave me a fright."

Raising his head, Angus allowed the woman to look into his eyes. "Go," he mouthed, moving past her into the room.

She wasn't young and she recognized affliction when she saw it. Closing her mouth, she took herself away.

Angus was already focused on his mark. Upon hearing the woman cry out, Walther Crane had risen from his desk. Angus saved him the effort of closing the door. Crane was in his forties, tall and thin and clever-looking. A knife belt slung crosswise across his chest held a sizable piece of steel.

"I have some questions," Angus said, lowering the latch and sealing them both inside the room.

Crane's sharp brown eyes assessed Angus. The surgeon was dressed in black wool pants and a cream linen shirt. A thick-banded silver ring mounted with a sphere of onyx gave authority to his right hand. It made his small gesture of compliance seem like a kingly concession.

Angus claimed more space in the room. "Forty days back a woman came to you with burned hands. How long did you treat her for?"

Crane moved back behind his desk and sat. "I have no

memory of such a treatment." His voice was cultivated and dismissive. He was calmer now he was in his chair.

Angus took himself over to the room's only window and closed the shutters. "Try and remember," he said, turning to face the surgeon. "It will be better for both of us."

The surgeon's gaze flicked to the door. A second, more subtle glance was directed toward his knife.

"The holster is loose," Angus told him calmly. "When you draw your knife you'll force the holster back and then have to yank it forward to free the weapon. You'll lose seconds."

The surgeon considered this for a moment and then nodded once, almost gently. He understood the new order in the room now. "Who are you?"

"Angus Lok."

When he realized there would be no more information, the surgeon nodded again. He placed his right hand on the desk, close to a collection of small bottles made of milk glass. "What do you want?"

"The woman with the burned hands, tell me about her." It was then, looking into Walther Crane's clever brown eyes, that Angus felt a moment of relief. Here it was at last: a path into the darkness. She had been here, perhaps in this very room, burned and hurting and at the mercy of this man. A chance comment from a healer in the village of Salt Creek had brought Angus here. *"If I were burned I'd head straight for White Kiln. Its surgeons are masters with burns. Those kilns spit out fire every day."*

Seeing a tendon in Walther Crane's hand twitch, Angus exploded into motion. Two leaps and he was across the room. Curbing his forward momentum, he slammed the heel of his hand into the surgeon's wrist. The desk jumped. Inhaling sharply, Walther Crane snatched his hand to his chest. Angus waited. Cradling his wrist, the surgeon began rocking back and forth in his chair. The apple of his throat was quivering.

Finally his gaze rose to Angus. Fear of the unknowable made him look like a small boy.

Angus considered explaining two things to him. First, when you are in the presence of an armed and dangerous man keep your body still. Allowing muscle to twitch close to a glass bottle that may or may not contain acid, bleach or poison was a mistake. Second, the force of the blow was controlled. The hurt could have been worse.

Instead, Angus said, "The woman."

The surgeon sighed. Fluid was rushing into his wrist and the flesh was beginning to swell. "She came here, in the middle of the night. She broke in. I was asleep." He glanced at the room's second door, indicating a second room where he slept. "Her hands were in a bad way. The skin was gone from the tips of her left fingers, damage across both palms. There was a ligament exposed. Those sort of burns, you only see when the skin has been doused with fuel. She must have been in a lot of pain, but you wouldn't have known it. She was exquisitely calm." Crane paused.

A softening of his expression told Angus all he needed to know about the Maiden's mental state. Magdalena Crouch was still at the top of her form, still able to manipulate any situation to her advantage. She had broken in to this man's residence, demanded medical attention from him under threat of violence, and here he was, forty days later, mooning over her like a yearman.

"What name did she give?"

"Delayna Stoop."

"What did you do for her?"

Crane massaged his wrist. "First thing I did was clean the wounds. She'd been wearing gloves at the time of injury and some leather still adhered to the flesh. This kind of procedure can be quite painful and it's my custom to administer blood of the poppy. She refused all painkillers—though she did pass out for a short while as I began to operate."

Confident now that he was talking about his area of expertise, Crane continued without prompting. "I stitched what I could and cut skin flaps to bridge the missing fingertips. The tendon was badly damaged and I did what I could." He shrugged. "I doubt if she'll ever be able to contract her left hand again, though the fingers appeared to retain some independent movement. And the thumb . . . below the second knuckle the thumb was fine."

"And the right?"

"The burns were more extensive yet more superficial. I've seen men with similar injuries lose use, but Delayna . . . she's so . . ."

Angus did not need to hear Crane's assessment of the Maiden's character. "How long did you care for her?"

"She stayed eleven days." There was an appeal for understanding in the look Crane sent Angus: an admission of frailty, man-to-man. When Angus gave nothing back, the surgeon hurried on. "The stitches and skin flaps had to be cleaned and dressed daily. It is my practice to dress burns with honey—it halts infection and aids healing—and Delayna was in no state during that time to care for herself. Anything touching her hands was agony. She had no desire to stay in public rooms and it seemed natural that she should stay with me so I could watch her. She was discreet.

No one knew she was here, not even my patients. She would withdraw to the bedchamber whenever I received patients."

It wasn't worth asking whether or not she had paid for his services. Money was seldom the reason people served the Maiden. "Did she send any messages?"

"None that I saw."

"Did she receive any visitors?"

Crane studied his wrist. It had not occurred to him yet to remove the onyx ring before the swelling spread to his fingers and sealed it tight. "No."

"What belongings did she have with her?"

"A small pack."

"Did you look inside?"

A beat passed. Crane dropped his gaze. "Yes."

Angus kept very still. "And what did you find?"

"A change of clothes. Boots with felt soles. Coins and jewels. A knife." He shrugged. "Nothing much."

"Where were the coins from?"

Crane thought for a moment. "Most were gold suns."

Morning Star then. It matched the rumor that the mountain city to the east was her base.

The surgeon hadn't finished. "The rest were those strange flattened coins from Spire Vanis."

Almsgold, flattened under the gate of the same name. The currency of surlords. Angus was not surprised. Penthero Iss had reason to punish him. As Iss had seen it, Angus Lok had stolen his daughter from Spire Vanis, took her north toward Ille Glaive and the clans. Iss had sent his chief henchman Marafice Eye to track them. Eye had pursued them as far as Ille Glaive.

Angus breathed deeply and wished for death. He should never have taken Ash and Raif to the farmhouse after Ille Glaive. There had been a sorcerer in Eye's party, someone powerful enough to part the mist on the frozen lake. A man like that had infinite ways of uncovering truth. Sarga Veys, that was his name. He'd acted as Iss's proxy in negotiations with the Dog Lord. And there had been some incident in the Bitter Hills, after the Dog Lord had transferred custody of Ash to Marafice Eye and his hunt party. Angus had been prisoner of the Dog Lord at that time, and he clearly recalled Hammie Faa, the man who brought him food twice a day, telling him that five of the party had died. Eye, Veys and Ash were the only ones who walked away.

For less than a second Angus thought about Ash March, considered the perfect symmetry of her face, and then shut away the memory in its deep and secret place.

"Was Stoop aware you looked through her pack?" he asked Crane.

The jittery energy that had possessed Crane upon receipt of the blow appeared to be draining away. His face looked tired and miserable. A lump the size of a quail's egg now bulged from the top of his wrist. "I don't think so. It was that first night, after the stitching, she'd pretty much passed out."

"What did she tell you about herself?"

Crane opened his mouth to speak and then hesitated. It was a phenomenon Angus had seen before. People thought they knew the Maiden, believed she had been as open with them as they had with her, but when it came time to list the results of that openness they came up blank. It was the same with her appearance. The Maiden hid in plain sight.

Angus moved on. "What state where her hands in when she left?"

"Still poor. I'd taken most of the stitches out. The skin flaps needed longer. They're tricky. Two of the three had begun to mesh with the damaged skin, but they were still in a delicate state. The wrong kind of pressure could shear them off, and she'd be right back to exposed flesh."

"That was four weeks ago. How would they be today?"

"She's strong. Healthy. Likely she's removed the remaining stitches: I showed her how. The skin flaps would need to be severed from their original blood supply once they're meshed. I advised her to visit a surgeon for that."

"Which surgeon? Where?"

For the first time it occurred to Crane that he was providing information that would be used in tracking down his patient. Angus saw the realization in Crane's eyes and was immediately ready to refocus the man's loyalties. Crane saw the readiness; by deliberately shifting his weight, Angus made sure that he would.

But he still lied. They always lied. "She was heading east for Morning Star. I gave her the name of a colleague in the city. Hermit Small. He's a fine surgeon, skilled in wound care. He's tended the Lord Rising himself. Of course he's not the lord's official surgeon, but . . ."

Angus let him drone on. Crane wasn't a good liar and was now spouting an unnecessary quantity of honest detail, as if by lowering his ratio of lies to truth he could somehow conceal the deceit. There *was* truth here though. The Maiden would never have let this man know her true destination. Whatever she had told him would be misdirection. So that meant she had revealed some other city as her intended destination—

probably Ille Glaive or Spire Vanis—and by speaking up and naming Morning Star, Crane sought to send her pursuer elsewhere. Which ultimately meant that Morning Star was still a fair bet. The Maiden was a wounded animal. Chances were she'd chose a familiar hidey-hole to lick those wounds.

"The clothes in the bag," Angus said, "describe them."

Sudden changes in the direction of the interrogation no longer surprised the surgeon. "A dark green wool cloak lined in velvet, a dark green dress, fur collar." He lowered his eyes. "Lace small clothes."

The fool hoped to see her again. Even now he did not fully understand two fundamental things. One, that the Maiden would never return to this place. And two, he was looking at the man who was going to destroy her. The surgeon lived in a world of cushioned privilege, one where his profession bestowed authority and respect. He knew how to heal wounds and stitch skin but he could not begin to imagine the deficiencies of the two people who had broken into his rooms. They did not live for the same purpose he lived for: for success, money, family, respect.

We live to end things.

Angus crossed to the door. Stand too long in one spot and his thoughts could unmake him. He was done here. Crane had nothing more to tell. The surgeon had thought himself an intelligent man and his encounter with the Maiden was slowly unraveling that illusion. Who falls in love with a woman who breaks into one's house, accepts help, shelter and confidences and gives nothing of herself in return?

Realizing Angus was leaving, Crane stood. Was it possible he looked disappointed? Once he'd begun talking about the Maiden was it difficult to stop?

Angus Lok had no sympathy for him. "Be glad you are alive," he told the surgeon in parting.

In under a minute, Angus had stepped from the building and made the turn east toward Morning Star. He'd already forgotten the look of quiet desperation in the surgeon's eyes.

CHAPTER 13

Enemies All Along

"Your mare has Sull in her," Chella Gloyal said, mounting her own glossy gray stallion. "Does she have a fifth gait?"

Raina patted Mercy's head. "Yes. When she has a fancy to she can move forward and sideways at the same time."

"That would be something worth seeing." Chella kicked her boot heels into her stallion's belly and walked the horse across the hard cattle court at Blackhail.

Raina followed on Mercy. Even though she was wary of the Croserwoman's flattery, she couldn't help but be pleased by it. Mercy had been a gift from Dagro: praise the horse he'd chosen and you praised him too.

"Have you been to the Wedge?" Raina asked, nodding toward the upland to the east.

"Several times. Let's go north instead."

Raina was surprised but did not show it. Chella had been in the roundhouse under twenty days yet had managed the four-hour roundtrip to the Wedge several times? Who had taken her? Glancing at the Croserwoman's cool, self-possessed profile Raina suspected she had an answer. Chella Gloyal had taken herself.

With a squeeze of her thighs, Raina coaxed Mercy into a canter and pulled ahead of the Croserwoman. It was an hour after dawn and the frost was still sparkling. Sheep were cropping tender shoots of oatgrass and wild carrot along the trail, and Raina grinned as the fuzzy creatures sprang into motion to avoid Mercy. She seldom rode due north from the roundhouse. The forest of great black evergreens did not please her. Yet that was what Chella had requested, and Raina was reluctant to let the Croserwoman know that she found the dimness of the blackstone pines unnerving.

They rode an hour in silence before entering the trees. Chella was a natural horsewoman, back straight, shoulders relaxed. Ewemen stopped in their tracks to admire her. Somewhere along the way her hair had slipped free of its ties and dark chestnut tresses spilled down her back. Raina envied her. She was young, beautiful, newly-wed to a good man who adored her. Her life stretched out before her, full of possibility and hope.

Was that how I looked when I first wed Dagro? Raina wondered. *Surely not. I was never that confident.*

Chella took the lead on the forest trail. Snow was still thick on the ground here. Dry, crunchy and littered with pine needles, it crackled as the horses' hooves punched its surface. Mercy followed Chella's stallion so closely their prints formed a single line.

"Is this one of the trails leading to the mine?"

Raina had been so wrapped in her own thoughts, she was surprised when Chella spoke. "Black Hole?" she said, buying herself a moment.

Chella glanced over the shoulder. "Yes."

Raina wondered about the question, but could see no harm

in answering it. "You can get to Black Hole this way, but most miners take the cart road to the east."

"I heard the mine is closing."

Raina looked at the back of Chella's head. She, Raina Blackhail, chief's wife, had heard no such thing. Quickly she searched her memory for recent mention of Blackhail's sole working silver mine, Black Hole.

"A party of Blackhail miners arrived at Croser just before I left," Chella said, reining her stallion to draw abreast of Raina. "They came looking for work in the iron fields. As they told it, the Hailhouse was full to the rafters and there wasn't enough room for them"

Raina got the distinct impression that Chella was well aware this was news to the chief's wife. "There is always room for tied clansmen at Blackhail," she said stiffly. "They were mistaken."

Chella executed the smallest possible shrug. "Of course you are right."

Agreement flummoxed Raina: she had been stirring for a fight. What was it about Chella Gloyal that provoked her so? She was an outsider, a clanwife whose only claim to respect was through her husband. Deciding to take control, Raina said, "The trail widens here. Let's stop and rest."

"If we ride on for a few minutes we'll find a clearing."

Raina blinked.

"You're correct," Chella said, plucking the question from Raina's face. "I've never entered these woods before, but I read trail marks. A while back they indicated a site to rest and water the horses."

"You hunt?" Raina asked, voice still stiff.

"A little," Chella turned in the saddle and smiled knowingly at Raina, "if I have to."

There was no way to reply to that so Raina didn't try. She was beginning to regret inviting the Croserwoman to ride with her this morning. In the stables three days back, Chella had told her she had made two mistakes. Raina had heard the account of her first mistake and could not fault it—she had no experience of planning a war party—and today she had planned on hearing her second mistake. Now she found herself wishing she hadn't given Chella Gloyal and her opinions so much credit.

As the Croserwoman predicted, the trail led to a clearing around a small creek. A log had been sectioned to form seats and another formed a bridge across the water. Raina dismounted and led Mercy to the creek. She could smell smoke and char from recent campfires. How could she have lived twenty years at Blackhail and never before stepped foot in this place?

Resisting the urge to question Chella about the clearing, Raina said, "You spent time in Morning Star."

Chella slid off her stallion and joined Raina by the creek. "You have been speaking with my husband."

It was not a question and Raina did not answer. Chella must keep close track of her information if she could be so sure that no one at Blackhail save her husband, Grim Shank, could furnish basic facts about her.

Crouching, Chella stripped off her gray leather gloves and tested the temperature of the water. Raina swore she could feel her thinking.

"My mother had family in the city and I lived there for three years."

"Consecutively?"

Chella raised an eyebrow. "No. Two separate visits."

Raina remained calm. She had hardly known where the question came from, but she knew it was to her advantage to pretend otherwise. She said quietly, "I will not tolerate you spying on me again. Your husband has gone to Bannen and you are alone in my house. Do not make me cast you out." *I have killed a man in cold blood*, Raina Blackhail thought. *If the Stone Gods are listening this moment they can surely hear it in my voice.*

Chella Gloyal rose to standing. She had a bow callus on her right thumb, Raina noticed.

"I apologize for my actions in the stables." The Croserwoman's voice was level and she looked Raina straight in the eye. "It won't happen again."

She hadn't been caught, Raina realized quite suddenly. If Chella had chosen to she could have kept her presence in the horse stall a secret. Which made her fine words nothing more than a promise to keep herself better hidden next time. Raina ran a hand across her forehead. *Gods, I'm no good at this.*

Waving the apology aside, she said, "You might as well tell me what you believe my second mistake was."

"You sent away your friends."

Wind moved the trees and lifted Raina's braid from the back of her neck. Overhead, she caught sight of a red-tailed hawk and she had a sense of how she must look from above: a figure isolated in a forest of dark trees. Orwin Shank and Corbie Meese: her two most powerful and loyal allies had departed the Hailhouse at her request. She had been so intent on caretaking Blackhail's treasure, she had not thought to caretake herself.

Dagro, come back to me my love. I need you.

The wind died and the hawk sailed west. Time did not reverse itself. Raina waited, but it didn't.

Looking carefully at Chella she said, "I can look after myself."

Chella's green-gray gaze was steady and knowing. "I don't doubt it."

They moved apart. Raina went to pay her respects to Chella's beautiful horse. The stallion had found fresh fern shoots on the east side of the clearing and was plucking them delicately with his lips. As Raina approached he raised his head in greeting. Raina patted and scratched him. Something about the sleekness of his cheekbones and nose reminded her vaguely of Mercy.

"He has Sull in him too. One eighth." Chella had come to stand beside her. "You can tell straightaway if you look in his eyes." Holding the horse's cheek strap, Chella turned the creature's head, presenting its right eye for Raina's inspection. "See the tiny flecks of white in the iris? The Sull call them *xhi a'lun*, the moon and stars."

Raina smiled with wonder.

Chella smiled along with her. "Mercy has them too. Just a few."

Something had happened between them at the creek and Raina was still trying to figure out what it was. They had both revealed something to each other, but she could not decide the nature of those revelations. Had they exposed hidden weapons or vulnerabilities?

Maybe both.

Raina reminded herself to be cautious. Chella was like no Croserwoman she had ever met. She was secretive and opinionated and too sure of herself by far.

"I have treats." Chella said, reaching inside her saddlebag, "to reward ourselves for coming this far." She pulled out a red tin box, well made with a crafty hinge and clasp, and a small flask insulated with rabbit fur. "Grab the blanket and we'll sit on one of the logs."

She was from Croser and perhaps they lived by different rules there, so Raina overlooked the impertinence of Chella directing a chief's wife. Raina took the blanket that had been rolled and fastened behind the saddle and spread it over the closest log. She was hungry. And she couldn't recall the last time she'd had anything that could be called a treat.

"Drink." Chella handed her the unstoppered flask and Raina did as directed. The liquid was cool and dry and tasted of pears. Raina felt it moving through her body like smoke through an empty house.

"My grandfather distilled it," Chella said, laying out items between herself and Raina on the log. "He owned a pear orchard on the south banks of the Wolf."

That meant wealth. "It's delicious."

"He would have been happy to hear that." Chella took the flask from Raina and drank. For a moment the Croserwoman's gaze lengthened, and Raina imagined she was remembering the past. "So. We have smoked trout, soft cheese and candied plums from Croser—and fresh bread purloined from the kitchens at dawn."

She had thought of everything, including little glazed dishes and a round-bladed knife for the cheese. Raina mashed trout into a hunk of bread. "At Dregg I used to eat smoked fish every day for breakfast. Hailsfolk have little taste for it. They don't care for water or anything that lives in it."

"No clan's perfect." Chella pushed a plum between her lips, chewed and swallowed. "Or any chief."

Raina turned her attention to the wedge of soft, ripe cheese and did not take the bait. Chella was forward—no one without due respect should speak of chiefs to a chief's wife—yet although Raina felt offense, she also felt the pull of the younger woman's lawlessness. Who was she? And why had she chosen to marry Grim Shank and travel north to his clan? Surely she would have seen more of her husband if she'd stayed at Croser? She had to know Grim would return to war.

"It's said that Wrayan Castlemilk took the warrior's oath when she was thirteen." Done with eating, Chella swiped crumbs from her skirt. "Her brother held her swearstone until his death. She took it from his corpse and now keeps it herself."

"Do you know Angus Lok?"

For the first time in twenty days, Raina saw Chella Gloyal look uncomfortable. Raina hardly knew what had made her ask the question—just some half-baked idea that the story about the Milk chief was the sort of thing Angus Lok liked to tell. Little stories with a purpose. With a push.

The Croserwoman began to wrap the remains of the food. "I have met Angus Lok, yes. He used to come to Croser to trade news and small goods."

Raina stood. "Let's head home."

She felt Chella's gaze on her back as she went to collect Mercy. For a reason apparent only to herself, Mercy was standing midstream in the creek and had to be coaxed to the bank. Ideas were swirling in Raina's head. She needed to ride so she could think.

Once Mercy had taken a trail she never forgot it, so Raina gave the horse her head. They didn't wait for Chella and the stallion. It was close to midday but the forest was still cool. Raina wondered if the snow between the pines would ever melt. Riding from the tree line into grazes and open fields was like punching into another world. The sun was warm here and the snow was slushy and mixed with mud.

So mention of Angus Lok had caught Chella Gloyal off-guard. Why? What did they have in common? Both were outsiders to Blackhail and both had lived in the Mountain Cities . . . and both liked to interfere with other people's lives. Oh, Angus Lok was a good deal more subtle about it, but then he had a good twenty years on this girl. And that was another thing. Grim Shank, Gods love him, was a fine warrior and a good son but he didn't match his new wife in demeanor, intelligence or looks. With all her charms Chella could have had her pick of men, yet she had chosen Grim. At the creek Raina had seen something in Chella's eyes. Intent, purpose: something.

Did she have something invested here? Certainly she found Raina Blackhail wanting and was not shy about pointing it out.

Enough, Raina told herself. Too much thinking. Dagro had rarely strained himself with excess cogitation—and he would never let it hinder his enjoyment of a fine ride.

Pressing her boot heels into Mercy's flank, she galloped the final league to the roundhouse. Chella kept apace, though her stallion could easily have outrun Mercy if he'd been allowed to. By the time they reached the cattle turnout, both horses were lathered. Raina turned to Chella and grinned, and Chella grinned right back.

"Wonderful," she said.

Raina agreed. They trotted their horses toward the stables in companionable silence. Cows had been turned out onto the hard standing and herders and dairymen were busy managing the herd. Raina was glad to see livestock on its way to pasture. It meant spring. Once the grass started coming in there would be less pressure on the dry stores and that was something else to be glad about. Raina decided not to worry about the grain level. Not today.

"Chief's." The dairyman, Neddic Bowes greeted Raina with the shortened version of the title "chief's wife." Dressed in a big red apron over dairy whites and knee waders, Neddic was hard to miss. "Back in time for the excitement, eh? Must have known it was coming."

The band of muscle between Raina's gut and lungs tensed. Outside she remained calm. "Well," she said, thinking furiously and beginning to regret her second helping of pear spirits. "Little happens around here without me knowing about it." Then, to the groom who had come forward to take possession of Mercy, "Box the stallion. I'll ride Mercy onto the greatcourt." She spoke loudly enough so that Chella, who was a length behind, heard the instruction. It was an order, and both the groom and Chella Gloyal understood it: the stallion and its rider stay here, at the stables.

Raina rode on. She felt as if she was leaving her old life behind, that the path to the front of the roundhouse was a tunnel and she would emerge from it into a remade world. She knew her clan. What she'd heard in Neddic Bowes' voice and seen in the face of the groomsman already told her much of what she needed to know: Harm was coming to Blackhail.

People were already gathering ahead of her. Stonemasons and builders had left their work on the new outbuildings and were forming small groups on the greatcourt. The clandoor was open and warriors, women and children were spilling out. Raina's eyes jumped to the Scarpes. Something was different.

Many of them were formally dressed, in black fronts, leather paneling and weasel pelts. All were armed.

Raina noted their numbers and felt fear.

You sent away your friends.

A mounted company was closing distance from the south. When they reached the gravel road, they fanned out in a classic "flight of geese" formation, displaying the high status of their leader. Two standard-bearers flanked the head rider. Six-foot poles held firm in saddle horns flew the black and brown of Scarpe. Weasel and poison pine.

Sweet gods. It was the Scarpe chief, Yelma Scarpe, sitting closed-legged on a huge brown mare fitted with a cushioned saddle seat. The instant Raina recognized her, Yelma Scarpe's thin lips stretched to something resembling a smile. *I'm ahead of you*, the expression conveyed.

Watching the Scarpe chief's face Raina made a series of decisions. Quickly she scanned the crowd. Singling out the young hammerman Pog Bramwell, she issued orders in a low voice. "Swift now," she told him, gaze flicking to the mounted company. "When you're done come and stand at my back."

Pog Bramwell, all of seventeen and still hoping to use a razor daily, bowed his head. Fine golden hairs at the back of his neck defied the jurisdiction of his warrior's queue. "Aye, lady."

Raina kicked Mercy forward so horse and rider stood ahead of the crowd. Yelma had gained the greatcourt and her party was slowing. Now they were closer, Raina saw that the saddle seat had armrests—like a throne—and Yelma's bony bejeweled fingers rested on leather pads. In a show of horsemanship, she held the reins in the crook of her left thumb.

Two months ago, on the day of Anwyn Bird's death,

Longhead had warned that the Scarpe chief was planning a visit. "When the snow is off the ground," he'd said. It did not take a wise man to scan the great rolling mass of the southern graze and see snow. It lay in gray heaps at the side of the road, in the northern shadows of hills and hummocks, in the wells of trees, and in slushy pools upon low ground. That meant Yelma had come early. So either she meant to take the Hailhold by surprise, or receipt of Stannig Beade's corpse had stirred her from the Weasel chair before planned.

It did not matter, Raina realized. *The one thing you need to know about weasels*, Dagro had once said, *is they eat the head first.*

Raina swallowed. The urge to dismount was strong but she fought it, making herself sit back in the saddle and relax. It was a declaration and she, Yelma Scarpe and everyone of the greatcourt knew it. There was no going back now. Raina Blackhail had declared herself equal to the Weasel chief.

Do and be damned.

Let my chiefship begin.

Almost on cue, Raina heard the sound she'd been waiting for: the bass rumble of the greatdoor sliding closed along its track. The sound tolled across the court, changing everyone who heard it. Warriors' pupils dilated as they checked the readiness of their weapons and the layout of the available space. Women drew their children closer. Old men wished for their youth. The bond between Blackhail and Scarpe snapped with force, creating enemies so hostile one could not doubt that they had hated each other all along.

You could not move time backward, Raina realized, but you could move it forward. With the order to shut the door on the Scarpe chief, she, Raina Blackhail, had made a new Age.

Out of the corner of her eye, she saw her guard assemble itself around her. Hardgate Meese, father to Corbie, was at her right. He had taken a kidney wound at Ganmiddich but she doubted he would let it show. Ballic the Red and Tannic Crow, the two finest bowmen remaining in the house, were at her left. Yearmen and graybeards made up the rest of her crew. Lyes and Murdocks, Ganlows and Gormalins, Bannerings and Onnachres: old families whose loyalty she was now counting on. Her two most valuable allies—Orwin Shank and Corbie Meese—were gone and she could not say what would happen here without them.

Yelma Scarpe gave a signal to her company, bringing them to a halt thirty paces from where Raina sat Mercy and leveling them to a single line. It occurred to Raina that an artist could render a likeness of the Scarpe chief without ever drawing a curve. She was dressed in stiff brown silk embroidered at the hem and cuffs with an unlovely design of weasel heads and pine cones. Her jewels, aggressively substantial, threw sparks.

"Welcome," Raina said. She could hear the ride to the northern woods in her voice, the flatness following a long exertion. Raina hoped it passed for calm. "We are glad you have come."

The sun was behind the Scarpe chief, making it difficult to read her face. Seconds passed. Was she looking at the crowd outside the greatdoor, head-counting the resident Scarpes? Her fingers curled against the armrests of her chair.

"Woman," she said. "I came here at the request of your chief, as a friend to Blackhail in time of war. It is an ill house that bars its door against its allies and an unsound mind that would issue such an order. Pray fetch the senior Hailsmen. I would speak with those in charge."

At her side, Raina's guard did not move. Raina listened for sounds from the crowd behind her—any sign that Hailsmen and Scarpes were dividing into camps—but blood was pumping through her ears and she couldn't be sure if anyone stirred. For a certainty she would not betray her fear by looking around.

She raised her chin. "You speak with me. The door is barred because we are full and will take no more Scarpes. We will be glad to have you camp on the west field." Raina raised her right hand toward the cleared ground to the right of the roundhouse. Grooms had been using it as a makeshift practice ring and dead grass, snow and horse pats had been churned into brown muck. "And will provide such tents as you may need."

Even before she'd finished speaking, Yelma Scarpe made a tiny signal with her index finger, lifting it from the leather pads. Straightaway, Raina heard the *snick* of steel drawn from leather. The sound came from the door. A half-second later, Yelma Scarpe's two standard-bearers threw down their flagstaffs and went for their weapons. Another half-second later the entire company drew arms. Raina inhaled sharply. All possible outcomes revolved in her mind. All consequences of issuing the command for Hailsmen to attack Scarpes were laid bare.

This meant war.

Raina Blackhail raised her arm.

Thuc.

An arrow sliced through air. *Thuc. Thuc. Thuc.* Three more hit in quick succession. Freezing in midsignal, Raina followed their trajectories. Two arrows vibrated in each of the Scarpe standards, pinning the black and brown canvas to the ground. Fletched with sparrow feathers and nocked with copper wire, the arrowshafts bore no identifying marks. Raina calculated they had been fired from the roof of the new construction that butted the roundhouse's eastern wall.

All was still for a moment. Yelma Scarpe closed both fists around her reins. The four shots had been expertly aimed— ten feet to either side of her mare—and it wasn't hard to imagine a fifth arrow in her chest. She and her company might win a pitched battle on the greatcourt, but she could not take on a bowman firing from high ground. Not without body armor. Not without a bowman of her own positioned on higher ground. She would die. The arrows told it as simply as that.

Seizing the advantage, Raina flung out her arm toward the standards. "Do not," she told Yelma Scarpe, "make the mistake of ordering an attack on Blackhail. Leave now before blood is spilt between allies and while my bowmen still possess the will to hold their strings." As she spoke the sun passed behind clouds and she received her first close look at the Weasel chief. Yelma Scarpe looked just like her nephew Mace Blackhail. It made Raina's voice as hard as nails.

Yelma Scarpe's gaze flicked to the new construction then back to Raina. "You will die for those arrows, woman. I came here in friendship, to offer protection to Blackhail while its warriors and chief are away at war. Now some clanwife with no authority or due respect dares order me shot. I am chief. And you have made yourself my enemy." Pulling on the reins, she turned the mare. The entire company moved in unison, reversing their formation on her signal.

Swiveling in the saddle chair, Yelma looked back at Raina. "Let your one consolation be this: You will not wait many days in dread of me."

With that, she drove a single, spurred heel into horseflesh and exploded into motion.

Steady, Raina warned herself as she watched Yelma's company follow their leader south across the grazelands. *Fainting would not look good.*

Behind her, the crowd began to move and speak. She heard angry grunts and worried whispers. A baby started to cry. Ignoring them Raina made herself watch the Scarpe retreat. If Yelma looked around she would see Raina Blackhail, chief, staring right back.

"You could have told me you'd put someone on the roof." It was Ballic the Red. Raina had forgotten the master bowman was there. "It was a fine strategy but it would have been good to know."

Raina said nothing. Instinctively she knew there would be nothing to gain and much to lose by informing Ballic that she had not directed the marksman to the roof, let alone ordered him to fire warning shots. She had to be practical now, and that included taking credit when it wasn't due. This thing she had set in motion would gain mass. The Scarpe chief would make sure of that. She was probably composing a message for Mace right now from her throne-like chair.

I am damned.

But she would not think about that. Turning toward the roundhouse, Raina scanned the roof of the new construction. Whoever had taken it upon themselves to shoot was gone. Good. That was another thing she would deal with later. Right now she had to eject every last Scarpe from the Hailhouse. She could not afford to have enemies on the other side of that door.

Quietly she addressed Ballic, Hardgate and Tannic Crow.

All three were grave. Armed Scarpe warriors watched as they spoke. Armed Hailsmen watched the Scarpes. Raina wished for the calm authority and practical experience of Orwin Shank. Chella Gloyal could not have spoken truer words this morning: It had been a grave mistake to send him to Dregg.

Was this a mistake too?

Raina surveyed the Scarpes in their black and braided leather with their dyed hair and poison pine tattoos. She could not stand them.

"Good riddance," she mouthed. It would be a relief to have them gone.

CHAPTER 14

Deadwoods

He had never liked them, but as a boy he had learned the paths through them—to this day he'd be hard pushed to say why. He'd been an ornery child, no doubt about it. If someone said, "Don't do this," he'd go right ahead and do it. Twice. That was part of it, Vaylo supposed. The other parts would be made up of pride and resentment and hope. No one had wanted him at home so he had simply taken himself away. The Deadwoods were one of the places he went.

That made him a braver child than he was a man, Vaylo reckoned. To camp alone here, in this tangled mosquito-infested netherworld of dead and dying trees, took jaw. Had he really come here with just a bedroll and hand knife? No.

He had brought the dogs.

Vaylo batted away a black fly and turned his thoughts to the now. They were walking their horses along a deer trail soft with melted snow and deer scat. A boar was baying to the south and the eerie sound was making the horses—and a fair portion of the men—jumpy. It took some getting used to. Horses and men recognized it for what it was—the territorial claim of a massive and dangerous beast—and only familiarity could temper that gut response. Same with the Deadwoods themselves. Instinct told you there were safer places to be.

What choice did they have though? They could hardly ride the Bluddroad and risk being cut down by Robbie Dun Dhoone's blue cloaks or Quarro Bludd's red ones. The Dhoone king had sent that mad axman of his, Duglas Oger, to test the Dhoone-Bludd border. Axes against swords usually made for an unlovely fight and though Vaylo rated his own chances in such a melee, he couldn't see his company escaping without casualty. They were a party of forty-five, including Nan, the bairns and himself. Every one was needed if they were going to pull off retaking the Bluddhouse. That meant survival took a second place to jaw.

Vaylo didn't like sneaking around the Bluddhold, but he was an old and unhoused chief with seventeen teeth, a dodgy heart and half a soul. He was getting used to doing things he didn't like.

As best he could tell they were three days northwest of the Bluddhouse. If they'd been riding at speed on open ground they could have gained the gate in two sunrises, but there were no roads through the Deadwoods and the paths were narrow and low, and no matter the size and makeup of your party you had to travel single file, afoot.

"Chief."

The voice belonged to the swordsman Odwin Two Bears. Odwin had volunteered for scout duty and had been traveling in advance of the party, surveying the intended route. One of the dogs was with him, the big black and orange bitch.

"Someone's made a new path ahead." Odwin's mother and older sister were wolverine trappers and Odwin had spent much of his childhood tagging along as they set and retrieved their lines. Wolverine furs were highly prized at Bludd and trapping territories were closely guarded. Marilla Two Bear and her daughter Yulia held claim to a small but significant section of the Deadwoods. Vaylo knew this because every year on Harvest Night the lovely honey-skinned Yulia brought him his chief's tribute: a dozen fine pelts with the heads still attached. Odwin had been ranging with Yulia in the Deadwoods as recently as last summer. When he said the paths had changed, Vaylo listened.

"Walk with me." The Dog Lord was reluctant to call a halt while the party was traveling single file. Word would have to travel down the line man-to-man — not a good policy to enact on a nervous company. Besides, halt now and the party would be spread across a quarter of a league, and Vaylo liked the thought of that about as little as he'd liked any thought he'd ever had.

Odwin Two Bear fell into pace directly ahead of his chief. Dressed for bushwhacking in a waxed coat and oilskin pants, the swordsman presented no edges for barbs to catch. His longsword was cross-harnessed against his back. Its crosshilts and pommel formed the head and claws of a steel bear. "There's a new trail heading due east. It's been head-cleared for riders."

Vaylo grunted. Clearing a trail to a height of nine feet to enable mounted men to ride with impunity took some doing. It didn't jibe with Gangarric's description of Quarro's steward-ship of the Bluddhouse. What had Gangarric said about his older brother? *Quarro grows fat and lazy — drinks ale all day and stays abed with Trench whores.* A fat and lazy chief didn't concern himself with clearing trails, especially if those trails were in the least accessible part of his holdings. Who had made them then? Did Quarro have a rival for the chiefship? Had some ambitious Bluddsman spent too many days watching his chief in his cups and begun laying plans to overthrow him? Or was it Dun Dhoone's blue cloaks, quietly clearing a path to the Bluddgate?

Neither was good. "How far did you scout?"

"About three leagues."

Vaylo did some reckoning. "Does the trail break south for the roundhouse?"

Odwin shook his head. "Could turn later though, above the grove."

It was beginning to sound like a secret path. Most trails through the Deadwoods radiated north from the Bluddhouse. Vaylo could think of a couple of reasons why a trail might ghost east above the roundhouse and he didn't like any of them. It still shamed him to recall Robbie Dun Dhoone's attack on the Sacred Grove six month's back. As Bludd chief, he should have been home to defend his house.

"Dhoone struck from the southeast," Odwin said, proving he was smart enough to anticipate his chief's line of thought. "They might figure *north*east'll be the charm this time."

"Are there clearings?"

"There's a beaver pond with some ground around it and another area that's pretty open. Trees. No bush."

Vaylo glanced over his shoulder. Hammie Faa was walking ahead of Pasha and Aaron and beyond them was the seasoned warrior Big Borro. Big Borro knew something was up. The message he sent to his chief was brief. *I'm ready.*

Receiving it in the form of a single steady look, Vaylo made his decision. "We'll take the new trail."

Odwin led the way. It was a few hours past noon and weather closing in from the north was darkening the spaces between trees. Red oak, red pine and hornbeam were slowly being killed by vines that Vaylo had no name for, man-thick tumorous growths that mimicked the trees they meant to kill. As the canopy lost cover, undergrowth had thrived. Dogwood, sumac, bearberries and thorns formed a tough, woody bush that was close to impenetrable. The Dog Lord had whittled himself a staff—he'd be damned if he'd call it a walking stick—and he beat back the branches with feeling. For a place hailing itself as the Deadwoods it had a grievous amount of life.

The boar howled like a creature from the underworld as the company slid through a break in the dogwood and onto the new trail. Cool and still, the trail tunneled through the undergrowth in a straight line. As Odwin had said, it was tall enough to accommodate riders but Vaylo found himself reluctant to mount. Behind him, he heard Pasha grumbling to Hammie about her sore feet.

"When the chief walks so do we," Hammie explained patiently, doubtless not for the first time.

"You did well to find this," Vaylo told Odwin Two Bear. "From the outside, it just looks like more trees to me."

Odwin nodded gruffly, pleased. The width of the trail made it possible for them to walk side by side and Vaylo could clearly see the warrior mark inked in red across Odwin's left cheek. "It took someone a while to do this. Months. A season even."

The Dog Lord agreed. Like most Bludd chiefs before him, he had been content to let the Deadwoods be. They formed a natural barrier to the north of the Bluddhouse and if

Bluddsmen themselves could barely traverse it what hope did foreign clansmen have?

No one had counted on the ruthless determination of the Thorn King, Robbie Dun Dhoone. As he moved along the trail, Vaylo became more and more certain. This was Dhoone's work. Had they already carried out strikes? For a certainty the trail had been used in recent days. The Dog Lord knew fresh horseshit when he smelled it.

I stayed away too long.

Ignoring the pain in his knees, the Dog Lord picked up his pace. What had he been thinking all these months? First he'd taken Dhoone then Ganmiddich, and when he'd been routed from both of those roundhouses what had he done? Gone north to the edge of the clanhold and played dog-in-a-manger with Dhoone. He should have come home. Three days, that was how long Bludd chiefs were chained to the guidestone before the guide accepted their chief's oaths. Vaylo recalled it as if it were yesterday, not thirty-six years in the past. He was young and hard-as-nails and he saw the Chief's Watch as something to be endured, not a sacred passage into chiefdom. He believed in himself, not the guidestone or the Stone Gods. He had not expected the visions. Certainly he had not wanted them. He had thought Maurice Penhandlo, the old clan guide, was trying to kill him. Maurice had that little bowl of water and he'd dip his long bird claws into it and shake the droplets onto Vaylo's face. Those droplets were the only thing that passed Vaylo's lips in three days. They just made him thirstier.

At first, he'd fought the mirages. They were fever dreams, brought on by cramping muscle, hunger and utter darkness. Gods, but the Bluddstone had been cold. Pressed against it for three days and it had never warmed to him, just kept sucking the heat from him, taking and taking, giving nothing but nightmares in return.

Of course Maurice Penhandlo would have called them visions. The guide left him alone that entire last day. He'd stoked the smoke fires, sealed the door and left. Vaylo supposed that he himself had fallen asleep—either that or been knocked out by the smoke. He remembered opening his eyes some time later and seeing . . . seeing things no man should ever see.

Was it the future? He had not thought so at the time. He had looked out on a dark and blasted land patrolled, *haunted*, by forces compressed into human form, dread beings that distorted the very space that surrounded them. Bludd was gone and its roundhouse was smashed into blocks. The great forests of the east were burning and the sky was red with smoke. The dread beings did not fear the flames, and they walked where no man, woman or animal could ever hope to stand and live. As Vaylo looked on someone came running from the fire's mouth, a young boy with flames on his back and legs. He was screaming in panic and fear. The dread beings moved toward him with their swords, and there was a moment when his gaze met the Dog Lord's and the Dog Lord understood all that it meant to be the boy. It was like ticking through a life. Hope, followed by surprise and then fear. There was a flash of sheer terror when the boy realized there were worse ways to die than being burned alive. And then pain.

He ceased breathing air and breathed pain instead.

The Dog Lord had recalled that moment countless times over thirty-six years. His dreams returned to it again and again. The two questions he asked were always the same. Did the boy, in that final instant, feel relief? Vaylo would never know the answer, for in the vision that was the point when the dread beings turned their backs on the lifeless form of the boy and perceived him, Vaylo Bludd.

They came for him, their forms rippling air, their swords sucking smoke from the fire. Vaylo had a choice then: flee or fight.

And that was the second question: What would he do?

For he had awakened at that moment and found himself back in the guidehouse, chained to the stone. He inhaled smoke, but it was from the smudgepots, not a raging forest fire.

Flee or fight?

Strange how you could think you were fighting only to realize you had actually fled. Was that what he had done by attacking Dhoone and then Ganmiddich? They had looked like fights, smelled like fights, but they had taken him away from his duty at Bludd. So weren't they really flights?

Enough.

"Bring forward my horse," Vaylo bellowed down the line. "Swift now." Think too long and you got yourself stuck in tricky little traps of your own making. He was here now, and he'd fight tooth and nail to make sure the Bluddhouse didn't fall into Dun Dhoone's hands. That was what he could do; things that he couldn't *un*do didn't matter.

Hammie brought forward Vaylo's stallion and held the reins while his chief mounted.

"Hand me the girl with the sore feet," Vaylo commanded.

Pasha was lifted from the ground and handed to Vaylo like a sack of grain. Undecided on whether or not she objected to this treatment, Pasha remained silent as the Dog Lord settled her in front of the saddle and kicked the stallion into motion.

"Eyes lively," he warned her, not trusting that all branches at saddle height had been cleared.

After a minute or so he began to relax. Dhoone had done a fine job clipping wood. What gall though, to make themselves a path right under Bludd's nose. And where were Quarro's patrols? Damn fool called himself the Bludd chief and didn't do anything to secure his house and clan? Well, the old chief was returning and the new chief would find himself turfed out along with the Dhoones. Vaylo was becoming less and less inclined to treat his eldest son kindly. Quarro didn't deserve respect. He'd be given one chance to surrender—that was it.

"Granda, there's a pool."

Pasha's high reedy voice broke through the Dog Lord's thoughts. They'd reached one of the clearings reported by Odwin, the beaver pond with a mud beach around it. Vaylo glanced at the sky. Two hours of daylight left. The desire to push on was strong but there was also a desire to be settled before dark. They had no choice but to spend the night in the Deadwoods and that meant planning and raising a secure camp.

Vaylo called the halt.

The beaver pond was, without doubt, one of the sorriest places he'd ever had the misfortune to spend the night. The mud around the shore was thawing and whatever had died there last summer was beginning to stink. Scrawny weed trees and rotten bulrushes with exploded heads were partially submerged in the water, and some kind of yellow scum floating on the surface was proving endlessly fascinating to flies. Pasha and Aaron quickly shucked off their boots and entered the shallows. Nan shrugged when Vaylo frowned at her accusingly. Children, water: her powers of control extended only so far.

Vaylo left them to it. His mind was on camp defenses and he consulted with Big Borro and Hammie Faa on the details. There would be a full black watch: half of the forty-two warriors awake at all times. Fifteen on the camp perimeter, and six—three pairs of two—concealed at lengths along the trail. Vaylo was quietly pleased when more men than needed stepped forward to volunteer for the first trail watch. He took a breath, about to tell the chosen six that the wolf dog would be patrolling the entire area, scribing a circle that contained them as well as the camp, safeguarding the watchers and providing a third level of security, when he stopped himself. The wolf dog was at the hillfort with Cluff Drybannock. It had chosen a new master to defend.

When facing good men who had just volunteered for dangerous duty after a full day on the road, it was unthinkable to show weakness. Vaylo set aside thoughts of the wolf dog and concentrated on preparing his men. Gods, but they were young and sharp. Drybone had attracted the best new warriors in the clan. The Dog Lord could see his eighth son in their solemn and thoughtful faces, hear Dry in their silences, in their unwillingness to engage in anything less than serious talk. It made his heart ache.

He assigned each pair one of the remaining dogs. Without the wolf dog as pack leader they weren't capable of organizing themselves as a wall around the camp but they would scout in a limited way as directed. Their ears and noses were still good.

By the time the watch was in place and the camp settled it was dark. No fires would be lit and no tents raised so there was little comfort to be had around the pond. Nan, smart woman that she was, had set aside a flask of Dhooneshine for just such a night. Everyone got a mouthful. It wasn't the liquor as much as the ritual of passing the flask man-to-man that helped. Even the bairns got a tasting.

Vaylo untied his blanket from his bedroll and took up position for the first watch. Facing west toward Dhoone, he pushed a cube of chewing curd between his lips and watched the black outline of the trees against the blackening sky. Mosquitoes smoked his head. He endured them. Behind him, the camp grew quiet as men slept. Vaylo felt deeply uneasy. Drybone was gone, the wolf dog was gone and here he was, camped two days north of his own roundhouse, about to order Bluddsmen to attack Bluddsmen, plunging his clan into civil war.

When the sound came he was half expecting it—something in him had been ready for hours—yet you could be expecting something and still be deeply and profoundly surprised.

The cry came from the north.

The Dog Lord rose and drew his sword. He had been still for too long and his muscles resisted their change in status. *Old* was the word that followed him as he tracked northeast along the camp perimeter. His night vision was not what it was and he was impatient with himself and the branches and exposed roots that slowed him. His mind was not what it was either, for he should have figured it out sooner.

The real threat was not from the west. Not tonight. Not any night. The real threat was from the North.

"BLUDD," Vaylo roared. "To arms!"

The first time he had battled the shadow beasts did not, in any way, prepare him for the second time. That first time at the hillfort, he and a small handpicked force had engaged nine Unmade horsemen who had fought in a way he had understood. As Cluff Drybannock had told it, the Unmade nine were the taken forms of his own men. They had once been Bluddsmen and although they were no longer recognizable as such, a shadow of their former existence glinted in the blackness like tooth enamel on a smile seen by night.

An infinitely small part of the horror had been knowable. The Dog Lord had not appreciated that at the time.

He did now.

They wielded *Kil Ji*, voided steel, but the Unmade metal had been forged into knives, not swords. And the lean and rippling forms who wielded them moved inhumanly fast. Vaylo recalled something Ockish Bull had once told him as they watched a fight between two city men at the Spring Fair. Cash and goods were riding on the outcome and over a thousand clansmen had gathered to watch. Vaylo had thought the rules too mannerly—all the fine stuff including headbutting and eye-gouging was disallowed—but once the fight got started and he saw the skill and brutality of the fighters his opinion changed. One man in particular caught his and Ockish' eye: a slight, dark-haired Vorlander on the far side of forty. His opponent had to have been ten years younger, with a pretty set of muscles and a sly face. The Vorlander had experience on his side though—and speed. Vaylo had never seen anyone move so fast.

"He's got the old mercury in his veins," Ockish had whispered in Vaylo's ear as the fight came to its grisly end. "It comes from a different age."

Watching the Unmade slice through the darkness around the camp, longknives of voided steel sucking air into oblivion,

Vaylo began to understand the full implications of what his eighth and best-loved son had told him about the Endlords. They were as old as the gods. Before there were clans, before there were even humans, the Endlords had been massing their armies. Other, older beings had been taken and unmade.

Was it Ockish Bull's mercury men who attacked the camp now? The Dog Lord doubted he would ever know.

The camp had mobilized and a core of twelve warriors formed a block around Nan and the bairns. Drybone had trained them well. The twelve hadn't needed to be told that their longswords would be a liability in the underbrush, and had staked their claim on the only open ground, the mud beach. Four were in the water. Vaylo gave them a brief nod as he cut across the camp. It was too dark to make eye contact with Nan, so he didn't try. She had her maiden's helper and pouch of poison. She knew what to do.

The remaining thirty warriors were in the process of cinching the perimeter of the camp. Ranks were already broken. Knots of warriors had formed as clansmen came to the defense of clansmen. The Unmade were blade-shaped forms striking in perfect silence. Their longknives were the best weapon for the underbrush. Vaylo could see his men struggling to swing their swords in the tangle of dogwood and sumac while the Unmade's knives pierced like darts.

"*Spear them!*" he screamed. "*Don't let them flank you.*"

Keeping his sword close to his body, Vaylo joined the line. Straightaway he smelled the sharp, sickly odor of chyme. Someone had been struck in the gut. Gods save him. A swipe at the elbow refocused Vaylo's mind. As he spun to protect himself he caught sight of his attacker up close. Its lips were curled back like a dog's and its eyes revealed the shatter-blasted remains of an Unmade soul. Vaylo shamed himself by stepping back. He pulled the stench of gas and ice along with him. A sword slid in to the space he'd vacated. At first he couldn't understand why, then he heard a high-pitched wail as live steel deflected voided steel, forcing both blades down and into the brush.

Vaylo cursed his eyes. The *Kil Ji* had come at him edge-on and he hadn't been able to spot the lean black line in the darkness. Glancing to his right he saw the blond swordsman Big Borro tugging his sword free from the brush. Vaylo drove forward to protect him, awkwardly bracing his sword hilt as he tried to isolate the blade from the snarl of sumac. A branch scraped along the lower orbit of his left eye and he could not prevent the reflex that demanded he close his eyes to protect them. He opened them perhaps less than a quarter of a second later but it was too late. Big Borro was opened by a single stroke of voided steel, traveling up from his hip, across his torso and along the right plane of his face. The violence and precision was breathtaking. Blood spattered Vaylo's hands and the roof of his jaw.

As Borro fell to the forest floor, something rippled in Vaylo's peripheral vision. Angling his sword cross-body as a shield, he stepped sideways and back. The Unmade shadowed him so swiftly it was as if it was accelerating through a medium thinner than air. Bending slightly at the knees and rotating at the hip, Vaylo presented the edge of his sword to the oncoming blade. Off balance and improperly braced, the *Kil Ji* hit him like a body blow, bringing him to his knees.

I am outmatched, the Dog Lord realized. It was the first time in his fifty-three years he had experienced such a revelation. It filled him with something that—if he allowed it—could instantly ignite into panic. He'd been head-to-head against opponents faster than him before now. He hadn't liked it but he'd survived. Always he had managed to be something *more* than his opponent. More experienced. More brutal. More lawless. This thing, though, this weighted shadow with knowledge of its own destruction in its eyes, was more relentless. And relentless beat everything else hands down.

The Unmade gathered itself above him like ink poured into a glass of water. Vaylo lost track of the voided steel as it moved with speed, black against black. Down the line to the west he could hear soft exhalations gentled by surprise. The sound of men receiving blades through organs.

"To the water!" someone screamed. It might have been Hammie Faa.

It was a good instinct, but Vaylo doubted it would help. The Unmade were too fast. Turn your back on them and you were dead. His hope lay in the block of twelve around Nan and the bairns. They had space to move their weapons and the chance to learn from their fellow warriors' mistakes.

Vaylo thought he heard hoof beats as he swung his sword to vertical, barring his face and heart. He did not have time to wonder what that meant as the Unmade flexed for a strike. Ice cold air riffled the Dog Lord's skin, and then time itself appeared to contract for *Kil Ji* was suddenly there at his chest and although he had watched and paid attention he had not witnessed its journey.

It did not find him unready though. On his knees with his swordhilt braced against his thighs, he had detached his right hand from the grip and pulled out his handknife. He was an old dog and he knew a few tricks, and he had guessed the Unmade would come at him from the side. The instant he saw the Unmade flex, he'd raised the knife to his chest, angling it parallel to the ground so that it formed a cross with the sword. The *Kil Ji* had been aimed at the exact space now occupied by the point of the handknife. The force at contact drove the flat of the handknife's blade deep into Vaylo's ribcage. He heard the soft crack of cartilage, felt a bolt of pain in his heart. His buttocks made contact with the forest floor as he felt a second riffle of cold air. The *Kil Ji* had been withdrawn, but the air meant it was returning and Vaylo was out of plans and luck.

We are chosen by the Stone Gods to guards their borders. A life long-lived is our reward. The Bludd boast, was that what he would remember at the last? An unfulfilled promise by the gods.

This was not a life long-lived.

Lacking the breath and coordination to wield the sword, he let it drop. The knife was his only friend now. Scooting backward on his butt, he braced the handknife against his heart, blade out. The Unmade moved like a cracked whip above him, and for one terrible instant the Dog Lord saw *Kil Ji* point-on.

It was the eye of an Endlord. The cold and black oblivion at the end of all things.

Vaylo knew for himself then what the boy in his vision had known. This was the worst way to die.

I should have guarded the borders.

Thuc. Thuc. Thuc.

Vaylo heard three shots, saw a line of black smoke shoot from the Unmade's torso. The creature rippled as if were made of water. For a moment Vaylo could see through it, see the sumac in the woods beyond. Its hand sprung open and the *Kil Ji* dropped from its grip. No thud marked the knife's landing.

The Dog Lord heard a soft hissing crackle as voided steel began its journey into the earth.

Above him the Unmade failed. It wavered and shrank, smoke venting from its wounds as it lost form. Vaylo dug his heels into the ground and willed himself to standing. He didn't have the stomach to watch that thing's final moments. All around him men were still as shots continued to blast across the clearing from the south. Vaylo did not need to turn to know who fired them. In a night of mistakes, this perhaps had been his worst.

The path they had taken hadn't been cleared by Dhoonesmen or Bluddsmen.

That path belonged to the Sull.

Filled with deep ambivalence and many kinds of fear and pain, Vaylo Bludd went to greet his saviors.

CHAPTER 15

Names

Ash stripped off her dress and waded into the lake. Underfoot the lake bed was muddy and each step raised a swirl of brown muck. When the water reached her thighs, she sucked in a breath and dove. Kicking hard, she swam submerged toward the center of the lake. It felt good, icy and shocking, the water filling spaces around her body that nothing but air and clothing ever touched. Something brushed against her leg and she opened her eyes. Pondweed floated in the murk. An ancient cannon-shaped catfish fled ahead of her into the depths. The lake bed dropped sharply and the catfish disappeared from sight. Ash was tempted to follow, swim into the place where deep water and darkness met, into that coolly shadowed world and never come back.

She floated a moment on the marchlands, her thoughts slowing to incomprehension as the freezing water closed down her mind. A spark of life-force firing deep within her core roused her, and pushing her toes into the mud she propelled herself toward the light.

March, that was the name her foster father had given her.

Not his own name, Iss, but something he'd made up. A march was a border, neither in one land nor the other. She had been named in anticipation of her abilities. She could move between worlds, or that's what the broken man in Ille Glaive had told her. The Blind, the place where the Endlords and their Unmade bided in the darkness, was hers to enter. She still didn't really understand. In the Blind they wanted to touch her, to be chosen and summoned by her, but in this world she could destroy them with a single touch. One hair from her head was enough.

Enough, she told herself, breaking the surface. *A name is just a name.*

Her body felt heavy as she waded back to shore. Afternoon light filtering through the cedars dappled her skin. The air smelled milky and damp. As she toweled herself dry, she could hear mosquitoes humming. She did not hurry to get dressed. Insects never bit her.

Green sheep bones and shards of egg shells littered the bank. The Naysayer said moonsnakes fed here. They were solitary feeders, he told her, except on nights where there was a full moon when they formed covens to hunt large game. Ash shivered and slipped on her dress. She had once seen a stuffed and mounted moonsnake in her foster father's collection: a thirty-foot-long monster with pale iridescent scales.

I wonder if it's mine now. Should I march back to Spire Vanis and claim everything Iss owned?

Frowning at herself, she tied her laces. The linen and whalebone bodice that cinched her dress was deteriorating. Stitches had come unraveled and one of the eyelets had torn. Continual washing had shrunk the fabric and it was tight around her belly and chest. Securing the final knot forced her breasts toward her chin.

Ash's frown deepened. Katia would have approved.

If Katia hadn't been dead.

Katia. Ark Veinsplitter. And now Penthero Iss. Dead.

Snatching up her lynx fur, Ash headed for the trees. The Naysayer had chosen a site in the woods. He would not set camp near open water. Cedars as big as watch towers instantly cut down the light. Walls of wet snow circled the trees, and Ash kicked them down with her boots. Her foster father was dead and there was a hollow place in her chest where feelings should have been. Not numbness, she decided. Absence.

When the Naysayer returned from his ride this morning he had told her the news. "The Surlord is dead. Another has been made."

You did not question the Naysayer. If he had wanted to say more he would have done so. Ash had nodded. She found she could not be still, and had made her way to the water. That was six hours ago, and as she returned to the camp now she was grateful to Mal Naysayer for not following her down to the lake. For most of her life she had been alone in a room. Sometimes, for her peace of mind, she needed to return to that state.

She could smell the Naysayer's cookery as she approached the camp, and guessed he had laid fresh meat across the hot stones in expectation of her return. The thought shrunk the hollow spaces in her chest, and she broke into a run.

The first indication that something was different was the third horse. Mal's blue was standing nose-to-nose with a glossy chestnut stallion. Ash's gaze darted to the center of the camp. Two figures stood with their backs to the campfire. One was the

Naysayer. The other was a stranger. He had a shortbow up and drawn and pointed right at her.

Ash froze. Her first thought was Lan Fallstar, but the silhouette did not match. This man was leaner, and there was something in his stance—a kind of settled awareness—that suggested the experience of age. Slowly, the man lowered his bow arm, easing the tension on the string. As the bow relaxed, the wings of its recurve popped into relief. Even though Ash could not see the man's face she knew he was Sull. All Sull bows at rest issued the same perfectly phrased threat.

The man tipped his head in greeting. He was standing close to the fire. Cold air kept the smoke at his heels. Mal Naysayer stood to the side. He too held a bow, though Ash did not think he had drawn it. Meeting Ash's gaze, he nodded an encouragement. *Come.*

Ash did not move. She realized that both men had been startled by her approach, uncertain of her identity until she cleared the last of the trees. But still. It did not make a girl feel welcome. It made whatever had shrunk in her chest spring back to its original size. There was no family here. Some Sull wanted to protect her. Some wanted her dead. The trick was telling one from another.

"I am Mors Stormwielder, Son of the Sull and Son of the Longwalker." The stranger pitched his voice in the low range men used to calm horses. He rocked the bow in his grip as he spoke, presenting the string toward her in the Sull sign of truce. "This Sull asks pardon for drawing his weapon against you."

Hadn't she heard that before, from Lan Fallstar? Ash decided the only thing that mattered here was the Naysayer's presence. He wouldn't allow anyone to harm her.

She stalled her response, a technique she had learned from watching her foster father deal with the grangelords. The longer Iss made them wait upon his word the more anxious they were to hear what he had to say. "I am Ash March, Daughter of the Sull. I've ridden one of your horses across breaking ice."

Stormwielder barely blinked, but she could tell she had surprised him. Vertebrae aligned in his upper spine. "Did she serve you well?"

"*He* did."

Ash understood then how her foster father must have felt during those long tense meetings when superior knowledge allowed him to score a point. It gave her confidence. The Sull might not be human but you could still better them.

And he knew it. Raising his eyebrows, he smiled softly and said, "A friend of Angus Lok's is a friend of mine."

So Mors Stormwielder had given away only one stallion. Ash remembered the beautiful bay horse that had belonged to Angus. That horse had saved her life. After she fled from Spire Vanis with Angus and Raif, Iss had sent Marafice Eye to pursue her. When Eye and his sept finally closed in on them at the Black Spill, Angus had sent Ash and the bay onto the fragile shore ice to escape. *"Trust him,"* Angus had told her. *"He'll lead you a fine dance. When all is quiet I'll call you back."* Ash had trusted Angus completely. There had been something in his face. He had not been prepared to lose her.

She took a step towards Mors Stormwielder. "Do you have news of Angus?"

The Stormwielder's eyes were the last color gray could be before it lapsed into black. His skin was deeply pigmented with metallic ores, and his cheek bones were so prominent they created undercuts all the way down to his jaw. A vertical scar sliced the length of his nose, perfectly centered like a seam. The scar was cured silver with age. Ash wondered if it was *Dras Xaxu*, the First Cut.

"Angus is *xalla nul*."

Xalla nul. Ash knew the phrase, it meant cast adrift. Orphaned. Suddenly aware that her hair was a wet sheet around her neck, she shivered. "His family?"

"*Mor n'ura*."

Ash had to think about the words. *Mor* meant dead. *Ura*, peace or rest. Dead without rest.

"They were murdered?" She couldn't keep the horror from her voice. She knew Angus Lok's family. His wife Darra had welcomed her into their home. Ash knew how his daughters looked when they ate their dinner, how they sounded when they teased one another and laughed. She had wanted to be one of them. She had wanted a piece of that life.

Mors Stormwielder did not speak his reply. He pushed back the cuff of his dark green saddle coat and bared the skin on his wrist. Four partially healed wounds cut lengthwise down his lower arm. Letting scars. The Sull paid for what they valued in blood.

Ash shuddered. She recalled the journey to Angus's house, the caution the ranger had taken along the way, the paths he had abandoned and the false trails he had laid. Angus Lok's greatest fear had been leading an enemy to his gate.

"Who killed them?"

Mors slid back his cuff. "This Sull does not know."

Ash heard the words as a warning. *Do not ask more.* She wondered if she already knew the answer. Marafice Eye had tracked her and Angus as far as Ille Glaive. Sarga Veys had been riding with Eye's sept, and Veys was capable of all kinds of inhuman acts. It was possible her foster father's sorcerer had tracked her all the way to Angus' door.

The setting sun made long shadows for the cedars. Mal Naysayer had said the largest trees were over a thousand years old. Ash was aware of the weight of them. A dark mass pressing down on the earth. "Where is Angus now?"

"*Emori.*"

The name, spoken by Mors Stormwielder, caused Mal Naysayer to lower his head. Both men held themselves still for a moment and Ash had the sense of comradeship between them. These men had knowledge of this place.

"Angus grieves," Mors explained.

Ash nodded slowly in comprehension. To the Sull grief was a location as much as a state of mind.

"Come. Eat," Mors said, stepping aside to make room by the fire. "The moon rises and we are three. Let us keep company in its light."

Ash crossed the clearing and sat on one of the rugs laid out before the fire. She was weary, and found herself content to let the Sull warriors tend the fire and feed the horses. Mors groomed the white with a bone comb. The little gelding whickered and nuzzled his neck. Mal Naysayer built up the fire, feeding it splinters of translucent coal. Ash wondered where he had been this morning. She had not seen any sign of habitation since they left the Fortress of the Hard Gate. Something must be close though. The Naysayer had possessed no such fuel last night.

The Sull were silent as they worked, their movements efficient and well practiced. A split and gutted deer carcass had been set to freeze on a snowbank. When Mors was done with the gelding, he pressed the carcass to test its lividity. Dissatisfied, he turned it over.

Ash tried to recall what else Angus had told her about Mors Stormwielder. She knew the stallion had been payment for a debt, and that meant Mors had owed a lot to Angus Lok. Blood and stallions were the highest currency of the Sull.

"You are not a Far Rider?" she asked as he returned to the fire.

Mors exchanged a glance with the Naysayer, and Ash guessed she had asked an impertinent question. When he spoke displeasure showed in his voice. "*Dralku* are called to different paths."

Dralu meant warrior, or something close to it. *Drakka* meant one who watches. *Dralku*, Ash decided, must be one who both watches and protects.

Accepting a cup of broth from the Naysayer, she tried another question. "Who is the Longwalker?"

Again, there was a glance between him and the Naysayer. Muscles in the Naysayer's left arm—his letting arm— twitched.

"She gave birth to this Sull," Stormwielder said quietly. "And the One Who Leads." Squatting by the fire, he turned his acutely-angled face toward the flames. Seeing his features this close, Ash had the sense that he was more alien, more wholly Sull than the Naysayer and Lan Fallstar. His pupils were fully dilated and something inhumanly intricate was visible at the back of his eyes. "The Longwalker accepted *Dras Morthu* at the Lake of Many Minks. The lake is far from our paths and we did not find her . . . remains for many days."

Several things struck Ash as he spoke. Although Mors had chosen the words *remains* for her benefit, she guessed the information about the lake and the body was not meant for her, but for Mal Naysayer. It was possibly his first time hearing the details. Second, Stormwielder spoke Common with an ease that the Naysayer lacked. He'd almost certainly spent more time in the West. Third, in most places in the Known Lands, Mors Stormwielder would be considered a prince. He was brother to the leader . . . which made the woman who had died mother to a king.

Ash finished the broth. It was rich with blood and liver juices and her body craved it. "I am sorry for your loss."

"*Xhalia ex nihl.*"

All becomes nothing. They were silent after that, eating organ meat seasoned with cardamom, and mushrooms fried in deer fat. The temperature dropped and ice mist sizzled as it drifted across the flames. Ash thought she tasted salt in the air and wondered if they were close to the coast. She knew so little. No Sull she had ever met liked to talk. To them, to speak of something was to reduce it. As she watched the moonlight turn the mist into silver haze Ash understood that mostly they were right.

They had not served her well, though. She had risked her life to become one of them—her human blood drained from her body to make way for Sull blood—but they had not helped her understand what it meant to be Sull.

"Your mother," she said to Mors Stormwielder, "will she go to the Far Shore?"

"What do you know of the Far Shore, Ash March?"

"I was told it's where Sull hope to go when they die."

"We dream." He paused. "In perfect proportion to our fear."

"That all becomes nothing?"

Mors Stormweilder's smile was brief and sad. He was sitting cross-legged on a worn blue rug he had taken from his saddle pack. A random field of stars was picked out in gray thread on the silk. "Did you ever see Raif Sevrance make a heart-kill?"

Ash blinked, barely understanding where the question had come from. What had the Naysayer told Stormwielder? She glanced at the Far Rider, but his ice-blue gaze gave away nothing.

Mors watched her decide upon her answer, as she weighed one loyalty against another. Motioning toward the freezing deer carcass, he said, "This Sull heart-kills also."

Oh. That changed things. Ash ran a hand through the mist. Tiny white moths had begun to gather around the flames and they fluttered in the current she created. "The first time I saw Raif Sevrance I watched him heart-kill five men."

Something in the glance Mors shared with the Naysayer made Ash wish she hadn't spoken. Thinking back on the events of last winter, she realized that the only thing the Naysayer knew for certain about Raif Sevrance was that Raif had heart-killed a wolf.

"Did he use a bow?" Mors' tone was brisk.

"Yes."

"And he killed them one after another?"

Ash nodded.

Mors was silent. Her answers had not pleased him.

"But you do what Raif does," she said, half challenging, half hopeful.

"This Sull does not heart-kill men."

"But—"

"Only game."

Ash felt tricked. "You can't do what Raif does then." It was not a question and Mors did not answer. "No one can. Is that why he's so important to you?"

Something shrieked in the darkness beyond the clearing. Something killing or being killed.

Mors said, "It is written *Mor Drakka* will destroy us."

Ash looked to the Naysayer. "Yet you helped us. You helped him. "

Mal Naysayer inhaled over several seconds, filling the deepest levels of his lungs with air. He had not spoken since she'd returned to the clearing and Ash guessed he did not want to speak now. His voice when it came was soft and weary. "Daughter, this Sull is proud to have saved you. Your companion . . . this Sull cannot say if it was ill done or well done. Word from the north is that the clansman has taken possession of *Sul Ji*, the God Sword. This fills us with fear and hope."

A moth *shush*ed past Ash's ear. "I don't understand."

"The Naysayer speaks of the sword humans call Loss," Mors said. "It is ours. We forged it in another Age, on another continent, in the Mountains of Giants. Hala, the First God, let his blood for its making. He sent its metals to us through the black void of space."

"A meteorite?"

Mors smiled, flashing strong blue-white teeth. "Yes, *xal ji*. Our most precious swords are forged with steel that fell from the sky."

"You want the sword back?"

Mors and the Naysayer exchanged a glance. In the silence that followed Ash understood the deep pride and sorrow of the Sull. If they wanted the sword back, they would take it. Raif Sevrance could not stand against them. How could he? He was one clansman, one human, against the might of the Sull.

He could heart-kill like a machine and still not stop them. Yet they wouldn't take the sword from him, and Ash was beginning to understand why. The questions Mors asked were her answer. Mors had needed to know for himself if the rumors about Raif were true. She had confirmed them: Raif was *Mor Drakka*, the one who could heart-kill men.

It wasn't hard to imagine a sword made from a god in Raif's hands. It wasn't hard to imagine what damage he could do with such a sword.

"Loss." She barely said the word out loud, but Mors heard it.

He absorbed it like a blow. After a minute or so he surprised her by speaking. "Thousands of years ago, during the Battle of Dammed Falls, a man, a human, wielding *Sul Ji* struck an Endlord. We do not say the Endlord was destroyed, but it was *xisa*. Displaced. It turned the battle. Until then we were failing and the enemy was pressing us hard. The armies of Men had called a retreat. When the Endlord fell all changed. The Unmade broke ranks. Thousands fell along with their Lord: we do not know why. We fought in chaos and darkness. The Sand Men lost seven in ten that night. We lost nine in ten. Yet we lived and the story of that night is told around the Heart Fires. Loss displaced an Endlord . . . and the one we believed to be *Mor Drakka* delivered the blow."

Here it was. The balance. Fear with hope. *Mor Drakka* might be the one who extinguishes the Sull, but he was also the one who could save them.

For a reason she did not fully understand, she thought of her foster father. It occurred to her that Iss had possessed some knowledge of Sull history—enough to try and enslave his own

Reach—yet Iss had used that knowledge solely for his own gain. The Sull were not like him. *They fight for us all.*

Out loud she said, "Why is it the Sull's duty to fight the Unmade?"

Moths had formed a galaxy around the fire, and soft hisses sounded as stray wings touched flames. Mors flexed his left hand. It was a small thing, something one might do to stretch out stiff fingers, but Ash knew straightaway it was more. Hairs on her neck rose, letting cool air brush her skin. The moths ceased orbiting and fled.

Mors took a breath and then spoke. "We fight because we have looked into the night sky and seen the absence there. Men call the nights when there is no moon new moon. We call them *mor lun*. The end of moon. Every two days in twenty-eight, we look up and see the future. The world is dark and the stars burn cold and give no light. We teach our children that what is created will be destroyed. *Xhalia ex nihl.* All becomes nothing. We fight to slow oblivion, not halt it. *Xana lun*, our warriors cry as we ride into battle. The moon will rise this night."

Ash was stirred but did not show it. She wasn't sure she trusted Mors Stormwielder, and she wasn't sure why he was here. "Why must you fight alone?"

It was the Naysayer who shook his head. "Nay, daughter. In other Ages we fought with men and those who are not men; the old races, the Ice Trappers and Sand Men and the Hounded. We seek allies, but we have learned caution. Allies turn. Territory is lost. We fight the longest and our losses mount more swiftly than our allies'. We are vulnerable at battle's end. Allies trusted with our maps are tempted. *If we do not take this land*, they tell themselves, *others will.*

"Opportunities are seized. Territory is lost and we retreat. North, always north, and east. What is left is mountains, forest and shore. Our Heart Fires have burned on the shore of the Night River for five thousand years. We will not give them up."

It was a lot of words for the Naysayer, and Ash could see they had unsettled him. He rose and walked from the fire. Within seconds he was swallowed by the darkness. One of the horses whickered as he passed the corral.

Out of respect for him, Ash waited before speaking. Silence, she was beginning to understand, was a language in itself to the Sull.

After a time, she said to Mors, "Even if you don't ally with the clans and Mountain Cities they'll seize your land. My foster father wanted a slice of it."

Mors looked at her carefully. "Are you Sull?"

She felt a beat of fear. The Naysayer was gone and she was alone with a stranger. Tilting back her head, she revealed *Dras Xaxu*, the First Cut, under her jaw. "Look at my eyes," she said, lowering her chin. "What color are they?"

"Blue."

"For seventeen years they were gray."

They weighed each other up. Age showed in the Sull as a hardening of muscle and skin. Mors Stormweilder's face had that hardness. Time and experience had sucked away unnecessary flesh.

"When you speak of us you say *you* not *we*."

"I am an outsider. Your people do not trust me."

"Choose a name."

Again she felt the prickle of hairs along her neck. She had thought much the same thing at the lake, yet as Mors spoke she understood it went deeper than distancing herself from her foster father. Mors Stormwielder was challenging her to be Sull.

He had come here as her judge.

Light dimmed as the fire shrank to a smolder. The forest was quiet. Mors rose to tend the horses. There was nothing to say. She either made herself Sull or she would never see the Heart Fires. Mors Stormwielder, brother to He Who Leads, was their gatekeeper. Strange how it was all clear now. This meeting was not by chance. The Naysayer had deliberately slowed the journey, waiting for Mors Stormwielder to intercept them. During the entire time they'd been speaking, Mors had been judging her.

And found her wanting.

Ash pushed her hands through her hair. The lake water had left it heavy and smooth. She felt tired, and sore in strange places. Her chest and armpits ached; probably from swimming. On impulse she stood and headed for the trees.

Moonlight bouncing off the mist lit the points of the cedars. Wanting to avoid the Naysayer, Ash turned north.

You will be able to walk the borderlands at will, hear and sense the creatures that live there, and your flesh will become rakhar dan, *Reachflesh, which is held sacred by the Sull.*

Heritas Cant's words, spoken half a year ago in Ille Glaive, kept repeating in her head. The broken man had not known why her flesh had value to the Sull. He had not anticipated that it could destroy the Unmade.

Jal Rakhar. The Reach.

The Sull *did* have a name for her, and she liked it about as much as the name March. So what should she call herself? She wanted to feel the warmth of the Heart Fires. She wanted to understand what the Sull saw when they looked at the night sky. She wanted to hear the word *daughter* again. It was a big lonely world and her foster father was dead. What had Mors said about Angus? *Xalla nul*. Cast adrift. She was one thread away from the same fate.

She had no family waiting back home. There was no home, just a place where she'd been held prisoner and hadn't known it. This was all she had.

Turning, she headed back for the camp.

She had chosen her new name.

CHAPTER 16

In the Star Chamber

They fed. Their great jaw detached and their teeth ratcheted on to the newborn foal and began pulling it down their gullet. Saliva jetted from the roof of their mouth to grease the motion, and when the head reached their throat banks of muscle contracted in waves. As the muscle drew the foal deeper, they began constricting its spine. When the head reached the digestive tract they allowed themselves to relax. The largest section was through. Everything else—shoulders, hips, legs—could be crushed.

They settled into a languor as the full length of the foal was enclosed. A half-moon was up and its perfect blue light provided a second, no lesser, nourishment. They felt heavy and overstretched and content. Horse blood pooled at the back of their throat and they would taste it later with relish. The night world was theirs. They owned and controlled it.

Sidewinding across sparkling snow, they returned to their den to sleep.

Cold water thrown at force onto his face woke him from profoundly strange dreams. He felt himself being peeled away from Moonsnake and grafted onto another life.

It was hot here. The world was crammed with too much color and movement. All stillness and purity was gone. Someone touched him and he lashed out. A startled cry informed him of the success of the contact. He received a single jab of pain to the meat of his upper arm in return.

The world immediately blurred. A word floated to him. *Drugged.* He blinked, remembered some things he had no desire to remember, then watched as they prepared him to fight.

Two Sull worked with the economy of men who had performed their task more than once. They pulled him upright, toweled him dry and strapped armor plates to the planes of his chest, arms and legs. It was like being buried alive. They ran a line of grease around his neck and plugged the helm against his face. Straps were cinched at the back of his head. Indignation was a fury in his blood, but his body would not obey the command to hurt the men who did this. Among the memories he recalled one that was useful: this state wore off quickly. Soon it would be possible to strike.

The Sull returned him to the pallet and left. A clangor of rusted iron echoed through the chamber as a bolt was engaged behind the door, and then silence. Raif, for he recalled his name now, lay flat on his back and stared at the traprock ceiling, waiting for the numbness in his limbs to wear off.

They, Moonsnake named the Sull. In the world of moon and stars they were beneath her. They claimed to own the night, but they could not see in the darkness as she could see in the darkness. They could not move and strike in perfect silence and live month after month upon the moon-blued snow. Her contempt fueled Raif's anger. How dare they hold him. He was *Mor Drakka*. They needed him to fight the Unmade.

Kill them and we will feed.

Current passed along Raif's body. His legs twitched and the tendons in his fingers contracted. Objects floating across his vision began to slow. His body was becoming his own again. They drugged him in different ways, he'd noticed, sometimes forcing sleep, other times subduing him while they worked on his body. He wondered if they still poisoned his water. His piss always smelled like the chemicals his mother used to soften hides.

Da.

The word helped hold him in place. It was the reason not to return to Moonsnake. Da was dead. Mace Blackhail had killed him. Through his, Raif Sevrance's own negligence, Mace Blackhail still lived and ruled in the clan.

Kill him and we'll swallow him whole.

Raif turned his head a fraction and looked around the chamber. Traprock blocks, blackened with age and damp, encased the tomb-like space. Moonholes in the upper wall and ceiling let in circles of pale gray light. Part of the chamber was sunk belowground, and water seeped through cracks in the mortar. The dome of the night sky had been deeply carved across the ceiling and walls. The quarter moon rising in the east was the only feature he recognized. The stars and constellations might have been from a different world.

A *thunk* sounded on the far side of the door as the bolt was drawn back. Raif looked wildly around the room. Where was the mark? Hadn't he kept a record of the time that had passed? He had a clear memory of scoring lines with his thumbnail— one for every day. Had they scrubbed it clean from the wall?

The door opened and the two Sull who had battle dressed him earlier entered. This time they did not need their hands free to tend him. Swords were drawn and the brilliant white light of meteor steel sent sparks across the room.

"Up."

The command was spoken by the Sull with the hard purple-blue eyes and copper skin. His nostrils flared fiercely as he spoke, and Raif wondered if his contempt was for his task or his prisoner. Or both.

Raif's own contempt rose in response.

They are beneath us.

He swung his legs off the pallet, fought the nausea. Stood.

"Out," the Copper One said. Both he and his companion stood wide of the pallet, leaving clear space between Raif and the door.

Raif noticed the other Sull, the younger one with golden eyes and deep slots cut in his earlobes, glance toward the water pail in the corner of the room. Was he checking if any had been drunk?

The thought slid away as Raif concentrated on moving his body. The drug was wearing off quickly now, but it left shocks and tingles and patches of numbness that had to be managed in order to walk.

As he passed the younger Sull, Raif calculated the probability of a successful strike. Nights hunting with Moonsnake had shifted the way he saw things. Surprise was everything to her. To achieve it she worked the angles and tangents, finding the blind spot and using it to lay a short and perfect line of strike. It was survival in its purest form. Calculate the correct angle and she would eat.

Raif headed through the doorway. He could see a possible

line of strike. The younger Sull was holding his two-handed sword with a single hand, his right. Smash the left quickly enough, driving close to his body, and the Sull could be thrown off center and denied sufficient space to wheel the sword. There were two problems with this though. First, Raif didn't know if he had the necessary speed while his body was still jerking back to life. And second, Copper One. The older Sull could cross the room while possession of the younger Sull's sword was still unresolved.

Climbing a short series of steps, Raif emerged into the forest. It was dusk. Broken sections of wall and paving tiles set amidst the ferns told him something had once stood over the chamber that had become his prison. Absurdly Raif recalled something Angus had once told him about Sull fortresses: *They cut perfectly aligned moonholes through every floor and ceiling so no matter what level they are on they can look up and see the sky.*

Bloodwood saplings as slender as reeds stirred in the wind. Raif smelled wood and tar smoke. The Sull camp was close and to the east, the rayskin canopy just to the west. A third Sull walked him at spear point to the paved circle he had first seen from the cage. A drum was beating and torches had been lit. Sull were gathering. Raif recognized the tall not-quite-perfect form of Yiselle No Knife. Her lips had been painted blue-red and her eyes were inhumanly bright.

Have I done this before? He felt a moment of free fall, as if the ground vanished from under him. The circle, the torches, No Knife: it all looked familiar but he couldn't be sure. Abruptly, he remembered the thumb marks on the chamber wall. Had he remembered to look for them? A muscle in his heart missed its cue and he felt the sickening suction of panic. What was happening here? He was Raif Sevrance from Clan Blackhail and this was madness.

Kill them. We must feed.

The spear point prompted the back of his neck, directing him into the circle. Raif spun and smashed the spear to the ground. His jaw sprung apart and suddenly he no longer knew what he was doing. He hesitated, and in that instant the Sull drew his sword. The body armor strapped across Raif's chest *bowed* as it took the point of meteor steel. The shock wave rolled across Raif's rib cage, punching his lungs. He blacked out, stumbled, somehow managed to keep on his feet. The Sull was on him, guiding his sword toward the crack between Raif's chest and back plates; left side, oblique angle, straight for the heart.

"Xaxu ull," the Sull murmured as he slid the point of his blade a third of an inch into the meat between Raif's third and fourth rib. First blood.

It took a moment for Raif to realize the blade wasn't going any deeper. There were rules here he didn't understand. Dropping to his knees, he waited for the pain to register. His body was working—blood was seeping through his undershirt—but although he was aware of the site of the cut he didn't feel any sharpness or sting.

"Into the ring." The Sull had cleaned his blade of blood and he used it to point the way forward. Raif didn't understand the rules but he understood that by tagging his opponent's heart the Sull had regained what had been lost when his spear was forced from his grip. Sull pride and clan pride were identical in this.

It seemed an important thought and Raif tried to hold on to it as he took up position in the center of the ring. A sword had been laid on the ground for him, its blade aligned with true north. Again he had the sense that he had done this before, fought here before, but the memory wouldn't dislodge. Night was falling and the surrounding forest was as deep and vast as the Rift. Impurities in the tar made the torches burn green. As Raif picked up the sword he caught sight of something on the blade. With a shock he realized it was his own reflection. The face plate made him a monster. The armor was thickly segmented like dragonhide and the person living behind it looked trapped. For the briefest instant Raif recalled Raven Lord. Armed and armored for thousands of years, dead beneath the ice.

Raif shuddered

"You failed last time, Clansman," Yiselle No Knife said quietly from just beyond the circle. "Failed yourself and your friend." She stepped to the side, revealing a small huddled figure behind her. Addie Gunn.

"Fuck them, Raif," he shouted. He was shivering and he no longer had a right hand.

Raif took a step back. Disorientation and horror hit him like a blast. What had he done? Addie's hand was gone. That was real—he could see the bandages at the stump of the cragsman's arm—but he couldn't remember how it had happened.

"You lost," No Knife told him. With a small movement of her gloved hand she ordered Addie to be removed. Raif's gaze jumped to the cragsman's face as he was pulled away. Addie Gunn was waiting for him. There was water in Addie's eyes but the gaze behind it was clear and searching. He was a sheepman, Raif understood instantly, watching out for his sheep.

Who would watch out for him?

I will. Watcher of the Dead.

You didn't have to understand the rules of a game to win it. Raif weighed the sword, and cut air to get its balance. Addie's face was no longer visible but Raif tracked the cragsman's silhouette as he was escorted away from the fight circle. A second silhouette caught his eye and he tracked that also as it moved in the opposite direction. His night vision was up and running and his body felt wholly his own. Even pain was returning to him. The wound on his side tingled unpleasantly. He welcomed it. It was unnerving not to know when you were hurt.

The Sull were silent as the figure who Raif now realized was his opponent entered the circle. He was a Sull warrior armed with meteor steel. His chest armor had been reinforced above the heart with a raised plate embedded with diamonds. Raif had never seen one before but he'd heard clansmen speak of them. Steel eaters, they were called. Even a passing glance could ruin a sword.

The Sull glittered like a form emerging from water. His gaze rose to meet Raif's as he drew closer, and information passed between them.

"*Xhalia ex nihl,*" the Sull murmured. All becomes nothing. It sounded like a promise, not a prayer.

Straightaway he struck, wedging his sword into the space below Raif's gut. Raif raised his guard. As steel chopped into steel, he leaned back. The Sull drove forward, pressing the advantage. Unwilling to use time retracting his sword for a full strike, the Sull needle-jabbed at Raif's thigh. He was low and he was off balance and his head and shoulders were wide open. Raif saw the angle. His jaw sprung apart. Wheeling his sword behind his back and over his shoulder, he sent it axing into the Sull's right shoulder blade. The Sull was in the process of darting back and the blow caught him a fraction of a second too late. Power was lost. His shoulder plate bowed, instantly distributing the force across the bone. Raif dislodged the sword as the Sull worked to keep his footing.

As Raif's muscles shortened for a second strike, the Sull found his balance and raised his sword. He was strong and he was fast and his armor was superior to anything cast in the clans. Raif registered a flicker in the Sull's iron gray eyes and anticipated the line he would take. Raif perceived the available space as a series of hollow shapes waiting to be occupied. *I've seen this before; done this before. Did I fail?*

Raif scanned the crowd, looking for sign of Addie. The Sull launched a series of brutal attacks, sending weight into the final foot of meteor steel and driving it into Raif's sword. Raif struggled to hold his guard. Each of his blocks was a split second too late and his body took a beating as it absorbed the full power of each blow. He could see what he had to do, but he didn't have the speed to do it. The heart was in his sights— red and close—and even with the diamond plate it was vulnerable. Every time he struck, the Sull exposed space above, below and to the side of his heart.

A better swordsman could have finished this by now. Frustrated, Raif swiped at the Sull's ribcage. A high-pitched screech sounded as a jagged edge of diamond peeled a curl of steel from Raif's sword. Raif smelled hot metal. As he pulled back his sword, he saw the brilliant flash of meteor steel. It was closer than it should be, he thought stupidly. Cold air whipped against his upper arm. He felt warm wetness . . . waited for the pain.

A single jab at the back of his neck made his knees buckle

under him. He hit the ground. Hard. It occurred to him as he blacked out that he still waiting for the pain.

Moonsnake wound through the darkness. She was close—closer than she'd ever been to the settlement. The Sull were away from their tents and livestock. Fires smoked, unattended. Solitary figures armed with bows patrolled the perimeter. They were alert and watchful but it was easy to avoid them. She tasted horse sweat in the air but her appetite didn't rise in response to it. Land fowl caged in a pen were more to her taste tonight.

Raif slid into her heart and she flexed in welcome. The cool and muscular substance of her body had become a familiar place. They were old friends now, co-conspirators and hunters. Without missing a beat of their shared heart they glided downwind of the camp.

Others were alert to the absences in the camp. Creatures with more reason to be wary of the Sull were testing the boundaries. Tasting fox and wolf on the night currents, they opened a gland in their underbelly and smeared a warning onto the snow. Ours. Keep away. The horse corral was a square mass ahead of them and they knew it would be easy to enter. In anticipation of moon snakes, Sull had hammered wood planks a foot into the ground. That did not concern them. With only one Sull guarding the corral, they could climb the fence and rip off a mare's leg before detection. Panicking horses—the need to release them and shoot around them—would aid their escape.

As they approached the bird pen, they read the wind and adjusted their line of strike. They, the Sull, placed high value on their horses and watched them even when the camp was deserted. The land fowl they valued only as food and the pen, though secured, was unguarded. A wolf was close, ghosting the same vector, staying behind the wind. It would not approach but would wait and see if anything could be scavenged once they were done.

Ignoring it, they hunted.

And fed.

Raif came to, blinking water from his eyes. A Sull with copper skin and cheekbones as blunt as shields, stood over him with an empty bucket. A second Sull, younger and more golden, stood in the open doorway. He was armed with a razor-edge spear.

"Up," commanded the Copper One.

Raif swung his feet off the pallet. His vision blurred as he moved and he sat still for a moment before standing. His clothes were soaking, and there was an uncomfortable tightness in his left arm. A thick layer of bandages prevented him from seeing what was wrong. As he gathered strength to stand a voice called from beyond the door.

"*Xhi hal.*" Leave him

The Copper One exchanged glances with the younger Sull and nodded. They left and bolted the door.

Raif sat on the pallet and waited. He had a bad feeling. Light traveling through the moonholes told him it was after midday. Suddenly he recalled that he had made thumb marks in the stone—one for every day he'd spent here—and he stood and searched the walls of the chamber. Nothing. Crouching close to the bloodwood door, he scraped a mark in the traprock with his thumbnail, exposing a line of lighter-colored stone. He looked at it a long time, thinking. Fixing its position in his head, he stood.

Two leather buckets stood on the opposite side of the door.

One was empty, the other full of water. He pissed in the empty bucket and drank from the full one. He wasn't hungry. It seemed his stomach was working on digesting something. He searched for a recent memory of eating, came up blank.

"Raif Sevrance of Clan Blackhail." He spoke so he wouldn't forget. "Drey. Effie. Da. Ash."

Inhaling softly, he remembered another name. "Addie."

You failed last time, Clansman. Failed yourself and your friend.

"No." Seizing his left arm, Raif tore off the bandage. A dark red wound, perfectly straight and expertly stitched with horse gut, ran along the muscle at the top of his arm.

No.

Small, jagged bits of memory returned to him. Addie's right hand. Gone. Barium-rich tar burning green. A swordfight. Lost.

Raif shook his head. He hadn't been fast enough.

Instinctively he began to move, pacing at first and then dashing the short distance across the chamber. If he leapt high enough, he could brush the stars on the dome ceiling with his fingertips. He picked one as he ran and jumped to touch it. His body ached and trembled, but he ignored it.

He hadn't been fast enough. And he couldn't bear to think what that meant to Addie Gunn.

CHAPTER 17

The Lost Clan

"That's the site of the old roundhouse."

Bram Cormac didn't need to follow Hew Mallin's direction to recognize the spot where the Lost Clan's roundhouse had once stood. A perfect circle of white heather marked the spot. So the legend was true then. Dhoone had raised it to the ground and then salted the earth to prevent anything from growing on the site. The white heather, it was told, had seeded three hundred years later. A blessing from Hammada, mother of the gods.

"What say we camp there?" Hew Mallin's hard, weathered face gave away nothing, but Bram suspected a test.

To spend the night sleeping on the white heather of the Lost Clan was the last thing any sane clansmen would want to do. Bram took a breath, exhaled. Ever since he had forsaken his oath to Castlemilk, he'd had the sensation he was falling.

A month later and he still hadn't come to land.

"I'll get some firewood." His voice sounded a bit strange so he covered it by sliding from his horse. "I'll meet you at the camp."

Nothing got by Mallin, but often it suited the ranger to act otherwise. Taking Gabbie's reins from Bram, he said only, "Take your weapon."

It was a struggle to free the big two-handed sword from its mounting across Gabbie's rump. Suspecting that another struggle would be necessary to cross-mount it against his back, Bram tucked the sheathed blade under his arm and quickly turned away.

He was beginning to hate Rob's sword.

The Lost Clan was in the highlands northeast of Dhoone and west of Bludd. They were on the northern edge of the clanholds with only a stretch of Copper Hills separating them from the Rift. The wind was high and fresh and half of the snow had melted. Needle-thin streams and glint ponds flashed in the late day sun. Bram was glad to be afoot, though the weight and bulk of the greatsword slowed him. Any time spent delaying camp on one of the most haunted and hallowed spots in the clanholds was just fine with him.

The ground was soft underfoot and most of the fallen wood was slimy. Tall, upright trees didn't grow in this part of the highlands; Bram had to make do with pieces of wind-stunted yew and white pine. Lines of smoke rose in the hills just to the east. He wondered if they marked the site of one of the settlements that had sprung up in the disputed territory of the Lost Clan. He liked the idea of new clans forming, though he was pretty sure it wouldn't be long before Robbie sent bluecloaks to wipe them out. *They know the risks*, Bram told himself. The question was: How would their removal change the game?

Bram thrust a length of yew with the needles still attached into his pack. Every day he was sounding a little less like clan and a little more like the Phage.

He glanced north toward the campsite. Mallin had set up

his tent dead center of the ring. Instantly aware that Bram's gaze was upon him, the ranger turned and tipped his bearskin hat. Knowing he was outmatched, Bram raised his hand in response.

Hew Mallin was breaking him, and he, Bram Cormac, had no choice but to be broken. He'd agreed to it. It wasn't enough that his oath and ties to the clanholds were severed. Old loyalties and ways of thinking had to be destroyed along with them too. Camping on the site of the Lost Clan's roundhouse was part of that destruction.

Strange how you could agree to something, know it was coming, and still be unprepared when it came. Stuffing the last space in his daypack with pine-cones, Bram headed for the camp.

The Lost Clan's roundhouse had been built on high meadowland with the River Sigh guarding its southeastern approach and the Copper Hills like a fortress to the north. Bram wondered how it had been broken. Surely it would have been difficult to take by surprise?

Mallin was skinning an ice hare as Bram approached. They'd been camping out for the past four nights and Bram fell into the routine of building the fire, setting water to boil and brushing down the horses. Both Gabbie and Mallin's stallion were grazing on the sacred heather. Bram frowned, but they ignored him. He hoped it would grow back.

Mallin was a good cook and once the fire was settled he laid the spiced and quartered hare on the hot rocks. Bram's mouth watered as the fat began to sizzle and the sweet aroma of thyme and wild garlic was released with the steam.

"Keep your bow at hand," Mallin said, leaning back against his bedroll.

Bram rose to fetch his bow and arrow case from his saddlebag. The sun was failing in the west, sending out a blaze of red light. He wondered what they were doing here, on the edge of the clanholds. When he had accepted Mallin's offer to join the Phage he had imagined they would travel to the mountain cities—Trance Vor, Morning Star, Spire Vanis, Ille Glaive—places that were worlds apart from the clans. Instead they had traveled through the very places he knew best: Dhoone, Wellhouse and Castlemilk.

It had been at Wellhouse where Mallin had made the decision to head north. They had been working their way east from Dhoone when they met a group of tied Wellmen on the Bluddroad. They were miners, heading west to look for work. Mallin had spoken to them at length. He was a good listener and he knew how to make people talk. Bram couldn't tell what piece of information had caught Mallin's interest—the ranger always held his cards close to his chest—but Bram did know that something Mallin learned from one of the old miners had been enough to change his course. Before the miners were out of sight, Mallin had turned north.

They'd spent the next five days and nights at Ebb's stovehouse on the River Ebb, north of the Wellhold. Hannie May, the stovemaster, had welcomed Mallin like an old friend. She'd turfed a Croserman from his quarters to make room for him, and always gave him the best table at supper—the one closest to her stove. Hannie kept a rookery above her stables and Mallin had taken Bram up there the first evening and showed him how the Phage sent messages by bird.

"That's my beauty there," Mallin said, pointing to a raven with glossy blue-black plumage and yellow claws and toes that was perched in a large bamboo cage with other corvids. "Take her out."

Bram had hesitated. The bird looked mean.

"Take her firmly by the breast. Talk to her. Don't hesitate."

Bram unhooked the little brass catch that held the cage door closed. He had no idea how to talk to a bird so he talked to her like a horse instead. "Easy, girl. Want some treats? How about some carrots, eh?" To reach the raven he had to slide his hand past a magpie and a blue jay. The blue jay looked ready to peck him so he quickly grabbed the raven.

"That's her throat."

Bram adjusted his grip. The bird was was lively and surprisingly light in his hand. She *chuffed* as he stroked her head.

"See the collar on her left foot. That's where the message goes. Here." Mallin slipped Bram a slender roll of paper. "Push it in."

Bram was aware he had not been asked to read it. The collar was made of a metal he wasn't familiar with; ash gray and very light. He molded the paper to fit the hollow ring and with a little bit of jiggling managed to slot it in place.

"Now we seal it with resin." Mallin took a small vial from one of the pouches in his saddle coat, uncorked it, and handed it to Bram. "Work quickly. It hardens on contact with air."

Pressing the bird's body against his lap to still her, Bram poured a line of resin onto the ring. It was yellow-red and smelled strongly of pine. Some got onto the bird's foot and onto his fingers. It tingled as it hardened, pulling on his skin.

"Wipe it off." Mallin handed him a strip of linen soaked in alcohol. "Otherwise she'll peck it and might damage the load."

"Won't she peck the collar anyway?"

"No. She's had it since she was a chick. It's normal to her, but bits of hardened resin aren't."

Bram took it in. He was hungry to know more about the Phage but had learned that Mallin never revealed anything before he was ready. "How will she know where to go?"

"She'll home." Mallin's yellow-green eyes narrowed and Bram guessed he wouldn't be learning where home was anytime soon. "And then we wait on a reply."

Bram thought about this. "Will the same bird be sent back?"

Mallin crossed his legs. He was sitting on a bale of hay, leaning against the dusty red-stained boards of the stable wall. "No."

"How will the new bird know where to go?"

"It will fly directly to this hayloft."

"How?"

Mallin smiled, his lips paling as he stretched them. "No need to ask why?"

Bram shook his head. This was a stovehouse. It was a place where people met, drank, talked, slept. Neutral territory in a land of warring clans. It made sense that the Phage kept birds here. "No."

"Good." The ranger took an apple from one of his pouches and bit on it. "Check the resin. If it's set take the bird to the window and release her."

Bram checked. "Is it meant to be rubbery?"

Mallin nodded

Taking the bird in both hands, Bram rose and crossed to the small triangular window at the end of the loft. The window faced southwest and Bram wondered if he could see the Dhoonehold in the distance.

"Throw her."

Bram did just that, tossing the raven into the cloudy afternoon sky. She opened her wings immediately and beat hard to keep aloft.

"Ravens home to where they were raised," Mallin said, surprising Bram. "When they fly from this stovehouse they are homing to the Phage. That bird was brought here overland in a cart and caged until needed. Now it's been released it will home. The person who receives the message will send a reply with a bird who was raised here, in this stovehouse."

Bram counted five major stovehouses in his head, and there had to be a dozen lesser ones. "That's a lot of birds . . . and a lot of carts back and forth."

Again there was that smile from Hew Mallin. Standing, he leant forward and fed the apple core to the magpie. "People work for us every day without knowing that they do so."

Hearing the low and pointed tone of the ranger's voice, Bram decided they weren't talking about birds anymore.

Mallin's gaze was surprisingly frank. *Yes*, it confirmed. *Everything you imagine is correct.*

Bram hardly knew what he imagined. He had an image of hundreds of tentacles reaching out and spinning things . . . and the spinning things did not realize why they spun.

The sun broke through the clouds sending a prism of light streaming through the window. Feathers and haydust stirred in the warm air as Mallin let his silence speak real and vital truths about the Phage: the scale and reach of its connections and resources, the subtlety and longevity of its plans.

"Let's get some food," Mallin said abruptly, ending the lesson. "Nothing makes me hungry like knowing I must wait."

Five days passed before the reply arrived. Mallin had spent the time grooming—he'd had a local woman rebraid his hair—bartering goods, extracting information from stovehouse patrons, eating well and often and bedding whores. Bram spent time with the birds. Hannie May let him feed them. It was a revelation. They were continually mounting one another and even the pigeons ate meat. It was Hannie who informed Bram the message had arrived.

"Got a live one," she told him as he was sitting by the stove, breakfasting on scrambled egg and trout. Mallin wasn't around. He'd spent last night with one of Hannie's girls. Bram decided to head to the hayloft without him.

The new raven was on top of the corvid cage, goose-stepping from bar to bar and screaming up a racket. Bram had learned a little about handling birds by then and bundled her in a blanket to calm her while he retrieved the message. Using his handknife, he broke the resin seal on the collar and winkled out the small roll of parchment. Ink had run through the paper and Bram could clearly see letters on the other side.

"I'll take that."

Hew Mallin climbed through the loft hatch. His expression was blank as he held out his hand. Bram had not heard him coming. Aware his cheeks were heating up, Bram handed over the paper and caged the raven.

Mallin read the message, rolled it back into a cylinder and fed it to the raven. "Get the horses ready," he told Bram. "We leave within the quarter."

As Bram saddled the horses on the stovehouse's hard standing, a party of Wellmen rode in from the south. Bram's mind kept slipping from its task and he was having trouble latching

Gabbie's belly strap. He kept thinking about the message, wondering what it said and where it was sending them, and worrying about what Mallin thought of him. Had he concluded that Bram was about to read the message?

Was I?

Bram's thoughts were interrupted by shouts from the Wellmen. They were sworn warriors, road-weary with a heavy complement of arms and armaments, and they made the assumption Bram was the stableboy. They were anxious to get inside to rest so Bram took their horses from them. The groom was out exercising Hannie's mare and would not be back for a couple of minutes.

The senior warrior threw Bram a coin for his trouble. Bram caught it and opened his fist to look at it.

"It's only a copper," the warrior said, mistaking Bram's silence for disappointment. "But I'll give you a gold coin's worth of news to top it. Robbie Dun Dhoone has taken the Withyhouse and crowned himself a king."

Bram couldn't recall much for a while after that. Gabbie's belly strap must have been successfully fastened and both horses saddled and loaded but he couldn't remember doing it. He hadn't even mustered much surprise when Mallin had informed him they'd be heading north.

Kingmaker, Bram kept thinking. Bram Cormac had helped Robbie Dhoone become king. He still wasn't sure what he felt about it. Mostly it didn't feel good, but there were moments when he felt small thrills of triumph. Power had shifted in the clanholds because of a message he had delivered.

To become king, Robbie had needed his brother's help.

Bram sat down by the campfire and strung his bow. It was dark now and the wind had dropped. Mallin was turning over the quartered ice hare with his knife. The juices were running clear.

"There's no need to unsheathe the sword."

Mallin was always watching him. Bram nodded toward the strung bow and half dozen arrows he'd taken from their case at Mallin's request. "I thought we had to be ready for attack?"

A sound came from Mallin's throat. Leaning forward, he speared the hare and set it on his plate to cool.

Bram was busy thinking. Why only a bow? What if they were surprised at close quarters? They'd need swords then.

Mallin transferred one of the hare pieces onto Bram's plate and handed it to him. "Why was the Morrowhouse built here?"

Morrow, the name of the Lost Clan. No clansmen worth his salt would speak it. Bram cleared his throat. "Good defensive position."

"And?"

"The river?"

"Eat," Mallin said. He might as well have said, *Don't speak.*

Bram ate. By the time he'd reached the bone he'd worked it out. "Good hunting."

Mallin wrapped the remaining hare, turfed the fire to extinguish it, and grabbed his bow. "Let's see what we can bring down."

It was a long night. They took up position by the river and then did a slow circuit of the meadow. Mallin, who was an excellent shot by day, compensated for poor nightvision with stealth. Bram was glad to have something useful to contribute: he'd always been known for his eyes. They brought down a goat, and a sheep without markings that Mallin said was probably part of a wild flock that had been founded by strays. By the time the carcasses had been split and bled the sun was up and it was another day.

Bram ran his hand knife along the whetstone, honing the edge. He was anxious to get the butchering done so he could bathe in the river. He was tired and he stank of goat.

"No skinning," Mallin said. "We're loading them onto the horses."

"Whole?"

Mallin threw his tent canvas over the back of his stallion. "They're gifts," he explained lightly, "for the Maimed Men."

Bram managed to close his mouth about an hour later, as they walked the horses through a pass in the Copper Hills. The Maimed Men. He had never imagined a future where he visited the world beyond the Rift. What was Mallin up to? What had that message said?

Excitement stopped Bram feeling weary for half a day. Mallin kept his own counsel, but Bram knew the ranger well enough to sense that he was anxious for the journey to be done. They stopped briefly at midday to rest the horses and reposition the carcasses. Both tent canvasses were stiff with blood. In the afternoon, the land began to descend and Bram spotted the thin black line on the horizon. He knew it instantly. The break in the continent, the Rift.

They walked toward it for the rest of the day and into the night. When they reached level headland the wind picked up, blowing hard into their faces. Bram began to notice lights in the distance and then, as they drew closer, he saw how heat venting from the Rift distorted those lights and the stars above them. A low current of fear kept him alert.

"What's that sound?" he whispered as they turned on to a well-maintained path that headed straight for the edge.

"Rift music."

It didn't really clear things up, but Bram could tell from Mallin's voice that no further explanation would be offered. Bram had never seen the ranger so alert. His hands and eyes were never still. As they approached the edge, Mallin slid his hat from one of his coat pouches and put it on. It was his badge, the means by which people identified him from a distance. He was the man in the bearskin hat.

It meant they were being watched. Bram dusted down his cloak and pants. It seemed to intensify the smell of goat. They were very close now and Bram could see the Rift spread out before him. It was the darkest object on a dark night, a gap that held nothing to please or rest the eye.

Yet something was moving across it. A light appeared to be suspended above it. As Bram watched he realized it was a torch. Somehow, someone was crossing the Rift.

The path ahead suddenly turned and they were there, on the ledge. Bram could smell the center of the earth.

"You're lucky," Mallin said, coming to stand by him. "A night crossing's always best first time."

Bram's gaze was on the torch. It was very close now and he could see the figure carrying it. He could also see that figure was walking on a rope bridge, not air.

"Take the kills off the horses and spread some feed by the rocks."

"Gabbie and Strife stay here?"

"Horses won't cross the Rift."

Bram found nothing reassuring about that statement. As he untied the sheep carcass from Gabbie, Mallin called out a greeting to the figure on the bridge.

"Welcome, friend," came the response. "I'll send a boy

over to watch the horses." The figure stepped from the bridge onto the suspension platform and looked with interest at Bram. "And who else do I greet?"

"Bram Cormac," Bram said, acutely aware of the space after his name where *of Castlemilk* or *of Dhoone* should have gone.

It seemed to him that the stranger from the Rift heard the space too. "Welcome, Bram Cormac," he said, raising the torch to reveal his face. "I am Thomas Argola, Rift Brother. Once of Hanatta . . . in a different time and life."

Seeing his features and hearing his voice, Bram realized the man was from the Far South. He was slightly built, with olive skin and clever features. A speck of blood floated in his left eye.

"Keep your gaze on the horizon," he told Bram, turning, "and don't forget to breathe."

Crossing the Rift with a sheep carcass slung over his shoulder after two days without sleep was something Bram would never forget. The rope bridge swung and some of the treads were gone and the light from Argola's torch was fitful. Bram's cloak filled with air and as he tried to flatten it he dropped a glove. Before a man could blink it was swallowed by the darkness. Bram stared at the spot where it had disappeared. He had an impulse to chuck away Robbie's sword, and let it fall for a very long time.

By the time they completed the crossing, Maimed Men had gathered in the landing area to inspect them. They didn't look friendly. Bram watched Mallin closely, following the ranger's lead.

"Meat," Mallin said, shucking off the goat carcass and letting it fall to the ground. "Brought down yesterday."

Bram copied the maneuver with the sheep carcass. He was glad to have it gone. A fire was burning on the ledge and the flickering flames made the Maimed Men look like ghouls. None of them made a move toward the carcasses but Bram sensed that some vital requirement had been met.

Argola led the way through them. "Stillborn will want to see you," he told Mallin. "He calls himself the Scar Chief now."

Mallin nodded tersely, and Bram followed him and Argola into the city on the edge of the abyss.

CHAPTER 18

Lost Men

They walked for an hour through the darkness. A group of Maimed children followed them. The eldest, a girl with stringy blond hair and missing teeth, threw a stone. A single look from Mallin prevented any further missiles from being loosed. The ranger cut quite a figure, Bram realized. Tall and lean in his long saddle coat, he moved like a man who knew what to do in a fight. Bram tried to follow his lead, keeping his chin high and his back straight. This was his first proper mission with Mallin and he didn't want to make any mistakes.

The cliffs were mined with caves. People came out of them to watch Mallin and Bram pass. A large bonfire was burning on one of the upper ledges and Argola led them steadily upward toward it. After two days without sleep, Bram's eyeballs ached and his leg muscles protested the climb. Mallin must have been weary too but you wouldn't have known it. He seemed focused and *alive*.

"Always one for a pretty hat, Hew."

They'd reached the bonfire and a big bear of a man with a

deep scar dissecting his face, and bullhorns wrapped around his bare forearms stepped ahead of the crowd of men to greet them.

"Stillborn," Mallin replied, inclining his head. "I hear you're calling yourself the Scar Chief now."

The one called Stillborn took a quick glance at his men. "It's a name. Some of us have many of them."

Mallin didn't take the bait. "Are matters well here?"

"We live by a godforsaken hole-in-the-earth. You tell me." Stillborn's voice was hard and his hazel eyes glittered in the firelight. Bram sensed the man felt threatened.

Mallin made no reply and the two men appraised one other in silence. "Hew and his friend brought meat," Argola said. "Two carcasses. A goat and a sheep."

For the first time Stillborn turned his gaze on Bram. "That must make you the sheep."

Bram felt the heat rise in his cheeks. Men with parts missing from their bodies and faces laughed at him. They were heavily and grotesquely armed.

"I'm Bram Cormac." His voice cracked a bit but sounded all right.

"And what clan did you fall out of?"

Was it that obvious he was clan? Acutely aware that Mallin was watching him, Bram said, "I fell out of a couple. What about you?"

For a wonder the Maimed Men laughed. Bram didn't dare take his eyes off Stillborn, but in the corner of his vision he could see that Mallin was perfectly still.

The bonfire roared as it burned, pumping out smoke and heat. "They threw me out of Scarpe. Me very own sister did the chucking. A lovely lass."

Was it possible this man was brother to the Scarpe chief, Yelma Scarpe?

Stillborn winked at him.

Bram concentrated on not letting his mouth fall open.

He could be me. The thought filled Bram with unease so strong it was almost panic. He did not want to end up here, desperate and out of choices like these men.

There was a tooth embedded in the scar flesh of Stillborn's neck. As Stillborn inspected Bram's face it began to twitch. "You lose your clan, and then you keep on losing. Next thing you know there's nothing left."

Bram took a step back.

Stillborn had taken a breath to continue speaking, but after a moment exhaled. He was shaking. So was Bram.

"Go to bed," Stillborn told the crowd. "Nothing to see here, just a sheep and a goat."

Maimed Men stirred. A handful walked away from the fire. Stillborn said to Mallin, "This time tomorrow you're gone."

Mallin knew when a show of submission was called for. "As you say."

Stillborn grunted. "Follow me."

As Stillborn took a lamp from one of the Maimed Men, Mallin exchanged a glance with Thomas Argola. It looked like a promise to Bram.

Later.

The whirring groans and shudders of the Rift followed them as they descended to a lower ledge. Bram wondered if the night would ever end.

He wondered about a lot of things.

"You don't use Traggis Mole's old quarters?" Mallin said

when they arrived at their destination, a shell-shaped ledge with a cave leading down from it.

Stillborn threw a hand through the air. "Place is full o' ghosts." He was dressed in a donkey skin kilt over black wool pants. Despite the coolness of the night, the only clothing covering his upper body was a leather waistcoat. He showed an even mix of muscle and fat that made him look as sturdy as a bear.

"Here, Cormac. Drink this." He thrust a pewter flask at Bram's stomach like a punch. "I'll see what I can scratch up to eat."

Bram and Mallin waited in silence as Stillborn rummaged in his cave. Bram tilted the flask toward Mallin. A question. Mallin nodded. *Go ahead.*

Walking to the edge of the cliff, Bram drank. Whatever stars had been out earlier had gone, and all that remained of the clanholds was blackness. Bram was dead tired and he wished he could forget Stillborn's words. He stayed on the edge while the Maimed Man built up the fire and cooked things.

After a while Mallin asked, "Have there been more attacks?"

"We're bleeding to death. Every couple of nights we're attacked, brothers are killed. I don't know what the fuck to do."

"Fight," Mallin said quietly. "There are no choices here."

Stillborn made a hard sound in his throat. Shadows settled into his scars like water finding its level in a trench. After a time he said, "Have you any word of Raif Sevrance or Addie Gunn?"

Mallin shrugged. "Never heard of them."

Stillborn nodded softly, and Bram was struck by the idea that this man was accustomed to disappointment. For a while Stillborn tended the fire and the food. "Raif Sevrance could kill those . . . *things*," the Maimed Man murmured, half to himself. "He knew what to do."

Mallin changed the subject and began giving Stillborn news of the clanholds and the mountain cities. A new surlord, a Dhoone chief who had made himself a king.

Bram stopped listening. He was wondering where he'd heard the name Raif Sevrance before. With a small jolt of surprise he realized it belonged to the Hailsman who had killed four Bluddsmen outside of Duff's after admitting to taking part in the slaughter of women and children on the Bluddroad. So he was a Maimed Man too? Bram took another swig from the flask.

The meal Stillborn prepared was good and surprisingly varied. Dates, almonds and dried apricots were heated in liquor and served over ptarmigan. Stillborn seemed pleased to see Bram eat and pushed the last of the dates on Bram's plate. "I've been keeping them so long," he said. "I've forgotten *why* I was keeping them."

Bram resisted liking him. He thanked him coolly.

Stillborn breathed in the coolness and stood. "You'll sleep in my quarters tonight. No doubt I'll miss you tomorrow, so farewell."

Bram was glad when he was gone. Carrying the torch, he headed into the cave. A quintain with a stuffed bear's head nailed to the top was suspended from the rock ceiling. Farther inside, there was a bed stacked with dirty blankets, and a great pile of rusted armor, metalwork, dusty clothes and pieces of furniture with missing legs. Bram was so exhausted he didn't bother conferring with Mallin about who would take the bed. He simply took it and slept.

Sunlight shining on his face woke him in the morning. Mallin was already up and awake. The ranger was boiling water for tea. It was about two hours past sunrise and Bram felt bad about sleeping late. Mallin appeared to be in no hurry, though and they sat and watched the mist burn off the clanholds as they breakfasted on leftover ptarmigan and way bread from Mallin's pack.

Seen from the north the clanholds were impossibly beautiful. The hills and highlands were purple and blue in the haze, and glinting lines of silver told of streams and waterfalls and melt ponds. Bram felt a strong desire to protect them. All of them, all of the clans.

He didn't want to look down and see the Rift, not then.

Mallin said, "Look along the cliff face to the east. Up a way. You see the door?"

Bram did.

"Find us a way to get there by the shortest route."

They killed the fire, left a token of thanks for Stillborn—a silver thumb cup from Hannie May's—gathered their belongings and made their way up from the cave. Bram was pleased with the task Mallin had given him and determined to do it well. The cliff wall was a like a termite mound. The ledges and cave mouths had no order and were staggered across dozens of different levels. Bram quickly realized that a direct route wouldn't work. Even if you were on a ledge directly below the door you wouldn't necessarily be able to reach it. It all depended on the network of rope ladders and hoists. Once they reached one of the main ledges Bram was able to walk to the edge and get a better look at the cliff wall. It was easy after that.

The secret was to go above the door and then drop down on to its ledge. Bram had them there within four minutes. "There's normally a ladder here," Bram said as they made the hard drop from a small outcrop about seven feet above the door. "See the marks where it should go?"

Mallin gave Bram one of his flat-lipped smiles. "Last time I was here it took me half an hour to reach the door."

It was as close to praise as Mallin ever came. Bram beamed all the way to his eyeballs, and then tried not to show it. As they walked toward the door, he risked a question. "Must you come here often?"

The ranger's nostrils flexed as he breathed in a great quantity of air. "More often than I used to."

Bram thought that was it—answers that gave nothing away were Mallin's stock-in-trade—but the ranger surprised him by continuing. "Need is greater. That's more than a crack in the continent. It's a split in the world. Things that should be sealed away are getting out. They're escaping in handfuls now. Half a dozen here, half a dozen there. That will change. Have you ever seen a crack that didn't get worse?" Mallin stopped and looked at Bram.

"No."

The ranger's yellow-green eyes darkened, and for a moment Bram wondered if Mallin hadn't hoped against hope that Bram would reply "*Yes*" instead.

Mallin gathered his fear so completely he left no trace of it behind. "The crack's running. If it gets deep enough the entire game changes. Right now we're fighting the Unmade. Pray we do not have to fight their unmakers."

Hairs on the back of Raif's hands and neck rose. An updraft from the Rift rose in a shockwave, distorting the air in a great sheet. Bram smelled sulfur and something secret and almost sweet. He looked down and saw layer upon layer of rock disappearing into a thin black line.

"The Endlords are down there?" He hardly knew he had spoken.

"It's one of the three places they will emerge if they break free of the Blind."

Bram thought about this. So they weren't down there, not really, but some sort of doorway *was*. "Where are the other places?"

"One is in the Want."

Bram heard the slight rise in Mallin's voice and knew what it meant. "The clanholds is the third place?"

Mallin nodded.

"Which clan?"

"We're not sure.

"Could it be Dhoone?"

Mallin shrugged, but not lightly. "It's one of the things we need to find out. Clans are notoriously bad at keeping records." Seeing Bram's expression, the ranger continued. "I would not lay coin on it being Dhoone. Unfortunately we lost two of our best people in the clanholds."

Bram frowned. "How?"

The look Mallin gave him was a lesson in the Phage. It was a dangerous fellowship to be part of. People were killed, hurt. Lost.

The ranger began walking. "We must busy ourselves to make up for our losses." Arriving at the gray door, he tapped softly, once.

A young woman opened the door. Her skin was olive-gold and her hair was glossily black. She looked boldly at Mallin and Bram but did not speak.

"We are here to see Thomas Argola," Mallin told her.

"Then enter," she said, moving only partly out of the way. Mallin slid past her without incident but Bram's arm touched the curve of her breast. He colored hotly. The girl just looked at him. Bram didn't think he'd ever seen anyone so beautiful in his life.

"Hew. Bram. It's good to see you." Thomas Argola rose to meet them. He'd been sitting on cushions on the cave floor. Bram wondered why he hadn't answered the door himself. "This is my sister, Mallia."

The ranger showed her little interest beyond a curt nod. Bram wished her good day and then attempted to follow Mallin's appearance of disinterest.

The girl wasn't fooled.

By either of them.

Swaying perfectly curved hips, she sauntered across the chamber and disappeared behind an embroidered silk screen. Bram stared at the space she had just occupied. It seemed emptier than normal air.

"Sit. Drink." Argola indicated the pile of cushions at the center of the space and then poured hot broth into three cups. "To luck," he said handing cups to Mallin and Bram. "When all else fails it must do."

Mallin accepted the cup without seconding the toast so Bram did the same. The broth was sharp and salty. Bram held it under his chin and let the steam roll over his face.

"You spoke with Stillborn." It was not a question but a request for information. Sitting cross-legged on the cushions, Argola appeared relaxed but Bram wondered if the outlander wasn't holding himself a little too still.

Mallin made Argola wait on a response by taking a long draught of broth. "He is worried."

"He has reason to be. We've lost seventy men and women in the past fifteen days. People are losing faith in him. He's a hard worker and a good fighter but he doesn't know how to lead." Argola set down his cup and looked frankly and expectantly at the ranger.

Mallin pushed a hand though his finely braided hair. It looked to Bram as if he was assessing Argola. And finding him wanting.

"Have you word of Raif Sevrance?"

Mallin said, "The Sull have him."

Bram concentrated on breathing—in and out, in and out—as he absorbed the evidence of Mallin's deceit. The ranger had looked the leader of the Maimed Men in the eye and lied to him. Suddenly everything that had happened last night looked different. Stillborn's dislike and distrust now seemed like a reasonable response to a snake in his house. Yet even wary as he was he'd still been fooled.

Mallin was that good.

You lose your clan, and then you keep on losing.

Stillborn hadn't just been talking about the Maimed Men.

"There is more," Mallin said. "Sevrance was taken by Yiselle No Knife and her Night Army."

Muscles in Argola's face slackened and the faintly amused expression he had worn since their arrival disappeared. "She's barely Sull. He Who Leads expelled her from the Heart Fires. What's she doing with Sevrance?"

"Breaking him. No Knife wants him in her army, riding at its head."

Argola stood. He was clearly agitated. "She can't do that."

"I wouldn't be so sure." Mallin's yellow-green eyes lost focus for a moment. When he spoke again there was uncharacteristic heat in his voice. "They're drugging him, isolating him. Playing with his mind. She wants him so far gone that he no longer knows who he is."

"How could he fight in such a state?"

"How did Raven Lord fight? By most accounts he was insane at the end."

Bram shuddered. He hardly knew what was he was hearing, but he understood there was horror here. Sull were torturing a clansman. And these two men, the ranger and the outlander, were not nearly as outraged as they should be.

As he looked from Mallin to Argola he saw the embroidered screen move. Argola's sister was listening. Quickly Bram glanced at Mallin, but the ranger was speaking and did not appear to notice.

"No Knife will use Sevrance to gain power. When she's finished with him he'll slay the Unmade better than any Sull. With *Mor Drakka* in her army, others will join her. She will win victories. He Who Leads will not be able to compete with her. He'll lose standing and power. And when he's weak enough, she'll strike and take his place."

Argola said, "Does Sevrance have the sword?"

"He took it from the ice. Yes."

There was a draw in the cave, Bram noticed. He felt its cool, upward current on his skin. Argola was standing close to the door, a slight man, plainly dressed with something that looked like victory in his blood-flecked eyes.

"Where is he?" he asked.

"In the Sway, northeast of Bludd."

Calculation passed like a tremor across the outlander's face. "You did not tell Stillborn?"

Mallin shook his head. "You could send five hundred Maimed Men there—they'd all die."

"And you need us here, don't you? We're your early warning, your bird in the mine."

Bram's head was reeling. The air in the cave was turning, spiraling as it rose toward the natural flue in the rock ceiling. He was only just beginning to understand the stakes the Phage played with. Argola wasn't Phage. They used him—wasn't that the point of the visit? Argola used them right back. It was a network, like the ledges, and you might be able to see where you wanted to go but there was no straight line to get there. Both of them—Mallin and Argola—were taking winding paths.

One thing was certain: Both of them wanted control of the clansman, Raif Sevrance. Yet the Sull had him.

And what the Sull had they never gave back.

Argola said, "What number does No Knife command?"

"A hundred."

Silence followed as both men gave the number its due. If it were clansmen or city men it would mean nothing. But Sull, on their home territory: a hundred were a wall of swords. Mallin had been protecting Stillborn then? If the leader of the Maimed Men went east to fetch Raif Sevrance, chances were high he wouldn't come back. Yet even that protection could be manipulation. If Argola was right, Mallin needed the Maimed Men to be strong.

Bram let all possibilities float in his mind. He was beginning to understand that there were things he might never know for sure. Looking up, he saw a sliver of Mallia Argola's face in deep shadow behind the screen. Their gazes met and Mallia put a slender, painted finger to her lips.

Everyone here was working their own angle. How could you know who was right or wrong?

"We have a problem then," Argola said, gathering the cups and copper kettle. "We can't help him so we must wait."

"He should not have been there." Mallin suddenly looked dangerous, like a fighter displaying his knives. "The Sull cannot bear him. They believe he will end their existence. How do you imagine they will treat him?"

Argola showed some weaponry of his own. Bram did not know how he did it, but something in the outlander shifted and the slight figure in the brown robe became a sorcerer. His eyes glittered and his fingertips moved in a way that looked barely human. "He had to possess the sword."

"Swords kill. As long as a blade is sharp one will do as well as another."

Argola smiled at this. "Really, Hew Mallin of the Long Watch. Would you take that very sharp sword of yours into battle with an Endlord?"

There were no longer two men in the chamber. There were two forces, standing off against each other. Bram realized he had made the mistake of assuming that Mallin, and therefore the Phage, was the superior power. He was wrong. Argola commanded something equally ancient and knowing.

Mallin *gave* under its force. "What is done is done."

Argola nodded in acknowledgment, and instantly whatever willpower or real power he had spooled into the room was retracted. "We watch and wait?"

The question sounded like an offering to Bram; a magnanimous victor sharing his spoils. Mallin shrugged. He looked old and weary and ready to leave. "We prepare."

"*Mor Drakka* fighting for the Sull is still *Mor Drakka*."

Mallin swung a hand into the air, pushing back Argola's words. "No Knife is renegade Sull. She's half insane, and she's attracted the worst kind of followers. I would not wish her on my enemy."

Argola did not disagree. Crossing to the door, he said, "We would all wish it different."

Mallin studied him a long time, and then stood. Bram followed. He waited for the ranger to say something but Mallin did not speak. Argola's words gained weight in the silence.

The outlander opened the door.

"He's a Hailsman." Bram hadn't known he was going to speak until his mouth opened. "He has clan and kin."

Argola and the ranger looked at him. Again, there was nothing more to say.

Bram stepped out into the cool brightness of a spring day. Not wanting to hear whatever words of parting the two men would say to one another, Bram walked to the edge of the cliff.

He stood there and did not think. Then, with slow deliberation, he unsheathed Robbie's great two-handed longsword and threw it into the Rift.

CHAPTER 19

A Day in the Marshes

Chedd's chin wasn't looking good. The cut under his jaw was black and wet-looking and his entire lower face looked puffy. His hands went to the wound constantly. "Doesn't feel right, Eff."

"Oh, it's fine," she told him impatiently. "Swelling's a natural response to injury."

"But that was five days ago."

Effie couldn't think of a reply to that so she changed the subject. "It's stopped raining. Let's see if we can get outside."

Chedd frowned. "But we're supposed to be on pump duty."

"You're too sick and I'm too . . . small."

"Buckler will come and find us."

"Let him. What did he do when he found you sneaking fishcakes from the kitchen the other night?"

"Put me on pump duty." Chedd thought about this for a minute, then grabbed his cloak. "Let's go."

The Grayhouse was dripping. The clinker blocks were like sponges that had absorbed their capacity and were now leaking. It had rained for the past four days, a cold icy curtain that hammered the marshwater into an unreflective surface and flattened great saddles of reeds. The Salamander Door was open and no one appeared to be on guard duty, so Chedd and Effie made a run for it.

Outside, the wind was up, pushing water against the roundhouse's platforms and blowing the flames off the gas vents. Men and women were out in the thin, peapod-shaped boats that were used to navigate the narrow channels of the Reed Way. The women were clearing reeds from the lake, a job that was done from dawn to dusk every day. The lake surrounding the roundhouse was the only open water for leagues. It was a precious commodity, ever-threatened by invasive, choking reeds. Clansmen were out trapping birds and game. Unlike other clans, trapping was men's work here. Big, complicated bamboo-and-bulrush cages were floated onto the islands and out into the sea of reeds. Effie spotted a man wearing green-dyed muskrat skins in one of the trapping boats.

"Is that him?" she said, elbowing Chedd. "The man who brought us in that first day?"

Chedd squinted. "His skin's kind of speckly. I think so."

"Let's get a boat and follow him."

"No." Chedd shook his head emphatically. "Double no."

Effie grabbed his shirt by the collar. "You promised. You spoke an oath and spit and clasped on it. Don't make me call you a turnie."

"I'm not a turnie," Chedd shot back. "I don't see how following Green Fur over there is going to help lift any curses."

"He's some kind of big cheese around here, but we never see him in the roundhouse. Wouldn't hurt to find out where he goes. And anyway. You said it's our duty to escape. If we follow him we might learn a secret way out."

Chedd's face told Effie exactly what he thought of her reasoning. "All right."

Finding a boat wasn't difficult. Dozens of craft were tied to the pilings and landings that clustered at the base of the roundhouse. If Effie thought about it she'd say there were more boats than people at Gray, but she wouldn't like to say why. Chedd chose a green skimmer with a curved nose and bow that was moored to one of the floating docks. Horse bladders filled with air barely kept the dock afloat. Effie got a soaking as she waited for Chedd to untie and turn the boat.

"Hurry," he told her when he was ready. "People are looking."

Effie glanced back to the roundhouse. Seen from outside you could hardly call it round . . . more octagonal. A couple of old timers were shucking mussels and sieving for shrimp on the main landing, and two tied clansmen were shoring mud at the base of the roundhouse, jamming bones and cane mesh into the ooze. No one was looking at the two people stealing a boat on the dock. Effie decided to hold her tongue: it was an experiment, she'd see how it went.

"Jump," Chedd commanded, and she did.

It was nice to be in a boat and not have one's legs chained together. Chedd appeared to appreciate it too and paddled with his feet up on the gunwales. It didn't make for a very good transfer of force, but Effie was still holding her tongue and didn't criticize. She felt almost serene.

The lake surrounding the Grayhouse was called the Stillwater. Tull Buckler had warned them that although it was mostly shallow it had sinkholes that were hundreds of feet deep. Slicks of shiny, sulfurous tar floated on the surface acting like flytraps for mosquitoes and riverboatmen. The wind drove the slicks toward the reeds.

"Why are there so many of these?" Effie asked as Chedd navigated a field of copper pipes, some with hissing flames at their tips.

"They vent the marsh gas, stop it from building up."

"What happens if it builds up?"

Chedd slammed the paddle against the lake surface, spraying water into the boat. "Explosion. They've lost a few clansmen that way."

"That could be the curse. Marsh gas."

Chedd turned to give her one of his special withering looks. "Gray's always been in the marsh. It may have sunk a bit, but it's always been here and it's always had to deal with marsh gas. You can't curse a clan with something it's already got."

She had to admit it: Chedd Limehouse had a superior grasp of the laws of cursing. "Over there," she told him. "Green Fur went between those rushes."

"Aye, Captain." Chedd did as he was told while sounding only a little bit sarcastic.

As they moved south toward the rushbeds, Effie realized she hadn't felt afraid once since they'd left the Grayhouse. Here she was—outside—with a big gray sky above her and open water and a jungle of bulrushes at eye level and she felt . . . what was the word she'd thought of earlier? *Serene*.

She glanced at Chedd. He was paddling hard and fat in his lower back and butt was jiggling. She loved him. He was crucial to her peace of mind. "You missed the turn," she told him. "It's back there."

Chedd grumbled. "Greenie's probably just checking his traps."

"So. We'll still learn something about the Reed Way."

"He'll knock our heads together and chuck us into the Stink."

"No he won't. He paid Waker Stone good money for us, remember? And what a man pays for he doesn't throw away."

Chedd grumbled some more. As he turned from open water into the rushbeds, light and wind dropped. Walls of bulrushes grew eight feet high on either side of the boat. They smelled meaty. Sticky white horsefly chrysalises were glued between the canes. Effie spotted a little yellow warbler perched above one of them, waiting for something to come out.

Paddling slowly and carefully to keep them centered on the narrow channel, Chedd was focused and silent. His feet were now on the deck. Effie wondered whether he was thinking the same thing she was: Escape was becoming more and more unlikely. As the crow flies they were a third of a league from the Grayhouse, but they couldn't see it. They couldn't see anything, only high cliffs of rushes.

"Eff, are you remembering the way back?"

"Yes." Up until then she hadn't been, but she was absolutely going to remember from now on. "You can see Green Fur's wake on the surface." She pointed to the gentle flow of ripples tapping the prow of the boat. "We have to keep them in our sights."

"That's dodgy logic," Chedd told her. "Ducks, wind, muskrats: anything could cause those ripples."

Effie knew Chedd was right. They'd lost sight of Green Fur half an hour back and although Effie was pretty certain he had turned in to this channel, she had no idea if he was still on it. The problem was the breaks in the rushes. Sometimes there were gaps between the islands, thin threadways that you couldn't spot until you were dead abreast of them, where a boat could just slip through and end up somewhere else. It wasn't hard to imagine there were breaks that you couldn't see, gaps curtained by canes.

"Should have brought a whistle," Chedd said. "Remember Buckler gave us that warning? Said even experienced Graymen could lose their way—especially after a storm. Islands can break away, crash into each other. Channels are lost overnight. New ones open up. Tangled rootballs can block—"

"Chedd." Effie poked him in the center of his spine. "Calm down. At worst we can turn the boat and back out."

"Five minutes," Chedd warned, "and then we're heading back."

The boat skimmed the marsh, barely breaking the dark brown water. Mergansers called from deep within the rushes, single hollow notes that sounded like the word *More*.

"That's it, I'm turning," Chedd declared, working the paddle backward. "No food, no water, no whistles. It's like being in the Want."

Effie helped Chedd turn the boat, pushing off against the rush canes. The clouds were getting darker overhead and she'd just felt the first spits of rain. Chedd put some real effort into paddling and soon they were gliding down the channel with the wind behind them. As they passed one of the gaps in the rushwall, Effie caught a glimpse of a raised mound in the distance. A hump of land with something built on it, rising above the rushes.

"Eff."

Snapping forward, she saw straightaway why Chedd had called her name. The channel had ended. A solid island of bulrushes blocked the way ahead. "Must have missed a turning."

Chedd shook his head emphatically. "We didn't take a turning. We've been on the same channel since we left the Stillwater." His voice was getting higher. "You were supposed to remember the way."

"Let's push through it."

The nose of the boat parted rushes as Chedd paddled forward. After a couple of feet the bow jammed in the tangle of roots. "It's solid. We can't go any further." He handed Effie the paddle. "Turn in your seat and back us out."

Effie turned. The way back was blocked.

"Come on, Eff. Hurry up." Chedd spun in his seat and saw what Effie saw. His expression froze and a strangled kind of noise escaped his throat.

Effie was about to tell him to close his mouth he might catch flies in it when she caught a glimpse of something moving out of the corner of her eye. Suddenly the bulrushes parted and Green Fur slid his craft into the channel directly ahead.

He did not speak. His small, dark face was tattooed to look like newt scales. As he brought his boat bow-to-stern against their boat and tied both craft into a line, Effie saw his hands were tattooed in the same pattern. She and Chedd sat tight as Green Fur expertly towed them from the rushes. Pulling their boat stern-first, he headed for the blockage straight ahead. When he was about three feet from the block, he pulled a long hooked pole from his boat, hooked a great chunk of bulrushes and floated the entire block aside, revealing the channel ahead.

Impressed, Effie glanced over her shoulder at Chedd. *Worried* would have been a better word for Chedd just then.

"What about the other block back there," Effie called to Green Fur. "We pushed against it. It didn't move."

Green Fur was silent as he towed the boat upchannel.

Chedd leaned forward and said in Effie's ear. "I bet he tied it in place."

Effie nodded slowly. She'd caught sight of the mound again and was beginning to suspect they were being pulled toward it. Green Fur executed a series of tight cuts, steering them onto a channel so thin it was barely as wide as the boats. Effie tucked her head low to stop bulrushes from whipping her face. She didn't feel afraid but couldn't be sure if that made her brave or stupid. *I wish the pike hadn't taken my lore.*

The channel turned and the mound was suddenly dead ahead. It rose ten feet above the water level and was gently rounded on all sides. A handful of alders grew just above the waterline and yellow weeds had sprouted in clumps across the surface. The closer they got, the more and more certain Effie became that the mound was man-made. As she'd floated down the Wolf, she'd seen a lot of islands and none of them were symmetrical.

Green Fur brought the boats to dock by the alders. He sprung ashore and tied the line to one of the branches. "Out," he told Chedd and Effie when he was done.

"First rule," he said as he helped Effie onto the steep bank, "is never travel in the Reed Way unless you know where you're going and at least two ways to get back." He helped Chedd next, moving lightly and exactly, doing just enough to help Chedd gain his feet. "Second rule. Water. Drink the marsh and you'll end up in the marsh. Third rule—"

"Food?" Chedd said hopefully. Seeing Green Fur's expression, he changed his answer to, "Spare paddle."

"Useful," Green Fur allowed, "but not a rule. You could rip out your boat's seat or gunwales if it came to it, use them to scull back to shore."

Chedd nodded with interest.

"Light," Effie said.

Green Fur turned his full attention on her. Beneath the motley of newt scales, his features were small and regular. His eyes were the color of bitumen—black with a little green in them—and it was easy to imagine you were seeing the surface of something deep. "Good," he told her. "You never want to be caught out here in the dark."

Effie beamed. Praise made her bold. "Why did you bring us here?"

Green Fur looked from Effie to Chedd and back again. The scale tattoos went all the way down his neck, disappearing beneath his muskrat-skin collar, and Effie wondered if his entire body was marked.

"We hope you will become clan."

It was not the answer Effie had expected. She didn't know how to reply. Green Fur was watching her intently. "You *bought* us," she said finally.

"We paid someone to bring you here." Green Fur's voice was level but there was some pride in it. "We do not own you."

"Then let us go," Chedd said.

Effie knew what Green Fur's response would be even before he spoke.

"You're free to go." Green Fur flicked his hand toward the marsh which surrounded them like a sea of canes. Sunlight breaking through the clouds sent a bar of gold running across it. "We will not hold you."

Of course you won't. Impatient, Effie said, "Who are you?"

"Rufus Rime, the Marsh Chief."

Dagro Blackhail had taught Effie the names of all the clan chiefs. Clan Gray was chiefed by Tournie Gray. She told Rime so.

Rime shrugged, not denying what she said but not giving it any importance. "Have you seen Tournie since you've been here?" he asked, his gaze focused on some faraway point in the marsh.

Effie looked at Chedd. Both of them shook their heads.

Rime let them think about that.

After a minute or so Chedd said, "Is he dead?"

Effie elbowed him. Sometimes Chedd didn't get things at all. "He's at Clan Hill, with the Gray warriors and horses."

A dragonfly wheeled in the air between Effie and Rime, its wings glinting cobalt blue. Effie thought she understood Rime's title, but would be hard-pressed to explain it to Chedd. It wasn't so much that Rime was Gray's chief-in-absentia — in fact she was pretty sure it wasn't about Gray much at all. It was exactly as Rime said: He was chief of the marsh. Its keeper.

Rime's black gaze stayed on Effie a moment longer, confirming half-formed thoughts. Abruptly, he turned and hiked the short distance to the top of the mound. Crouching close to the apex, he beckoned Chedd and Effie to join him. As they approached he put a finger to his lips.

Turtles, over a dozen of them, were basking in a small depression at the peak. Chedd lay flat on his stomach to get a good look at them. "Spotteds," he said with feeling. To Effie's disgruntlement, this evoked a similar look of praise from Rime as when she'd correctly guessed the third rule: lamps.

"If they're lucky they'll get some sun afore the day's out," Rime told him.

Chedd nodded, transfixed. The turtles were small and green with yellow spots. A handful were hatchlings.

"Why do the newborns die?" Effie blurted. "There's been four funerals in ten days."

Chedd groaned. Effie glared at the back of his head. Wasn't he supposed to be busy escaping?

Rime moved away from the turtles. Effie followed. "If children and newborns die here that means Chedd and I are goners too."

The scales on Rime's face rippled as he breathed. "You will live, though the cut on your friend's face needs attending."

"How do you know we'll live? You're cursed. Your whole clan's sliding into the—"

"Do not," Rime warned, cutting her off, "speak ill of this clan. You do not know of what you speak."

Effie hung her head. You could hear the pride again in his voice. They were facing south now and Effie could see humps of land above the reeds, tiny isles covered with trees that looked as if they were under assault.

"You're from Blackhail?" Rime asked. Effie nodded. "Be glad of it. Be glad your kin and clansfolk are safe."

"They're not safe." Da and Drey were dead. Raif was lost. Raina had been hurt in terrible ways by Mace Blackhail.

"Still better there than here," Rime said in his faintly accented voice. "All things being equal, safer in Blackhail than Gray."

The words made Effie feel old. Pushing the thick black mud aside with the toe of her boot, she realized the ground she was standing on was stone. A stone dome. She looked up.

"Are they all so clever at Blackhail?" Rime asked, reading the word *roundhouse* on her face.

Effie didn't think it would be polite to answer truthfully so she practiced her new talent of silence instead.

This made Rime smile. His teeth were greenly white. "Yes. We're standing on the top of the old Grayhouse. It's been sinking for over a thousand years. Come back next spring and it'll be gone and rushes will have closed the water."

"Rate of sinkage must be increasing," Chedd said matter-of-factly from his position on the ground by the turtles. "Twenty feet every year for a thousand years would make for one tall roundhouse."

Effie blinked at Chedd, but he didn't look up from his turtling. Nor did he say anything else.

"They say it was the most beautiful roundhouse in the clanholds, built of green granite carted from the stone fields of Trance Vor, surrounded by walled gardens and blue pools and weeping willows. The marsh was drained for a league in all directions and clansmen built breakwalls to keep out the water. They grew flowers and wheat, and cows grazed on rich grass. Slider Gray, the Turtle Chief, raised a path through the marshes all the way to Trance Vor. He called it the Grayroad. Two stovehouses sprang up along the way. Any clan with goods to trade came here and Slider charged them a toll to take his road. Gray grew rich and powerful and began to look west to Otler, Hill and Halfbludd. Dry land there, no need to keep shoring the dams."

Rime's voice began to fade. "Slider took Hill and moved half of his clan there. They say he was fixing to take Otler when the water started rising and the wralls came."

Effie shivered. She'd once heard Anwyn Bird and Dagro

talking about wralls. When they realized she was there they'd fallen silent. "What happened?"

Rime moved to the top of the mound, crouched next to Chedd and seized the largest turtle. With a twist of his wrist he broke the creature's neck. The remaining turtles scampered into the water.

"Gray failed," he said, chucking the turtle into the front of his boat, "and we've been fighting the water and our own bad luck ever since."

Effie glanced at Chedd. He was standing up and his face looked kind of crumply. He'd been turtling the day Waker kidnapped him. Turtles were one of his favorite things.

"Was that when Gray was cursed?" Effie shot at Rime.

"This land was cursed before we got here. We just didn't know it."

Chedd had come to stand next to Effie. She put her hand on his shoulder. He felt hot.

Worry made her forceful. "Why do newborns die?"

"The air is bad. The swamp gets into their lungs and they can't fight it."

"What about us?"

"You're older. You're strong." Rime beckoned them to the boats. "Those who come to us after the age of five or six rarely die."

Chedd and Effie went to board the green boat, but Rime made it clear they'd be traveling in his craft with him. As soon as they were settled, Rime untied the rope and cast off. The green boat followed them on its line.

"We'll just escape," Effie said, faking confidence. She'd taken the front seat because that's where the turtle was and she didn't want Chedd having to look at it on the trip. Now she found she didn't want to look at it either. Its little black eyes were still open. "We're not stupid. We can learn the Reed Way."

Rime paddled deftly through the water. "Of course you will. Our hope is that by the time you learn it Gray will be your home."

Effie thought about the Croser girl in the kitchens. She hadn't appeared to want to get away. Was it possible that if you spent enough time in a place it became your home? "We'll never forget we're from Blackhail and Bannen," she said defensively.

"No. And I'll never forget I was a landsman from Dhoone."

Effie turned to share a glance with Chedd. *Dhoone?*

Rime, who was in the middle seat, intercepted the look. He smiled. Turning his left hand toward the sky, he revealed a newt's-head tattoo on the palm of his hand. "They got me early. I was six. At first I felt like you—that Gray's too wet and broken-down for me—then I began to pole around in one of the boats. No one ever stopped me, though I was warned about the four rules. Once I got the hang of it I'd be out here for days, floating from island to island, sleeping under the alders, toasting turtle and sweet mallow for breakfast.

"Gray is like no other clanhold: no two days are ever the same. She changes. Islands rise and sink. Water opens and channels close. Beavers dam downstream and suddenly there's a flood. Every morning I come out here and I'm not certain what I'm going to see. I'll never go hungry, I know that for sure. Fish, waterfowl, muskrats, turtles: a boy or girl with a cage can catch many things."

As he spoke, Rime turned onto the main channel and headed back toward the roundhouse. His paddle strokes were light and swift, propelling the boat at surprising speed. "By the time I learned the Reed Ways it never occurred to me to leave. This is my home. Dhoone doesn't need me. She's strong. Gray needs me. This marsh needs me. The people in the round-house need me. And that being needed, that's what makes a life worth living."

Rime fell silent as he paddled onto the Stillwater. The wind had died and the lake's surface was glossy and black. Fishing craft glided across it, heading home ahead of the dark.

"You are needed and wanted here," Rime said, guiding the boat toward one of the landings. "It is our hope that Gray will become your home."

Effie spoke the word *Blackhail* to herself as Rime tied up the boat. She felt a bit sorry for him and Clan Gray, but couldn't imagine this place ever being home. And she wasn't sure she trusted him either. There were things he wasn't telling.

"What's the fourth rule?" she asked as he helped her off the boat. "You only gave us three."

Rime gave her a long, speculative look. When he blinked, you could see that even his eyelids were tattooed with scales. "Never head more than an hour east. The Sull border is no place for a clansman."

CHAPTER 20

Hailstone

"Robbie Dun Dhoone has crowned himself a king."

Raina walked through the roundhouse, thinking about the latest news from the south. Warriors had arrived an hour earlier. She had settled them in the Great Hearth and and spoken with them at length, and now left them in the company of Ballic the Red and the senior clansmen. Her face burned at the thought of what Ballic might be telling the four warriors at this very moment. *Raina's closed the house to Scarpes. She's turfed out every one of them, and Yelma's camped by the Oldwood, spoiling for a fight.*

Raina snorted. Either she was going insane or it was somehow possible to feel worry, fear and delight at exactly the same time.

Gods, but the roundhouse was better without them. No more stinking cookfires and foul witches' brews. No more hard-faced children hissing "Bitch" behind her back. No more pigs and chickens running wild in the hallways. No more being watched and criticized and accused.

If time could freeze in this moment, as she walked through

the peaceful and orderly halls of Blackhail, passing Hailsmen and Hailswomen who greeted her with respect, it would be a good kind of life. She wished she could live it and not have to think of the future, and the terrible things waiting there.

Dagro, my love, I miss your wisdom today. Reaching the entrance hall, Raina took a turn toward the kitchens. She needed to think what effect this latest news had on Blackhail. Dun Dhoone was now a king. Bludd forces had been occupying the Withyhouse and according to Glynn Sellwood, one of the warriors newly arrived from Bannen Field, Dhoone had annihilated them. Two of the Dog Lord's sons—Thrago and Hanro—had been slaughtered. Glynn had mentioned a third son, Gangaric, who had managed to flee south with a small force. Raina crossed the kitchen, nodding absently at Merritt Ganlow and the head cook. What could she learn from this? Dun Dhoone was ruthless and ambitious. And he kept winning.

Arriving at a small flight of stairs, Raina unhooked a safe lamp from the wall and headed to the underlevels of the Hailhouse. How would Mace react to Dhoone's victory? He would probably make a push for Ganmiddich, try and gain the Crab Gate before Dhoone marched south. It was possible that he might turn and head for home, but he'd lose standing with his fellow warriors by doing so.

Hailsmen did not back down from fights.

Raina moved quickly through the narrow corridors belowground. The Hailhouse was aging. The explosion in the guidehouse had opened huge cracks in the foundation. First water came in, and now the earth itself was forcing its way through. Black mud oozed from the walls. Raina could see insect carapaces and bones in it. She tried to avoid stepping in the sludge as she made her way to the foundation space and the small, airless store room where she had hidden the last fragment of the Hailstone.

It sung to her in her dreams. It told her not to forget it existed and warned her that a guidestone hidden from sight was an affront to the gods. As soon as she entered the store room, she could feel it pull on her. How it had remained hidden all these months was a mystery. Surely any clansman or clanswoman walking above it would feel the steady discharge of power?

Raina knelt. The room was cool and dry, like a tomb. Setting down the lamp, she studied the wedge-shape fragment of granite. Dust had not gathered on it. It was an exterior corner piece and you could still see the chisel marks. Raina reached out and ran a finger along the ridges. Something deep beyond the stone, and older than the clanholds, reached back. She wasn't afraid or surprised . . . she was sad. The Stone Gods and whatever power they laid claim to were retreating from the world of men. They still occupied space, would continue to occupy space, but that space was getting smaller as an Age turned. She did not question how she knew this. It was guidestone. Touch it and truth was revealed.

Withdrawing her hand she waited as the knowledge worked on her mind. She had hoped that Orwin would return soon with Blackhail's new guide, some earnest young boy or girl who had been trained by the fierce mind and drill-sergeant tactics of Walvis Harding, clan guide at Dregg. Orwin's return was no longer a simple thing though. A man in a cart loaded with food and grain would not be allowed to pass Yelma Scarpe's line. The Weasel chief had already intercepted shipments from tied clansmen. Farmers bringing winter kale, storehouse roots vegetables and dried grain, ewemen bringing the first new lambs of the season and cattlemen bringing calves: the armed camp at the Oldwood had blocked and seized them all.

It was a problem, and one Raina knew she would have to deal with. She had caused this, and if she had thought in advance about the implications of sending Yelma and her Scarpers from the Hailhouse she would have—*should* have— acted with some diplomacy. Instead she had got angry and let herself react to Yelma's pinched and unlovely face. Now she had an unlovely mess on her hands. A thousand angry and hungry Scarpes were on her threshold. And short of declaring out-and-out war she could not think how to be rid of them.

What was becoming obvious with every passing day was the fact that Yelma was digging in for the long haul. Trees were being felled, shanties were being raised. Rumor had it that a fight-and-tourney circle had been cleared. And why not? Why not claim the old briar meadow and ruined farmhouse east of the Oldwood? Scarpes did not possess a roundhouse: they might as well camp here instead of there.

Raina rubbed the tip of her finger. It was still tingly where it had touched the stone. Camp here and Scarpes could feed their hungry, lazy selves by seizing Blackhail-bound goods coming in from the east or south. So far they had not killed any tied Hailsmen in the process of relieving them of goods, but they had not treated them kindly. One eweman had taken a spear through the side. Laida Moon was tending him. She said he was lucky the blade missed his gut. Raina's heart ached to think of it: a man alone and outnumbered protecting his sheep.

What had she created? And how was she going to fix it?

Yelma Scarpe was contending that she, Raina Blackhail, was illegally occupying the Hailhouse. According to Yelma, Mace Blackhail had asked the Scarpe chief to look out for Blackhail while he was away, and by barring the door to her and her Scarpemen, Raina was effectively usurping Blackhail's chiefship. So by staying close to the Hailhouse and monitoring the situation, Yelma was simply acting in Mace Blackhail's interests.

Raina took a deep breath. Yelma Scarpe was driving her to her wits' end—literally. She did not have the wit to deal with her. Raina supposed she should be grateful that Yelma had so far refrained from intercepting sworn warriors returning from Bannen Field. Such an act would be an irreversible act of aggression. But Yelma was slowly gathering power at the Oldwood and Raina wouldn't put anything past her. She had looked into the Weasel chief's eyes and seen the treachery there.

Yelma Scarpe wanted Blackhail for herself.

Leaning forward, Raina grabbed the last fragment of the Hailstone in both hands and lifted it a foot above the ground. With a small downward movement of her wrists, she drove it into the floor. A single piece broke off and shot across the storeroom. Raina released her hands from the Hailstone and stood. She could see the path the splinter had taken. It had cleared a straight line in the dust. Bending at the waist, she picked up the fragment. It was the size and shape of a grain of wheat. She looked at it a moment, turned it to see all sides, and then slid it under her tongue.

"I pledge to defend Blackhail and stop at nothing to save us and give my last breath to the Heart of Clan."

The old words of oathspeaking had power, even now, as the

gods who heard them were withdrawing from the clans. It was First Oath, spoken by young warriors who were not yet deemed ready to commit themselves wholly and for life to one clan. *For one year and a day*, ended the oath.

Raina Blackhail of Clan Blackhail stood in perfect stillness, thirty feet belowground, within the roundhouse of her adopted clan and tasted the bitter salts in the guidestone. She would never see the walled gardens and painted halls of Dregg again, she knew that now. Her hope of returning to her birth clan and living a peaceful and sunlit life was dead.

Peace was not in her future.

War was.

Raina opened her mouth and spoke the words that would seal her fate. "I give myself wholly to Blackhail for one lifetime and a day."

The stillness did not break, nothing on the surface of the world changed, so she couldn't understand why tears sprang in her eyes. After all that she had been through, wasn't this a very small thing? She loved Blackhail, loved it with a fierce and possessive love. Now the clan she wanted to possess, possessed her back.

Raina brought her hand to her lips. This was where the oath's second should step forward and take possession of the swearstone. She had no second. No one to keep the swearstone. No one to support her oath.

I keep it alone.

Closing her eyes, she swallowed. Muscles in her throat contracted, pushing it down. She felt the swearstone pass down her esophagus and enter her stomach, felt it sink against her gut wall and start burning a place for itself in her body. Within a day it would seal itself off, her flesh closing in around it: a piece of Blackhail and its failing gods in the center of her being.

Somewhere Inigar Stoop's body was turning in its grave.

Raina's smile was shaky. Dagro, Anwyn, Inigar, Orwin away at Dregg: all the wise people of Blackhail had gone. That left the unwise to rule.

I'd better get started then. She scooped up the lamp and exited the chamber. As she made her way up through the underlevels she couldn't understand why the swearstone made her feel lighter, not heavier. Did it not increase her burdens? When she passed a narrow, recessed flight of stairs leading up toward the chief's chamber, she began to understand what the gods had given her in payment for her life.

A clear conscience.

Any act, big or small, hot-blooded and reckless or cold-blooded and ruthless, was justified in defense of her clan. Ancient words now commanded her to *stop at nothing* to protect Blackhail. Stannig Beade's slaughter fell within their mandate. Just like Yelma Scarpe, Beade had been a threat to Blackhail, sneaking power while its chief was away at Bannen Field.

Some long-held tightness in Raina's chest—she did not know if it was guilt or shame or fear of being caught—relaxed. Sworn warriors did not weep over their kills or worry what others though of them. They slept well and deeply at night.

Raina ran up the stairs to the kitchen. Funny how you could have a burden and not know it until it was suddenly and surprisingly removed.

Merritt Ganlow was overseeing the cleanup and removal of Scarpe debris from the roundhouse. Today she had turned her considerable attention toward the kitchens, where she was supervising a handful of pretty girls as they scoured butcher blocks, fire irons, cauldrons and cook pots. Raina considered most of it a waste of time. The girls could be better used in the kaleyard planting greens or in the Wedge setting traps. Merritt knew this and as Raina walked toward her, the clanswoman folded her arms in expectation of a fight.

"We'll be doing the entrance hall next."

Raina looked at Merritt's clever face, with its green eyes and wrinkled skin, and realized that the clanswoman was in some fundamental way *different* from her now. Merritt's folded arms and bristling manner in no way engaged Raina. In the past Raina knew she would have bristled right back in response and a battle of wills would have ensued. Today, in the kitchen, with the swearstone burning a hole in her core, she said only, "Good."

Merritt blinked. Her eyes and ears registered a change in Raina, but she did not understand what that change was. Raina saw worry in the older woman's eyes.

She had no time for it, and bowed and left Merritt to her domain. She was so anxious to be outside that she took the kitchen's rear door. With its bloodstained sawdust and chicken feathers, the kitchen court was not a place she cared to be. A boy was collecting eggs from the chicken coops. Raina bid him stop and find Chella Gloyal. As the boy ran to do her bidding, Raina walked off the kitchen court and turned toward the kaleyard.

She had not been in the yard since Jani Gaylo's death. The poor, silly misguided girl had fallen under the spell of Stannig Beade and ended up dead in a well shaft because of it. Raina's gaze went to the well as soon as she opened the wood gate. Beautifully cut and fitted rosestone surrounded the wellhead, and two curved stone benches hugged it on either side. They looked as little used as any tomb, and Raina found no desire to approach them.

She was pleased to see vegetable beds had been raised. Crossing to inspect them, she searched for the first shoots of the season.

"Just as well there's nothing yet. The frost would only kill them."

Raina looked up to see Chella Gloyal standing next to her. She had not heard the Croserwoman approach.

Surprise made Raina sharp. "It's too late for frosts."

A single look, not ungently given, reprimanded Raina for making the mistake of applying the past to now. Chella looked healthy and alive. Color was glowing in her cheeks and her lovely dark hair was loose. "Glynn brought me a message from Grim," she said, explaining her high spirits and color and perhaps making an effort to change Raina's mood. "He, Corbie, Stellan and Drew are safely at Bannen. But then, of course, you would know."

Raina did know. Mace had received delivery of the Blackhail treasure, and by at least one account was ill pleased. He had expected more gold. Raina wasted no thought on that. "Is Grim settling in for the long siege?"

Chella Gloyal was sharp. She knew, she just knew, what the question really meant. "Oh, I would say so," she replied, keeping that gray-green gaze of hers on Raina. "I don't expect him back anytime soon."

So Chella thought that Mace would stay put on Bannen Field. Raina was glad to hear it. She was beginning to suspect that Chella had access to sources of information that she, Raina Blackhail, did not. This morning, while she was settling Glynn

Sellwood and the other three clansmen in the Great Hearth, Glynn had handed her a leather satchel.

"I'm sorry, lady, to trouble you with this task, but I normally give them to Anwyn."

The satchel contained messages for people in the clan. Raina had never spared a thought for who controlled delivery of messages in the roundhouse. If she'd stopped to consider it she would have said that returning warriors either delivered the messages themselves or set children, or whoever was close and unemployed, to the task. She would have been wrong. Sweet Anwyn Bird, always ready with beer and fried bread whenever warriors walked in the door, was the one who took possession of all messages entering the roundhouse. Raina reeled to think about it. Had Anwyn opened and read messages sent to her by Dagro, Mace, Shor Gormalin, Drey Sevrance? Were a clan's worth of secrets sharing Anwyn Bird's grave?

Even without opening the messages you could learn things. Emptying the contents of the satchel, Raina had discovered three separate letters addressed to Chella Gloyal. One of the messages had Croser's pike seal upon it and another had the thick parchment and fancy blue ink of something sent from a mountain city. Chella Gloyal had a faraway friend, one who had gone to the trouble of sending a message onto Bannen Field.

Raina had passed the messages to Jebb Onnachre for distribution. Next time perhaps she would open then. *Stop at nothing*, commanded the oath.

Now it was time to see if Chella had learned anything else from either Grim or Croser or her blue-inked city friend. "Glynn thinks Dun Dhoone will march straight to Ganmiddich without first returning to Dhoone."

"It seems likely. Robbie Dhoone is on winning streak, though things *have* fallen in his favor so far."

"How so?"

"When he took Dhoone from the Dog Lord he only had to battle a force of forty men. Withy was harder—they say its house is built like a sealed tomb—but somehow he managed to locate and break a secret door."

Glynn had mentioned nothing about this. Raina began a circuit of the kaleyard. It was only noon, she noticed. She'd felt as if she'd lived a year in half a day.

"What do you think will happen at Ganmiddich?"

Chella, who was keeping abreast of her, shrugged. "Bludd will lose it for a certainty. Pengo is a fool. It's a wonder he's held out for so long. As for what happens when Blackhail meets Dhoone . . . who knows? One thing's for certain: When it's over things will be settled in the clanholds for a very long time."

Raina shivered. Suddenly she did not feel like walking and stopped. "Because of the losses?"

"Because of the losses," Chella repeated.

The Hailstone burned in Raina's gut.

Stone Gods save us.

To Chella she said, "Why did you fire on Yelma Scarpe?"

The Croserwoman had either the sense or decency not to deny it. She had been the marksman on the roof that day; Raina was certain of it.

"When I heard the Scarpe chief was arriving, I anticipated a problem."

I bet you did. "Go on."

"At Croser we know the value of a well-placed bowman. I didn't think there was much to lose by slipping on the roof and keeping watch."

"You shot at a chief."

"I aimed to miss."

"You took my authority from me."

"I did not. I backed it up."

"What is the truth of you, Chella Gloyal? You come here and start pushing me—*why?*"

The Croserwoman took a breath. She was vibrating at a high frequency, like a rung bell. "You do not know how great you are. I see it. Others see it. There is no one else like you, Raina Blackhail. Hundreds and hundreds of clansmen and clanswomen would follow you with full hearts to their deaths."

Tears stung Raina's eyes as she looked at Chella's strong and beautiful face. Could what she said be true?

No. No.

I am coping, just trying to get from one day to the next and not think about what happened in the Oldwood or fall apart when I remember Dagro's face. There's no greatness here, just struggle. Any woman in this clan could have done a better job.

Chella's eyes were fierce, her chin high. "Why do you think it was so easy to clear the Scarpes out of the Hailhouse after Yelma withdrew?"

Raina was surprised at the question. "Hailsmen and women were eager to have them gone."

Chella shook her head. "No, Raina. They watched you on the greatcourt, standing up for their clan and sending off an enemy chief, and it stirred them. They were filled with pride for Blackhail and love for its chief's wife. They would have ridden into battle for you that day."

No.

"Blackhail loves you that much."

Stupid tears rolled down Raina's cheeks. This was not true. It could not be.

"I'm doing what everyone here wants to do: comfort you, help you. Follow you."

The cold wind of treason dried tears on Raina's cheeks. It did not cancel out Chella's words as much as weigh them down so they fell to earth. Raina looked at Chella, saw that the young woman was now wearing the silver-and-black of Blackhail at her waist and throat. Raina thought she could almost trust her.

Chella waited. She was very young and she thought the future was something to be seized.

Raina knew you could seize something and still have it slip away. The Hailstone, as if in agreement, sent an ache through her gut.

Steadying herself, Raina thought about the future, how it could unfold in many ways. She made a decision.

"Teach me how to use a bow."

CHAPTER 21

He Picked Up the Sword and Fought

They brought him in. Pain was like a wild animal, tearing at the soft sections of his body, pulling him apart. He did not understand how he could bear it. Anticipating blacking out, he suspended most forms of thought. They dropped him on the bed. He blinked at the ceiling and it began to turn like a giant millwheel, slowly at first as it juddered into motion, then more quickly as it gained momentum.

He was dazzled by the sight. It was the night sky, rendered in perfect moving form, wheeling clockwise as it should, turning around the pole star. This must be what the Sull had intended when they carved the constellations into the chamber's ceiling, this instant when a world of pain and loss could be soothed by a world of stars.

Like sorcerers they paid no heed to their enchantment. They moved above him, unfastening buckles and latches, not ungently stripping him of armor and clothes. White hot pain burst across his rib cage as they peeled off the breastplate. It had an indentation as big as a fist, and the cartilage of his ribs had collapsed around it. Words were exchanged. Beautiful Sull words that sounded like spells.

He lost time.

Moonsnake bided in the darkness, her pale and massive form curled around itself forming a solid disk of snake. She waited for him now, he'd noticed. At some point in their acquaintance he had ceased to be extra weight. *Let us hunt*, she bid in language so primal he had to translate it into words. Images and tastes flashed across his eyes and tongue. A deer shivering as it died. A longbone snapping in two. The sugar-sweet spray of bone marrow.

No, he told her. Something, some half-remembered promise to himself, warned him to resist.

She hissed.

He opened his eyes. The stars had stopped turning and the pain returned. Night air descending through the moon-holes chilled him. They were working on his naked body, stitching flaps of skin together with black thread, smearing yellow-red ointment on open wounds, bandaging his ribs and wrist. *Did I lose another fight?*

Memories of swordfights floated in his head. There was no order to them, no way to be sure which one had occurred most recently, just a procession of beatings and stabbings and slicing where steel points came at him from all sides. Slowly, over the course of an hour, one of the memories settled into place.

"Addie."

The figures tending him stopped to look at his face, and he realized he had spoken out loud. Saddles of muscle in his lower back and thighs fired as he tried to sit up. Sull pressed him down. One of them put a hand on the damaged cartilage of his ribs. Pain seared him.

He lost more time.

Voices lured him back. A woman was speaking, and even though he did not fully comprehend what she said he could tell from the tone of her voice that she was speaking about him. Keeping his eyes closed, he listened. She spoke Sull and he could not understand all the words.

"He grows faster."

A male voice said something in response.

"It is not important. He heals well."

"*Sul Ji?*"

"Not yet."

He shivered, and the voices fell quiet. He could feel their owners inspecting him. He ignored them. Something the woman said had pushed a thought adrift in his mind. *Faster.* Suddenly hands seized his jaw and yanked it apart. Liquid flooded his mouth. Head snapping in panic, he coughed up the liquid, choking and spluttering. The hands grabbed him again. One slapped against the back of his head, the other cupped his lower jaw. More liquid was forced in his mouth.

"Drink."

He drank. Aware that he was about to black out, he fixed together his two words and repeated them as he spiraled into darkness. *Addie. Faster. Addie. Faster. Addie. Faster.*

Moonsnake was waiting for him. All it took was a loosening of will to enter her heart. She acknowledged him with the slightest delay between breaths and then they were one. Uncurling the great length of their body they struck north for the hunt. A half-moon hung low in the western sky. Time was short. Rich scents filled the air, but one stirred them more than the rest: fresh blood. The snow was melting to water beneath them as they cut toward the scent. As they drew nearer they tasted something unexpected in the air. Fresh blood meant a predator feeding on prey and they had been prepared to send off a rival . . . but this. This was an affront to their being. It was a half-moon, not a full one, and another of their kind should not be in their territory this night. They flicked out their tongue. Thrice. Tasted the creature's age and size and sex. It was female and inferior to them in every way. They increased their speed in proportion to the deficit.

Righteous fury filled them. They knew the instant their rival perceived them—the strong musk of snake fear spored the air—and knew an instant later their rival was helpless. She was gorging. Her prey, a newborn deer, was part-in and part-out of her body. The fawn's head and neck had been consumed but its legs and abdomen lay quivering on the snow. Its chest was in the snake's mouth. Immediately she began disgorging, contracting muscles in a wave from abdomen to head, forcing out the meal. Her milk blue eyes tracked the threat. Her scales *mirrored* in defense, making her instantly more difficult to perceive. It was not a strategy that worked when you were attached at the mouth to a deer.

They struck, their fangs fastening onto her abdomen and yanking her and her prey furiously through the snow.

Coven Mother. The rival begged in terror and pain. *Spare me.*

They yanked her again, but their fangs sunk no deeper. The taste of snake blood did not please them.

I beg you. The force on her abdomen had aided the disgorgement and as the rival pleaded for her life, the deer's head popped from free from her jaw. It was encased in a sheath of saliva.

Take it, Coven Mother.

Deer scent charmed them. It was late and dawn was

coming and this snake had been taught a lesson in prece-
dence. Withdrawing their fangs, they warned it, *Do not enter
this territory again unless you come with your sisters at full
moon.*

Yesss, Mother, the rival replied as she sidewinded away from
the kill. Bleeding and in terrible pain, she headed for the sheltering darkness of the forest.

They did not spare her another thought and fed.

Raif awoke. Mist and soft morning light poured through
the moonholes. Something was making a scratching noise in
the corner of the chamber. *Rat.* He was pleased to find an
appropriate name. Turning his head, he looked toward the
source of the noise. A figure dressed in gray was crouched
close to the chamber's oak door, smearing dirt on the wall.
Raif watched him. He had a small pot and kept dipping his
finger in it and dabbing the stonework. Raif calculated the distance between the figure and the bed, and then struck.

He had not accounted for the drag caused by pain but he
still managed to reach the figure before the figure could form
a defense. Hissing, Raif grabbed him by the throat and yanked
him away from the wall. The pot he held went skittering
across the chamber.

"How many?" Raif cried, pressing his thumb and fingers
into the sinews of the man's neck. "How many?"

As he spoke Raif heard the retort of the bolt being pulled
back on the other side of the door. A shout sounded. Footsteps
followed. Raif increased his pressure on the man's throat. He
was old and almost bald and his skin had the patchy dullness
of a Trenchlander. "How many marks have you covered?"

The man's eyes were wide. Spittle foamed at the corner of
his mouth. Muscles in his neck strained as he tried to shake

his head. Furious, Raif threw him across the chamber. Old bones cracked with the soft snap of wet twigs. Air wheezed from a punctured lung. Raif stood upright. He was breathing hard. The door burst open and three armored Sull rushed the room. Two held him a swordpoint while the third dragged the body from the chamber.

Raif felt hate so powerful he might have taken them on, swords and all, if it hadn't been for two words circling in his head.

Addie. Faster.

He could die here and he could not say that would matter much at this moment, but his friend's life depended on him carrying on. And getting faster.

Raif let the Sull direct him, allowed them to force him back onto the bed. By the time he lay down, the one who had removed the body returned. It was the Sull with copper skin. He had a needle dart in his hand, the kind they used in their blowguns. Raif knew what was coming. He braced himself.

Addie. Faster, he repeated, determined to retain possession of the words as whatever substance coating the point of the dart was jabbed into his veins.

He dreamed he was back at the Hailhold. Drey and Effie were walking up the stairs toward him. They were smiling. Effie was talking in her fast excited way, telling Drey some complicated story involving the Shankshounds, the remnants of her supper and Anwyn Bird. Drey was trying his best to keep up. Raif waited for them, his heart aching with love and joy. Drey looked older than he remembered. His brown eyes were darker and there were lines on his brow.

"Brother," Raif called to him, unable to wait any longer. "I'm here."

Raif awoke. A tightness in his chest made it difficult to breathe. Opening his eyes and looking up he saw the ceiling of the chamber, stonework carved with stars. Despair threatened to swallow him but he could not say why. He rose and relieved his body in the bucket provided for the purpose. As he went to drink, he caught sight of a small pot on the far side of the chamber. He set down the bucket and retrieved the pot. It was the size of a duck egg and made of brass. Something dark and greasy was drying to a cake inside. Raif smelled it. Linseed oil. He dipped a finger into the pot and looked at the substance. It was the exact same color as the chamber walls.

A memory slid into place. They had been covering up his marks, erasing them so that he had no record of the days he'd been imprisoned. As he tried to make sense of this, his gaze rested on the wall close to where the pot hand landed. The chamber was belowground and water was dripping through the cracks. Raif saw that one of the leaks had made a small puddle of water on the floor. Thrusting his hand in the brass container, he scooped out the contents and threw them in the waste bucket. He unraveled the bandage from his wrist, looked at it, decided that although it was not exactly clean it would do, and then used it to wipe the last of the pigment from the bottom of the pot. Carefully, he centered the empty pot on the drip. Satisfied he sat and watched it. It was going to take a while to fill, days probably, and even then it would only provide a single drink of water.

Still. It was something. It was a start.

Thirst made him rise and drink from the water bucket. It was strange swallowing something he knew was tainted, but it didn't make him take any less. He had a strong memory of what it felt like to collapse from thirst. It was worse than any wound inflicted by the Sull. As he finished drinking, the bolt was retracted and the door opened. Food was pushed a short distance into the chamber and then the door was drawn closed. A loaf of bread and a whole roasted ptarmigan rested on the stone floor. The ptarmigan was still hot and leaking juice. Raif sat and ate it methodically, gnawing all the meat from one bone before starting on the next. He didn't know whether or not he was hungry but he knew his body was hurting and needed fuel. When he was done he pushed the carcass and its loose bones into a pile against the door.

Feeling his thoughts getting softer, he repeated his two words. *Addie. Faster.* He knew what they meant. They meant he had to get faster for Addie. He had to start winning fights.

He began moving through his forms, darting into empty air, twisting to avoid imagined blows, and searching for the perfect line of strike. The stars on the domed ceiling and walls were his targets and he picked a quadrant and began slaying every star within it. As he moved he realized his body knew how to do this. It had done it before, practiced before. It made him understand he was losing his mind.

Later, when he lay aching and winded on the bed, he tried to string together his thoughts. Addie. Fights. Drugged water. The effort required was staggering. It was as if each thought came with a thousand-pound weight. Closing his eyes, he let himself drift. Briefly he touched Moonsnake. She was dormant while her body performed the great work of digesting a whole deer. The deepness of her languor affected him and he fell into a peaceful and dreamless sleep.

Even before he was fully awake he knew they were preparing him for a fight. Hands touched his body with firm efficiency, strapping felt padding in place before they armored him. The bruising on his ribs and wrist was taped, hinge and chafe-points were greased. He watched the two Sull moving above him and knew what it was to be a corpse.

When he was ready and standing, they opened the door. It seemed a change in routine, that closed door. Hadn't they kept it open when they'd prepped him before? Did that mean they were more wary of him now?

Three Sull, two armed with swords, one with a spear, walked him up the stairs and into the forest. It was dusk—it was always dusk—and a cold snap was crisping the air. The trees were giants and the moon breaking over the horizon sent their shadows racing to infinity. *Da-dum. Da-dum. Da-dum.* Sull drums were beating. Their achingly hollow notes were filled with loss.

Raif wondered when he would lose the part of his mind that felt fear. The heat of burning torches distorted the air, turning the Sull who waited for him in silence around the fight circle into horrors from another world. No one who saw them in this light could mistake them for human. Their skin, their eyes, the shape of their heads and the very *weight* of the space they occupied marked them as inconceivably different to men. Raif realized then that even if he possessed a whole mind he would never understand them.

Unprompted he entered the ring. Green torches circled him and it took him minutes to grow accustomed to the light. He searched out and found the figure of Yiselle No Knife, clothed in silver tissue like a queen.

"*Mor Drakka,*" she named him.

A line of fresh blood underscored her left eye like war paint. She spoke some words in Sull and then said, "Pick up the sword."

Raif could see the sword on the ground before him. It lay on a circle of blue cloth to protect it from frost. The blade did not possess the blue-white brilliance of meteor steel, but it was patterned in the design known as 'heron walks on sand' and was beautiful in every way. His fingers twitched at the sight of it.

"Where's Addie?"

No Knife raised an eyebrow and the new wound below her eye expelled a perfect tear of blood. She waited, allowing him time to understand that she could not be commanded, and then made a small gesture with her gloved and misformed left hand. Raif spotted movement in the crowd and tracked it. He could see Sull but not Addie. It gave him a sickening feeling in his gut.

Two Sull approached the low and broken wall of the fight circle. After a moment Raif understood they were carrying something between them . . . a stretcher. He spotted the sandy-grayness of Addie's hair as an armed figure in a greathelm entered the ring. Raif took a step forward, desperate to see Addie's face.

The cragsman turned toward him.

Oh gods.

Addie's skin was gray and slick with sweat. The fat had gone from his cheeks and lips and he looked an old man. He was covered with a blanket but it had fallen down around his chest. His right arm was gone.

Slowly, Addie's gaze rose to meet Raif's. The gray eyes were dull with pain but comprehension still lived behind them. Raif looked into them and saw he was known. The cragsman knew all his names and the acts he had done to earn them. Addie Gunn knew Raif Sevrance and still loved him like one of his sheep. Raif's one hope then was that Addie knew he was loved back.

Yiselle No Knife's smile was knowing as Raif bent at the knees and took possession of the sword. He ignored her. An armed figure was moving toward him and he needed those handful of seconds to read the weight and balance of the blade. It was surprisingly heavy, as if there was tang of pig iron as its core. Were they training him up? Providing a heavier sword for each fight? He did not pursue the thought. For the first time in what seemed like months, he perceived the raven lore at his throat. Plate armor was pressing the small black piece of bird ivory into his collarbone. He was glad of it. It reminded him of who he was.

Watcher of the Dead greeted his opponent with a set of blistering strikes. Sparks flew as steel smashed steel. The Sull was wearing the same diamond-reinforced breastplate that other opponents had worn and it sprayed a glittering spectrum of light. Raif knew that if he were wise he would keep his blade away from it, but he was not wise. He was furious. The Sull were killing his friend.

The Sull's heart was large in his sights. Every line of strike led straight to it and the sword *homed* along the line. The Sull's blocks were surprising in their speed and savageness. To have your forward momentum stopped by one was like being slammed against a wall. Raif absorbed blow after blow. Diamonds filed his sword. He was beginning to see a pattern, to understand that his opponent's blocks fell into three categories and he, Raif, could dictate which one his opponent deployed by shifting the angle of his heart-strikes. He began testing, sending out his sword but cutting each blow short. Raif saw the open space below his opponent's two-handed forward block as an opportunity. He just had to calculate the right line, hit just below the diamond reinforcement, on an angle to reach the heart.

Let us feed.

Raif feinted forward and withdrew ahead of the Sull's block. Stabbing his toes into the stone floor of the fight circle, he rebounded forward, sword in motion, and claimed the open space and the heart beating behind it.

The Sull's eyes widened as air and blood pumped through the hole in his chestplate. Even before his eyes dimmed, his legs gave way and Raif was left holding the body upright with his sword. Raif threw the sword and the Sull away.

The crowd gathered around the circle were quiet and still. A hundred drawn swords glittered in the moonlight. Somewhere beyond them the drummer changed his rhythm, slowing the tempo so that each beat existed alone. Raif searched for Addie, but could not see him or the Sull who had carried him away.

Yiselle No Knife stepped into the space he searched. "*Mor Drakka.* Pick up your sword."

Raif was shaking in violent bursts. He didn't understand what she meant. The sword was in his opponent. He'd won.

Spotting movement out of the corner of his eye, he turned. Two figures armored in matte-black plate and greathelms entered the ring. One was armed with meteor steel. The other carried a six-foot spear and a shield.

"Pick up your sword," No Knife said quietly. "You do not want to fail your friend."

Hatred for the Sull entered Watcher of the Dead's soul.

He picked up the sword and fought.

CHAPTER 22

Morning Star

Local belief held that it was good luck to enter the city of Morning Star during the few seconds of sunrise on cloudless days in late winter and early spring when the sun first appeared in the east and before its rays had a chance to extinguish the morning star in the west. Angus Lok entered the city at such a moment but he didn't believe in luck.

The city on the red lake glowed pink and golden in the early light. Angus entered by the West Gate, and as he was traveling without horse, pack, or serious weaponry he was waved through without examination. The Morning Guard's interest had fallen on a group of mounted HalfBluddsmen. In an earlier life Angus might have stepped in to aid the fierce yet nervous-looking clansmen. In this life he slid quietly away.

The Star, as the city was known to its residents, was split in two by the Eclipse River, which ran north from the lake. Entering by the West Gate placed you in the West Face of the city and to cross to the East Face meant taking a short ferry ride or crossing one of the half-dozen bridges and paying the Lord Rising a copper penny for the privilege. Angus Lok was just fine where he was. It was the poorer half of the city, peopled by fishermen, workmen, beggars, bidwives, mercenaries, men-at-arms, prostitutes and market traders. He knew this place, knew its streets and its dangers, knew where to go to get the best ale in the city and where to avoid unless you were spoiling for a fight.

The area just north of the gate was known as the Crater. A shantytown of wood huts, tents, cabins and lean-tos had been raised in a bowl-like depression on a mound above the Eclipse. Spring was flood season and not all the streets were passable. Angus took what routes he could. Boards had been laid across the mud in some places. In other places the brown-red mud flowed like lava, its surface slowly hardening to crust.

Money was Angus' first order of business. Since Ille Glaive he'd been spending coin raised in the sale of his sword and he was down to his last coppers. Normally money wasn't a problem. The Phage were many things and poor wasn't one of them. Any city in the North, most large towns, some villages and even some one-room alehouses on the road: Phage gold could be had in all of them. The brotherhood held wealth in many locations. A word in the right place to the right person and a purse with enough currency to live on for a year would be dropped discreetly into your hand. The Phage hoarded Sull gold, Forsaken gold, Forsaken property, Bone Temple riches, treasure sneaked from failing kingdoms, jewels given for services rendered, and others taken when debts went unpaid. They sat on their wealth like an old, suspicious man, stashing it in different places so that no one could get everything if he died.

Morning Star was the Phage's main staging ground in the North. There were rooms in this city that, if you were to enter them with a lamp, you'd swear you'd walked into an enchanted palace made of gold. Angus had been in those rooms—they were belowground, always belowground: you could not trust the weight of gold on wood planks nailed across a frame—but they were not his destination today. Phage currency came at a price. Take it and you would be tracked. Somewhere someone would stick a pin in a board and think to himself, *There is Angus Lok*.

Even now, careful as he had been, Angus rated his chances of evading the eye of the Phage as low. This was their city. Even if the Morning Guard had not marked him, a walk down any street might be enough. Angus knew to avoid certain places—the arms market in the west, the scribes' quarter, river gardens, and courthouses in the east—but you could not plan for a chance encounter on an unlikely street as someone who knew or worked for the Phage was out buying fresh fish or hothouse melons for his or her family. Angus accepted this risk. There was a point in most missions where stealth had to be cast aside.

The shortest route to the money-lending quarter required crossing the silk market. Angus foresaw no problem with this and entered the colorful tents and stalls of the largest clothing market in the North. It was early and vendors were still setting out their wares. Merchants and bidwives were draping their stalls with red-and-gold ribbons, bolts of turquoise cloth, embroidered belts and boned bodices, horn-and-paper fans, fake jewels, silk purses, lace collars and straw hats. Angus felt the skin on his face tighten as he walked between the stalls. A hole opened up in his chest and it was suddenly difficult to breath. Stopping, he put a hand on a tent pole for support.

"What's the matter, lovey? Too much of the black stuff last night?"

Angus raised his head and regarded the woman who spoke. She frowned, not unkindly.

"Need to get some food and tea in you."

He pushed himself off from the pole and left without a word. The quickest way out of the silk market was to retrace his steps south. So that's what he did. As the stalls thinned, he began to breathe more steadily and by the time he was clear of the market he was back to normal. Or something like it.

He had not expected ghosts.

Any man who had daughters and who traveled away from home carried directives with him at all times: *Daddy, I need ribbons. Daddy, can you bring me back a dress? Father, not that I really, really want a purse, but if you were to get one make it red.* Angus had been to countless markets in countless towns and cities and always—always—he'd spent time shopping for his best girls. It made him stupidly, grumpily happy. Baffling conversations with stallholders concerning the girls' ages, sizes and tastes. Paying through the nose for goods that to him looked like pieces of tat. Swapping vaguely embarrassed looks with fellow men. Most of all, it was the pleasure of anticipating his daughters' delight. Often he bought them something extra, some little surprise, because after they'd opened their expected packages it created unexpected delight.

And delight meant laughter and kisses and hugs.

Angus shut away the memory of his girls. He could not live and think about them. He simply could not live.

Taking the river route to the money-lending quarter, he skirted the banks of the Eclipse. Fishermen were casting nets and mudmen were digging the margins for clams. After the Eclipse left the city it flowed into a delta. Some of its waters streamed north to flood the extreme southeastern clans, some flowed east to fill Drowned Lake at Trance Vor, and one outlet, legend said, flowed northeast to the Night River and to the Heart of the Sull. Angus considered this legend as he walked. It seemed as good a place as any to rest his thoughts.

The money-lending quarter was quieter and more orderly than the Crater but it was doing just as good business. Trance Vor, Morning Star's closest neighbor, was a rich but lawless city, unstable in many ways. Smart Vor money went west for safekeeping. The mine owners and landowners who earned it weren't prepared to trust it to the whims of the notoriously volatile Vor Lord. Vor's loss was Star's gain, and Star's banks and moneylenders were some of the richest in the North.

Angus moved swiftly through the cobbled streets. Custom suited him here. The rules were keep your head low, do not look anyone in the eye and do not acknowledge acquaintances. When he came upon a small blue door with the sign of three tears drawn upon it in white chalk, Angus glanced over his shoulder and then entered the building.

Sitting behind a desk, sliding beads on an abacus, was a beautiful ebony-skinned woman. Two mirrors positioned at angles to the room's only window provided her with an unobstructed view of the street. A slender rope strung on a series of loops connected her left wrist to the latch on the door. Only fools and first-timers thought they entered Morning Star banks uninvited.

The woman lowered the latch, barring the door to the outside world. Raising an eyebrow she waited for her customer to speak.

Angus knew the woman and knew that she knew him, but form had to be maintained so he spoke his name and business.

She smiled, displaying even teeth. "I remember you now, Angus. Of course. Sit. Sit. Would you care for a glass of wine. No. Of course not. I see." Her voice was soft and aimed to charm but it was all business underneath. "Of course you realize that I can only release a portion of your funds. Your original request was that they be split between the Star and Ille Glaive."

Angus nodded, though in truth he recalled paying extra for the privilege of being able to take his nest egg—in its entirety—from either location. This was not a place for disagreement or threats though. Break the woman's neck and he would never gain access to the saferoom behind her desk and therefore not receive a penny of his money. The bank's security was layered like an onion, and just as the woman watched the street, someone else watched the woman from the saferoom.

"A third, is that all right?"

He told her it was. During his twenty-five years in the Phage he had managed to set aside a small sum for his family, enough to provide modest dowries for the girls and to keep Darra and himself comfortable in their old age. Now only one future he currently imagined resulted in him growing old.

The woman tapped on the inner door with fingernails as long as needles. She was admitted into the saferoom and the door was closed behind her. In under a minute she returned. Sitting, she slid a small cloth bag across the table. "I'll need you to sign the ledger," she said, indicating the book and stylus that lay next to the abacus.

"I already did." Angus took possession of his money—silver, judging by the weight of it.

The woman checked for his signature and found it. He

could see her wondering what, if anything, the other dates and signatures in her ledger might betray.

He let her worry for a while before asking, "Do you know where a woman called Magdalena Crouch lives?"

Of course she shook her head. Discretion was a reflex in her line of work.

"Maggie Sea? Delayna Stoop?"

She stood, indicating the meeting was through. Angus made her wait on that also, taking his time finding a safe spot on his body for the new purse. By the time he reached the door she was impatient for him to be gone.

As he went to touch the door handle he winced. "Damn arm. They stitched it but it still isn't right."

The woman gave him a perfectly disinterested look. Her gaze flicked to the door.

He didn't move. Rubbing his elbow, he said, "I think one of the stitches is about to pop. Shit. Who's a good surgeon round here?"

Distaste crossed the woman's lovely face. She gave him a name and address to be rid of him.

Angus let the door slam shut behind him. The surgeon's address was to the north, so that's where he headed. He purchased a fried fillet of trout stuffed in a hard bread roll from a street vendor and ate as he walked. Morning Star was fully awake now and its streets were jammed. A chaos of mule-drawn carts, dog carts and horse carts made it imperative to watch your feet. Angus gave way for carts but not men. He didn't know the exact location of the surgeon's house but the woman had mentioned Spice Gate, so he followed his nose.

As he turned from a narrow street onto a open boulevard, he got his first glimpse of the Burned Fortress. It dominated the north of the city, bridging the Eclipse. The river disappeared beneath it, subducted underground for four hundred feet. Some said that was how the river got its name, for the fortress literally blocked it from sight, but Angus knew the Sull had once held this river and the land surrounding it and had named the river *Lun xi'Cado*, Hidden by the Moon, before the fortress ever existed.

The fortress itself was not a pretty sight. It had been burned and parts of its exterior casing stone had hardened to glass. Other sections were the matte black of scorched earth, and there were some places near the base where you could still see the original tan-colored stone. History gave two versions of the burning. In one, Magrane Stang, the fifteenth Lord Rising, had set light to the fortress to harden its soft sandstone walls against the armies of Trance Vor. In the second version, Stang had set light to the fortress for no other reason than to see it burn. Angus was inclined to believe the latter. The past Lord Risings of Morning Star had not, on the whole, been sane.

Angus had no interest in the current Lord Rising or the politics of the Burned Fortress and the river gardens. They were relics of another life. The great scheming machine that was the Phage would continue rolling forward without him.

Reaching Spice Lane, he cut west away from the river. Scents of pepper, vanilla and lemon filled the air, making the day suddenly smell like Winter Festival. Angus purchased a sliver of fresh ginger and a cup of quince water from a girl with a handcart. He drank the water and returned the cup and then chewed on the ginger as he walked. It was his intention to gift the surgeon with fresh breath.

The cart girl had provided excellent directions to the

surgeon's address, and he arrived at his destination by midday. Signs of saws cutting bone and leeches attached to earlobes lined the street. Angus walked the length of the district and back. Passersby looked sickly. An unusually high portion had limps. The bank woman had named a surgeon who was not only located dead in the middle of the street, but also appeared to be middle in rank as well. His house was more modest than some, better than others, and his sign, though not old, did not look especially new.

Angus waited in a doorway across the street and watched for someone to enter or leave. When the better part of an hour had passed and the house remained undisturbed, he crossed over and rapped on the door. A small viewing window slid back in the door's upper panel, revealing a pair of youthful but bloodshot eyes.

"I'm here to see the surgeon."

"He's not here. You'll have to come back."

Angus made a calculation. "You're his apprentice. Maybe you can help."

The young man who the eyes belonged to shook his head. "Can't do it."

Angus shook his new purse. "It will only take a minute and I'll pay well. No questions asked."

Thinking took place behind the eyes.

Angus said, "If the surgeon comes back before we're finished I'll just tell him you and I are old friends, and you can keep the money."

No man or woman should ever agree to collude with a perfect stranger, yet to Angus' constant amazement they did.

A bolt was drawn and the door swung open to reveal a

short and burly youth with twice his share of facial hair. "Be quick."

Angus obliged. The boy looked strong and he had a nice weapon fastened with correct tension at his waist. He was standing in a square hallway with two doors leading into the house's interior. The boy glanced nervously from door to door.

"What say we go into the kitchen?" Angus suggested. "That way we won't disturb His Highness's domain. Hurry, now, I'm hurting up a storm."

The boy acquiesced, turning to open the door at his back. Angus followed. The boy hadn't asked for his money yet. He was making a lifetime's worth of mistakes.

Angus was led into a narrow kitchen with a door and two windows at the back that opened onto a tiny walled courtyard. The adjoining wall was lined with heavy shelving. At the corner of the room, a flight of stairs led belowground to what appeared to be, judging by smell alone, a root cellar. A chopping block laid with fresh green herbs and a wet knife told exactly what the boy had been doing before he was disturbed.

The boy cleared his throat. When he spoke his voice was lower and more formal, possibly mimicking his master. "What appears to be the problem?"

Angus moved to the chopping block, pushed back the left sleeves of his coat and undershirt, exposing the entire length of his forearm, and rested his knuckles on the table.

The boy's mouth fell open.

"It burns," Angus said, looking the boy straight in the eye. "I need something for it."

Nodding absently, the boy regarded the foot-long scar that ran from an inch above Angus' wrist to the tender inside skin of his elbow joint. Proud flesh had formed two thick ridges along the original wound and the scar was hard and raised and shiny. "Looks old," the boy said, tentatively touching Angus's arm — but not the scar — with his index finger. "It healed clean."

Angus pushed down his sleeve. "If you could give me something for it."

The boy's face changed as he finally understood the request. It was possible a shade of disappointment slid across his eyes.

Angus moved so that the coins in the purse clinked.

"Blood of the poppy?"

Angus nodded softly. "Whatever you have."

"Two silver pieces."

The boy was finally thinking. Angus laid the cloth purse on the table and pulled apart the drawstring. Dozens of small silver coins streamed onto the chopping surface. Looking carefully at the boy, Angus pushed three coins his way. It was probably more than he earned in six months.

"I'll get the poppy." The boy moved around the kitchen, pulling a set of wooden steps from the corner by the stairs and setting them under the heavily laden shelves that lined the kitchen's east wall.

"What's your name?" Angus asked as the boy climbed the steps and sorted through various pots and glass vials.

"Jeddiah."

The boy was busy and did not think to ask the question in return, and Angus Lok never volunteered information. "Is your master tending anyone with badly burned hands? A woman."

Jeddiah's head shook. "No." He'd pulled down a jar, uncorked the stopper and sniffed. Satisfied with the contents, he descended the steps.

"Have you got something for a sore gut while you're there?" Angus sent him up again. He liked his subjects distracted. While the boy considered the appropriate remedy, Angus said, "Do you know most of the surgeons on the street?" The boy nodded as he reached for a jar. "And I bet you talk with the other apprentices?"

Locating what he needed, the boy jumped down. "I see them, yes. What's it to you?"

Angus let his gaze drift to the table. The purse was still open, its contents glittering in the dim kitchen light. "You can have it all if you find me the woman with burned hands. A doctor in this city will be seeing her. She needs stitches and skin flaps removed. Burn care. Ointments. The hands are in a bad way. Talk to the other apprentices, find out who's tending them."

The boy placed two jars, one glass, one made from glazed brown pottery, on the table. He was eighteen or nineteen and if Angus Lok had to guess he'd say the boy's master was working him too hard. The swollen veins in his eyes were from lack of sleep.

"Why do you want to find her?"

Angus knew the boy was his then. "She's my sister. She's led a less than perfect life . . ." Angus let the sentence trail off, letting the boy write his own end to it. Prostitution, thievery, stupidity: whatever appealed the most. "With the burning it's gone too far. My father and I are trying to find her, bring her home."

The boy's glance moved from the coins to the glass jar containing the blood of poppy. Angus could almost hear what he was thinking: This man and his family are deranged. "What's her name?"

Angus made a seesaw motion with his head. "Magdalena Crouch, though you understand she may use other names."

The boy wasn't about to admit he didn't understand. He nodded curtly, with force.

"Maggie Sea. Delayna Stoop. She usually picks names that have some relation to her real one."

"Like Magda Kneel?"

Angus smiled. "Just like that."

The boy's glow was touchingly girlish. A noise from the front of the house halted it midblush.

Angus scooped up the purse and the coins spilling from it, slid them inside his coat and moved to the back door. "In three days I'll walk down this street at noon. If you have an answer come out and meet me."

The front door creaked open and a voice rang out. "Boy!"

The boy rushed to the table, pocketed the remaining three coins, and then picked up the two jars and thrust them at Angus' chest. Angus accepted them, though in truth they had slipped his mind. He opened the back door.

"What does she look like?" the boy whispered.

Angus slid outside. "Why me, of course."

The boy looked surprised. Perhaps he wasn't so foolish after all.

"Three days," Angus reminded him in parting.

Clouds were closing in from the north as Angus scrambled over the courtyard's back wall and into the alleyway behind the house. The jar containing the sore gut remedy had cracked as he crested the wall and he emptied out the powder as he walked. It was, fortunately enough, the color of dirt. He set the empty jar on the ground against a nearby wall and transferred the second jar containing the blood of poppy to the interior of his coat. Reaching the end of the alleyway he turned south. He needed to find a place to stay. Somewhere in the maze of the Crater would do.

Angus Lok ghosted through Morning Star as the day turned cold and gray, not sparing a thought for the dangers that either Magdalena Crouch or the Phage could visit on the boy.

CHAPTER 23

This Old Heart

Big Borro was dead. Midge Pool dead. Wullam Rudge. Quingo Faa, who had been some convoluted cousin of Hammie's. Thirteen Bluddsmen dead in all, and a couple not likely to make it. The numbers kept mounting and Vaylo wondered what had happened to his jaw. Right now he could not think as a Bludd chief should think: *I'll get the bastards who did this.*

The enemy was a phantom. You could not kill what was already dead. There was no glory to be claimed on this field, no satisfaction in bettering the foe. Just horror and uncertainty, and no sense that the battle was won. How many had attacked in the Deadwoods? Four? Five? Against *forty* men. The Dog Lord did not understand odds like that. When Bluddsmen outnumbered their foe they won.

Vaylo began a circuit of the camp. It was one of those bleak spring days where the wind whipped at ground level and the rain turned into that persecutor of spirits: sleet. They were just northwest of the Bluddhouse, tactfully camped on the edge of Quarro's sights on the slope of a west-facing hill. Four hours ago at dawn Odwin Two Bear and Hammie Faa had left on a mission to parley with Quarro, and Vaylo was awaiting their return.

On the whole he didn't hold out much hope.

Nan was sitting by the campfire doing something with her hair. As soon as she caught sight of his face she stood. Vaylo waved her down. Her comforts would not work on him now. Idly, without thinking, he whistled for his dogs. Together he and the three animals headed upslope to look at the house they'd once called home.

Some said it was the ugliest roundhouse in the clanholds; Vaylo reckoned they might be right. He'd certainly ruled his fair share of them. Dhoone was like an ice palace, cool and blue, built to impress. Ganmiddich looked like something out of a fairy tale, with its tower and green walls and beach upon the Wolf. Bludd was a steaming mound. Ockish used to call it the Dunghouse, but he'd beat you senseless if you agreed with him. Vaylo had always thought the woods surrounding it were pretty. He found them beautiful today.

They used to say that if you wanted to make friends with a Bludd chief gift him with the seeds of a rare red tree. The saying appealed to something in Vaylo, though he suspected it had never been true. There were some nice trees in the woods and a couple of them you wouldn't see anywhere else in the North, fancy things with leaves like red lace and others with bark like rusted metal, but you could have given the rarest tree in the world to Gullit or his father Choddo and you would have got a smack in the teeth for your trouble.

Abruptly Vaylo turned away. He had spotted Odwin and Hammie riding back on the hill trail and he did not think it was a good sign that they brought no one with them.

"Tell Quarro I come in peace. The chiefship is his and I

*make no claim upon it. Allow me entry so that together we may
defend our house against all threats."*

That was the message Vaylo had bid Odwin and Hammie
deliver to his oldest son, Quarro Bludd. Odwin had got it
straight away but Hammie had to repeat it a few times to
make it stick. A second, no lesser, appeal concerned the Dog
Lord's injured men. *Allow them entry or send out Wendolyn
Salt.* Wendolyn was Bludd's healer now that her father Cawdo
was gone.

Vaylo tried not to worry but failed. He had begun to feel his
age, not in his bones or weakening eyes or loose teeth, but in
his heart. The mistakes he had made lived there, pressing
against the walls. Make any more, he suspected, and there'd
be no room for his blood.

To bide time before Odwin's and Hammie's arrival, he
made another circuit of the camp. They were still burning
some of the strange Sull fuel on the campfire. It was smokeless
and released long, amethyst-colored flames. Of course,
Bluddsmen had thrown wood in there too so the smokelessness
was currently disguised, but the flames were unmistakable;
slender swords of purple amid the choppy red fire.

The Sull had left in the night. The camp had awakened to
find them gone. No one, not even the dogs had heard them
depart. They left a gift of fuel and fresh meat—a night-killed
fox with an arrow point still in its heart. Vaylo had not known
what he felt about their withdrawal. He had walked the earth
their tents and horses had occupied only hours earlier, staring
at the flattened grass and dirt, waiting to feel what? Relief?

He had not felt it. The Sull had stayed with them for two
days and nights, setting their tents across the fire from Bludd
tents, fetching water from the stream, hunting, butchering,

caring for their horses, doing all the small and large things it took to survive in the wild, yet even seeing them eat and work at simple chores Vaylo still felt no closer to them. They were Sull. They were made of something different.

So why had he not felt relief when they left?

If any clan had reason to fear the Sull it was Bludd. Bludd shared the longest and most aggressively defended border with the Sull. Vaylo himself, as a new-minted chief, had learned a lesson in Sull might when he and a small force had penetrated the Sull border at Cedarlode. To this day Vaylo could not figure out the swiftness of the Sull response. Cedarlode was in the back of nowhere, a Trenchlander logging town in the middle of a burn zone. How had two hundred armed and mounted Sull managed to respond so quickly? The conclusion Vaylo had drawn over the years was that they had been watching him, waiting for the opportunity to warn the new Bludd chief against testing their borders. To this day, though, he still wasn't sure. For all he knew the Sull might have forces stationed at every league along the border.

That was the thing with the Sull. No one had any intelligence on them. Their numbers, movements and tactics were a mystery. Sull territory was the Great Want for scouts: they entered and never came back. Absence of information caused fear. Every clansman in the east had Sull stories but none of them had hard facts.

It should have been stranger to sit around the campfire with them. But then again perhaps there was nothing like a battle with the Unmade to level men. Sull, clansmen: it had been the living against the dead. The silent and formal camaraderie that had formed around the campfire later had been hard fought for and hard won.

Vaylo threw a stick for the dogs, sending them scampering downslope into the tough yew and alder brush. He did not like to think about what would have happened in the Deadwoods if the Sull hadn't arrived. Bludd had been failing. *He*, the Dog Lord, had been failing. The Unmade were viciously fast. They had surprise on their side. Their weaponry was better suited to the close combat of the bush. And their night vision was vastly superior.

To clansmen, the Dog Lord amended. Not Sull.

Those arrows, their trajectories, had been things of perfect beauty. A man could die happy having seen a Sull arrow find a heart. It was a revelation of God.

The big black-and-range bitch had returned with the stick, so he hunkered on his knees and wrestled her for it. She was getting thick around the waist and he wondered if she was growing pups. Releasing the stick, he clicked his teeth for her and she plonked herself across his lap. Her furiously wagging tail was a magnet for the sleet.

No doubt about it, the Sull had saved their lives. Bluddsmen were not equipped to fight in the dark at close quarters. The Sull *were*. Vaylo had to admit that afterwards the Sull were quiet about it. Sober. That was the word he would use to describe that first meeting. There had been formal introductions, swiftly followed by the necessities of tending the injured, the dying, the dead. There too the Sull had proven invaluable. Stretchers and splints were quickly fashioned, tourniquets expertly placed to stanch bleeding, fires were built, torches lit, and then the Sull, with a discretion that Vaylo had come to believe came from centuries worth of experience, withdrew to let Bluddsmen rest their dead.

Nan and the bairns washed the bodies. Dawn broke as

Vaylo closed the circle of powdered guidestone around his lost men. He hoped the fact that they had fallen on Bludd land would bring comfort to their kin.

Later, as the sun rose in a cloudless sky, the Sull had led them to one of their campsites—*in woods ruled by Bludd*. Vaylo wondered if his limit for amazement would ever be reached. Here, within a day's travel of the Bluddhouse, the Sull had established a camp. Naturally, Vaylo had ordered Odwin to keep his eyes lively, keeping track of the route and distance. Vaylo suspected the Sull had outwitted him even in this as the path they took seemed . . . circuitous and Odwin said later there were points on the journey they appeared to pass twice.

Within their campsite, the Sull were more at ease. Food was laid on the fire, water boiled for broth. There were four of them, three male and one female. The one who spoke for them was named Thane Foebreaker, and by silent and mutual agreement he and Vaylo waited until nightfall to speak.

"This Sull grieves for your losses." The sky had remained clear and the moon and stars lit the Sull—*the Bludd*—grove. Bats were in flight above the canopy, whirling and dipping as they fed on the wing.

Vaylo looked at Thane Foebreaker. He was small for a Sull, and no longer young. Perhaps that's what made it easier to speak with him. "I am sorry for your losses too."

The Foebreaker lowered his head. No Sull losses had occurred during the skirmish in the Deadwoods, but he accepted the larger meaning of the sympathy.

It was a good start.

"We have spilled blood."

Vaylo heard a world of truth in those words.

Only when the Foebreaker turned his wrist to the light, did Vaylo understand their specific meaning. A fresh wound cut crosswise against the veins of the Sull's wrist.

For my men. Vaylo thanked him. He knew then that he would not question the Sull's residency on his land, their secret network of trails and camps. How could he? Its smallness would only shame him.

Thane Foebreaker's night-dark eyes regarded Vaylo, seeing much that wasn't said. Wind stirred the trees. "The shadows rise and your house is not safe."

Gods, do not speak this. Fear squeezed Vaylo's chest.

"You should return home and secure it."

So much in so few words. Never in his life had Vaylo experienced a conversation so profoundly condensed. The part that came later, the offer and the tiny starling in its tiny cage, were secondary. Even now, three days on, Vaylo was still discovering new meanings in the Foebreaker's words. One thing that was clear was the fact the Sull knew all about Vaylo Bludd and his intention to take the Bluddhouse from his son. It boggled a man's mind.

On the second day, the Sull had led them from the Deadwoods and onto the rolling pasture northwest of the Bluddhouse. On the third day they were gone. It was strange, no one except the bairns had mentioned them since. Everyone was thinking of them—the Sull's solemn formality had affected the entire camp—but no one wanted to be the first to speak of them. It was possible the men were waiting upon some signal from their chief. *The Sull are still our enemies. The Sull are now our friends.* Truth was Vaylo did not know what the Sull were to Bludd. Trespassers, certainly, but as the Sull had once held Bludd land who was trespassing where?

"Granda. He's drinking the milk."

Four heads, one human and three canine, turned toward the camp, where Pasha and Aaron were lying on the grass, poking a milk-soaked rag through the globe-shaped starling cage. Vaylo frowned at that lot of them—dogs, grandchildren, bird—and then standing, went to sort two of them out.

"Easy," he warned. "It's a bird. Not a toy. And who says it's a he?"

"The Sull did," Aaron said, not the least bit ruffled by his grandfather's rant. "His name is *Mir'xell*. Homecomer."

So his grandchildren were now speaking Sull?

Vaylo watched as the bird walked forward, rolling the flexible leather cage around itself as it moved. It was a tiny thing, black with a bit of green in its wings. Vaylo scooped it up and delivered it to Nan. "Seeds and water, only," he told her.

Nan gave him one of her looks which just about said it all. She was beautiful today. Her long silver hair was dressed with ribbons and there was a fine chain around her neck. Vaylo touched her shoulder. As apologies went it would have to do.

"Chief," came the cry he'd been dreading. "Hammie and Odwin have returned."

Forty-five had left the hillfort in northern Dhoone. Now, including Nan and the bairns, they were down to thirty-two. Three were bedridden and two more—if they had any sense— should be lying right along with them. That left twenty-four able-bodied men. A good number for a chief's personal guard. A laughable one for a strike upon a roundhouse.

There was a very strong possibility that Quarro Bludd had laughed.

Vaylo composed himself. As he took up position at the top of the hill, he was aware of his men forming a line behind him. All were silent. Their families and loved ones lived inside that house in the far distance: sisters, mothers, fathers, wives. The men wanted home.

Odwin Two Bear was young but he'd learned a bit about diplomacy and his face, as he approached, was a neutral mask. Hammie Faa, gods love him, gave away the game. His slumped shoulders were an open book. Dismounting before they crested the hill, both men approached on foot.

"Chief," Odwin Two Bear said in greeting. A muscle pumped beneath the warrior's mark on his left cheek as he looked at the men behind Vaylo.

"You delivered the message?"

"Aye." Odwin glanced at Hammie who nodded for him to continue. The young swordsman met Vaylo's eye and then looked down. "Quarro denies you entry to his house."

Men inhaled. Someone murmured, *"Bastard."*

Vaylo stood and absorbed the blow.

Hammie could not bear the silence. "He thinks the stuff about you not being chief is just a sham to gain entry, and that once you're inside you'll knock off his head."

Vaylo was touched by Hammie's indignation, even though he knew Quarro was right. It had been a nice theory—the old chief retiring to second place to back the new chief—but in reality it would never have worked. Why then had he sent the message? An appeal had to be made, yes, but it was more than that. The Sull said his house was in danger. What was biting his tongue and taking second place to his worthless first son compared to that?

"They know our numbers?"

Hammie nodded, but it was Odwin Two Bear's face that Vaylo was drawn to, its stillness. Vaylo's gut began to turn.

"Will they accept the injured?"

This time Hammie's nod was a confused, diagonal affair. Odwin Two Bear remained still.

Vaylo looked straight at him. "What are Quarro's conditions?"

The swordsman swallowed, found his strength. "Quarro says he will accept everyone in this party except you. Or no one."

Men gasped. Out of the corner of his eyes Vaylo saw Nan drawing Pasha and Aaron away. She had brought the bairns forward to listen to the parley but now . . . Now this was no longer children's talk.

Vaylo closed his eyes, shutting out the light and the sleet. He had five men here who needed a healer's care. Twenty-four who hadn't seen their families in the better part of a year, two children under ten whose mother was dead and whose father was hundreds of leagues to the south, and one woman whose dearly loved sister Irilana was waiting in that house.

The decision made itself.

"Tell Quarro I accept his conditions."

"No, chief," said Odwin Two Bear. "I will not."

Hammie stepped forward. "Nor I."

Vaylo shook his head, but even as if he did so the roll call started behind him.

"Nor I," said Jud Meeks.

"Nor I," said Boddie Bryce, brother to Yuan.

"Nor I."

"Nor I."

And so it went on as every man in the camp refused Quarro's terms. The injured were carried over on stretchers and those who could speak did. One man moved his fingers. All understood what he meant.

Vaylo continued shaking his head at them, but some unlikely condition of the throat prevented him from speaking. When Nan stepped into his line of view and declared "Nor I" the men cheered. Pasha and Aaron followed, pushing themselves to their front, their small faces grave.

"Nor I."

"Nor I."

After that the dogs began howling and Hammie exploded into laughter. The dogs howled even louder to compete with him and began jumping like crazy things in the air. Then everyone began laughing, deep belly laughs that made your ribs ache. The dogs were insane. The men were insane. And they had an old and crazy chief.

Vaylo looked at them, all thirty-five including the lunatic dogs, and he felt the pressure ease in the part of his heart where his mistakes were stored. He had been many things in this life—his brothers' killer, a poor father, a bad chief— but he had always had the good fortune to lead fine men. There were the fine men who had helped him steal the Dhoonestone from Dhoone, those had faced off against the Sull at Cedarlode, and the thirty-six who had died defending the Dhoonehold. Bluddsmen were fine men.

Bludd was a fine clan.

Now how the hell was he going to save it?

CHAPTER 24

Stillwater

"I'm not putting my feet in that water," Chedd said, sitting next to Effie on the dock. Instead of swinging his legs over the end like she had, Chedd scooched up his knees, tucking his heels against his butt. He didn't look very comfortable but that was Chedd.

Effie ran her toes through the water. "It's cold but it wouldn't kill you if you fell in."

"As long as you keep your mouth closed and don't drink any of it." Chedd sent a chunk of clinker spinning parallel to the water. "No good for skimming," he commented when the stone dropped, without bouncing, into the lake.

His voice sounded a bit despondent so Effie turned to look at him. The cut where his chin met his jaw, despite numerous washes with alcohol and witch hazel, was still looking puffy. All of him looked a bit puffy. And pale. To cheer him up, she pointed across the water. "Look. He's bringing up one of his traps. Let's take bets on what's in it."

Chedd's gaze followed the direction of her finger. "That's easy. Eels."

They were sitting on the Grayhouse's east landing, facing

east. The Stillwater, the freshwater lake that surrounded the roundhouse, was looking especially murky and black. A handful of fishermen were out on the water. The one Effie had pointed to had just removed his float from the surface and was hauling up his trap. The trap was so heavy that it was chained as well as roped and big sinews popped out on the fisherman's arms as he pulled it from the water.

"Turtles," Effie said quickly before the trap broke the surface. "Loser relinquishes their rights to his or her midday meal."

"Done."

They watched in silence as the fisherman brought in his catch. The trap was a cage woven from cane, and weighted at the corners with little balls of iron. As the fisherman swung it onto the boat, water flooded from the trap. Slimy yellow pondweed clung to the cane and the fisherman pulled it off as he settled the cage in the bow of his flat-bottomed boat. He was wearing heavy boar's hide gloves.

Effie saw something twinkling in the corner of the cage as the man ran his fingers across it. Swinging toward Chedd she bumped him with her shoulder. "What's that?"

"Gold," Chedd said as if it should be perfectly obvious. "All the fisherman use at least one gold weight on their traps."

"For luck?"

"No, for *weight*. It's heavier than iron. Makes the trap sink right into the mud."

"I bet it's for luck too."

Chedd didn't dispute this as the fisherman was sculling his boat toward the dock and the contents of the cage were now clearly visible. Black and shiny snakelike fish thrashed against the canes. "Eels."

Effie couldn't say she was surprised. Animals were Chedd's *thing*. He knew stuff about them, knew whether they were male or female, where they were when no one else could see them, and sometimes what they were intending to do. It was the first thing she'd liked about him: he had some of the old skills too. That's what Mad Binny called it. Clewis Reed said it was sorcery, but Clewis Reed was dead, killed by Dhoonesmen on the banks of the Wolf. Judging by the eel call, Chedd's skills were still going strong. Effie was less certain about her own skills. Things had never been quite the same in that way since she lost her lore in the river.

"Look, Eff. There's a pike in there too."

Effie felt a chill around her heart. It was a pike that had taken her lore, snapped it from her neck when she fell overboard from Waker's boat. She hadn't told Chedd about it—*a pike took my lore* being the kind of thing that crazy people said—and she had managed to squeeze the memory into a very tiny and underused part of her brain. One word brought it back.

"It's a beaut," Chedd said. "A redfin."

She looked and immediately wished she hadn't. Now the boat was closer you could see the eels were torn and bloody. The pike was flipping among them, its gills huffing as it died.

"Must have followed the eels into the trap." Chedd spoke with deep satisfaction. "And then the beast itself was trapped."

Effie stood. "Stupid pike. What's it doing here anyway? In the middle of the stupid marsh."

Chedd shrugged. "They're strong swimmers and they'll move upstream against a current. Could come from anywhere—even the Wolf."

A snort of disbelief let Chedd Limehouse know what Effie Sevrance thought about that. She began to pull on her boots.

Chedd remained unruffled. "All this water drains into the Wolf. That's how we got here, remember?" Swinging around to face her, he said. "Eff, you have to dry your feet before putting on your boots. You don't want swampfoot."

She most certainly didn't want swampfoot. Groaning as if she were doing him a big favor, Effie rubbed her feet with the hem of her dress. It was getting a bit mucky down there. No one had thought to give them fresh clothes. Thrusting her feet into her boots, she said, "Looks like rain. Let's get going."

They ran along the landing and entered the roundhouse through the Salamander Door. The Salamander Hall was dim and smoky. It had taken Effie a while to understand why a room named after a salamander was tiled with turtle shells, but now she decided that if you squinted just right the lighter turtle shells formed the shape of a four-toed salamander stretched across the ceiling and the walls. It was subtle and kind of stylish: well worth the squint.

As she headed for the stairs, Chedd stopped her. "No. Kitchen," he said in his nonnegotiable voice. "You owe me food."

He was sweating hard for a boy who had only run about a hundred paces. "All right."

The kitchen was about as busy as any place ever got in Clan Gray. Women and a half dozen children were sitting at the far end of the long table, eating heaping bowls of garlicky mussels and sopping up the juices with toasted bread. A handful of old-timers—aging clansmen and fishermen—were supping ale and chewing on reed heads while recreating some ancient war across the lower half of the table. Pieces of

bleached bone represented warriors and there was some disagreement about placement and numbers. One of the
children kept stealing a chief.

Effie and Chedd received helpings of mussels and bread
from the Croser girl and then went to sit at the other table.
Chedd ate quickly, breaking open the mussel shells and lipping
out the meat. When he was done with his bowl, she pushed her
bowl toward him and he took it and carried on eating. Once
he'd reached the halfway point of the new batch, he said to her,
"You can dip your bread in my old bowl if you like."

Effie picked up her hunk of break, looked at it, considered
mashing it into Chedd's face, and then said, "You have it. I'm
going to call over the Croser girl."

Chedd's mouth was full but he still managed a groan. "Not
now, Eff."

Ignoring him, Effie caught the girl's eye and nodded. The
girl was peeling apples and she brought over her bowl and
knife so she could continue working. She didn't sit.

Effie said to her, "What was it like at Croser?"

The girl shook her head. She was dressed in a high-necked
green shift with an apron pinned over it and the tattoo on her
breast wasn't visible.

"We know you're from Croser," Effie said in what she
hoped was a low voice. "Chedd's from Bannen and I'm from
Blackhail. Hardly anyone in Gray *comes* from Gray. I don't
think it's a secret."

The girl stoutly continued peeling her apples; little dusky
gold ones with worm spots. Effie watched her closely. She
was a pale thing, but the color in her cheeks was steadily
rising.

"You know what I think?" Effie said. "I think you'd rather be here than Croser. I think at Croser you were different. Here, no one takes any notice."

Done with her apple, the girl put it in the bowl. The color had gone as high as her ears. She looked at the apple, took it out of the bowl, and began to core it.

Sensing victory, Effie stood, rose on her tiptoes, leaned in close and whispered, "I think you're like Chedd and me. I think you can do sorcery."

The girl dropped the knife. The old-timers turned to look at her. Smiling at them nervously, she retrieved the knife and began chopping the apple into little bits

Effie addressed Chedd. "Come on. We've got chores." Confident he would follow, she left the kitchen without looking back.

As soon as she and Chedd reached the Salamander Hall they broke into a run, racing up the stairs and through the house. By mutual agreement they did not speak until they reached Effie's room and closed the door.

"Holy bird fart," Chedd said, wheezing for breath. "You were just like a clan guide. No. You were like Behethmus, searching for the truth." He collapsed onto the bed like a felled tree. "Where did it all come from?"

Effie thought he was looking a bit green but didn't want to spoil the moment by telling him so. "Inigar Stoop, Blackhail's guide, wanted me to be his apprentice you know. If I hadn't been kidnapped I'd have been grinding the Hailstone by now."

"I wouldn't want to be Bannen's guide."

"I don't want to be Blackhail's."

This struck them as funny, and they laughed for a bit. Effie was relieved that Chedd was laughing and also relieved that he hadn't been embarrassed at the things she'd said to the Croser girl. He could be sensitive about his skills.

"So what made you think she was . . . you know?"

"The eels." Effie saw Chedd was looking blank so she said, "Come on, you know you had an unfair advantage on the bet."

"Did not."

Realizing she'd made a mistake, Effie put a hand up to placate him. "Sorry. I didn't meant that. It just got me thinking, that's all. Then I was remembering Waker and his crazy father. Crazy Da definitely had the old skills—remember how he vanished my teeth?" Chedd nodded. "Didn't you ever think there was a reason why Waker chose us?"

Chedd shrugged. "We were both on the river."

"It was more than that. Crazy Da was like a sniffer dog, sniffing us out."

"No."

"Yes and the kitchen proves it. That Croser girl's got the old skills too."

Chedd thought for a few moments. "She did look pretty uncomfortable."

"And that stuff Rufus Rime was saying about how he hopes it will become our home? Remember, he was so sure of himself? That's because most people who have old skills feel like outsiders in their own clan. Coming here's a relief. No one cares if you're strange. Everyone's strange." Seeing she was losing Chedd she added. "Not you. You're different. You've sworn to return to Bannen. Just everyone else . . . and me."

This was a lot for Chedd to take in. He put his head back and rested.

Effie was quiet for a moment but it didn't last. "They're bringing magic-users to Gray because of the curse. I can feel it. Either magic can help us withstand the curse or they hope we're going to lift it."

"Rime said there wasn't a curse," Chedd said sleepily. "Death happens because we're living in the marsh."

"Rime's lying through his teeth. Not about *every* thing but some things. He's tricky."

Chedd started snoring. Effie frowned and then clambered on the bed.

"Make room," she told him.

She slept and dreamed of the dome of the old Grayhouse, sinking slowly into the marsh.

"You two. Up. *Now.*"

Effie was immediately awake. Tull Buckler stood above the bed. Her skirt was hiked up and he was looking at her bare legs.

Effie scrambled to her feet. She and Chedd were supposed to be on pump duty. How long had they been asleep?

Chedd didn't move so Buckler grabbed his shoulder and shook it. "I said up."

A queer noise, like the sound of air escaping from a water-skin, came from Chedd's mouth. Buckler went to grab him again.

"You leave him alone," Effie screamed, thrusting herself between Chedd and Buckler. "He isn't well."

Buckler's brown-black eyes appraised her. With no effort at all, he pushed her out of the way. "Up," he said to Chedd.

Chedd moaned.

"He's sick." Effie put herself right back in the same place. "His cut got infected."

Buckler pushed her away again. This time he touched Chedd's neck. Swearing softly to himself, he checked Chedd's forehead and temples. After that he just stood and breathed for a moment and Effie felt a bit sorry for him.

"Stay here," he told her. "I'll be back with the healer."

Effie watched him leave and then got back on the bed with Chedd, spooning against his back. He was burning up. "Chedd," she said in a soft voice she hadn't used on anyone else except the Shankshounds. "Where's my Chedd?"

Chedd didn't reply but he moved a bit.

"There you go, there you go," she told him.

His shirt and tunic were soaked and as she pressed against him she could feel the front of her dress getting wet. Her teeth started chattering, though she wasn't cold, not a bit. "Chedd," she said into the soft skin and baby hair at the back of his neck. "Please don't be sick."

Crazily, improbably she fell asleep. The next thing she knew hands were upon her, peeling her like an apple skin from Chedd. She was placed on her feet and so she stood. She was surprised at the effort it took to do this.

Three people had entered the room: Buckler, Rufus Rime, and the woman who must be the healer. She was old, which seemed a good thing, with striking white hair and an austerely beautiful face. As the two men took up position by the wall, she examined Chedd. First she laid a hand on his forehead, then she used both thumbs to test for something at the points where Chedd's neck connected to his jaw. Next she stripped back his shirt and tunic and put her ear against his chest. The last thing she did was probe the skin around Chedd's chin wound, pressing lightly to test for give. During all this her expression remained the same, impassive. Effie took this a good sign. With Laida Moon, Blackhail's healer, you knew straightaway if you were a goner.

When she was finished with Chedd, the healer turned her attention on Effie. "Do you have any open wounds?" she asked in a voice that could only be described as queenly.

Effie shook her head.

"May I?"

The meaning of this question failed Effie. Her lips flapped.

"May I examine you?"

The flapping lips managed a "yes" and Effie found herself in receipt of a near identical examination to Chedd's. When the bit where the body was listened to came around, the healer turned Effie's back to the room before baring Effie's chest. It tickled. The healer smelled of water locust and mint. Effie thought of the jokes she could share with Chedd about receiving an earful.

Finished, the healer said to Effie, "You are well. You can leave."

Effie glanced at Chedd. His body was jerking slightly as he breathed. "I don't want to leave."

"I'm not giving you a choice." The healer made eye contact with Tull Buckler, who immediately started toward Effie.

Effie backed against the door. "I'm going." She opened the door and stepped into the hallway. Three pairs of eyes watched her. Buckler rested a knuckle-ringed hand on his knife. Effie looked past him to Chedd. "But I'm coming back."

She slammed the door before anyone could say anything. She was breathing hard and couldn't think.

"I should have been called sooner."

The healer's queenly voice passed through the cane-and-alder door, muffled but still audible. Effie froze. She heard footsteps and then rustling. Rufus Rime said something but she couldn't make it out. Suddenly the door swung open with force.

Effie ran. Buckler pounded after her, but fell back once she reached the top of the stairs and began descending. He probably figured he'd scared her enough. Effie kept running, taking the stairs two at a time. She dashed past the Flood Door and down more stairs. Her brain still wasn't working and she didn't know where to go. If she'd been at Blackhail it would have been easy: she would have gone to the dog cote and holed up with the Shankshounds. Old Scratch wouldn't have been there, because Old Scratch was dead, but the others would have come and jumped on her, piling on her legs, chest and lap until she was squashed by seventeen stone of dog.

Unable to decide what to do, Effie went outside. She had a bad feeling in her chest next to the place where her lore used to sit, and she didn't want to think why. Old Scratch, Clewis Reed, Druss Ganlow, Da, Raif, Drey: people and dogs she was close to ended up gone or dead.

The sun was setting over the marsh and the Stillwater was steaming. A luntwoman was lighting torches along the landing and fishermen and marshmen were tying up boats. One man was bringing a crop of bulrush heads ashore; Effie didn't know why. She needed to be alone but didn't want to take out a boat so she walked around the exterior of the roundhouse, moving clockwise from south to north. Some of the planks on this side were soft and rotting. Others had gone completely, lost to the lake. Effie watched her feet. The island the roundhouse was built on sloped sharply here and the water looked deep.

One of the benefits of walking to the west of the roundhouse was the sunset. It was orange and green and you could feel it on your face. Effie spotted a kingfisher diving into the water. It emerged a few seconds later in a different place, but she couldn't make out whether or not it had caught a fish so she turned to consult with Chedd.

You could really get used to someone.

Effie jumped onto a lower platform that abutted the Grayhouse's northern wall. Fewer boats were tied up here and no lanterns had been lit. Effie thought she was alone until she spied a movement by the clinker wall. Someone was hunkered down against the base of the roundhouse, rocking back and forth on the balls of her feet. As Effie drew closer she was saw it was a little girl and as she drew closer still she recognized the child's red hair and freckles. It was the girl she and Chedd had wanted to speak to all those nights ago after pump duty. They'd been so busy since then they had clean forgotten she existed.

The girl watched Effie approach. She was about six or seven, small for her age and thin. Her thick copper-colored hair looked more substantial than she did.

"Aren't you cold?" Effie asked, coming to a halt a few feet away from her.

The girl was wearing a brown wool dress without sleeves. A wisp of a shawl was the only thing close to covering her bare arms. She shook her head.

Effie wondered why she and Chedd hadn't seen the girl in so long. She used to be out every day on the front landing. "Mind if I sit?"

The girl made a little shrugging motion with her mouth. Effie took it as a yes and sat. "My name's Effie, Effie Sevrance. What's yours?"

The girl stared ahead. She was silent for a long time. "Flora."

"Like the Dhoone queen."

"No, like my mother."

There was no reply to that. Effie stared ahead for a bit, thinking. The stars were coming out; gas venting from the marsh made them ripple. "Do you put your cages out here now? I never see you at the front."

"No." There was something missing from the girl's eyes. It took Effie a while to figure out what it was: focus. She was looking so far in the distance she wasn't seeing anything.

Effie shivered. For some reason she thought of the pike. "What happened to your brother? I heard you crying for him once." She hoped she didn't already know the answer, but she did.

"He's dead."

"Did the marsh kill him?"

This questioned appeared to interest the girl. Her breathing pattern changed, speeded up. "They never found his body."

Effie didn't like the sound of this one bit. "Perhaps he'll come back."

The girl puffed a hard pellet of air through her nostrils, and Effie suddenly felt as if she were the younger one here.

"My friend Chedd's sick," she blurted out. "I need to lift the curse."

For some reason this brought down the girl's breathing. Some of the tension she'd been holding in her bent knees relaxed. "There is no curse."

"Yes there is. Gray's the Cursed Clan, everyone knows that. People are dropping like flies."

"It's the marsh. Makes people sick."

"That's what Rufus Rime said, but he's just dodgy." Even as she spoke Effie knew she couldn't say the same thing about

Flora. The girl was too far gone for dodgy. She was so pale you could already anticipate her ghost. "Is that how your brother died?"

Flora did not answer this question and Effie sensed she was losing her. The girl's focus was spooling further and further into the distance.

The only strategy Effie could come up with was to raise her voice. "There's some big problem here. *What is it?*"

The girl blinked. The spooling paused. "Magic to find it. Magic to block it."

Effie watched as Flora departed. She didn't stand, didn't move a muscle, but she left.

A sense of solidarity made Effie sit for a few minutes before departing. Get up straightaway and it would feel like desertion. So the nine-year-old and the six-year-old sat and looked at the swamp for a while.

It was full dark as Effie made her way along the landings. Water lapping against the pilings was the only sound in the night. Effie hurried to the Salamander Door. The marsh was a place where unspeakable things happened and she no longer wanted to be out here. Reaching the door, she discovered it closed and pounded hard on the wood.

"Let me in!"

The warriors who opened the door were amused by her fear. "We pulled a live one from the water," the older one quipped.

Laughter followed Effie up the stairs.

She had meant to go to the kitchen, find someone and tell them about Flora so that the girl could be fetched inside, but Effie forgot all about Flora as she raced through the house. She desperately, *desperately* needed to see Chedd.

Her heart quivered when she spotted the spearman posted at her door. Running toward him, she cried, "Is he all right?"

The spearman barred the door. "No one enters. Healer's orders."

Effie stared at him wildly. "Is he *all right*?"

"Sorry, love. I don't know."

Effie's knees gave way as she fainted.

CHAPTER 25

Target Practice

"I t's the heart," Chella Gloyal said, raising the tip of Raina's right elbow. "All archery targets are the heart. Release."

Raina released as she had been instructed, lifting her three middle fingers from the string. Air cracked against her ear as the arrow exploded from the plate. The string ricocheted forward, thrashing her left wrist. Raina winced. A C-shaped line of blood instantly appeared on her skin and she looked at it with a kind of puzzled wonder. She'd had no idea archery was so violent.

"Here. You can put this on now." Chella took the bow from Raina and handed her a three-inch-wide strap of leather, a wrist guard.

Raina wiped the blood on her sleeve and began the awkward struggle of fastening the guard against her wrist. Chella watched. Raina's fingers felt big and her wrist was smarting. A series of scars, at different stages of healing, stretched from her wrist to her lower arm.

"They're like widow's weals," she murmured, thinking about the cuts widowed Hailswomen inflicted upon themselves to relieve the pain of losing husbands.

Chella Gloyal wasn't impressed by this comparison. "They're a lot more useful," she said.

Raina let the remark go unchallenged. Chella was young and her husband was alive. What did she know about the very few ways the pain of loss could be eased? Finished with the wrist guard buckles, Raina said, "Hand me the bow. I'm taking another shot. I notice you didn't pass comment on the last one."

"Silence is louder."

Raina couldn't help but agree with that as she took her next shot.

They were on the graze north of the Hailhouse but south of the northern woods. The Leak, the stream that ran past the roundhouse, was flowing high at their backs. Chella had set up a target on the trunk of an oak: a melon-sized circle drawn in chalk. Raina had taken two shots already, but both of them had missed. Only one had hit the tree. It was her fourth archery lesson and this time Chella had made her stand at a distance of thirty feet—ten feet farther than yesterday. To add to the difficulty, the wind was shearing from the east.

"Let the bow follow your eye not the other way around. Elbow higher. Your knuckle should graze your ear. Hold."

Raina held. The string was cutting into the meat of her fingertips and her entire body was at tension like the bow.

"Release."

The arrow shot from the plate. The string whacked her arm but the guard protected it. *Thuc.* The arrow hit the tree, a foot above the target.

Chella did some more of her silent instructing, letting Raina work out for herself what she had done wrong. She needed to lower her bow arm and not overpower the shot. She said, "If the target's the enemy's heart at least I would have got his head."

"No. You would have missed the head. The head's small and there's always more air around it than you think. That's why we never target it."

"But the heart?"

"Miss it and we might puncture a gut or blow a lung instead. Miss the head and while we're reaching for another arrow we'll get shot through the arm—if we're lucky."

It occurred to Raina that the more she got to know Chella Gloyal the less she sounded like a clanswoman. Was Croser that different than Blackhail? Or was there something more to Chella? Raina thought she'd better watch her just to be safe.

Chella handed Raina another arrow. "Only use one eye to sight the target this time and keep your chin down."

Raina did as she was told and managed a serviceable shot, grazing the target's upper boundary.

"Fair," Chella told her. "We probably need to release some of the tension in the string. It looks a little tight for you."

Raina handed off the bow. It had belonged to Anwyn Bird. Raina had found it, still strung, in Anwyn's workshop. She watched Chella as the Croserwoman expertly unpicked the complicated array of knots at the tip. "Who taught you to shoot?"

"My father. He wanted a boy."

"He taught you well."

Chella's fingers danced along the string. "I practiced a lot. I used to bowfish in the Wolf." She smiled when she saw Raina's expression. "You can't call yourself any kind of bowman until you've shot a fish in running water."

"I've never heard of fishing with a bow."

"It's a Croser thing. Our bowmen are a little mad."

Raina laughed. She had begun to enjoy her mornings with Chella. The girl was full of surprises. "Did your father give you your bow? It doesn't look clannish."

Chella glanced at the shortbow strung over her shoulder. It was a built bow, Raina knew that much, made from pieces glued together, not a self bow carved from a single piece of wood. "You have a good eye," Chella said, biting off a piece of string with her teeth. "It's a Morning Star weapon. I got it while I lived there."

"That must have been something, to live in a city," Raina said. "All those people. None of them clan."

"That should do it." Chella handed back the bow to Raina. "Whoever used it last had shorter arms than you, so when you drew it there was too much tension. Give it a try."

Raina took an arrow, knocked it against the string and drew the bow. Chella was right. Drawing was easier now and the string didn't bite into her fingertips as much.

"Breathe," Chella reminded her. "Exhale on release."

For a wonder she managed a credible shot, the arrow entering the upper left quadrant of the target. Raina jumped up and down. "I got her."

Chella grinned. "It's a tossup between heartburn and heart-kill."

It was good to laugh. It was good to shoot targets. "Now I've got to learn how to do it again."

"Practice," Chella said. "Every day. That's the secret."

Raina's smile faded. There were no shortcuts here. It would take her weeks, *months*, to become a serviceable archer, let alone a decent one. And in the meantime the Weasel chief was sitting in Blackhail's western meadow, gathering Scarpes around her like a queen bee, and acting as if she had a right to be there. Only yesterday she had intercepted returning Hail warriors and questioned them as if she were their chief. Then she had the gall to suggest that someone needed to remove Raina Blackhail from the Hailhouse before she did any more harm. "Dangerously volatile" was the phrase Yelma had used. And then in the very next breath she had pondered aloud, "We still don't know who killed our guide."

Raina's cheeks heated. She could imagine the entire scene, the rich silk tent, the jewels on Yelma's fingers, the small pause as she allowed the warriors to connect the two statements into one big indictment. Luckily, the party had included Dunkie Lye and Marten Gormalin who had paid the Scarpe chief little heed and returned to the Hailhouse to tell all. Still. Whispers had started. There were some here— Merritt Ganlow and her widows and Gat Murdock and his old-timers—who night be secretly pleased at the Weasel's words.

"Release."

Raina blinked. She was hardly aware she had drawn the bow. Sighting the arrowhead on the tree, she lifted her fingers from the string. As soon as she released she knew the shot was bad. The string skinned her arm above the wristguard on the recoil and the arrow shot into the earth, ten feet short of the tree.

Chella set off to retrieve the arrows. "You held your draw too long. Lost concentration."

Raina heard kindness in the words. "I'll never be good enough to—" She stopped herself. "To shoot consistently."

Chella dug up the turfed arrow and pulled the others from the tree. "My father used to say that before you bring down your first deer you have to shoot a lot of rats." Sliding the arrows in her bowcase she went in search of Raina's first arrow, the one that had gone astray. "Of course, he didn't mean just rats. He meant anything close to home that wasn't afraid of the smell of humans—but should be."

Was she trying to tell her something? Raina studied Chella's profile as the girl searched for the missing arrow. Chella didn't look up. Raina would have liked to ask her, *What's your lore?* But that question was taboo in the clans so she went to butter up Mercy instead.

The two horses had walked upstream. They had found and investigated a small pond and had the frogspawn on their noses to prove it. Raina unfastened her wrist guard and used it as a scraper. As she removed the last of the jelly-like eggs from Chella's stallion she saw two mounted figures heading out of the northern woods. A little prickle of apprehension traveled up Raina's spine. *What now?*

The riders were unarmored and neither appeared heavily armed. They were riding at a trot and it was obvious that both had skills with horse. It was also obvious, though Raina would be hard pressed to say why, that at least one of them wasn't clan. He was wearing a saddlecoat rather than a cloak, though it was more than that. Something in his stance—a sort of relaxed keenness—marked him as different. He was wearing a bearskin hat.

Raina looked to Chella, who nodded and came to stand in a formal position at Raina's back. It was a signal to anyone who knew the clans: someone of high rank here.

In silence they watched the riders approach. The one with the hat was lean and ice-tanned; Raina could not imagine his age. The other rider was young and small, dark haired and dark eyed. Not quite a man. Reaching a distance of about a hundred feet, the older rider removed his hat and used it to wave a greeting. The unexpected and slightly countrified gesture warmed Raina and she smiled in response. At a distance of fifty feet the man cried out, "It's Hew Mallin and I do believe we've met, Raina Blackhail. I had the pleasure of knowing your very fine husband, Dagro."

Without a discernible signal passing between them, both riders dismounted and closed the remaining distance on foot.

As they came toward her Raina thought that perhaps she did know Hew Mallin, that he had visited the Hailhouse long in the past. A lot of people came to meet with Dagro and she had not always paid attention to them. Coming to a halt, both men waited upon her word as was proper. With Chella behind her, Raina felt as if she had a warrior at her back.

"Greetings, Hew Mallin," Raina said. "It's been a while."

His smile was quick and it was followed by a deep and courtly bow. "Ten years since I was last here, lady. Much has changed."

It was true enough. Mallin's yellow-green eyes looked straight into hers and she found common experience there: things lost.

He said, "This is my companion, Bram Cormac. It's his first time at Blackhail."

Raina welcomed him. He was a good-looking boy, watchful and guarded, with the dark hair and complexion of the wild clans. The fact he was a clansman was not in doubt. How could Raina put it so someone who was not clan could understand her certainty? There was a *vacancy* after Mallin spoke the boy's name where a clan should have gone.

"Lady." The boy's bow reached the same depth, if not the elegance, of Hew Mallin's.

Looking at the baby-fine hairs at the back of his neck, Raina decided not to pursue the matter of his clan. She sensed the question would be unkind.

With a small movement of her wrist, she brought Chella forward and introduced her to the two men. The girl was so fine and strong Raina was proud to name her a Hailswoman.

Chella, for her part, was subdued. Her nods to Mallin and Bram Cormac were brief and she did not speak. Raina was surprised, but her attention was quickly taken by the horses. The boy's horse, a fine black stallion, had slipped from his master's control and had gone to sniff Mercy. The boy raced after him but it was too late, Mercy had begun to rear. The stallion was young and interested, but Mercy wasn't having any of it. Grabbing the reins, Bram restrained it and pulled it back. Then, from a distance, he started speaking words to calm Mercy. Raina was surprised when the mare settled down. Usually when Mercy was vexed she did not take to strangers.

"Sorry," Bram said to said Raina once Mercy was still. "Gabbie's a bit willful at times."

There was high color in the boy's cheeks and Raina felt for him. "Has he had a long day?"

Bram glanced at Mallin.

"Many long days," Mallin said, taking the question away from him. "We've been riding south from the Rift."

Raina didn't know what to say about that.

"The Maimed Men pay coin for fresh meat," Mallin explained. "So we went to earn some pennies. Now we're heading back."

Raina nodded. She had heard the Maimed Men always needed meat. Dagro used to say they were terrible hunters. Certainly Mallin and Bram looked equipped to hunt: excellent horses, and two longbows, braced and ready, tied to the cantle of Mallin's horse.

Quite suddenly she realized they were waiting. Mallin, Bram, even Chella. They were waiting upon her word, just like men and women would wait upon Dagro's word in such a situation. These two men were passing through her clanhold. She could give them her blessing and let them pass, or invite them to enjoy the shelter of her roundhouse. What would Dagro do here? The answer was clear straightaway. Dagro was social and he loved company, and he also loved gathering information from different sources. He'd laugh and drink with visitors but you always knew he was chief.

Raina looked from Mallin to Bram. The wind was lifting Mallin's thin gray braids and filling Bram's patched wool cloak with air. It was a strange feeling, not unpleasant, having people apply for her hospitality. When she spoke she thought of Dagro and tried to do him proud. "Come and break your journey at our house. Blackhail will keep you this night."

The response, the gratitude and pleasure of it, kept her warm during the return ride to the Hailhold.

The moon, three quarters of it, rose early while the sun was still in the west. It was good to ride in the company of three skilled riders, good also to see the massive dome of the roundhouse silhouetted against the southern sky. You could find many faults with the Hailhouse, but size wouldn't be one of them, and Raina felt pride as she accompanied the visitors onto the stable court.

Jebb Onnachre came out to take the horses and, as was

often the case with grooms, knew Hew Mallin on sight. "Been a long time, Sir," he said. "Got yourself a new pony?"

Raina was pleased Jebb was acquainted with Mallin and also pleased with Mallin's serious and respectful response. This was no high-and-mighty city type with no understanding of the value of working men.

Bram Cormac was different. Raina could not fault his respectfulness, but he was silent and wary. She fell in beside him as they walked to the front of the roundhouse. They could have entered through the new construction on the east wall but Raina recalled that Dagro liked first time visitors to pass through the greatdoor. "A bit of awe never hurt," he used to say.

Altering her pace so that Mallin and Chella, who were walking side by side, pulled ahead, she said to Bram, "We don't bite."

His head was lowered against the wind but she thought perhaps he smiled, just a little.

"Where are you headed to next?"

Bram looked up. They had just rounded the front of the house and she could see the western sunlight traveling through the holes in his eyes. "Lady," he said. "I do not know."

She thought of that answer later, as she bathed and dressed for supper. Perhaps it was foolishness but she wished she could keep him here. He was young and she'd seen something vulnerable in him, and a life when you did not know where you would be tomorrow was no kind of life for a clansman.

She dressed with some care, loosing her hair and brushing it until it shone, and selecting a dress of fine blue wool. It was habit, from the old days when Dagro had visitors. The simple, womanly ritual soothed her. When she was ready she made her way to the Great Hearth.

The great doors were open and fire was dancing in the hearth. Torches ringed the room, creating a warm bright light. Raina wished that more of the benches were occupied, then checked herself. Only ten days ago they'd been full of Scarpes.

Food and had been laid out on the table close to the fire and Raina was pleased see that Merritt Ganlow and Sheela Cobbin had done a fine job. Platters of roast pork and spring lamb were set beside bowls of whole roasted onions and fried bread in gravy. Warriors helped themselves. Some were sitting at the table and other were at their regular spots on the benches. All were drinking. A fresh keg of ale had been tapped and malts of various ages and pedigrees claimed the floor at the end of the table. Some women and children had taken places near the rear and Raina hoped more would come later. It was tradition that when the doors of the Great Hearth were held open women, children and those without oaths were welcome.

Raina entered at will these days.

"Chief's." The welcome came from Hardgate Meese, Corbie's father, and she returned it with a smile. Hardgate was sitting in the company of a half-dozen hammermen and her smile prompted a general raising of mugs and a toast.

"Chief's."

Grinning, Raina crossed toward Hew Mallin. The visitor was deep in conversation with master bowman Ballic the Red, but broke off conversation as she approached. "Lady," he said rising and offering his chair.

Raina took it. She also accepted the cup of malt he poured for her. Tasting it she discovered that Mallin had somehow managed to lay his hands on the best malt in the house.

Ballic left to fetch some food.

While it was still fresh in her mind, Raina asked Mallin, "Where are you off to next?"

Mallin shrugged. He had taken off his saddlecoat, revealing a fawn brown tunic and intricately knotted linen shirt. "Maybe Spire Vanis."

Raina wondered how soon the boy would know. She said, "Has Ballic been telling you of our troubles with the Scarpe chief?"

Leaning back in his new chair, Mallin said quietly, "Word gets around."

Raina inched forward. They were sitting in the rear of the room. Mallin's back was to the wall. Smoke from the torch above his head was being drawn toward the hearth's chimney, forming a line like a spoke on a wheel. She said, "What have you heard?"

"The Weasel Camp's a thousand strong. More are on their way."

Dunkie Lye had mentioned a similar number. "How many are coming?"

"Word is she's sent for the entire clan."

Dear gods. Raina forced herself to think. "You mean all those remaining at Scarpe?"

Mallin nodded. "She won't pull any of her warriors from Bannen Field. It would be too . . . risky."

Raina saw the point. If the Scarpe force at Bannen was to suddenly pull up tents and head north Mace might start to get worried and turn right around and chase them. That was not what the Scarpe chief wanted. Yelma wanted to be well ensconced in the Hailhouse before Mace realized her true intent.

Taking a sip of malt, Raina let the information sink in. The alcohol existed at the divide between fire and smoke. She breathed more of it than she drank.

Mallin poured himself another cup but didn't sup. His eyes were green in the lamplight. "Yelma's a Scarpe through and through. She won't strike until everything's in her favor."

"So she'll wait upon the extra men from Scarpe."

"And she'll be counting cards as well."

Raina didn't understand.

"She'll be keeping track of your numbers. How many come. How many go. The less warriors in here the better. And remember, she knows the house is not secure. That new construction's not done. Half of it's still wood boards."

He was quick and he was right. A brief walk past the construction and he'd figured that one out.

"If I were you, Raina Blackhail, I'd strike that camp hard and soon. Take it by surprise and tear it down."

Raina stared at Mallin. Something in her gut was tingling and she wished she hadn't drunk the malt. She had wanted to be ready before she took action against Yelma Scarpe, ready to shoot from the saddle and lead men. There was no time for ready though, that was what Hew Mallin was telling her. She had to strike before Yelma's reinforcements arrived.

Mallin stood. "She has superior numbers but inferior position. And she doesn't think you have the jaw to strike.

"Prove her wrong."

With that he bowed and walked away. Raina watched as he stopped by the food table and served himself a plate of lamb. Within seconds he had fallen into conversation with the swordsman Stanner Hawk.

Raina put a hand on her belly. The pain wasn't the malt,

she knew that now. It was the guidestone, stirring in its pocket of flesh, reminding her of the oath.

I pledge to defend Blackhail and stop at nothing to save us and give my last breath to the Heart of Clan.

Raina rose and left.

CHAPTER 26

Small Game

They hunted close to the den and only tracked small game. They cornered an opossum in its set and dragged it into the moonlight to feed. Things were shifting within them and this would be their last meal before the full moon. Digestion took the largest toll on their life-force and they need to conserve, to rest. Releasing musk from their scent gland, they returned to the den, trailing a welcome in the snow.

Watcher hissed when they woke him, and lashed out as they tended his wounds. The Copper One reacted quickly, but Watcher was quicker and he took out a piece of neck. A dart jabbed his arm straight after that, and he found himself staring at the ceiling, aware of activity and hushed voices around him but unable to move. Someone brought a wet rag and cleaned the blood and tissue from his fingers. His nails were humped and yellow like claws.

A female reached over the bed to tend his left arm. Watcher regarded the curve of her breast, followed it to the bare, golden skin at her throat. Sull. The word jumped nerves in his heart. The female backed away, responding to the unexpected motion of his chest. She said something to one of the others, Sull words that he made no attempt to understand. They lied. That was all he needed to know.

Next they dressed him for battle. They took less care now and did not bother with chest padding or leg armor. They turned him to strap on the back plate and then left him, stomach down on the bed. Gradually, over the course of an hour, his body returned to him and he rose and drank water from the bucket. One of the moonholes was directly overhead and he looked up and saw the three-quarter moon above him.

He did not go gently when they came to take him to the fight circle. The Sull prodded him forward with their spears. Copper One was not among them. Watcher was glad. He wished him dead.

The forest smelled darkly green and full of meat. Moths spiraled in hopeless circles toward the moon. One of the spear holders released a hand from his spear shaft to brush away a moth close to his face. Watcher smashed the Sull's hand into his jaw and yanked the spear from his grip. The Sull gasped in pain, stumbled to his knees. Blood welled from the collapsed cave of his mouth. Arming the spear, Watcher turned. The two remaining Sull, one male, one female, pinned him with their spearpoints. Watcher heaved his spear at the female, plunging it into her chest. As she collapsed in a fountain of blood, Watcher released the shaft and stepped back from the male's spearpoint. Grabbing the socket just below the blade, he jerked it back with force. The wings of the blade punctured the heel of his hand and little finger as he dragged the Sull in a quarter circle and then impaled him with the spear butt.

"No more."

Watcher yanked the spear from the Sull's gut and turned

toward the voice. A wall of blades aligned along his back. As he moved, one touched the space an inch from his eye. He sprung his jaw at it. Dropped the spear.

The wall of blades pushed him toward the fight circle. Three down, he told himself. With Copper One maybe four.

The fight circle was a ghoul hall, domed in green torch-light. He entered and went straight for the sword. It was Heron Walks on Sand. It was familiar and that was good.

"*Mor Drakka.*"

Watcher did not acknowledge the name. It was Sull and he rejected it.

"Your friend Addie Gunn is ill. He needs your help."

He turned to face the owner of the voice. It was her, the queen with the damaged hand. If he were to feed on her he would sever it before gorging. He would not want that malformity in his gut.

"You won some of your matches last time," she said to him. "So you saved Addie from being hurt. However, regrettably, you lost the final match." The eyes glittered. "So we could not administer the medicine he needed."

Watcher hurled the sword at her. Shields closed around the queen. The weight of the pommel and crosshilt raised and gyred the blade and the sword crashed against the circle wall, short and to the left of the queen.

The queen made a motion with her head and the shields were lowered. Her den mates were armed with thick blades of meteor steel. Watcher counted them, made a calculation, and then charged the queen anyway. The swords came to meet him like a single opponent, an enemy made from points of steel. The blades were neck choppers. Let one take your head and you'd been killed by a falling star.

Watcher did not want to be killed. Watcher wanted to live to kill Sull.

He backed away from the blades, his gaze fixed on the queen. There had been one moment as he charged when he smelled her fear. Her face had the fixed stillness of prey not wanting to betray its position.

And then she smiled. Muscles along Watcher's spine contracted in a *rearing* response, snake to rival predator. His shoulders came in and his back humped below the neck.

The queen's smile widened. "Now you've gone and made things more difficult, *Mor Drakka*." With a wave of her hand she directed one of her den mates to pick up Heron Walks on Sand and throw it at his feet. Its point was chipped, sheared by the wall. "You've gone and damaged your sword. It'll be so much harder to pierce armor now. I'd make an early start if I were you."

Her glance darted behind his back. "Addie was screaming last night. We would have liked to give him something for the pain . . ." She sighed. "But you lost and our hands were tied."

Watcher felt hate so pure it narrowed the edges of his vision. He was aware of an opponent closing in from the far side of the fight circle but it did not concern him. He had calculated the opponent's trajectory and speed and knew when the enemy would strike and what he, Watcher, would do to counter it.

"Show me Addie," he said to the queen. The voice was low and hoarse and hardly seemed to belong to him. Dimly he knew that he had not always sounded like this. Once he had had been younger and less harmed. Once he had lived in a world where one tried to understand people and their motives, tried to find sense in terrible things. That illusion had gone. There was just predator and prey.

Feed or be fed on.

It was simple and it governed everything, and the only question you had to ask yourself was: *What do I have to do to stay alive?*

Watcher exploded into motion, dipping to seize the sword and at the same time pivoting on the balls of his feet. His opponent had been in the process of delivering a high blow to Watcher's back and that momentum carried forward into vacant air, throwing the opponent off balance and opening a cone of space around his core. Watcher rose into it, searched for and found the break between his opponent's chest and skirt piece, and powered the blunt sword through his heart.

Sull around the fight circle caught their breath and stirred. Watcher released his grip on Heron Walks on Sand, leaving it in his opponent, and took his opponent's sword as his own. It was heavy and cheap-looking but at least it had a point. The opponent had not been Sull.

The Sull had stopped sending their own to die. Instead they sent Trenchlanders: part Sull, part something else. They varied in skill, size and willingness to fight. Watcher had slices of memory, disconnected images that showed him some of those he had fought. Three figures moving in concert, their big cross-and-hook-bladed halberds boxing him in. A man with mottled skin, no helmet or body armor, jumping like a demon on his back. Something, some kind of giant man, who had hugged the fight wall and not wanted to move to the center. Watcher recalled the extra chamber in its heart. Fight after fight, always more than one in a night. Had there been one time where he'd stumbled from exhaustion and two armed figures, perfectly twinned, had each put swords to his ears? And had the only thing that had saved him been a stay from the queen?

Watcher said to her, "Show me Addie."

The queen looked at the body at his feet. The force of the heart-kill had sent blood through the man's nostrils and mouth. Her gaze stayed on the black wetness and after a time she nodded an assent.

Den mates left to do her bidding. Watcher saw and noted the big warrior with the cheekbones like undercut cliffs and the purest, bluest sword. The consort. He was the most dangerous Sull of the hundred. Watcher knew that to feed on the queen he would have to kill the consort first. Watcher calculated the probability of bringing him down, running sequences of events in his head. None achieved the desired outcome of Watcher alive, consort dead, so he sent his mind elsewhere as he waited.

Two Sull carrying a stretcher made their made to the front of the crowd. When they reached the fight circle, they maneuvered to align the stretcher with the wall. Watcher took a step forward.

Light cracked like lightning as dozens of swords rose as one to form a defensive barrier around the queen.

The queen said, "Drop your weapon and you may approach."

Watcher dropped his weapon and approached.

There was a smell that all hunters knew. It was not present during the hunt or the butchering but would rise later, on the journey home, if the carcass had not been properly prepared. Smell it and the hunter knew the meat had turned and had to be discarded. There was no other odor like it on earth.

Watcher told himself he did not smell it. Watcher told himself many things as he approached the stretcher and when he reached the wall he was calm.

Addie Gunn's slight and unwhole form was cradled in the center of the stretcher. He was on his left side, his knees tucked close to his chest. A large and clean white bandage capped the shoulder where his right arm had once been attached. He was dressed in a loose linen shift, also clean. Where the fabric ended at his neck you could see the swollen fever veins. His breathing was quick and shallow, his chest quivering like a bird's.

Watcher waited for the gray eyes to find him and focus.

Around him, Watcher was aware of a semicircle of swords tracking his movements. Sull were silent. No wind stirred the forest and its owls and night creatures were still. Moonsnake slept.

The gray eyes, their gaze, rose to meet Watcher. The cost of that movement, of the sheer expenditure of willpower, would remain with Watcher for the rest of his life.

When he looked into the gray eyes he saw that nothing stood between him and Addie's soul. It was there, all of him. Maimed Man, cragsman, eweman, clansman. Son. Friend. All the goodness, all the hurts and losses, heartbreaks and hopes were present. Watcher knew this man had hoped for very little, wanted so very little. A few sheep, a scrap of land, a wife.

The gaze held until it could be sustained no longer. Dimming as it withdrew, its owner, Addie Gunn, sent out a final message.

Watcher received the message, locked it away, locked it deep.

With swords swirling around him like long grass, Watcher bent and kissed his friend. Addie was sleeping now, resting. Watcher wanted to stay and keep him safe until the end.

It was an impossibility. The queen signaled the stretcher-bearers and the two Sull raised Addie and began to move him away. Watcher pressed forward and the wall of swords pressed back. Their points clinked against his chest armor. One touched the space between his nose and mouth.

Watcher watched as his friend was borne way. Watcher told himself again he hadn't smelled the hunter's smell. He told himself that if he fought hard enough and long enough Addie Gunn could be saved.

Almost belief was not belief . . . but it was not disbelief either.

It would do.

Watcher watched until his eyes could no longer perceive the H-shaped form of the three figures. Then he watched the darkness left behind.

The queen spread her fingers as if she were sowing seeds. Movement occurred behind Watcher's back. Watcher turned, assessed the opponents the queen had summoned into the fight circle, and went to retrieve his sword. Three men, slight and quick and wielding longknives, fanned out in formation as they moved toward him. Watcher had not thought it possible to be glad when faced with three enemies armed with blades. He was wrong. Something in him sparked. Swiftly he made the calculations, and then moved to take out the strongest man first.

He killed and kept killing through the long night. Opponents fell and bloodied him. Some ran, some begged for their lives. All died quickly, Watcher gave them that. It had become easy. Opponents attacked in predictable ways, creating patterns of open space. Watcher tracked the open space. Anticipated it, and used it to create a line between the point of his sword and the center of his opponents' hearts. As the killings mounted he wondered why he felt no relief. The answer came to him as he pulled his sword from a poorly armored Trenchlander chest.

He was not killing Sull.

Suddenly, the queen, who had barely moved during the killings, raised a fist. Watcher saw one of her den mates raise a blow gun to his lips. A soft *thuc* sounded and Watcher felt a sting on his neck. The night blurred. Haloes formed around the lamps. Watcher staggered, fell to his knees. Puzzled, he tried to stand. He had to keep fighting—for Addie—but his legs were no longer working. He tried to force them, but they gave even more and he slid onto his butt. His right hand released his sword and it clattered onto the ground between him and the Trenchlander. He looked from the weapon to the face of man he had just killed as his vision began to fade.

"He's ready for God's Sword," the queen said in Sull.

Sul Ji.

They were the last words he heard before he joined Moonsnake and slept the deepest sleep of the year, the one before the brightest full moon.

CHAPTER 27

The Phage

When Hew Mallin came for him in the morning Bram was ready. It was an hour before dawn but he had already been awake for hours. He wasn't certain he'd slept, and he was sure that if he *had* slept he hadn't enjoyed it or found it restful.

A night in an enemy clan was not conducive to rest.

"Plans change," Mallin had warned yesterday as they crossed the open ground between the northern woods and Blackhail roundhouse. Bram realized later that Mallin had already identified the two women archers by the creek and meant to use this chance meeting to his advantage. Bram also realized later that in some subtle and shaming way he had been a small part of Mallin's plans.

"Would the young sir like a spot of breakfast?" A voice spoke over Bram's thoughts. "I can hop over to the kitchens and have you fried bread and a sausage in a minute."

Bram's stomach grumbled. He was standing in the Blackhail stables where he'd spent the night sleeping in the hayloft—with the bats. Dinner had been trailmeat and carrots and he would dearly have liked something hot. Looking at the kindly and well-meaning man who offered this luxury, Bram Cormac shook his head. "Thank you, but my master and I need to be on our way."

The man, who was as far as Bram could tell some kind of senior groomsman, was quick to nod in understanding. "Master Mallin, he's a busy man. Always going more than coming."

"The road's my home, Jebb," Mallin said, stepping from the box stall and leading out his horse. "It's what you get for being a ranger."

Jebb pulled down Mallin's saddle from one of the tack hooks. As he handed the oiled and supple tan leather saddle to Mallin he cleared his throat. "You wouldn't happen to have word of Angus Lok, would you? He's a ranger, just like yourself. Fine man. Promised me he'd be round this spring to check the foals."

Mallin sucked air through his teeth. "I recall the name but . . ." He shook his head. "Can't say that I know anything about him."

"Aye." Jebb's nod was soft and deflated. "Big world. Don't know what I was thinking."

"Bram," Mallin said briskly. "Saddle Gabbie and get the bags. I'll meet you out front."

Bram did as he was told, climbing up the ladder to the loft to retrieve the packs and then bridling and saddling Gabbie. Jebb helped. Gabbie liked the groomsman a lot and even picked up his hoofs for Jebb's inspection.

"You've got a beauty in this one," Jebb told Bram as he filed Gabbie's heel. "He's got the look of the Castle about him."

Bram made no reply. He reminded himself that horses were traded across the clanholds and just because a horse had the look of Castlemilk about it didn't mean that it belonged to a Castleman. Or a Dhoonesman. "Could you help with the belly strap while I center the packs?"

Jebb was quick to do his bidding, crouching below Gabbie's belly to fasten the cinches. "Done."

Bram's hand was already on the reins. "Thanks for your help, Jebb." Looking around, he thought for a moment. "It's a fine stable." Bram could feel Jebb beaming against his back as he walked through the stable doors and onto the horse court.

The predawn air was chill and Gabbie's breath blew in clouds. An orange line above the headland known as the Wedge predicted the sunrise and to the north the ptarmigan were calling, staking early claims. Mallin was already ahorse and his stallion was lively and kicking, spoiling for a run. Bram mounted and they trotted the horses south around the massive dome of the Hailhouse.

He was glad to be gone. Of all the things he had imagined upon waking up yesterday morning, spending the night in the Hailhouse had not been one of them. Right now, hundreds of leagues to the south, Dhoone was preparing to face Blackhail at Ganmiddich. Robbie wanted to take the Ganmiddich roundhouse from Bludd. Before he could do so he had to contend with the Hail armies camped on Bannen Field. That meant he, Bram Cormac, half-brother to Robbie Dun Dhoone, had just accepted the hospitality of the enemy.

They did not feed me, Bram told himself as he and Mallin cut across the Blackhail greatcourt and onto the southern road. And he had slept not in the Hailhouse itself but in the stables along with the horses.

It had probably saved his neck. If he had supped and slept in the Great Hearth with Mallin and the Blackhail warriors, someone at some point would have recognized either his face or his name. *Cormac? Wasn't that Robbie's name before he plucked a grander one from his mother's side of the family?* Or, *You have the look of that mad swordsman from Dhoone, Mabb Cormac. What was your name again, boy?* Bram imagined that both questions were equally likely. What he couldn't imagine was how he would have answered them. To be uncloaked as a Dhoonesman in the heart of Blackhail; Bram wasn't sure he would have lived out the night.

Mallin had been no help, of course. The ranger had warned early on he wasn't Bram's keeper and Bram now had a pretty good idea what that meant. Bram Cormac's neck, keeping it whole and above water, was entirely Bram Cormac's affair. Mallin took care of his own business, allowing Bram the privilege of tagging along and sometimes even helping him, but Bram better expect nothing in return. They were the rules of the game, take them or leave them. Bram took them. He was learning. *How to stay alive in an enemy clan when you've been introduced to the chief's wife by your real name* was a lesson more or less worth receiving.

Keep your mouth shut, your head low, and duck out of sight when no one is looking: that's what Bram had learned last night. The only moment he wished he could have taken back was the moment when Raina Blackhail asked him a direct question and looked him straight in the eye as he answered.

Where are you headed to next?

Bram felt his cheeks heat so he kicked Gabbie's ribs, commanding the stallion to gallop, so he could generate some air to cool them. Mallin had already left the path and was was riding for the woods in the southwest. Bram followed.

Trouble was he had liked Raina Blackhail. She was beautiful, like a queen. When she smiled at him he had felt it all the way down to the bones on his face. Her words, *"We don't bite,"* were the first kindness he had received in months. When it came to it he had not been able to lie to her. His answer about where he was heading was the truth.

Lady, I do not know.

He didn't know now. Sometimes he didn't think Hew Mallin knew either, though the ranger appeared to have something in mind today as he had found a path leading west through the grazeland. Bram knew better than to ask. Direct questions to Mallin rarely yielded the truth. Mallin had lied outright to the groomsman. The first time Bram had met Mallin, the ranger had claimed friendship with Angus Lok. Today he had denied that friendship.

Bram didn't understand, but he was watching and he was learning to emulate. He just hoped Mallin hadn't overheard his reply to Raina Blackhail. I do not know, was hardly an answer worthy of the Phage.

Seeing that Mallin had slowed to a trot, Bram reined Gabbie. The rising sun sliced light through the grass and found all the standing water for leagues. Bram spotted a lake to the north, and for a wonder Mallin actually volunteered information about it. "That's Cold Lake," he said. "One of these days we'll have to go and see old Mad Binny who lives on it."

Mallin knew a lot of women. For some reason, not yet apparent to Bram, females liked him. Bram was no expert but he thought Mallin was a bit old. He was still wondering what the ranger's relation was to the young Hailswoman Chella Gloyal. Something had passed between them. As they had entered the stables yesterday evening while Raina Blackhail was walking ahead, Mallin had slipped something into Chella's hand. It was gone in an instant, lost so quickly to the folds of Chella's gray cloak that someone watching may have doubted its existence, but Bram had good eyes. He knew what he saw.

Sometimes Bram thought he'd never get to know the secrets of the Phage. Other times he thought they were being revealed right in front of his eyes and all he had to do was watch.

Glancing at Mallin, who was buffing his fingernails with a shammy as he rode, Bram decided to risk a question. "Do most rangers work for the Phage?"

Mallin didn't look up. "Rangers are rangers. They trade, trap, do day work." He held his fingers to the light to inspect them. "They travel, get to know people. Mobility like that can be useful."

Especially in the clans, Bram added. Was that what he was becoming then, a ranger?

Satisfied with his fingernails, Mallin tucked the shammy in his saddle pouch and regained the reins. "Let's go find some weasel," he said.

Bram followed Mallin's stallion off the trail and through the brush. Last night, lying on his bedroll in the straw as the bats began to stir, Bram had listened to the stablemen talk. He guessed where they were headed now.

They followed an old trapping path that was soft with mud onto an open field that backed against a dense forest of hardwoods. Before they got twenty feet into the field, they were challenged and forced to dismount. Two Scarpe hatchetmen demanded their weapons for ransom. Bram looked to Mallin. The ranger was calm, offering both his sword and knife freely so Bram did the same. The weapons were stowed unceremoniously in a sack. Mallin appeared unmoved by this fact . . . but Mallin was not a clansman. He did not feel the insult of having one's ransomed weapons removed from one's sight.

"What have we got here?" The smaller of the two hatchetmen pushed open the flap on one of Bram's saddlebags. He was pale-skinned and black haired with part shavings above both ears. Casually he picked out items, sniffed them, tasted them, threw them away. Bram could not recall which pack contained the Dhoone cloak.

"Gentleman," Mallin said easily. "If you're looking for the Dhooneshine it's in the other pack. Brown flask. The one with the label on it saying A gift from me to you."

The hatchetman grunted. Glancing at his companion, he walked around the horse and flipped the second pack. Thrusting a hand deep, he found what he was looking for. Silent, he drew out the flask, uncorked it, sniffed and nodded. His bigger, older companion addressed Mallin and Bram.

"Straight ahead. Lead your horses. Your weapons stay here until you're back."

Bram thought he'd like to pick up his bedroll and spare pants from the dirt but now didn't seem like a good time. Abandoning them, he headed for the Weasel Camp.

Tents and wood shanties had been raised around a series of small buildings that had once been a farm. A house, a wood barn, a roofed well and cattle run were still standing, though the house was black around the windows as if it had been burned. Young trees had been logged and split to make posts and big square-shaped tents had been raised on a network of tensely strung ropes. Poison pine banners were flying from every point. The brown-and-black weasel standard, the personal badge of the Weasel chief, was stretched over the large central tent.

"Weasel's in her lair," Mallin murmured. He seemed close to happy.

Bram reckoned the numbers. There were a lot of people here; women, children, elderly. A surprising number of warriors—more than at the Hailhouse. Women were cooking, washing, drawing water from the well. Men were eating breakfast, brushing horses, repairing leather and honing steel. Children were crying, rubbing sleep from their eyes, squatting to relieve themselves, and running around the camp. A big vat of liquid was boiling on one of the fires. It smelled like chemicals, not food.

A single warrior, dark and lean and armed with a bastard's sword, came out of the chief's tent to greet them. His hair, eyebrows and lips were dyed black. "You intrude upon our camp."

"Yes we do," Mallin agreed.

"Leave, then."

"May I present a gift to the chief first?"

The Scarpe warrior didn't find much to like in Mallin's easy manner, but he couldn't find much to object to either. "Give the gift to me."

"I'll let you look at it."

Suspecting a trap the warrior sent a hand to his sword. It was exquisitely sheathed in basket-braided leather. "Go on."

Mallin opened his mouth and pointed to his tongue. "It's right here and it's called information."

The two men looked at each other as a camp full of people watched. They could not have overhead what had been said but the battle of wills was plain to see.

The warrior was no match for Hew Mallin's confidence. He made a jerking motion with his head. "Follow me."

Bram slipped in step behind Mallin and they were escorted to the Weasel chief's tent.

The interior space had been partitioned and they entered a large and empty reception area. A mink rug sewn from hundreds, possibly thousands, of individual weasel hides, floored the chamber. A high-backed chair made of a solid piece of oak with carved weasels for armrests stood in the center of the rug. Low braziers burned to either side of it, smudging the air with greasy smoke. No other furniture or ornament graced the space.

Mallin looked at the chair and slid something soundlessly to Bram. "Probably best if we stand."

Bram accepted the item, tucking it under his sleeve as he pushed back his cuff. The warrior had gone ahead into the interior of the tent and Bram heard him speak and a female voice respond.

They waited. An hour passed and then another. Mallin walked around the chair, tapped it with his cleaned and buffed fingernails, and then did something with one of the braziers. He extinguished it.

"Gentleman." Yelma Scarpe, the Scarpe chief, stepped through the flap in the interior wall. "I have kept you waiting."

It definitely wasn't an apology, Bram decided, not even an observation. It sounded more like a boast. The Scarpe Chief had kept them standing in her reception room for the better part of two hours and she was pleased to have done so.

"Uriah," she said to the warrior who followed her into the chamber, the same one who had accompanied them to the tent. "Relight the brazier. It's gone out." She glanced sharply at Hew Mallin, who was all innocence.

As the warrior left to retrieve whatever was needed to tend the brazier, Yelma Scarpe took her seat on the weasel chair. She was clothed in a black dress embroidered with pine cones that was tightly cinched at her scrawny waist. Her neck and hands were heavily corded with sinews and veins, and also heavily dressed with jewels. Bram had no idea what age she was. Her eyes were clear and her face was tinted with rouge and colored pastes. She could have been anything between fifty and a hundred.

"I know you," she told Mallin.

The ranger bowed. "Hew Mallin at your service." Unfolding a hand in Bram's direction, he added, "And this is my traveling companion Bram Cormac."

Hard black eyes studied him. "You're Dun Dhoone's brother."

"*Half*-brother."

Yelma raised an eyebrow at the force of his reply. It appeared to give her pleasure. Jewels on her knuckles glittered as her fingers drummed the weasel armrests on her chair.

Bram kept himself still. Inside his stomach had turned to liquid, but if he could just keep the shell hard no one would know. He had just denied his brother.

"So we have a half-baked, oath-breaking Dhoonesman and a ranger so old he should be walking on sticks. Is there is no end to the pleasures of this day?"

"We've come from Blackhail," Mallin said.

"I know," replied the chief.

The warrior returned from the inner room, doused the brazier coals with fuel and used a taper to transfer a flame from the second brazier. Air *whumpf*ed as the coals ignited.

Yelma Scarpe stirred the fresh wave of smoke with her little finger. "How do you find Raina Blackhail?"

"Afraid."

"Really."

Looking from the Scarpe chief to Mallin, Bram realized they were playing a game. Yelma may have kept Mallin waiting two hours but she wanted very much to hear this. Why would she trust him? Bram wondered. Then he tried out some answers. Because she'd received information from Mallin in the past? Or because she was hearing something she already believed?

Bram concentrated on keeping still. The smoke was itching his throat. He had an urge to cough and had to suppress it.

He had an urge to run and suppressed that too.

Mallin looked the Weasel chief straight in the eye. "Raina Blackhail doesn't know what's she's doing. She's a fool who shouldn't be anywhere near a chiefship. Half the people in that house want her out."

"Yet they helped her evict us."

"I don't think I said that Blackhail now loves Scarpe."

Yelma lowered her head slowly in something that might have been a nod. "She won't strike."

It was not quite a question and Mallin said nothing.

Suddenly Bram couldn't help himself and coughed.

Yelma looked at him, curled her lip, and looked away. He was a clansman without a clan: he was nothing to her.

"What's the bitch's defenses?" It was the warrior who, done with the brazier, had come to stand at the Weasel chief's back. There appeared to be a family resemblance.

"She's got that big hole in her wall," Mallin said. "And she's planning to dispatch a company of warriors to Dregg to escort Orwin Shank and the grain she sent him to purchase back to the roundhouse."

Both the warrior and his chief thought on this. The warrior said. "I was there the morning Shank left. He was heading for Dregg all right."

Yelma made a little sound in her throat.

"She knows she'll have to send a decent-sized crew," Mallin continued, raising his gaze to the roof of the tent, "to assure the grain's safe passage."

It took Bram a moment to realize that the thing stretching across the Weasel chief's face was a smile. "Unfortunately," she said, "there are a few new obstacles along the way."

Like this camp. Bram started coughing again. The smoke was scratching his throat.

Mallin and the chief ignored him.

The warrior said, "When's she going to send this crew?"

Mallin shrugged. "Soon. A few days give or take. You'll know when you see them."

In the silence that followed Bram tried to control his cough. And failed. His lungs were burning and his diaphragm started contracting and he just couldn't stop.

All three were looking at him now. Bram's face burned.

"Get the hell out," hissed the warrior. "Control yourself."

Mallin frowned at Bram. Bram could tell he was annoyed. "Go on," he said impatiently. "Get yourself some water from the well."

Bram left. The talks between the remaining three resumed even before he cleared the tent flap.

Outside everything seemed bright and busy. Scarpes stared at him. A child ran past him and poked him in the shin. A group of women standing close by found this funny and laughed. Bram rubbed his eyes and cleared the last of the smoke from his throat. He was glad to be out of the tent.

Glad to have something to do.

He went and got some water from the well.

Bram met up with Mallin a quarter later and together they walked their horses back across the field. Mallin was humming. Bram didn't recognize the tune. It was midday and the sun was peeking through silvery rain clouds. Bram's mind turned to his pants.

For a wonder they were still where the hatchetman had thrown them, though they were sporting extra boot marks now. Bram picked them up along with his bedroll as Mallin claimed their weapons from the hatchetmen. Both Scarpemen were drunk.

"Dhooneshine's potent stuff," Mallin told them without rancor. "You're supposed to sip not gulp."

The smaller hatchetman burped his response.

Mallin handed Bram his weapons. He had never commented on the loss of the mirror blue longsword. "Let's get away from here," he said.

Bram couched his weapons and mounted Gabbie, and they trotted off the field. When they reached the trapping path, Bram looked to Mallin for direction: north or south?

The ranger thought about this. "You know, I told Raina Blackhail I'd be heading for Spire Vanis. What say I keep my word?"

They headed south.

CHAPTER 28

In the Guidehouse at Clan Gray

They carried the body in on a stretcher woven from reeds. It was uncovered and it was clear from its pallid nakedness that it had been pulled from the water. Two Graywomen sang a death song, ululating like marsh birds. The clan guide had grayed his face, smearing it with a mask of mud and leaving it to dry. As he walked beside the body, he dropped tiny gold skullcap seeds in its wake.

Effie stood on the stairs above the Salamander Hall and watched. The corpse's long red hair spilled over the edge of the stretcher and whipped in the air like flames. Flora, not named for a queen. Effie knew she wasn't to blame for the the girl's death, but she also knew she should have told someone about the girl sitting alone on the northern dock. An adult had been needed, someone motherly enough to wake Flora from her daydreams. Or someone strong enough to pick her up and carry her in the house.

Instead they had needed to haul her from the water. She had been found after sunrise by a woman in one of the reed-clearing boats. No one had mentioned how she died.

And no one seemed surprised.

Feeling a little flutter of worry, Effie glanced upstairs, toward Chedd's room. She had tried to see him again earlier but had been refused. Bruises were forming around the rebuttal. She'd rebutted the guard quite a bit. Now she had to wait until the guard was changed to try her new, improved strategy on someone who didn't know she was trouble.

She *had* managed to learn that Chedd had slept through most of the night. She took this as a good sign—sleeping through the night seemed a healthy thing to do—and she held onto this fact. Tight.

Spying the Croser girl making her way toward the kitchen, Effie thought she might as well go and speak to her. Flora's words from last night were still on her mind. And besides, she was hungry and it wouldn't hurt to get some food.

The mourners who had gathered to watch the body being transferred to the guidehouse were dispersing. Effie could hear the skullcap seeds popping under their boots. It sounded like shots being fired.

No one questioned her as she walked to the kitchens. Between Flora's death and Chedd's sickness she supposed they didn't have time to worry that the roundhouse was sinking and no one was manning the pumps. Happily they didn't appear to have time for food either and the kitchen was close to empty. Effie glanced out of the room's only window, an x-shaped opening in the clinker-and-timber wall. It was a few hours after midday.

"You never told me your name," Effie said, approaching the Croser girl who was standing over a pile of fish so fresh you couldn't detect a smell.

The girl looked nervously to her right, where the cook was telling one of the kitchen boys the correct way to scour a pan.

Noticing the girl's gaze upon him, the cook halted the lesson to address her.

"Lissit, before you start on the fish, go to the buttery and get me a block of lard and some mustard seed—and a hand of ginger if you can find it."

That was that then. Lissit.

"I'll help her," Effie told the cook as she followed Lissit out of a low alder door in the kitchen's west wall.

If the cook told her not to do so Effie didn't hear him. Unfortunately she made a lot of noise closing the door and that might have blocked out the sound.

Effie had never been in this part of the roundhouse before and was surprised she had to crouch to move along the low-ceilinged corridor. Light came from a series of slits in the wall. "What's the other way?" she asked Lissit when the corridor branched out and Lissit took the fork to the left.

"Guidehouse," Lissit told her flatly. "Sometimes we bring the guide hot coals from the oven." The branch ended abruptly, blocked off by another alder door. Lissit turned. Her delicate face and pale hair looked wan in the dim light. "You shouldn't have said that to Cook. I'll get in trouble later."

"I doubt it," Effie replied. "They need you here. They're dropping like flies."

Lissit had nothing to say to this and opened the door. Good smells and a few strange ones wafted straight to Effie's nose. The buttery was like a larder, she realized, full of things a person could eat. Following Lissit inside she looked around, deciding what to start on first. She was devising a plan to punish Clan Gray for kidnapping her and Chedd. It required eating them out of house and home.

Chedd's special powers were needed to make it succeed.

Chedd thoughts made Effie mad and she closed the door, sealing her and Lissit inside. It was dark. The slits in the wall had been covered with canvas panels to prevent sunlight getting through. "Did you know Flora, the girl they found today?"

Lissit's glanced jumped to the door. "A little. Everyone comes in the kitchen."

"Do you know what happened to her?"

"No."

"What about her brother?"

Lissit closed her mouth. She was wearing a scoop-necked dress and the tail of her tattoo was visible on her left breast.

Looking at it, Effie wondered how old Flora's brother had been. She'd assumed he was her age or Chedd's age, but what if he was older, like Raif or Drey? "What was his name?"

"Gregor."

Like the king. "How old was he?

"Seventeen." Lissit looked at her feet. "Like me."

Effie heard something in those words. It sounded like the noise made when two things stuck together were pulled apart. She said, "What happened to him?"

Muscles in Lissit's throat moved but she didn't speak. She was still looking down.

"Flora said the marsh took him."

The girl looked up. Her eyes were full of water. "He paddled east and didn't come back."

"But what if—"

"No. They found the boat. They found one of his boots."

Effie watched two big tears rolled down Lissit's cheeks. They moved as if they were thicker than salt water.

"Was he trying to escape?"

Lissit shook her head.

Effie frowned. She was trying to be understanding and everything, but nothing was making any sense. The round-house juddered. An apple rolled off a shelf and Effie and Lissit watched it scoot across the floor like a mouse. Effie tried again. "Where were Flora and Gregor from?"

"Dregg."

Raina's clan. "And they both had . . . the old skills. Sorcery."

Lissit pinched her mouth; Effie took it as a yes. Clan did not believe in sorcery and they certainly weren't going to talk about it or admit to possessing any sorcerous abilities. "You know the children they kidnap always have the old skills? You, me, Chedd, Flora, Gregor."

Lissit blinked a nod.

"Why?"

"I've got to get the lard. Cook's expecting it." Lissit spun on her heel, sliding a wet box from a low shelf. Chunks of lard wrapped in linen were floating in the water. The girl fished one out and set it on the counter.

"Mustard and ginger," Effie told her. She didn't think Lissit had the best memory.

As the girl searched for the ingredients, Effie thought about Flora. Those first days after she and Chedd had arrived, Flora had always been on the roundhouse's main platform, looking east. The girl had probably been watching for her brother's return. Effie could understand that after a while she might have to look in a different direction, take herself some-where else.

Raif. Drey.

Effie felt her lore, or rather a tightening of the muscle in her throat where her lore used to be. For some reason she recalled what the old clan guide had said to Raif when Raif threw away his raven lore and the guide found and returned it. *Did you really think it would be that easy to be rid of it? Here it is, Raif Sevrance. One day you may be glad of it.*

What if she couldn't get rid of her lore either? What if it found a way back?

Looking carefully at Lissit, Effie said, "Why was Gregor paddling east? Rime warned us never to head in that direction. The Sull border's out there."

Lissit now had the mustard and ginger. She slid the block of lard from the counter, pressed it against her chest and walked toward the door. "I have to get these to Cook."

Effie blocked her. "What was Gregor doing?"

Lissit moved to the side. So did Effie. Quite suddenly she knew she would hurt this girl.

Even if she got hurt back.

Perhaps Lissit saw it in her face or perhaps she was just getting anxious about being missed, for she blurted out, "He was looking for the break. It's in the east—he knew that much—by the border. He was trying to save everyone." She pushed against Effie. The lard was melting through its cover, depositing a dark stain on her dress. "Including you and me."

Effie gave, allowing the girl to move past her. "He was trying to lift the curse?"

Lissit opened the door and then swung around to face Effie. She was breathing hard. "It's not a curse, you stupid girl. It's a doom. *The Endlords will walk Gray first.*"

Effie watched as Lissit fled.

She felt as if she had been slapped. All she could do for a time was stand and absorb the blow. *Stupid girl* stung because it was right. Effie Sevrance was a stupid girl who didn't know it—the worst kind. Everyone kept telling her there wasn't a curse, but she hadn't believed it. Gray was the Cursed Clan. She had thought that meant that people were dying *because* of a curse, like Maudelyn Dhoone's unborn babies. But people were really dying because it was a marsh, just like Rime had said. Cuts got infected. People got sick. The marsh got inside their lungs.

Like Chedd's. It wasn't a good place to raise a family—it was risky—and people left. Warriors took their families to Otler, HalfBludd and Hill. Then, when they were older, some came back. That was why there were so many oldtimers here—because your clan was always your clan.

Finding she was free to move again, Effie searched the shelves for something to eat. Locating a wet box containing dairy products, she picked out a huge wheel of cheese and bit on it. *That'll cost them*, she thought, putting it back.

So, some people died because the marsh made them sick. And others, like Gregor, died because they were trying to prevent the doom. Lissit said he had gone east looking for what? The break?

Magic to find it. Magic to block it.

Effie recalled Bitty Shank telling her that he could still feel the two fingers he lost to the bite. He said they got cold and hot and tingly even though they weren't there. That was how she felt about her lore right now. It tingled.

Things were starting to make sense. Effie picked up the fallen apple from the floor, dusted it off and stuck it down her dress for later. Deep in thought, she left the buttery and took the fork in the corridor toward the guidehouse.

The Grayhouse was cool and quiet. A faint mist stirred at

her feet as she walked, and she was glad when the corridor gave way to stairs, glad to climb above waterlevel. As she approached the guidehouse door, she slowed, unsure whether to knock or enter unannounced. Then she recalled that Flora's body had been brought here only a few hours earlier.

No point in knocking for the dead.

Raising the latch, she entered a room so thick with smoke she couldn't tell its size or shape. The only thing she knew for certain was that the Gray guidestone was here. She could feel it pull along the small bones in her ear. Closing the door softly behind her, she waited for her eyes to grow accustomed to the darkness.

Over the course of several minutes the Graystone emerged from the smoke. With a shock of wonder Effie saw that it wasn't oblong like the Hailstone or other guidestones. The Graystone was round.

And it looked as much metal as stone.

It gleamed in the dull red light of the smokefires, a smoothly rounded lump of strangely sheared metals fused with scorched and flinty stone. *How would you grind it,* Effie wondered, *without producing sparks?*

Because it didn't seem as if she had any choice, she walked forward and touched it. For a brief instant she saw her hand reflected in the metal and then she saw *through* the guidestone to the place on the other side.

Things immeasurably old and powerful waited. Effie didn't have a word for them—gods would not do. They were more like storms, black and destructive, lit by metallic flashes of lightning. Only they were aware and they knew her and they turned their great thunderheads toward her, and Effie felt her bladder loosen and wetness streak down her legs. As she yanked back her hand, they followed her, cracking like thunder, bolting toward her, their clouds forming the shape of a . . .

"*Girl!*"

Effie switched. She was somewhere *other* and then she was back in the roundhouse, and her dress was wet and she was shaking and she thought she might just as well faint.

"Sit." A chair was thrust with perfect precision under her bottom and she dropped onto it. Luckily it had a back. Unluckily, someone yanked her and the chair round, sending its legs screeching over the stone and propelling Effie forward so that she had to stay alert and pay attention to prevent herself from careening to the floor.

A face covered with mud and not at all friendly thrust itself in front of her eyes. "What the hell are you doing in my guidehouse?"

Effie blinked. Spittle had landed on her mouth and eyelids. "Visiting?"

The guide, for that's who the face belonged to, thumped the back of the chair and stalked away. Effie just sat. She didn't smell so good, she realized, and her skirt felt yucky.

"Here." The guide thrust something at her. "Take off your dress and put this on."

She hesitated.

"*Now.* I will turn and I will not look. Your child's body does not interest me."

Effie believed him. She was surprised by the effort it took to leave the chair, undress, and slip on the robe provided by the guide. The apple she had stowed in her bodice went flying. Its fate seemed to be to roll across the floor. The guide, who was indeed facing away from her, tracked it as it trundled past his feet.

Unsure what to to with the discarded dress, Effie dropped it tactfully under the chair. She sat again. The robe was as heavy as a dog.

"Are you dressed?"

Effie nodded, realized the guide wouldn't be able to see her so spoke instead. "Yes."

He turned and the smoke revolved with him. All guides were physically strong—they spent their days grinding stone—and Gray's guide was no different. He looked ready for a brawl. "How did you get in?"

"The corridor behind the kitchen."

"How long were you touching the stone?"

"Don't know."

"What did you see?"

Effie couldn't understand why her eyes began to sting. Stupid eyes. Stupid sting.

The guide moved closer. The dried mud on his face was cracked around his mouth. When he spoke he made a sentence of each word. "What. Did. You. See."

"Storms," Effie said, aware she was sounding a bit hysterical but unable to control herself. "Things coming. Bad things."

"The Endlords?"

Effie felt a prick of fear. There was that word again. "I don't know."

The guide breathed heavily and deeply as if she had given him the worst possible answer. "Were they close?"

She closed her eyes and saw them tearing through the guidestone. In a whisper she said, "They're almost here."

Clan Gray's guide put his hands over his face and rested. His bulk and his vitality appeared to shrink, and when he removed his hand and spoke to her he was in some fundamental way a different man from the one who had challenged her by the stone.

"Go," he told her.

"What does it mean?"

"It means we'll be the first to fall."

"But—"

He looked at her with eyes that held terrible knowledge. "Do you think what you saw will stop at the border of Clan Gray?"

She did not. She rose, picked up her dress.

"Go the way you came," he said as she made a move toward the front of the guidehouse. "We keep a three-day deathwatch on Flora Dunladen and you will not disturb her peace."

Effie looked into the smoke. Perhaps she saw a table with a dead girl upon it; she didn't know.

She turned and left the way she came. The guide watched her. In some sense she felt she deserted him.

As soon as the door was closed she broke into a run. It was suddenly vital to her peace of mind to see Chedd. Chedd would know what to do. Chedd would calm her down, point out exactly where and how she was being silly. And they'd laugh about her peeing her dress—in front of the guidestone, no less. Couldn't you be damned in the seventh circle of hell for that?

She raced though the corridor and into the kitchen. Lissit was heading the fish and Effie made her wipe her hands and fetch a jug of hot water.

"Put some mustard seeds in it," Effie told her, making a last minute improvement to her sneaky get-in-to-see-Chedd plan. "And some of the ginger too."

Lissit didn't look happy at this but she was accustomed to taking orders and did as she was told. Cook was busy cranking spitted muskrats above the hearth flames and paid no heed to Lissit grating ginger and cracking seeds.

You couldn't run with a jug of hot water, couldn't even walk quickly, Effie found as she plodded through the Salamander Hall and up the stairs. Steam from the water coated her face. It smelled just about perfect. Medicinal, definitely medicinal.

Luck stayed with her as she turned into her hallway. The guard outside Chedd's door—which was really *her* door—had changed. Composing herself, she approached him.

"The healer sent me to fetch this," she said, holding up the jug. "Said I have to give it to him straightaway."

The guard didn't look at the jug. He was gray-haired with hard belly fat and a soldier's useful muscles and she knew straightaway she hadn't fooled him. He wasn't unkind, just firm. "Go away, girl. There's sickness here and you don't want any part of it."

She looked at him. "I need to see him."

"Can't do it."

"How is he?"

"Healer's in with him now."

"Let me wait."

He sucked in a thoughtful breath. "How old are you?"

"Nearly ten."

For some reason this answer made him smile. "Set down the jug and go and sit against the wall."

Effie did as she was told. She was tired out and shivery and the guide's robe itched the back of her neck. More than anything in the world she wanted to see Chedd.

She waited. If she concentrated hard she could hear voices. It sounded as if Tull Buckler was in there too. She listened and listened but couldn't hear Chedd. After a while she got thirsty and drank some of the water.

Footsteps pounding toward the door made her start. Voices were suddenly louder. The latch was lifted and the door swept open. Effie made a run for it, aiming head first for the opening. She bowled right into Tull Buckler. The warrior pinned her by the shoulders as if she weighed next to nothing and then calmly moved her aside. His face was grim. He nodded to the guard, who took Effie by the arm and pulled her away from the door.

The healer came out. Her expression filled Effie with fear, and Effie bucked against the guard, slamming and grasping, desperate to get free. "Let me see him," she screamed. *"Chedd! It's me. Eff."*

The healer pushed her lovely silver hair from her face. "Let her see him," she said.

Instantly Effie was free.

Forever she would remember those seconds, the four seconds it took to get to Chedd's bed. Four seconds when the world hadn't collapsed and she was moving with purpose, not thinking, just moving, and possibilities still existed and as long as she didn't arrive at her destination everything hung in the balance, undecided.

She got into bed with him. He was still warm and he still felt like Chedd.

Softly she said in his ear. "It's me." She told him she loved him and then waited patiently for his reply.

CHAPTER 29

An Uninvited Guest

Angus Lok left his room in the Crater, taking his very few possessions with him. He hadn't yet decided whether or not he would return, but his policy was the same either way. Be ready.

The room was acceptable to him in all essential ways. It was in a private lodging house, not an inn, located at the front of the building with a window looking down on the street. It had a bed, a washstand and a chamber pot, nothing else. Its landlord catered discreetly to men and women who were taking the Holy Cure; a middle-aged, hopeful, soft-bodied clientele with just enough money to finance a trip to the city for the required twenty-nine days of the cure. Angus could imagine the Phage looking for him in many, many places, but in a house filled with mildly religious, gout-ridden invalids stinking of sulfur he felt relatively safe.

If they found him they would strike him down.

You never left the Phage.

You never killed the Phage.

And you never interfered with their plans.

That was three and counting. For a certainty they were on

his trail. He knew how they operated. He had lived this life from the other side. He had *been* the tracker, the one quietly making inquiries at inns and alehouses, blacksmiths and feed stores, slipping into stables at night and checking the boxes, swapping stories with local whores. When necessary he had done more than track. Stay alive in the Phage long enough and sooner or later you'd find blood on your hands.

They dressed it up, of course, wrapped themselves in cloth-of-gold. They were the Brotherhood of the Long Watch and they pushed back against the darkness, taking the long view, identifying threats, consolidating strengths, moving in ways subtle and unsubtle to remake and prepare the world.

The question was, who watched the Phage?

Angus wished them harm, every one of them. And they wished him that harm right back.

He was careful as he made his way north through the Crater. It was God's Day and the streets were quiet. In Morning Star any copper coins exposed to daylight today were God's due. It meant business went inside and candles and lamps were lit early so that coins could be exchanged in man's light, not daylight, and God could be denied his piece. The barter market was open by the river but Angus avoided that particular noisy busyness and instead took a route that followed the city's west wall.

Chapel houses were open and the low and monotonous bellow of horns urged people to come and pray. It was still early and the light was golden as it cut along the streets. Apart from a brief excursion for food Angus had not left the lodging house in three days and he experienced the morning and the city as separate from him. Waiting was not a thing he did well, but in this he had little choice. All normal avenues were closed in this city. People he would typically use for information could not be trusted. The Phage was one conversation away from them all.

His best chance of finding the Maiden was through her hands. This was her city and she had lived, secreted within it, for many years. Angus could only imagine what duplicities she practiced to keep herself hidden in plain sight. She was the Crouching Maiden and that was what she was known for: staying still, keeping low, letting the shadows gather around her mutable female form. Describing her to strangers was impossible: no two people looking straight at her saw the same thing. That was why the hands were so important. She could not work her magic on the imperfect substance of burned flesh.

And she was hurting. Somewhere the Maiden was hurting and in pain and somewhere a doctor was treating her. Her hands were the tools of her trade and she would not entrust them to some backstreet drunken healer. Mobility could not be lost. Lose her grip on a knife and she was dead. She would have no choice but to seek out a fine surgeon, and Angus' instincts told him she would do so in Morning Star. This was a city with hundreds of doctors to choose from. This was her home.

Even on God's Day, Spice Gate broadcast its location for all to detect and Angus turned east, away from the wall, when he smelled the odors of pepper and garlic. His intention was to approach the surgeon's street from a different direction than his last visit. Caution ruled the game this morning. He could not dismiss the possibility that the woman in the money-lender's had passed along word of his arrival to the Phage. Nor could he dismiss the fact that by simply inquiring about a woman with burned hands, the surgeon's apprentice had drawn the attention of Magdalena Crouch herself. Burned or unburned the Maiden was the most dangerous assassin in the North.

Angus Lok moved through the city's northwestern corner like a specter, gray-coated, toeing the shadows, avoiding open spaces. He scribed a quarter-league circle around the surgeon's house and moved no closer until he had circumvented it. A six-story building with a dovecote open to the sky was the tallest structure in the area and he looked at it closely, but kept walking. He rejected the second tallest structure—a tower manse with a roof of domed copper—and settled on the third tallest, a four-storied timbered house with windows looking across to the surgeon's building and street. Angus entered the building's back courtyard and tried the door.

It opened into a kitchen. A pretty maid with blond hair barely contained by a white cap turned to face him. "They all out?" he asked, not giving her time to think.

"They're at chapel, yes."

"I'd better wait then."

The girl looked uncertain. Her slender fingers danced across the surface of her apron.

"Very well, I'll go," Angus told her, "but *you'll* have to tell the master that I'm not sure when I can return." He turned, put his hand on the door.

"Wait. Stay."

Angus completed a full spin. "I'll wait upstairs. I know the way."

She followed him nervously as he crossed the kitchen to the interior door.

"What time do you expect them back?"

"They just left."

Two hours then. Good. "Fetch me a cup of hot broth to the solar. Quick now, girl. I've had a long journey."

The maid reversed her course, heading back toward the stove, and Angus took the doorway, looked around, and then made his way through the house. Young maids were a knowable commodity. Give them orders and they had a tendency to obey.

She found him ten minutes later, nodding off in a padded chair in the house's large and comfortable primary common room, the solar. All houses of a certain size and prosperity possessed such a chamber.

"Leave me now," Angus told the maid, accepting a cup of hot fragrant liquid from her delicately shaking hands. "Wake me when the master returns."

The maid bobbed a curtsy and left.

Angus listened to her footsteps descend the stairs, set the cup down on the floor, and then exited the room. A hallway led to stairs which led to the third and fourth stories. He climbed both flights of stairs, took a moment to orient himself within the geography of the house, and then selected a door which opened onto space at the front of the house.

It was an attic room with a sharply slanted ceiling and unplastered wood walls. A stained mattress and a handful of wicker boxes, piled unevenly against the interior wall, were the only contents. A single window faced south. Its shutters were tightly closed.

Angus opened one of the shutters gradually over minutes, easing it back, keeping in the shadow behind the second shutter. The rear of the surgeon's house, its walled yard, kitchen door and window, were clearly visible. Beyond that the south end of the street and a small bar-shaped section at the north end could be viewed through the spaces between houses.

Angus spread his weight evenly between his feet, settling in for a long wait.

An hour passed. The surgeon's kitchen door opened and a man with gray hair—probably the surgeon himself—came out and pissed against the wall. The street was quiet. People walked its length, either alone or in groups of two or three, with purpose. No one loitered. An old man with a cane took his own good time reaching a house at the street's north end, but Angus found nothing in the man's appearance or behavior to raise alarm.

In the second hour two children, boys of about eight or nine, ran into the center of the street and began playing a game that involved hurling a sealed waterskin at one another. Angus didn't like this. When people stayed in place he got worried. And the Phage were not above using children.

He watched the boys, increasingly aware that time was running out. *Go*, he told them silently.

They stayed. He could hear their excited laughter and the crude one-upmanship of their taunts. The taller of the boys was dark-skinned and black-haired with a dusty tunic and no cloak. The other boy was smaller but perhaps older with red hair and pink skin. He was wearing the kind of roughly pieced deerhide favored by bush hunters.

Angus closed the shutter. Time to go.

Swiftly and quietly he made his way down through the house. The maid was in the kitchen—he could hear her clacking pots—so he took the front door and slipped out into the street. The sun was still shining but a smoky haze rising from the city stopped it from being bright. Angus walked to the corner, cut a turn, headed for the south end of the surgeon's street.

Years of training did not prevent the acceleration of his heartbeat. This could be simple. Or not. Making the turn onto the surgeon's street, he deliberately slowed his pace. The arrangement with the apprentice was that the young man would walk out to meet Angus at midday. It was a minute before midday. Angus wanted to give the apprentice plenty of time to see him, to observe him perhaps for a moment or two, to set his young mind at ease.

The boys were still playing. They were engaged in an unheated argument over the rules of the game. "Possession's mine," claimed the taller, younger boy. "You dropped it."

Angus tracked all the movements on the street. The boys, a woman walking with a cane, a girl leading a horse laden with milk pails. Two crows were pecking through dirt that had accumulated in a wheel rut. Angus' gaze jumped from the birds to the surgeon's door as light streaked across the varnished wood. The door was opening.

He did not reach for one of his knives, though the instinct was there. He continued walking, easily, almost jauntily, toward the house and its door. A figure was emerging from the dimness of the entryway and every nerve in Angus' spine was trained upon it. Size was right . . . shape was right. The figure stepped into the light.

It was the apprentice, looking younger and softer than Angus remembered. The young man had shaved and donned stiff-looking formal clothes, probably his best. Angus peered into the dim interior behind the apprentice. He saw nothing, but knew better than to allow himself the luxury of relief.

The apprentice raised his gaze and made eye contact. Angus returned it. The apprentice closed the door. Angus adjusted his pace, timing it so that he and the apprentice would fall into step as they met. You could tell a lot from a man's neck, see what muscles were working in his throat and jaw. Angus could tell the apprentice had information. You could see it weighing down the muscles in his tongue.

They fell into step, walking north. The apprentice was the first to speak. "How's the arm?"

Angus made a seesaw motion with his head. "Been worse." Moving his hand against his coat, he made the silver coins stored there jingle softly. "Have you found her?"

The apprentice kept his gaze ahead. His eyes were still bloodshot from lack of sleep. "Money first."

He was learning. Angus took out the cloth bag and tamped it into the apprentice's cupped hand. More money than he would earn in five years. Maybe ten.

The apprentice slid the bag under his good half-cloak. A second passed while he seated it.

Angus said, "Where is she?"

He wanted to talk, that was the thing about information. Once you had it, it was a pleasure akin to relief to pass it on. "She's calling herself Anna Roach and she's—"

Angus slammed into the apprentice as the word 'she' left his mouth. The red-haired pink-skinned boy had hurled the waterskin directly at the apprentice, and as Angus and the apprentice slammed into the ground the waterskin burst right by the apprentice's face.

It was not filled with water.

The two boys tore off down the street.

Angus rolled onto his knees and dragged the apprentice away from the lye. He could smell it burning the young man's face. He felt pinprick sizzles on his own face and hands where the splash had caught him.

"Who's treating her?" Angus said.

The apprentice looked at him. His just-shaved face was beginning to singe as if it were being held to a flame.

"Who?"

"Sarcosa."

Angus heard the *tht* of a crossbolt lever being released. Grabbing the apprentice by the back of his cloak, Angus hauled the young man's torso against his own, using the apprentice as a shield. A crossbolt lanced into the apprentice's shoulder with such force that Angus' teeth smashed together.

Rising, he threw away the young man.

The crossbolt had come from the tower manse with the copper roof. Angus knew exactly how long it took to crank and cock a crossbow and as he sprinted away from the apprentice he worked out the bowman's angle of sight. Reaching the first alley between houses he darted into the gap. As long as he was close to a building on an east-west axis he was safe.

He ran east toward the river, scrambling over walls, jumping fences, tearing through courtyards and private spaces. He had been a fool. He *knew* the two boys hadn't been right. Someone had paid them to play there. Someone had given them a water-skin lined with God-knew-what so that it could hold lye, and instructed them to throw it at the two men meeting outside the house. It had been a diversion, something to slow down the mark. Once he, Angus Lok, was on the ground he was a sitting target.

Of course they weren't interested in the apprentice. He was just the means, the lure.

This had the Phage written all over it. The Crouching Maiden would not have set such a clumsy trap. Crossbolts at distance weren't her style. She played with superior odds.

Out of breath, Angus slowed to a walk. He calculated he had put half a league between himself and the manse tower and as there was no sign of pursuit he felt safe. Lungs pumping, he headed for the riverbank.

The big black maw of the Burned Fortress swallowed the Eclipse two hundred yards upstream. Angus watched the water swirl above the drop. He jumped the floodwall and hiked down the bank. Kneeling in the mud, he splashed water on his hands and face. It cooled the burned specks on his skin. He rested for a while, not thinking.

He wasn't young anymore. How much longer could he outrun threats?

Not for the first time he wondered if he was doing this in the right order. If Cassy was alive, if the lack of her body at the gravesite meant that she hadn't died that night, then wouldn't it be better to track her first?

It had seemed clear: Take down the Maiden at all cost. Anyone who knew anything about the Maiden would tell you that she never failed to kill a mark. Once she took a commission with your name on it you were dead. Sooner or later you were dead. That meant Cassy was in grave danger.

He was a father; he had to take that danger away.

Abruptly, he stood. He could not think of his daughter, of the possibility of her being alive.

It was too much for a man to hope for. It would drive him insane.

Angus peeled along from the river, heading south. He needed to wash, and mend and launder his clothes. There were wormholes in his coat where lye had burned through the fabric. He considered returning to the lodging house—he had paid for ten days—but he knew from being a tracker that it was a mistake to follow patterns. Once someone identified a pattern in your behavior they could anticipate your next move. And there was no doubt in his mind: The Phage were on him.

It was not worth worrying about how they had come to learn of his arrival in the city. Anyone—gate guard, market stall holder, drunk in the street—could have identified him and passed along the information to the Phage. They watched for their enemies. The important question was: Did the Phage know what the apprentice knew? Did they possess the Maiden's latest alias and the name of her doctor?

Angus Lok knew and didn't care for the answer. He had to proceed as if the Phage knew everything. They had known enough to lay a trap at exactly the right place and time. And although their traps left something wanting their intelligence rarely did. That meant they were likely ahead of him. Even aware of that fact, what choice did he have but to continue? He would not, *could* not, stop looking for the Maiden. Angus Lok and Magdalena Crouch could not exist in the same world. It would not continue to happen.

Finally he was getting close to tracking her down.

Anna Roach.

Sarcosa.

She was here. Somewhere in this city she was rubbing ointment into her burned hands, sipping tea to slake her thirst, speaking to people who could not see the truth of what she was. She would be cautious, but it was too late. She had already made the fatal mistake. She had followed a pattern. She had returned home.

Angus Lok took the Turret Bridge and crossed to the east side of the city. It was God's Day and the bridgekeeper could not charge a toll for passage so the fact that Angus had no money made no difference. He had abandoned the purse containing his savings at the exact same place and time he'd abandoned the apprentice.

He did not care about the money . . . and he could no longer remember the young man's name.

CHAPTER 30

Heart Fires of the Sull

Ash Mountain Born rode in formation with Mal Naysayer and Mors Stormwielder across forested headland. The trail was wide and clear, formed from soft gray clay and gravel freighted with quartz. No saplings or ferns grew on it though the forest was feet away. The sun was high and in the west and a haze of cloud silvered it, anticipating the full moon.

Ash rode at the head of the formation. It did not seem an honor as much as a right. The two Sull warriors rode at her shoulders, their recurve longbows strung and ready on their saddle horns, their longswords cross-harnessed against their backs. Ash knew they were ready to defend her. She knew she needed defending. Lan Fallstar was one Sull who wanted her dead. Chances were there would be more.

The farther she got into Sull territory the greater the risk. She was *Jal Rakhar*, the Reach, and the Sull could not decide whether they wanted her alive or dead.

Ash glanced down at her hands as they worked the reins. They *looked* like normal hands, with veins and tendons and horse dirt beneath the nails, but they weren't. They were *rakhar dan*, and if they were chopped into pieces they could kill the Unmade. So the question for the Sull was: Did they kill her and divide her corpse, or keep her alive and farm her?

She didn't much like the sound of either of those and rejected both of them. Ash Mountain Born was determined to decide her own fate.

A pair of blue herons flew over the path, whooping as they beat their blade-shaped wings. Ash wondered if they were close to water. She couldn't see anything beyond the massive, shaggy cedars and the fern gardens below them.

"Hear that?" It was was Mors Stormwielder. He was speaking Sull.

Ash looked over her shoulder. The Naysayer was nodding in response. She hadn't heard anything.

"Listen," the Stormwielder bid her.

Ash listened. She could hear wind moving the cedar boughs, the distant echo of the herons, and a coolly repetitive drilling sound that was possibly some kind of bird.

The Stormwielder nodded. "That is it."

She listened again. The drilling sound repeated, this time farther away.

"It's the rattle of a male moonsnake. It means a coven is forming."

Ash felt a chill rise along her hands and up the sleeves. "He's joining it?"

"No. The covens are females. After they feed, the queen may allow him to mate."

"It will be a big moon," the Naysayer said quietly. "We guard our horses tomorrow night."

Mors Stormwielder said something in response, but Ash didn't catch it. She did not have all the Sull words. For the first time since her human blood had been drained to make way for Sull blood, Ash felt the urge to open a vein. The desire to let blood was so strong she could feel where the knife should break her skin.

Quickly she glanced from the Naysayer to the Stormwielder. What would they think? If either were to ask why, she had no answer. It might be the forest, the rattle of the moonsnake, her new name.

Mountain Born. It was strong and it was true. She had been born twice; once on a mountain, once within one. The first time she had been a human newborn and the mountain was Mount Slain. The second time she was reborn as Sull, in a mountain cave east of Ice Trapper territory as she floated in a pool of her own blood. The name honored both births.

It was a strange thing, the name. By taking it she had claimed her own identity. What she had not expected and what she would not tell the Stormwielder was that it made her, not more Sull, but more herself.

She was no longer Foundling, no longer March or almost-daughter. She was Mountain Born, she was herself. Choosing a name was just the start.

"We must stop," she said.

The two warriors exchanged glances but did her bidding, shortening reins and bringing their horses to a halt. They kept their saddles as she dismounted, watchful but not alarmed. Perhaps they thought she needed to relieve herself; she had been doing that a lot.

She searched her saddlebag for the letting knife, the silver dagger Ark Veinsplitter had given her after she had become Sull. The weapon was wrapped in lynx fur. Its blade was so sharp that to touch it was to be cut. The grip was silver metal, with a design that had been worn to almost nothing by years of handling. Like all letting knives it felt right in the hand. Ash pushed up the sleeve of her dress, baring the skin of her left wrist.

Now the warriors understood. With tactful respect they lowered their gazes and quieted the horses. The Naysayer laid a hand on Ash's white gelding.

"Gods judge me," Ash murmured in Sull.

She pushed the blade across her skin. There was no pain, just a sense of opening, of becoming somehow larger than herself. Her body was no longer contained by her skin, and the insubstance that shimmered on the edge of existence touched her from the other side like a kiss.

Live.

Blood welled in a perfect line. Ash looked at it. The presence which she felt, the insubstance, withdrew. She swayed for a moment toward it, chased it, but it was gone.

Blinking, she watched her blood roll her wrist and drip onto the gravel. Time passed—she did not know how much of it—and the Naysayer moved forward on his horse.

"Daughter," he said, holding a small square of fabric toward her, "press this against the wound."

She took the fabric and did what was asked. She felt as if she were waking from a dream. Was this what it meant to be Sull?

Mors Stormwielder broke the spell. "The Heart Fires lie ahead," he said once she had stanched the bleeding, "It is fitting you have honored them. Come, we leave."

Ash dropped the square of bloodied fabric onto the path and went to relieve herself in the trees. She could not see what would be gained by telling Mors Stormwielder that she had not let her blood for the Heart Fires so she kept her peace when she returned and mounted her horse. As the gelding walked over the spot where her blood had fallen, she spoke a word to herself. "Raif."

She did not know where he was or whose company he kept, but she suddenly knew with great certainty that the blood she had spilled was for him.

She did not rush to return to her horse. Stormwielder might have commanded Ash March, Foundling, but he did not command Ash Mountain Born, the Reach.

The party was quiet as they continued their journey south. Ash sensed a shift in the two warriors, an easing of tension. The Naysayer edged back in his saddle and his beautiful blue stallion began kicking out its heels. Mors Stormwielder's chestnut fell in step, matching the blue's movements so that both horses' hoofs struck the ground at the same time. Ash felt the white getting jumpy and gave him the reins, and the gelding immediately synchronized its gait with the other horses so all three kicked their forelegs in time. Ash turned to the Naysayer, smiling and full of wonder.

"This they do for themselves," he told her. "They dance for the Heart Fires."

Ash's heart swelled. The light from the sun was warm on her face. She heard running water in the distance and began to see glimpses of something silver-blue moving between the trees. The path climbed and turned, tilting itself toward the sky. It was so wide now ten horses could ride abreast. Ash saw other paths leading west and east through the cedars. She smelled sweet smoke and river water and something deeply and wonderfully strange. She smelled the night, its stillness and deepness. And the dark eternal space between stars.

The cedars fell away as the path climbed, and they rode through a cut in a rocky bluff. Banks of bluestone mined with jet formed the walls. Ash caught glimpses of carvings cut at the base, simple shapes, simply made: Moon. Raven. Stars.

And then the headland ended, fell away directly ahead of the path. Mal Naysayer and Mors Stormwielder reined their horses and dismounted. Ash watched and did the same. Water was roaring to her left, crashing so loudly she could not have heard the warriors speak. Ahead she saw sky colored a shade of blue she had not known existed. Somewhere close by water was taking to the air. She felt its fine droplets pebble her skin, and caught glimpses of the shimmering and ephemeral rainbows it created.

The two Sull warriors stood silent, heads level, nostrils flaring as they breathed in essential air. Ash sensed that they were waiting, wanting to allow her the privilege of being the first to walk to the ledge at the end of the path.

Releasing the reins, Ash moved forward. She felt the world was turning, revolving into place below her. To her left, beyond the ledge, a river was discharging down a sheer cliff face. It fell for half a league. The water formed a milk-white torrent that crashed into a plunge lake at the base of the cliff. Clouds grew there. Ash could see the mist gaining mass and roundness, separating itself into individual clouds.

Ahead she saw the Heart Fires of the Sull.

Icewoods towered in the valley below, their impossibly tall and slender forms shaped like flight-feathers. The great Night River snaked through them, blue-black and wide as a city, its surface alive with water birds, its meanders terraced with black shale. It was the night sky, and the icewoods were its stars. And the Heart Fires that burned on its shores and in the forest were pieces of the full moon.

Ash Mountain Born guessed that if she were to spend a lifetime traveling the continents of the world she would not view anything to match this sight. She stood, letting the mist soak the front of her dress, and rested her gaze on the reason why the Sull fought.

Here. The Heart Fires.

Some time later Ash turned into a remade world. The Sull warriors were still in their places. Mal Naysayer had opened a vein. He had been away for many months, she realized, and he returned without his *hass*, Ark Veinsplitter. Ash tore off the sleeve of her dress.

"Here," she said. "Press this against the wound."

The Naysayer's ice blue eyes held hers, and she knew that in the only way that counted they were now equals.

He knew it too.

She would never hear the word *Daughter* from him again. Their relationship had passed beyond father and child.

If Mors Stormwielder hadn't been there they would have spoken. Mal Naysayer would have promised her his life. Ash Mountain Born would have accepted the promise but offered nothing of her own in return. It was his misfortune to love her.

The Far Rider and the Reach looked at each other and understood each other, and then Mors Stormwielder called them forward to descend the cliff.

Large broad steps had been cut into the cliff face directly beneath the ledge and the path wound down, curving west away from the waterfall and descending onto the cleared ground west of the lake. The steps were slick, but thick ridges cut into their faces aided traction. The horses were alert but not afraid. Ash hiked up her skirt. She was surprised to discover the height made her feel a bit dizzy and possibly sick. She had been hungry earlier and had been planning to munch on trail bread, but now the thought of food made her queasy.

The light, sweet smoke from the Heart Fires seemed to help. Ash asked the Stormwielder what was being burned.

"You smell the dann of the icewood," he told her. "The wood that is laid down in late spring and summer. We use it for two things: our sacred bows and the Heart Fires."

As they drew closer to the valley floor, Ash saw there were buildings set between the trees, stone circles and domes and round towers. All were open in some way to the sky. Most did not possess roofs. Beautifully pieced tents colored in white and gray and pale blue occupied the stone circles, their skins and canvases ripping in the breeze. Guideropes formed shimmering silver webs between the icewoods.

Seeing the city laid out beneath her, Ash began to feel nervous. This was real. It was happening. She had been traveling for so long, running away for so long, she had hardly imagined the journey could end.

Home, she tried out the word. Perhaps it was the fact she was still feeling queasy that stopped it from sounding right.

Two people, a male and female, were waiting for them when they reached the plunge lake. The female was striking with black hair pulled back in a top notch and clay-colored skin. Ash still wasn't good at working out the age of Sull, but the female appeared young. Ash envied her sureness. The male had the kind of metallic cast to his skin that she associated with the purest Sull. Both of his earlobes had been removed and his head was shaven clean except for a quarter moon of short growth in the center of his scalp. Two swords were harnessed to form an X against his back.

"Do not address him and do not look him in the eye," warned the Stormwielder. "He is *Mor Xana*."

The Walking Dead. Ash understood the words but not their meaning. She knew so little. The Sull were a mystery to the people of the north. How many non-Sull had stood at the Heart Fires? Had Angus been here? She did not know. One thing was for certain: every step she had taken since she'd crossed the Easterly Flow had been permitted expressly by the Sull. You could not arrive here without sanction.

Light prismed across the female's face as she watched Ash descend the last of the steps. Fine droplets of water released by the waterfall did strange and beautiful things with the light. Ash felt giddy. Not trusting herself to avoid *Mor Xana's* eyes, she averted her gaze from both him and the female, so at first she did not realize that the female was prostrating herself on the ground at the base of the stair. The female was dressed in fine doeskin pants and tunic and when she lay belly-down on the rocky shore, Ash could see the line of her spine.

"Rise," Ash told her curtly, halting on the final step. She would not have this.

"*Jal Rakhar*," the female said, quickly moving to her feet. "This Sull is glad you are here."

"I am glad also," Ash replied in Sull.

The female's smile was lovely and brief. "I am Zaya Mistwalker, granddaughter of the Longwalker, daughter of He Who Leads and Daughter of the Sull. My father asked me to welcome you to our home and tent."

Ash had to think about the information in this statement. After a moment she turned to Mors Stormwielder who stood above her on a separate step.

His keen gray-black eyes instantly registered her query. "Zaya is my niece."

Ash understood from his manner that he would not greet the girl until the formal welcoming of the Reach was completed. There were protocols to be observed.

She turned back to face Zaya. "I am Ash Mountain Born, Daughter of the Sull, and I accept your father's invitation."

"It is good," replied the girl, flashing her teeth.

She saved her real smile, a long and warm beam, for her uncle. Moving past Ash, she went to greet him. Ash descended to the lakeshore with the horses. While Zaya had been performing her greeting, *Mor Xana* had been standing at the break of the water, facing east. A single muscle in his neck was twitching. He was safeguarding someone and she did not think it was her.

When all the greetings were complete, the party headed south along the lakeshore. Sull had staked their tents in cleared and walled circles along the paths. Their horses and animals grazed on tender grass and their fires burned with fierce silver light. Some came out to view the Reach, their expressions serious and probing but not lacking in respect. The children were slender and quick. Icewood branches ticked like drawn bows.

Zaya led them along the plunge lake's outlet, down toward the river. The sun was sinking and herons and geese were in flight above the water. Somewhere to the north a wolf howled for the moon.

The Night River created its own tow. Ash felt the wind change as she approached it. She could see the buildings now: a fastness deep within the trees, a tower set back from the black shale of the rivershore. As they approached a dome built from opalescent stone, a man came out to take the horses. The Naysayer greeted him with a touch to the arm, and dropped back from the party to speak with him. Ash felt a tremor of fear. In a land of strangers the Naysayer was her only friend.

She did not yet trust the Stormwielder or his niece, and she thought it quite possible that *Mor Xana* might kill her. He was a ghost along the path, always walking within blade's reach of her heart. She tried not to show her relief when the Naysayer rejoined the party.

"Here," Zaya said to Ash indicating a switch in the path. "My father awaits you in his tent."

All in the party stopped. Ash glanced at the Naysayer, who nodded.

They meant her to go alone . . . except for *Mor Xana*, who moved forward when she did, and who walked in the grass while she took the path.

A moon one sliver short of full was rising as Ash Mountain Born entered He Who Leads' rayskin tent. Outside a white-hot Heart Fire was roaring. Inside a single lamp shaded with amethyst marked the center of the circular space.

A Sull was standing in perfect alignment between the lamp and rising moon. He did not speak as Ash and *Mor Xana* entered, but waited until the tent flap they disturbed fell still.

"Welcome," he said.

For a moment Ash struggled with the simple translation. Nothing in this man's face or manner supported the courtesy of that word.

"I am Khal Blackdragon, son of the Longwalker and Son of the Sull."

Instantly she realized the natural conclusion to her earlier thought: if every step of the way here had required sanction, every step back would require it as well.

Khal Blackdragon's skin was so darkly metallic his face looked cast from iron. His black hair was pulled back and notched in three places. It was tied with lead clasps. He was dressed plainly, in dyed deerskin, and his only decoration was the torc around his neck formed from soldered arrowheads.

Ash saw no reason to return his welcome. "I am Ash Mountain Born, Daughter of the Sull." As she spoke *Mor Xana* slipped into position behind her and against the tent wall.

He Who Leads did not acknowledge him in any way. *Mor Xana* did not exist.

"I have one question, Ash Mountain Born," Blackdragon said to her in a hard and quiet voice that revealed age. "Do not reply until you are certain of the answer."

Ash felt dead tired. She wanted to wrap herself in blankets and sleep. She did not want to face this man and his dangerous question.

Blackdragon waited. Beneath his feet, blue and silver silk carpets shone like old jewels.

"Ask," she said.

The eyes were the surprising thing about Blackdragon's face. The skin was gray iron but the eyes were amber, the color of low-burning flame.

"Can the Reach control herself?"

The three people in the tent were still. The only thing that moved was their shadows, kept in motion by the shifting glow of the amethyst lamp.

Did Blackdragon know she had reached at Fort Defeat as the two Sull assassins approached her with drawn swords? How was it possible? She had not spoken of it to anyone, not even the Naysayer. Looking into Blackdragon's eyes she decided all things were conceivable with this Sull.

He had asked the only question that mattered.

If she could not control her Reach power she would reach again, tear down more of the wall, let in an army of Unmade and clear a path for the Endlords. This went beyond Lan Fallstar and what he had wanted from her body—its flesh. This went to what she was capable of if the Sull kept her alive. Ash had no answer.

"Leave now," Blackdragon told her, removing the need for her reply. "Refresh yourself after the journey. We will speak again."

Mor Xana rose like a spirit summoned by a sorcerer. As Ash moved so did he, floating to her side so that she would exit first.

She pushed back the tent flap and turned to look at He Who Leads. Khal Blackdragon had shifted his position to retain alignment with the moon.

Ash and the ghost left to join the Heart Fires.

CHAPTER 31

Watcher of the Dead

They carved a large circle in the last of the spring snow, trailing the scent that called the coven to order, soundlessly tracing and retracing the circle, laying down the old magic, waiting for the daughters to arrive.

"*Up. Now.*"

Watcher was instantly awake. He was in the chamber with the false stars. His body was aching. His shoulder muscles felt ripped to shreds.

"Up."

Two Sull females stood above him. A third Sull, a male, stood sentry by the door. He had a blowgun ready at his lips. The younger, riper female held a sword to Watcher's throat as he swung his feet onto the floor and rose to a sitting position. The second female held a bowl and a cloth and moved to tend an injury on the back of his shoulder.

Watcher allowed the tending. He kept himself still and did not wince when alcohol was poured into the open wound. He did not want a blow dart to the neck. The females were nervous, expecting a strike. Watcher wondered what had happened to Copper One. Could a Sull survive without a neck?

"Armor him," said the male Sull to the older female.

The younger female took a step back while the older female clamped a backplate against Watcher's spine. The metal was heavy and warm. A dent that had been improperly hammered bit his skin. Watcher raised his arms to aid the female as she fastened the backplate to the breastplate at his underarms and waist. Her face was right next to his as she cinched the shoulder joins.

Watcher restrained himself. As she moved away, the female looked him in the eyes. Her gaze did not lack penetration.

"We play with fire," she said under her breath in Sull.

Watcher blinked at her. He thought about Moonsnake resting after a kill and allowed his body and expression to follow his thoughts.

The Sull female read the change. It was possible she was not convinced but she and the other female turned and left the room. The male followed a few seconds later and the door bolt was engaged.

Watcher continued to sit in the same position. He continued to blink. The Sull had not provided a helmet but part of him felt as if he were already wearing one. It was as if a hard layer of steel was encasing his face.

The light in the chamber shifted as sunset seesawed with moonrise. The walls blued. Watcher stood, crossed to the water bucket. As the moon broke the treeline it aligned with one of the moonholes in the ceiling, casting a perfect circle of light onto the floor. Watcher looked at it and saw a small brass pot on the ground near the wall. He set down the bucket and walked to the pot. It had been set beneath a slow drip and was full of water. Watcher thought about it. He glanced at the door. It was possible the Sull entering the chamber had not noted it. Shadows this far from the door were deep.

Watcher squatted and drank. The water tasted flat and stony. As he stood, he realized he was waiting for something— a kind of blurring and redrawing of the space. It didn't happen. Edges remained firm.

Watcher relieved himself and returned to the bed. Some time later the bolt was drawn.

"Out," came the command. There were four of them now. One male had been added to the rank. The new male and older female were armed with spears.

Moving slowly so not to startle them, Watcher rose. They had no idea how vulnerable they were, the sheer volume of killing space surrounding them.

As he climbed the steps to the forest path, the moonlight found him. It felt like a warm meal. The forest was alive with three-chambered hearts. Strange cravings and old magic were loose among the cedars, conjured by a snake sidewinding a circle in the snow.

Watcher was placid during the walk to the fight circle. He let himself be led. The crisp air went deep into his lungs and he felt strong and clear-headed and ready to fight.

A special fire had been lit at the head of the circle. It was white-hot and fragrant. Sull glittered like an army made of metal in its light. Torches were barely needed. The full moon was as big as a world and the sky was clear. The lightest breeze pushed air against Watcher's skin.

The queen was dressed in her finery. A blue gown cut in a V to her waist revealed the curves of her breasts. She was armed with a small recurve, slung from her neck like a jewel. Her consort stood at her side, armored and battle ready. Watcher met his cool gray gaze.

The consort did not blink.

Watcher reappraised, and entered the fight circle.

Sull were silent as he approached the center. Some did not appear to breathe. Watcher saw his weapon laid out on a cloth and understood why.

Loss waited in the darkness like a bear trap. It had been ground and filed, polished and remade. The rusticles had been chipped away, the grip wound with leather, the edges—for there were two of them—honed. It was not beautiful. It was big and its blade was sunk with whorls. The crosshilts were fashioned as raven wings, flight feathers partially spread. A raven head formed the pommel.

Take it and we will feed.

Watcher hesitated. He wanted it and did not want it in equal measure. The sensation of looking out through a thick layer of armor was strong. He recalled Raven Lord, headless under the ice.

History had not remembered his name. Had he even been able to remember it himself?

"Pick up the sword, *Mor Drakka*. Your friend needs to be saved."

Watcher heard the lie. The queen forgot who she spoke to. He had seen Addie Gunn's face, smelled him and kissed him.

He was Watcher of the Dead.

He picked up the sword, felt the shocking heft of it, and fought.

The moon rose toward its zenith as Moonsnake finished her circle.

The coven has formed.

Watcher struck in the margin where the white light of the Sull fire and the blue light of the moon met. The sword was hard on his wrists. It was perfectly balanced but heavy at both ends and it required more control to wield it. The Sull had shown him mercy with his first opponent. A quick and savage child could have slain the aging Trenchlander. The man had the muscle and gut of a tavern brawler, and he barely knew how to hold live steel. Watcher used him to learn the reach of the sword, killed him as an experiment in the sharpness of its blade.

The second and third opponents were better but he was already becoming capable with the sword. Loss's weight could be used, he learned. The sword had a downswing like the chop of an ax. Set in motion, it almost killed by itself. Loss's reach created new possibilities. There was so much vacant air around the third man, Watcher plunged into it like a diver into water. By then he had learned the keenness of the blade and he gave the man a swift end.

"You do well, *Mor Drakka*," the queen said as he freed the sword. "Win the next bout and we will bring medicine to your friend."

Watcher was breathing hard. He moved toward her, Loss trailing behind him in a one-handed grip. "Show me Addie Gunn."

The queen dared not move her face.

He lunged at her. A barrier of swords fell between them like a gate. He pressed into them because he wanted her dead. He stopped before the points took veins because he had to stay alive to kill her.

Bleeding from a dozen puncture wounds, he backed away. The queen's eyes were carefully blank. Watcher looked and looked but she would not acknowledge the challenge in his gaze.

Watcher turned his back on her. Addie was dead. The Sull had killed him.

Fancy a journey east. Got a hankering to see trees—real ones, not piss-thin bushes. I imagine I'll set off soon. 'Magine when I do no one will try and stop me, it being a free world and all and a man being free to travel where he pleases.

The words came from a different life. Watcher heard Addie speak them. The cragsman had been throwing in his lot with Watcher of the Dead. *I'm with you*, the words said.

Taking Loss in both hands, Watcher walked to the center of the fight circle. The enemy entered and it was Sull. The queen had sent in her consort.

Spinebreaker, that was its name.

Watcher hissed. A hundred twenty moon snakes heard him.

Meteor steel met the hard and unforgiving metal of Loss with a grinding clash. Edge squealed against edge, throwing sparks. The consort was fast and solidly strong. Raining strike upon strike, he forced Watcher back. Steel hacked Watcher's ear and the top of his hand. The consort, sensing the advantage, kept pushing. He was moving swiftly, varying his strikes. The space around him was rarely open.

Watcher glimpsed lines of strike, and followed them with his sword only to be met with blocks. For the first time he realized it was possible for an opponent to see the same lines as he did, perceive a vulnerability and close it. The consort was the better swordsman. He was quicker and stronger, and decades' worth of experience moved his hands.

Their gazes met. The consort was focused, not yet struggling for breath. He touched his swordpoint to Watcher's neck roll to prove it.

Watcher warded the blow. He was thinking of Addie, recalling the meaning of the last look the cragsman had shared with him from the stretcher, the force of the message in Addie Gunn's eyes.

Do not forget who you are.

Watcher heard goodness and caution, and pushed it aside. It interfered. The words themselves though had use. He was Watcher of the Dead. No one could match him at finding hearts.

It was simple after that. Spooling his sights, he locked on to the consort's heart. It burned his retinas like a glimpse at the sun. The consort's exterior concealed how quickly it was beating. Watcher took satisfaction in that. He feinted, let the consort come to him. As he accepted the blow he edged back, creating the space he needed.

Using everything he was and everything he had learned, Watcher thrust Loss through the Heart of the Sull.

It entered with a sigh and dimmed the light of the moon.

The night darkened. The queen screamed. Meteor steel flashed like an electrical storm as Sull moved to protect her.

"Kill him," the queen cried.

Blades rushed at Watcher as he yanked free the sword. Blood arced from the tip. Sull were coming at him from every point in the circle, cinching it closed. Watcher turned, using Loss like the arm of a sundial to mark his defensible space. It occurred to him that at least this way they would not blow-dart or shoot him. Anything fired into this circle could hit Sull.

The first blow came to the back of his shoulder and he spun on his heels to address it. He had to get to the queen. She had to pay for Addie Gunn.

A sword entered the back of his thigh as he parried the Sull at his shoulder. He stumbled, rotated Loss. Pain showered his visions with red dots as a third sword punctured his chest plate at the belly. He went down on one knee and the Sull closed the circle. They were grave and proud. Bringing this death did not please them, but a death would be brought all the same.

Watcher accepted a second blow to the damaged shoulder. He watched as a single sword peeled off from the wall of steel and rose with momentum for a downstrike. It was a heartkill; he of all people knew that.

He felt air whiffle, saw the point come for him.

The coven feeds.

And the night of snakes began. Pale, glistening monsters reared around the circle. They struck like wingless dragons. A white and streamlined head lashed forward with the force of a cracked whip and clamped its jaws around a Sull's arm. Snapping back, the creature lifted the Sull from the ground and tore off the arm at the shoulder socket. A second snake immediately struck the twitching body, snatching the Sull away.

The Sull surrounding Watcher turned in formation, swords rising, armor glittering, faces deathly blue in the moonlight. The Sull who had been setting up the heart-kill locked gazes with Watcher. He was not young; there were deep lines around his mouth. His eyes were surprisingly brown.

"*X'all sano*," he said.

Fight with us.

Watcher rose and slew him, coring the Sull's heart with Loss.

As the warriors began battle with the rearing, lashing moonsnakes, Watcher made his way toward the queen. The fight circle was a living nightmare of razored teeth and mirroring scales. Moonsnakes reared like serpents. Blood sheeted across the ground as Sull and snakes took harm. Watcher remained untouched.

Den mates had formed a guard around their queen. Moonsnakes streaked through the trees toward her, sidewinding in absolute silence, the great girdles of muscle in their abdomens contracting in sinuous waves. The queen's den mates were forced to step away from their queen to defend her. Watcher waited until a snake strike diverted three of the mates and moved to occupy the available space.

The queen spotted him and screamed. She was the only Sull who did so, Watcher noted. The rest were silent in battle. Some den mates turned and heeded their queen's cry but the coven was in full assembly now, striking with viciousness and speed. One of the den mates lost her head. Another fell and was torn into three pieces by three snakes.

The queen raised her bow toward Watcher. Watcher walked straight toward it. Behind the queen he had spotted the coven mother, his heart mate. Moonsnake. Her scales shone silver in the moonlight and her eyes were milky blue. Her jaw sprang open in greeting, and Watcher felt his own jaw muscles respond. In tandem they worked to take down the queen. She knew, Moonsnake *knew*, that this was his kill and she deferred to him. With her beautiful streamlined head as big as a wolf she punched the queen's arm, knocking her forward and throwing her aim. The queen released the string and the arrow shot into one of the den mate's legs.

Watcher spun Loss into motion. As he came for the queen her mouth opened and she spoke some words in Sull that might have been a prayer. She dropped the bow and her gloved and malformed right hand went to her heart. He would pierce it to kill her.

In the end she died well, her eyes open and filled with knowledge of her own mistakes. Watcher drove Loss to its crosshilts. Blood welled over his knuckles as he accepted her dead weight. Moonsnake waited at the queen's back, her head weaving air. Watcher's gaze rose to meet her.

And the world changed on him one final time.

Kill an army for me, Raif Sevrance. Any less and I just might call you back.

Death returned his gaze through Moonsnake's milky eyes. She had been waiting there all along, laying her plans, biding time.

She laughed. It was a sound so cold and gentle it could turn a man to stone.

Did you think I was done with you? she asked.

Watcher took a breath. He did not know what else to do.

Death withdrew, trailing her soft laughter and claiming the last words.

Who watches the Watcher?

I do.

He did not know how long he stood there with the queen impaled on his sword. Moonsnake moved into the fight circle to feed. The Sull were nearly gone now. Lone holdouts battled in the darkness, growing weary and making mistakes. It wouldn't be long before all were gone. The air smelled sharply of snake. A raven landed on the fight wall and goose-stepped around the carnage. Watcher wondered what it was doing out at night.

Dropping his sword point, he let the queen slide to the ground. The black body of the forest seemed the only place to go. Squatting he wiped Loss's blade with the hem of the queen's dress. It was not meant as a dishonor. A blade must be cleaned: simple fact.

Rising, Watcher turned his back on the fight circle and

the coven. He took the queen's shortbow and a sheath from one of her den mates and a few other items. A moonsnake lay dead and seeping along the path. Its body stretched for thirty feet. Watcher walked alongside it, heading north. As he moved he stripped off his body armor and strapped the sword and bow against his back. Now he could travel faster.

He ran. Moonlight lit the spaces between the bloodwoods and cedars and it was easy to see the way ahead. He kept running, faster and faster, adding more distance between himself and the Sull.

Finally there came a time when he could run no longer. He slowed to a walk but did not stop. Gradually his wounds bled out and began to seal. When he grew thirsty he stopped at a stream, put his head in the water, and drank.

Do not forget who you are.

What if you wanted to forget? What if when you looked back you saw all that you had lost and all the terrible things you had done? Was that how it had been for Raven Lord? Was it a mercy when he forgot his own name?

Watcher started running again and the moon began to set.

He ran until he could no longer think and then lay down and slept.

CHAPTER 32

Strike Upon the Weasel Camp

"Here. Let me dust your face with this."

Raina looked at the charcoal powder mounded in Chella Gloyal's cupped hand and hesitated. "Surely the enemy will see me regardless of my brightness? Where is the stealth in a charge?"

Chella did not disagree. "Sometimes we arm not against our enemies but against ourselves."

Raina had to think about this. She glanced at Chella. The young Croserwoman—no, Hailswoman—was dressed in leather chest armor, snugged close to her breast and waist, and a split and leather-panelled riding skirt that fell a mere foot below her knees. She appeared young and dangerous and Raina could only imagine what looks she must have received as she traveled across the entrance hall and up the stairs toward the chief's wife's chamber. Tongues would be wagging.

Female ones.

Which was exactly part of the problem.

"The Hammermen of Blackhail were once famous for coloring their teeth with iron juice," Chella said. "So unless they were smiling as they smote down their enemies it would appear not to have a functional use."

Raina laughed at that. Chella somehow managed to be wholly clan and immersed in clan but able to see it from a distance as well. Where did she get it from, this respectful disrespect?

"So why did the hammermen do it?"

"You know why."

To make themselves fierce. Raina inhaled. "Do it."

Raina Blackhail sat in front of the fancy city mirror bought for her as a gift by her first husband, in a chamber she had not used in a year, and watched as her face was darkened with charcoal and spit in readiness for her first battle.

Chella worked quickly and efficiently, her touch light. "Close your eyes," she bid. With two sweeps of her thumb she blackened Raina's eyelids.

It looked and felt strange at first, perhaps even faintly ridiculous, but as the saliva started to dry, pulling her skin tight and making it prickle she began to change the way she thought. She didn't look like herself anymore. Dagro would not have recognized his wife.

Chella pulled back Raina's hair and braided it in a single queue. Over Raina's simple linen chemise, she drew a padded, fitted shirt. Expertly she cinched the laces. "Stand," she said, voice low.

Raina stood as armor made for the Dhoone queen, Flora Dun Dhoone, and seized at the Battle of Standing Point, was strapped to her breast and spine. It was like plunging into ice water. The steel was cold and unforgiving; heavy, though Chella said with wonder, "It is so light."

She was not wearing it.

The armor had been powdered so it did not reflect light. Brog Widdie had reshaped it for Raina in his forge and at some point during his hammerings he had seen fit to remove the thistle badges and blue enameled panel, center front. How must that have felt for him, she wondered, an exiled Dhoonesman defacing the artifacts of Dhoone?

Following some instinct she could barely identify, Raina refused the armored kirtle that would have covered her hips and thighs. She was wearing the black skirt with the silver panels. Hatty Hare had cut it down from the dress that had been singed by the Menhir Fire. Hatty had cleaned up the silver panels, made the skirt beautiful and new.

Hailsmen needed to see it. They needed to know who they followed and why.

"Give me my helm," she commanded Chella. It was a half helm that matched the chest armor. Raina tucked it under arm.

"Do and be damned," she said to the mirror. The woman looking back said the same.

The torches were lit as she descended the stairs. Raina could not recall when she'd last seen them burn so brightly. Everything was crisply vivid. Colors were deeper, edges sharper, shadows as black as the clan's name. People had lined the stairs and halls to view her. Most were quiet and unblinking as she passed. Merritt Ganlow's mouth fell open and she hissed to Sheela Cobbin, "Who does she think she is?"

"Blackhail," Raina said without stopping. *I have the guide-stone in my belly to prove it.*

Sarolyn Meese, Corbie's lovely wife, blew her a kiss. The baby was suckling at her breast. Masha Horn, little sister to

Florrie, burst into tears; it appeared from fright. Raina resisted the urge to smile. Fright was good.

The tall double doors of the Great Hearth were open. The fire was out and the chamber empty. The sight of row after row of vacant benches sobered her. Sworn warriors were waiting upon her arrival.

She forced herself not to rush. Clan needed this. The women and children and tied clansmen who remained behind needed to believe in their . . . chief. They needed to know she was not fearful or light-of-heart and they needed to see her pride in herself and her clan.

Raina was shaking minutely as she crossed the entrance hall. Chella was at her back.

"May I ride with you?" she had asked last night, after the plans for the raid had been finalized between Raina and the sworn clansmen. "Will you grant me that honor?"

Raina had not answered then and there and had taken the question to bed with her, to her clean and refurnished wife's chamber. It occurred to her then that she would like to better know the histories. Women were chiefs. Women had been warrior queens. Look at Wrayan Castlemilk. By all accounts she was ten times more capable than her brother. Blackhail was different though: stouter, older, more reserved. Raina did not know the names of its women chiefs. She did not even know if it had any.

In the end she had decided she must do as she pleased. There would always be Merritt Ganlows and Gat Murdochs who did not like her. A chief could not satisfy all.

And Blackhail needed manpower. The last scouts had mentioned Scarpe numbers past eleven hundred. Raina had already discussed with the sworn clansmen the logistics of including unsworn men in their ranks. It had been agreed that those who were able-bodied, skilled at horse and vouched for could be given positions in the rear of the van. Raina still did not know the numbers; planning and assembly had happened so fast.

She had only been certain she would act the day after Hew Mallin's visit. *If I were you, Raina Blackhail, I'd strike that camp hard and soon. Take it by surprise and tear it down.* The ranger's words had given her a sleepless night. She did not know for certain who Hew Mallin was, and knew only a fool trusted a stranger, but she could not argue with the ranger's assessment. He told her what she already knew. Out loud, where it counted, where it could not be ignored.

Raina's greatest fear was that Scarpe would strike the roundhouse. As Mallin had pointed out, the house had a hole in its wall. Raina had ordered it filled but such detailed masonry took time. Even if there were no hole Yelma would still strike. She needed to claim Blackhail as her own before Hail warriors began returning from Bannen Field. The Hailhouse was weak now but it wouldn't always be. When Blackhail met Dhoone on the field everything would change.

Raina did not care to think about what some of those changes meant to her. Right now, tonight, her thoughts must be narrow. Scarpe was trespassing on Blackhail land, intercepting its goods, harassing its farmers, slaughtering its livestock and interrogating its warriors. Such transgression could not—would not—continue.

The Weasel chief needed to be sent home, back to her poison pines and her burned down house and her vats of caustic hair dye. Raina Blackhail would make it happen. She was about to execute the boast.

We are the first among clans, and we do not hide and we do not cower and we will have our revenge.

The great armored Blackhail door and its pullstone were open. Although the sun was still setting in the west, the court was ringed with torches. Their orange and red flames toward the sun, it looked to Raina as if they were homing. The battle party was met within their borders. Warriors were ahorse, and the sounds created by their war harnesses and hammer chains filled her with dread. Armor sawed against armor. Ax cradles creaked. Horses tossed their heads and danced.

The warriors were grave, their gloved or gauntleted fists at tension on their reins, their jaw muscles twitching like crane flies. The mass of their armor and war cloaks made them into giants. People would be afraid at the sight of them. Raina felt pride.

Their ranks parted as she made her way out of the Hail-house and on to the court. Ballic the Red, Stanner Hawk, Cleg Trotter, Hardgate Meese and the hammermen were there. Cleg's father, the tied clansman Paille Trotter, was sitting on a big plow horse. Raina wondered who had vouched for him. He was a sixty-year-old farmer with a gamy leg. All the sworn old-timers were present; Gat Murdoch, Turby Flapp, Mungo Kale who, although possessing an oath, had probably not left the clan forge in years. They had all come out for her. Pig farmers, warriors, old men.

Raina held her head high as she moved through the space they had created, a corridor leading to the center of the court.

Jebb Onnacre walked forward with her horse. The stable-man was clad in a motley assortment of armor; unmatched chest, shoulder and back pieces, and what looked to be a leather cast around his neck. Raina could hear Jebb's mother, the bossy but good-hearted Hillda Onnacre. "Here, put it on. I made it special. All the sworn warriors will be wearing them."

Raina accepted the reins. She was glad of Jebb's assistance with mounting Mercy. The Dhoone armor made her upper body stiff. As she settled herself in the saddle and received her primed and unlit torch, the war drums began, sounding a stark four-quarter beat. When Raina seated her helmet she could feel the rhythm vibrating through the steel.

Dagro, my love. I wish you were with me tonight.

The sun was sinking below the horizon as she turned Mercy and surveyed her army. They were waiting on her word. Seasoned veterans like Ballic the Red and Hardgate Meese were watching for her signal to move out. She loved them fiercely.

And at this moment it wasn't hard to imagine she was loved just as fiercely in return.

Raina Blackhail had never ridden in a war party, had not once led a company of men, but she had stood with her back to the clan door and watched as dozens of raid parties and armies and battle groups had departed. She knew how it was supposed to happen. There would be no speeches, no fine words designed to fire and motivate. Hailsmen did not require them. They just required a leader to lead.

The ranks parted for a second time as Raina walked Mercy to the western edge of the court. Behind her she was aware that Chella Gloyal had mounted her glossy gray stallion and fallen into line. The warriors barely noticed: all gazes were on their chief. When Mercy's hoofs encountered the soft give of turf, Raina took a deep breath. Her breasts pushed against the plate armor. Her heart felt big and nearly whole.

Kicking boot heels into Mercy she cried, *"Kill Scarpe!"* and led the charge from the Hailhold.

An army moved on her word. Horses leapt into motion. Drumbeats quickened. Warriors took up the call.

Kill Scarpe. Kill Scarpe. Kill Scarpe.

A waning moon one day short of full lit the graze. Raina could see for leagues. The world was colored black and silver like the clan badge. Around her she was aware of the hammermen, matching but never exceeding her pace. They made half a fortress for her, kept her dead in the middle, kept her safe.

She had not known riding to war could be thrilling. In all the intimate conversations she had shared with Dagro as his wife, he had never spoke of this. The charge conjured powerful and elemental magic. The night was alive with the possibilities it created. Anything could happen. Armed men were riding at force.

They traveled west along the farm road and then adjusted their course north. Cold Lake glowed blue in the distance; a barn owl was in flight above it. As Raina made the cut onto the old trapping path, she felt a tightness in her chest. The last time she'd taken this path had been the worst day of her life.

Dagro was dead and Mace Blackhail, his foster son, had raped her. After it was over she had walked this path back to the roundhouse. She recalled the sun had started shining. It had melted the snow that caked the back of her dress.

Aware her pace had dropped, Raina squeezed Mercy's belly with her thighs. She could smell the Scarpes now. Their smokefires always stank. Behind and abreast of her, the mood of the army was changing. Men fell silent. Visors were lowered. Hammers, axes, longswords and riding bows were drawn. Raina considered her own weapons. Anwyn Bird's bow was strapped to Mercy's back along with sufficient arrows to kill a score of Scarpes. Mounted at her waist were her knives. The maiden's helper had been a parting gift from her uncle at Dregg. *This will keep the men away*. It hadn't, of course, but Raina supposed that was more a failing of herself than the blade. She'd been wearing it when Mace raped her.

Quickly, Raina moved her hand to the second knife. The handle of Dagro's hand knife felt warm and smooth. When the time came for her to draw a weapon it would do. It had already killed one Scarpe. It knew the drill.

The party slowed as they entered the bush. The wet ground was steaming. Slowly and silently, the bowmen began to fan out through the low trees. It was a shock when Raina heard the first discharge. She had known Ballic and his crew would pick off sentries around the camp, but knowing and experiencing were different things in battle.

Raina swallowed.

She heard the cry. "Intruders to the east."

Raina's entire life had been lived on the other side of those words, and it took a brief but perceptible moment to realize, *They mean me*. And then she called the charge.

KILL SCARPE!

It was like rolling on a giant wave. You could not stop it once it began. You could only hope to keep breathing and survive. Raina went crashing forward with the hammermen, as the bowmen lit their fire arrows and rained them on the camp. Mercy was a mad horse, bucking her head and keeping pace with the stallions. One-sixteenth Sull, Raina reminded herself. That percentage was paying off. At her right, the fine old hammerman Hardgate Meese was swinging his hammer into motion. Raina felt the air it displaced, heard the terrible rattle of its chains. At her left Cleg Trotter's mighty four-foot war hammer was already a blur. His teeth were black, she realized. And Chella was wrong about the smiling: Cleg was grinning from ear to ear.

The camp lay directly ahead across Thwater Field on the site of the old Thwater Farm. Safe lamps made the tents glow like orange blocks. Black figures were rushing across the camp, pulling on clothing and strapping on weapons as they ran. Women and children were screaming. The fire arrows had started to hit, and flames were running like primed fuses.

Raina yanked her torch from her saddle harness and swung it behind her as she rode, begging for a light. Some kind bowmen touched its primed tip with the point of his fire arrow and the torch ripped into life. With one hand on the reins, the other on a flaming torch, Raina Blackhail charged the Weasel camp.

She stepped into another life.

It was a violent and flaming hell. Horses reared. Fire roared. Men killed. Women raced for the trees. Children and animals caught fire and were burned alive. Hammers moved like vengeful gods, swift and full of malice. Swords sucked at flesh, holding on to it, cleaving as they withdrew. Raina rode straight for the large central tent and charged it with her torch. Scarpemen moved from her path. A woman shrieked in fear. It was a revelation. She had become an unstoppable force.

She hurled the torch into the tent canvas with all her bodily might. Mercy compensated for the abrupt shift in balance with a clever little dance that Raina had not known the horse had in her. Together they watched the flames sheet across the canvas and race along the guide ropes. Raina was screaming at the top of her lungs. *Kill Scarpe. Kill Scarpe.*

She wanted each and every one of them to die.

Spotting an old man fleeing around the side of the tent, she drew Dagro's knife and rode him down. Bending low in the saddle she stabbed him in the shoulder. He cried softly with surprise and then turned. He had something shiny in his hand. It was a sword. Raina froze. Her capacity for thought fled. She watched the edge of the blade come toward her and knew it was not a good thing, but could not imagine how to stop it. Her training ended here. The sword came up. Muscle charged in the old man's arms as he struck. She thought, *This is it.* And then suddenly something grew from his eye.

Raina looked at it stupidly, trying to understand. The old man dropped the sword midswing and clutched his face. He was making an odd chuffing sound, like a dog about to be sick. *Feathers,* Raina identified. There were feathers sticking out of his head.

It was an arrow, she finally understood, as the man swayed and fell to the ground. It had been fired with such force she had not seen or heard the shot.

Chella.

Raina turned, and there was the Hailswoman sitting calmly astride her gray stallion, her bow already drawn and at tension, ready for another shot. With a small upward movement of her draw elbow, she acknowledged Raina's glance.

Like bowfishing, she mouthed over the distance between them.

Raina did not know if she smiled or grimaced, only that something happened to her mouth. Swiftly, she turned Mercy and rejoined the van. She was shaking. Sweat had made her warrior face start to run. Black drops fell on her skirt.

Realizing her mistake, she joined the hammermen. She had pulled too far ahead of the line, leaving herself vulnerable to strikes. Adjusting her grip on her maiden's helper she warned herself to have more sense.

The camp was a stinking inferno. Foul chemicals favored by the Scarpes had started to burn, sending up chimneys of black smoke. Drums of lamp fuel were exploding. Most Scarpe warriors were ahorse now and the battle was met head-to-head. Scarpes preferred longswords to hatchets, and melees were brutal and intense. Raina recognized the lean form of Yelma's nephew, Uriah Scarpe. He was mounted on a piebald gelding that she recognized as having once belonging to Bitty Shank. This annoyed her on behalf of Orwin. How dare this man steal a bereaved Hailsman's horse?

Making eye contact with Cleg Trotter and Hardgate Meese, Raina charged him. This time she knew the hammermen were with her. She had learned that she did not possess martial skills, and that it did not matter as long as she kept her head.

No one here with the possible exception of Chella Gloyal was keeping count of how many Scarpemen Raina Blackhail brought down. All saw her though. With her Dhoone queen's armor and skirt of black-and-silver she was the most prominent figure on the field. That was what counted: to be seen and marked. Word needed to be carried all the way to Bannen Field: Raina Blackhail rode at the head of the line.

It was the final, vital step to becoming chief.

And Raina was fine with that. She was just as fine as fine could be.

Uriah Scarpe had been engaging the pig farmer Hissup Gluff. He had drawn blood and was closing for the kill. The sound of charging horses caused him to slow and turn his head. His expression in that moment, his confused and slightly irritated disbelief, was something Raina would keep with her for always. It was one of the most satisfying moments of her life.

Yes, Scarpeman. It's me.

Her hammer crew took him down in a precise concert of blows. Raina stabbed him as he was falling, and then winked at Hissup Gluff.

The pig farmer said one word.

"Chief."

Raina and her crew moved on to the next mark.

She would never know how long the battle lasted. The Weasel camp burned to the ground and many took to the woods. Yelma and her crack swordsmen made a stand in front of the well. The Scarpe chief was mounted, and armed with a sharp and needle-like sword. She knew how to drive her horse in circles and ward her own space. As her bodyguards began to fall she made a tactical decision.

Addressing Ballic the Red, who had come forward with his bow now that the battle had turned, Yelma Scarpe cried, "I yield."

Ballic the Red turned in his saddle to look at Raina. He was the senior clansman present, and in that Yelma Scarpe was faultless.

Unless she was in the presence of a chief.

"Disarm her," Raina said.

The chief's bidding was done. Ballic the Red shot an arrow into the Weasel chief's knuckles, forcing the fingers apart. Yelma sucked in breath. The sword dropped.

Raina wiped the maiden's helper on her sheepskin numnah and then charged the Scarpe chief. Yelma was defiant, her chin high, her small black eyes unblinking. She did not believe Raina Blackhail had it in her. She did not realize until the last moment that she was dealing with a chief.

That instant of reappraisal would be buried with her. Her mouth opened, the recognition of a threat dilated her pupils, and then the Hail chief took her life.

Raina felt no pity for her as she freed the knife from her chest. Yelma had misjudged her enemy and failed to protect her clan. Raina swore she would never make the Scarpe chief's mistake.

The battle ended quickly after that. Flames burned low as farm buildings, tents and shanties were reduced to ruins. Warriors surrendered and were granted quarter. Blackhail took no hostages, allowing those who fled to the woods the privilege of freedom. Raina doubted they would return. Their camp was gone, their chief was gone. No good reason existed for them to stay.

Just as she'd led the line in battle, Raina led the return to the roundhouse. Men were weary. Their hands and faces were coated in a black mix of blood and soot. Raina was dead tired. Victory was hers, and as she took the trapping path toward home she felt she could finally breathe.

Snapping the buckles on her breastplate, she sat back in the saddle and rested. She was chief now.

Do and be damned.

CHAPTER 33

Floating on the Sull-Clan Border

Rufus Rime's rules for traveling in the Reed Way were: Don't travel unless you know where you're going; take water; take a lamp; never go east.

Two out of four wasn't bad.

Effie Sevrance had a lamp and water waiting in the boat.

Now she had one final thing to fetch.

It was dusk as she walked from the dock to the roundhouse. The sky was green and pink, like it could only get over the marsh. The sun was a big blurry shape, no longer round. Reeds were swaying like corn in a field and marsh birds were calling for the night.

Effie entered the roundhouse and headed straight for the kitchen. The Salamander Hall was quiet but people had begun to gather in the kitchen for supper. Effie had to push past them to get to Lissit.

The girl saw her coming and tried to duck. Only she couldn't, not really, as she was serving up some sort of broth with chunks of fish in it, stirring and ladling it into bowls. All she could do was sort of tuck her head low and train her gaze upon the broth. As if that was going to help.

Effie walked straight up to the broth pot and pushed her chest against the rim. "You're coming with me," she told Lissit through the steam. It was strange how flat her voice sounded, like there was no longer any air puffing it up.

Lissit pushed back a strand of blond hair from her face. She looked at Effie.

Effie Sevrance, sister to Drey and Raif, daughter of Tem, glared back.

Lissit dropped the ladle into the pot. "I can't be away for too long."

They took the back door and headed for the guidehouse. Lissit was dressed in pretty gray-green linen that swished at her ankles as she walked. She had the good sense not to ask any questions. Answers would not help here.

The narrow corridor was cool. Swamp water seeping through the walls created puddles that had to be navigated. When they reached the guidehouse's rear door, Effie wondered briefly if she should knock. Raising the handle, she went straight in. Gray had never extended any courtesy to her so why should she extend any in return?

The guidehouse was empty and dark. You could tell straightaway the guide wasn't present. No one was stirring the smoke. Lissit gave a little yap of worry as she entered.

"What should we say if they find us?"

The question was so irrelevant it seemed to hail from another world. Effie did not even attempt to respond to it. Her mind was on other things.

The Graystone gleamed red in the exhausted light of the smoke fires. Its metal planes looked like glass. Effie averted her gaze from them. She knew what was in there. She wasn't about to forget.

Quickly she moved beyond the Graystone and into the front of the guidehouse. Smoke had formed horizontal layers in the air. Effie's mouth was aligned with the space between so she could breathe without drawing it in. Lissit was taller and not so well aligned. She coughed softly as they approached the stone table. She had given up asking questions again. She had probably guessed what they were about to do.

Chedd's head and chest were covered with a white cloth so fine you could see the contours of his face. He was laid out on the low stone table—maybe the table was an altar; Effie did not know. The woven cane stretcher lay limp beneath him, its guide poles perfectly aligned with Chedd's body on both sides. Effie touched the edge of the table. The granite was very cold. Chedd had been lying upon it for two days. Tomorrow they would come to take him away.

Only Chedd Limehouse would be gone; Effie Sevrance was taking him. He was her love and Gray could not have him. And only she, in the entire world, knew what to do with Chedd's body.

"Open the door. Then take the end," Effie told Lissit, nodding toward the stretcher handles by Chedd's feet. "I'll take the head."

Lissit was someone who responded well to being told what to do. She ran to the front of the guidehouse, opened the door between the guidehouse and the Salamander Hall and then moved into position at the end of the table. She grabbed the stretcher handles by Chedd's feet. Effie took the other side.

"On three."

The hardest thing was getting the body off the table. They had to shimmy the stretcher sideways, moving awkwardly with their arms outstretched and their hands on the butts of the poles. Chedd's feet came first. Once they overhung the table by a sufficient margin, Lissit moved into position between her poles. Once there, she swung the stretcher around, pushing it forward at the same time so that the stretcher and Chedd formed a cross against the table. Effie could then take her position between the poles, and together she and Lissit edged Chedd sideways and clear of the table.

The weight was on the far edge of bearable. Effie would not have had it any other way.

Arms straining, fists white around the poles, Effie and Lissit bore Chedd Limehouse from the Grayhouse. Perhaps there was a kind of sorcery here, perhaps not. Effie knew for certain that no one would stop her. Even if they challenged her she would not be stopped.

No one challenged her. People must have seen the two girls shuffling through the Salamander Hall with the stretcher, yet no one prevented their passing. Perhaps it was such an incredible sight that they did not believe their eyes. Or perhaps they realized: Yes, *this must be done.*

The old warrior at the Salamander Door did not meet Effie's gaze. He was idly rubbing rust from his blade with his fingernail and did not look up. Outside it was nearly dark. A halo of green light lit the west.

The loons were calling.

Effie led the way along the dock. She wasn't sure how it was going to work—getting Chedd into the boat—but in the end it turned out to be easier than pulling the stretcher off the table. Lissit must have learned some things at Croser, for she was the one who showed Effie what to do. Dropping down to their haunches they lowered Chedd and the stretcher onto the wood slats of the dock, at a right angle to the water. Following Lissit's direction, Effie boarded the boat and turned it so that it formed a line with Chedd's body. Crouching, Lissit pushed the stretcher so that Chedd's head extended over the dock and above the boat. When they were in position, Lissit raised her end of the stretcher and Chedd's body slid into the boat. It *thunked* a bit but Effie wasn't stupid. It didn't matter. Dead was dead.

Lissit pushed off the boat and then stood on the dock and watched as Effie paddled across the Stillwater with Chedd.

Effie headed east, away from the setting sun and toward the rising moon. She wasn't coming back.

Flames from the gas vents cast yellow light upon the water. You could hear them hissing softly, spending fuel. Effie watched the moths and crane flies orbit the flames. Only skill kept them from death.

Some didn't make it. Effie paddled easily and lightly through the water. Chedd was in the stern of the boat and her supplies and the lead weights were in the front. At some point during Chedd's transport the cloth covering his face had fluttered away. Smoke from the guidehouse fires had cured his skin, but apart from the change in color he looked exactly like Chedd. Not creepy. Not squelchy. Just Chedd.

Part of her wanted to lie down beside him and sleep, but that wouldn't get them anywhere. They'd just float into a bank of reeds.

Reaching the margins of the Stillwater, Effie rested her paddle and lit the safe lamp. She'd thought of everything: flint and striker, extra fuel, a blanket for when she got cold. The weights. Perhaps she should have brought food, but dead bodies and bread and cheese didn't seem a good match. She had eaten beforehand, forcing herself to chew and swallow, and to drink when her throat got dry. She had chosen not to eat anything tasty, like pastries or fried fishcakes, because she knew that whenever something good passed her lips she had an urge to go and tease Chedd. He was smart until he saw food, and then he was dumb.

Look how easy it had been to maneuver him into helping her lift the curse. One sweaty pastry was enough. Chedd Limehouse was very, very dumb.

Effie frowned her way through something dodgy happening behind her eyes. It was stinging back there, but when she scrunched up her forehead tight enough it stopped.

Chedd would have been impressed by how she got the weights. She stole them. Easy peasy, from a fisherman who left his traps unattended on the dock. She had taken her knife and cut them from the trap line, then transported them two at a time to her boat. She didn't get them all, because the fisherman returned, but she thought she'd gotten enough for the job. And she took his gold weight too. It was funny, watching him realize what had happened. His traps were exactly where he left them, but most of the weights to keep them sunk in the water were gone. Scratching his chin, he had circled the traps as if another angle of view might help. Effie was sitting nonchalantly on the edge of the dock, and when he looked at her accusingly she'd played dumb. Her dumb was better than his smarts and he'd strided off in the opposite direction looking for someone else to blame.

It was amazing what you could get away with if you were brazen and didn't care about getting caught. What could the fisherman have done to her that would be worse than losing Chedd? Beat her? She could jump into the water. Shout at her? She could shout right back, tell him exactly what she thought about his mangy, sinking clan. She was glad she'd got his gold weight. What did he need it for anyway? Catching fish?

Realizing she wasn't paying enough attention to the way ahead, Effie concentrated on steering. She was in one of the channels now and rushes formed walls to either side of the boat. The safe lamp was up front on the deck, its light creating a twelve-foot orb. She couldn't see very far ahead, but she wasn't paddling fast. She still wasn't sure where she wanted to go.

East would do for now. East was right and good.

She wasn't a bit afraid or nervous. That was the other thing about when bad things happened to you: They didn't leave much space in your head for the stuff you normally felt. And besides. It was better to be doing something than nothing. And it was definitely better being here with Chedd than at Gray.

She wasn't doing this for them. She was doing this for Drey and Raif and Raina and everyone back at Blackhail. She was doing it for Bannen and the fine and honorable Limehouse family who lived there.

She was doing this for herself and Chedd.

He had promised to help her lift the curse, and the fact that she now knew more about the curse's true nature didn't change that promise. Its spirit remained the same. He was helping her to prevent something bad from happening. They were helping each other in that way.

Magic to find it. Magic to block it.

That was the reason Gray stole children with old skills, because they were hoping one or all of them could prevent the bad thing from happening. Bairns with old skills were born throughout the clanholds but Gray was increasing those odds. There were probably more magic users in Gray than in the entire western clanholds combined. Flora, Flora's brother Gregor, Lissit, Rufus Rime. They'd all been hauled from other clans in the hope that someone would find the weak point where the Endlords would ride through, and block it somehow with magic. Gregor Dunladen had died trying. Poor Flora had gone insane. Lissit was reduced to a scared mouse, and Rufus Rime had become a recruiter, finagling people into becoming part of the Gray crew with his stories and mysterious rules and lessons in marsh lore. Effie imagined that's what happened when you'd been here too long. You got to imagine it was a fine place and wondered why so few people thought the same.

They'd probably miss the curse when it was gone. How hard could they have really tried to change things? She knew what to do and she'd been here less than two months.

Reaching a confluence in the Reed Way, Effie chose a channel at random, turning the boat southeast. The moon was rising so quickly you could almost see it moving. It wasn't full but it was bright. Clouds closing from the north would eventually put a stop to that.

Effie wondered if a prophecy was the same as a curse. *Only if it's bad,* she decided. It seemed more accurate to call Gray the Doomed Clan, but the longer she thought about it the more certain she became that the doom didn't really have much to do with Gray at all.

They'd just picked a bad spot for their clan. It was like mountains. Uncle Angus said that mountains were mostly mountains but once in a while one blew, just plain exploded out of nowhere. Gray had chosen a bad mountain: one that was about to blow its top and spill out terrible stuff.

The trick was to find the spot where the stuff was set to escape.

And the second trick was to stop it.

That's what Gregor Dunladen had been up to when he was drowned. Perhaps he'd made the same connections she had— he had been named after a king and all. And the name Gregor *did* sound smart. Trouble was he couldn't have found the spot. At least not the way that she could find the spot.

Her way was unique to Effie Sevrance.

Feeling a bit cold, Effie reached for the blanket. Mosquitoes had begun to dance around her hands and face. She swatted them with the paddle. They flew a short distance and then came back.

The rushes smelled like broth. They swayed in great waves, but Effie didn't think it was the wind that moved them. The breeze was blowing a different way. For some reason this made her think of the Graystone.

How was it possible that only three days had passed since she'd touched it? She could swear she'd been having bad dreams about what it showed her for ten times longer than that. Somehow Chedd was mixed in with the dreams. In them, the terrible force that reached through the stone came and snatched him right from his bed.

Effie had to do some forceful frowning for a bit to stop a sudden stinging behind the eyes. The force didn't *care*. It just destroyed things. It wouldn't rest until everything was gone.

Do you think what you saw will stop at the border of Clan Gray?

"No," Effie said out loud, recalling the clan guide's question. You couldn't see what she had seen and not know the answer.

She turned the boat—she did not know why—and took a narrow channel that was little more than a crack between the rushes. The first fingers of mist were rising from the water and the clouds had caught up with the moon. Effie glided through darkness, keeping the boat centered on the channel and avoiding the thick roots of the bulrushes

After a while she adjusted the blanket. It didn't appear to be working.

The channel led to a second needle-thin passage and Effie didn't think, didn't make any conscious decision, just let her arms do the paddling. They paddled her due east. Once she caught a glimpse of something rising above the water—a mound, either an island or partially sunk building—but knew it didn't concern her and paddled on.

The boat seemed to weigh nothing at all. It skimmed over the marsh like a damselfly. Effie steered and paddled and thought of nothing or thought of Chedd. She had fallen asleep next to him that final night and she recalled a moment as she was falling into unconsciousness when she imagined that the arc of her fall and the arc of Chedd's greater, deeper fall intersected. The healer woke her soon after that and she was made to leave while they tended the body. They had closed the door, as if that would make any difference.

Skirting a bed of reeds, Effie took another channel. Mosquitoes were feeding on the back of her hands. Mist was rising along the hull and pouring into the boat. She increased her speed, growing more and more certain. She could feel it now, the tow upon her body.

The stone lore was calling her home.

Did you really think it would be that easy to be rid of it?

Raif had not been able to throw away his raven bill; gone was not gone when you were a Sevrance and lost your lore.

Of course it had come here, brought by the pike that was not a pike, carried back toward the darkness that spawned it. Chedd was the one who had helped her understand that part of it. *All this water drains into the Wolf. It's how we got here, remember?* The pike had snapped the lore from her throat and swam hundreds of leagues against the current to reach the place in the marsh, the weak spot where its masters would rise. In a way it had been homing too.

Effie would not think about why a force of destruction had bothered with something as simple a girl's lore. Instinctively she knew the answer would not help her.

The Endlords themselves had revealed the final piece of the puzzle. As they moved toward her through the stone, their massive forms spinning like storm clouds, they had formed a shape to strike her. It was the streamlined head of a pike. She hadn't realized it properly at the time because the clan guide was there, shouting, and her dress was wet, and there were lots of other things to remember. But she thought about it later. She hadn't forgotten.

The Endlords had revealed themselves to her. They were the pike that had taken her lore.

Effie seated the paddle in the locks at the side of the boat. She was close now. Momentum would take her where she needed to go. The marsh water was running quickly and the current caught and carried the boat. The first sign of open water was the overhead mist: it had formed a white disc low in the sky. Mirroring, that was the name for it. Rufus Rime had told her that water in the air, either clouds or mist, would often mirror the shape of the pond or lake below it.

The rush walls fell away on both sides of the boat, and although Effie couldn't see very far she had a sensation of opening space. The air smelled different, like metals in Brog Widdie's forge. A line of palely glowing posts formed a string across the water.

Effie wondered if it was the Sull border. The posts had that look to them, the silent authority of a boundary. She didn't know what made them glow, for they weren't alight or burning. She *did* know some minerals shed light in the dark. Perhaps the posts were made from phosphorescent stone.

As the boat moved toward them Effie readied Chedd. He had been dressed in his own clothes: wool pants and tunic and the gray leather cloak of Bannen. Someone had cleaned them, but the smoke from the guide fires had sort of canceled it out. Effie took the rope from the front of the boat and began winding it around Chedd's waist. It wasn't easy as Chedd needed to be tilted a bit when the rope passed under his back. The shape of the boat helped. The V of the hull provided a small but crucial space beneath him. Effie pulled the rope tight with each pass, cinching Chedd's belly. A little gurgly noise puffed from his lips as she did the final cinching but it was surprisingly easy to ignore. Dead was dead, remember.

As she tied the weights to the rope, she was aware of the current turning and slowing the boat. Black water was swirling between the glowing posts, and it wasn't hard to guess where the boat was going to end up.

Effie worked quickly, using knots Mad Binny had taught her, complicated beautiful knots that would hold fast in water. When she was done she sat and waited for the boat to come to rest. She could feel the thinness of the world now. Forces on the other side were close and waiting to kiss her. It was not a good kind of kiss given in love or kinship.

But it was a welcome.

The boat stopped skimming forward. The current began to turn it on its axis, slowly spinning it like a bottle. Effie rose in the center of the boat and took off her clothes and boots. Naked she stood, spinning as she gathered the old magic around her. And then she knelt and slid her fingers around Chedd's waist rope and with a mighty heave capsized the boat.

Down they plunged into the cold black water, joined together like an anchor and its line. The force of entry punched air from Effie's lungs. It was shockingly, stunningly raw. Chedd's body dropped so quickly it yanked at Effie's finger joints and armpits, and she set everything in her—all thoughts, willpower and strength—to the task of holding the rope.

They fell through darkness. Deeper and deeper, sinking to a point on the thinnest edge of the world. Effie could feel them, the Endlords, moving to meet her, pushing from the other side. They were a storm the size of the world, spinning with perfect violence, tearing apart everything in their path to intercept her.

No, she told them.

No.

Time passed. She opened her eyes. All was black. She could not remember who she was and why she was here. A speck of light existed below her. As she plummeted toward it, the blankness in her mind formed a word.

Lore.

It lay there in the black, marking the edge of an infinitely deep abyss. One inch farther and it would have fallen into the crack in the world. *Stop here*, the lore said to her. *Effie Sevrance stops here.*

It was telling her it was the end of her and Chedd. She did not want to release him, but what choice did she have? Effie relaxed muscles in her fingers. Her skin sawed against the rope. For a second they cleaved, her and Chedd, holding together for one final moment in this world. And then she let him go.

Chedd Limehouse sank into the abyss.

Magic to find it. Magic to block it.

Chedd Limehouse was magic. He knew things about birds and turtles and fish and bears that no one else could know. The old skills ran in his veins, they strengthened his bones and sharpened his eyes. He would block the Endlords. He would keep his Eff safe.

Aware that she was bottoming out, her body slowing and beginning to buoy, Effie flung out her hand for her lore. With her fingers closing around the small piece of Hailstone, she began to rise.

When she reached the surface, she found, turned, and boarded the boat. It took a while. Many of her belongings were floating on the surface and she fished them aboard with the paddle. Not long after that she fell asleep.

She dreamed of Chedd. A good dream. There were turtles in it.

The current took Effie south.

CHAPTER 34

Watcher of the Damned

Angus Lok lay in the stinking filth of the drain culvert and watched the street. Men's bodies were pushed to either side of him, huddling for warmth in the darkest and stillest hour of the night, the one before dawn. The men reeked of urine and the sourness of unwashed flesh. One man was jerking rhythmically, either insane or pleasuring himself. Maybe both. Angus ignored him.

He was waiting as he had waited every day and night for the past four days, watching the crossroad of two streets, scanning for Sarcosa.

The surgeon's rooms were located in a house along the east-west-running street. Angus had arranged it so that whenever the surgeon left his home he had no choice but to move through this corner, which was to the east of his rooms. The way to the west, the end of the street which led down to the river and the water gardens, was flooded.

Angus dismantled small sections of the city's flood walls discreetly every night. It was the time that caused him the most anxiety—not the crow-barring of masonry and the resulting possibility of detection, but the fact that he was away from his watch. Anything could happen at night. Surgeons were called out for the dead, the dying, the sick, the hysterical, the seizing. A call might come at any time, a messenger sent running to the surgeon's door. *Come quick.*

It was Angus' greatest fear that a call would come while he was maintaining the flood, and that call came from the Maiden. Sarcosa would leave and go to her and he, Angus Lok, would never know.

Angus lived to know. The Maiden was hiding in this city and he needed to know where so he could send her to hell. The woman who had slain his wife and daughters in cold blood could not continue to live.

He would die rather than allow it.

Shifting his position, Angus warded against numbness in his feet and legs. He needed to be ready to depart any time. Any figure passing in the darkness might be Sarcosa.

It was easy to find information once you had a name. Surgeons needed income like everyone else. They could not afford to keep themselves hidden. Inquiries, lightly pressed, at the gold market north of the water gardens and the Great Round east of the fortress had supplied the facts that Angus had needed. Sarcosa lived on the east bank, on this street. He doctored an exclusive clientele of lords and ladies, rich merchants, bankers, and captains-of-the-guard. He was said to have paid visits to the fortress. By several accounts he was a fine-looking man, silver-haired, dignified, striking in his black cloak and boots. His rooms were modest, as he chose to spend his money in other areas of his life—young prostitutes, Angus understood—and because of that, he rarely saw patients there. Sarcosa was a beck-and-call surgeon, attending the rich and privileged of Morning Star. He came to you.

Armed with this information, Angus had investigated the street. He was cautious in his movements, as he could not rule out the possibility that the Phage knew exactly what he knew. The surgeon's rooms lay directly east of the water gardens, the park of man-made canals, fountain walks and lily ponds where the rich and well-dressed displayed themselves on fine days. The street was quiet and boasted few businesses. Its character varied depending on its closeness to the water gardens. West was good, east bad. Drainage was a problem in the eastern section, and great ditches and culverts had been dug to divert floodwater. The sheltering walls of many of these culverts had attracted the most desperate men in the city. As soon as Angus had spotted the community of ragged, dirt-eating beggars on the far corner of the surgeon's street, he had begun to design a plan. The beggars stopped water from running down their culvert by building a makeshift dam of scrap wood, rotten clothing, animal hides and dung.

If they could block water, he could free it.

It was easy. The west part of the surgeon's street lay below the high-water level of the Eclipse. Break the floodwall downstream and water came pouring into the water gardens and the street, blocking off roads to the north, west and south. East was the direction the surgeon now had to turn to leave his street. East to this crossroads, past the watcher who was waiting there.

Angus had followed Sarcosa on every trip he had made over the last four days and nights, ghosting behind him, an unremarkable figure in a dun-colored coat. The surgeon had tended rich dowagers in their manses while Angus had stood outside in the shadows, looking in. When the surgeon had taken dinner in a well-favored tavern, Angus had waited at a safe distance, far down the street but in sight of the tavern door. He had accompanied the surgeon to a mummer's show and followed him later as he stopped at a small house to leech a patient. Later still the surgeon had visited a pleasure hall. Angus joined him for the long walk home.

When the sick called for Sarcosa he no longer arrived alone. A shadow trailed him, sometimes at a distance as far as three hundred feet. Look and you were unlikely to see it. But the shadow always saw you.

Angus barely slept. He ate scraps off the street, bread slid from vendors' stalls in passing, chunks of boiled meat thrown into the culvert as a charity by the Bone Priests. He drank the water. With every day he became more invisible, as if dirt and raggedness and desperation were magic concealing him from people's eyes, and the more he gathered about him the less detectable he became. He recognized this and used it. Above and beyond that he did not care.

He lived for one thing.

Men and women in the culvert, the beggars, the shit-eaters, the insane, did not question his right to be among them. They recognized their own truth in his eyes. All here were lost or losing something.

No one challenged him to a fight.

Angus lay in the collective warmth of their bodies and did not rest. Dawn glowed in the eastern sky and the city stirred. A street vendor rolled out his brazier and set it upstreet and upwind of the culvert. Business had been good since the flood. A group of maids in white caps and white aprons headed for the markets, empty baskets in hand. They crossed the street well before the culvert and averted their gazes as they passed.

A runner boy came racing down the street from the north and muscles in Angus' belly tensed. Runner boys meant messages. Messages could lead to calls.

The surgeon's rooms were located in a house a third of a league down the street. Angus could not track the boy to the address. To follow him down the street would leave himself too exposed, so he waited. If the Phage knew what he knew and wanted to assassinate him, they would watch the house.

After a quarter hour the runner boy returned, message delivered, and headed back north. Angus stayed in position. Men in the culvert were rising, scratching their beards, shaking themselves off, pissing downstream. Few spoke. The smell of sausages grilling on the brazier was a shared torture. Not for the first time Angus wondered why the men in the culvert didn't simply rise up and overpower the vendor.

He decided they weren't quite desperate enough.

Spying a tall figure moving east, Angus stilled. It was Sarcosa in his black cloak, gloves on, boots polished, slender leather satchel slung sideways across his chest like an arrow case. He approached the crossroads and turned north. Angus forced himself to wait.

As he counted to twenty, he watched for other watchers. He had been Phage himself once; he knew the deal. Satisfied that all was normal, Angus rose and left the culvert. He did not look back.

Morning Star was still coming to life. Geese on the riverbanks honked as a small and pale sun rose through clouds. Delivery carts hurtled along the streets, draymen warning bloody murder if the way ahead wasn't cleared. Angus kept to the walls. Sarcosa was a hundred feet ahead, walking briskly with a sense of his own importance. He turned east, away from the river. Angus turned along with him.

The area here was comfortable; manses and law courts, whitewashed taverns and stables, temples with stonework carvings showing the sun and morning star in opposition. Sarcosa stopped abruptly and rapped on the door of one of the manses. He was granted swift entry and the painted white door closed behind him. Angus glided past and kept going.

Five minutes later he approached the house from behind. The back door was swung open and the courtyard was in use. A laundry girl was boiling blankets in a bath over a fire. Angus continued moving along the lane. Sarcosa's daylight visits could be a problem.

Two houses down he spotted a fat and ancient maid sitting on a bench in her master's courtyard, doing little save looking exhausted. "Day, Mistress," he called to her.

She turned her stately head and inspected him. "We give our alms to the chapel house. On your way."

Angus ignored the direction. "Just saw the doctor step into the house two doors down. Bad business?"

Information, its receipt and transfer, were irresistible. The ancient head nodded. "That so? Can't say I'm surprised the way that poor man's heart's been playing up."

"Wife driving him hard?"

The woman chuckled. "Not unless she's doing it from the grave. The only woman he has to contend with is the maid. Runs herself ragged for him, she does."

"Blond girl, the one doing the laundry out back?"

"Sounds about right."

Angus made a swift farewell and left. The woman watched him with some suspicion as he walked down the street.

He took a slow circuit of the house. This time as he passed the door he stopped and rapped hard on the wood.

"Elise!" came a cry from the front of the building. "Can you get that? The surgeon and I are busy."

Judging the cry was loud enough—and intended—to reach the laundry girl in the back courtyard, Angus moved on. His concerns over who had answered the door when Sarcosa arrived were now gone. The master had answered it himself.

Sarcosa took his own good time at the house, emerging over two hours later. He treated himself to a midday meal at one of the fine whitewashed taverns and then headed north to make another call.

The Fortress District was the most monied part of the city. Here, in the shadow of the Burned Fortress, lived the city's most venerable occupants. High lords kept houses within call of the Lord Rising, and rich and powerful public servants lived within walking distance of Burned Bridge. The streets were so quiet you could hear the fortress gate descending. When horns broadcast the Lord Rising's movements, the Fortress District learned of them first.

Angus had never liked it; bricks made for high walls and unfriendly neighborhoods. He liked it less now. Fewer people on the streets meant he was more detectible. Private guards posted outside private manses watched him as he approached and kept watching until he moved on. He slowed his pace, dropping back from Sarcosa. Crossed the street.

Sarcosa approached a house at the far end of the street, a limestone manse with the kind of detailed stonework that took masons years to complete but in reality just trapped the bird shit and the dirt. It had actual glazed windows, diamond-shaped panes set in lead. The door was clad with iron panels.

To the left stood a guard wearing the kind of bright, gilded uniform that undercut a fighting man's dignity but pleased rich ladies. The guard knocked for Sarcosa, as if it were a dangerous endeavor better taken care of by a professional. Perhaps it was. Knuckles on an iron door.

Entry was granted and Sarcosa disappeared into the house. Angus wanted a look in those windows. He re-crossed the street.

The guard saw him coming and flexed his weapon arm. He was holding a steel halberd with a nasty hook assemble under the blade.

"Got any coppers," Angus said, holding up his hands to show they were empty, "for a veteran of the Morning Guard?"

The guard shook his head. "Sorry, friend." He didn't sound sorry and he wasn't a friend.

Angus walked past him, toward the window. Unable to resist, he approached it and peered in. An old and bewigged lady was sitting on a high-backed chair with Sarcosa at her feet. The surgeon was unwinding a stained bandage from around her black and swollen ankle. Detecting movement they both looked up, but Angus was already gone.

The guard called out a choice selection of curses as Angus paced down the street.

An hour later Sarcosa left the house. Angus followed the surgeon as he made a third call to a tower manse on River Hill to the east. This call was also unproductive—a man with a thickly bandaged head met Sarcosa at the door—and Angus waited in the next street until the surgeon was done.

It began to rain. Angus took no shelter. When Sarcosa came into view at the end of the street, Angus fell in his wake. It was getting late now. Taverns lit their lamps in expectation of the night. People were dashing home with the day's purchases, cloaks pulled over their heads. Mothers stood on doorsteps and called children out of the rain and into the warmth. Angus turned his thoughts away from the dangerous territory they represented. He thought about his man-made flood. The rain would be good for it, maybe even remove the need for an adjustment later tonight.

Sarcosa stepped down a side alley and into a pleasure hall. It was different place than the one he had visited last night. Angus was immediately alert.

The hall's big ground-floor windows were open to the alley-way. Angus hung in their shadows and watched as Sarcosa took a seat at one of the benches. An alewife brought the surgeon something in a tiny glazed cup. As Sarcosa drank, a fair-skinned girl sat beside him. She was dressed in a tight sky-blue bodice cut low. Her cheeks and the exposed curves of her breasts were rouged. Her hair and skin was baby-fine; she couldn't have been more than fifteen.

Sarcosa called for more drinks in little glazed cups. He and the girl sipped and chatted as the hall filled with patrons. After a while they stood in unison and headed for the back of the large high-ceilinged room.

Angus entered the hall. Light and heat from the stove dazzled him. Steam rose from his coat. A woman wearing a red silk dress whispered something to her friends and an entire table of people turned to look at him. Angus saw, judged and dismissed them.

The alewife who had served Sarcosa began wending her way through the crowd. Angus continued moving. He had spotted a door in the back of the room and was heading toward it. The alewife saw this and moved at a tangent to intercept him. She was middle-aged, just turning to fat, and carried herself with some authority.

She was trying to catch someone's eye. Angus tracked her gaze to a burly man standing at the counter, chatting merrily with two girls. The man was unaware of the alewife's attempt to hail him and he had not yet seen Angus Lok.

"Hey, lovey." The alewife was brisk as she approached Angus. She probably dealt with undesirables every day. "Outside, eh? We don't want no trouble here."

Angus turned his head and looked her straight in the eye. "Go away."

It was spoken quietly, perhaps not even spoken at all. The alewife's entire demeanor changed as she realized this was not every day. Her mouth closed. She glanced at the counter man. Angus did not need to look over his shoulder to know that he wasn't looking back.

The alewife gave ground.

She swallowed and then said hoarsely, "I'm going to fetch the keep."

Let her fetch, Angus thought as he took the final steps to the door.

It opened, and his heart beat with force in his chest.

He closed the door. Swiftly and quietly he broke and jammed the lock. The door was flimsy, its hinges better suited to rabbit hutches than public places, but it was something. It gave him time.

Turning, he surveyed the interior space. He was in a corridor lit by a pretty mica lamp that made the wood-paneled walls glow. Four doors led off the corridor; two on either side. A single chair stood against the east-facing wall. Some kind of dyed and decorative feather shawl lay upon it.

Angus tried the first door, swinging it lightly open. The room was dark. It contained a posted and canopied bed, nothing else. He moved on.

As he crossed to the second door he heard Sarcosa's voice murmur softly, "This will not hurt."

There was a world of possibilities in those words, but Angus Lok recognized the tone. This was not a man talking to a very young girl he was about to bed. This was a surgeon talking to his patient.

Angus Lok drew his longknife from the sheath that snugged his thigh. The blade gleamed orange in the mica light. It was two feet long, double edged, and forged by the Sull. They called such knives ghostmakers.

Behind him, someone tried the door between the corridor and the hall.

Angus exploded into motion. Give the Maiden an instant to react and you were dead. She was quicker, more skilled and more calculating than any other assassin in the north. Take her by surprise or do not take her at all.

Angus kicked the surgeon's door with such force he sent it upright into the room like a shield. Three figures occupied the small, dim space. The girl with the sky-blue dress was standing by a little table next to the bed. In some deep and intangible way she looked different than she had five minutes earlier when she had sat and coaxed Sarcosa on the bench. Not older, but wiser. Sarcosa himself was kneeling on the floor on the opposite side of the bed, a needle threaded with black surgeon's silk in his hand. Both he and the girl were still, stunned with shock.

The third figure was already in motion. She had been sitting on the bed with her dress sleeves rolled up to her elbows. Her hands were skinned. Angus could only imagine the pain she received as she drew her longknife.

The Maiden did not blink.

She rose like smoke, swaying and indefinite. There was a blur around her profile, an *uncertainty*, that was not human.

As the pleasure hall door was kicked down in the hallway behind them, Magdalena Crouch and Angus Lok performed a dance.

She knew who he was. She knew he had been after her. The business with the young girl and the pleasure hall, which meant Sarcosa never knew where the Maiden was going to be or when she would contact him, had been set in place to avoid detection. The Maiden had not wanted this. She was damaged. She wanted to lick her wounds in the dark.

With eyes that might have been brown or blue she watched him. The door had landed partway across the foot of the bed like a ramp. Angus did not want to step on it to get to her. It might slide or break under his weight.

Moving around the fallen door he came for the Maiden. He had been ready before her, and she was caged on three sides by the bed, the door and Sarcosa: all advantages were his. It did not matter that she blurred from side to side. Her core, her chest, was constant.

Along with the skinned hands.

Angus Lok was prepared for this moment. He had lived it in his head a hundred times. All he had carried since the day he had rode up to the farmhouse with spring flowers for Darra, his wife, came forward with him. The weight of it made him unstoppable.

He could not stop or be stopped.

He went for her hands, raking his longknife into flesh that looked like raw meat. She inhaled. And that fraction of a second, that instant of weakness, cost her life. Their longknives slid against each other creating a strange high dissonance that was heard throughout the pleasure hall and talked of for years. She was strong. She nearly managed to head off his blade. But he was stronger. Darra, Beth and Little Moo—pray not Cassie, pray Gods not Cassie—were the weight, the unbearable weight, behind the blade. It went straight from his heart to hers.

In the end her eyes were brown. Her pupils were fully dilated and hell could be glimpsed in the black space behind them. She was damned. They both were, but he was alive and she was descending to hell. Later those thoughts might mean something to Angus but for now he was content to watch her fall.

Her form settled and diminished before him. She was just a woman with brown eyes and brown hair, still young, still capable of bearing children. Angus waited to feel relief as she slumped from his blade and onto the bed.

He waited.

He stood for a moment in that small room, with Sarcosa and the girl watching him and footsteps racing down the hall, and just breathed.

As the footsteps reached the room, he turned. It was time to find his daughter.

A shuttered window led outside so he took it. It opened onto a narrow drainage ditch running between the pleasure hall and the next building. Angus picked his direction and hurried south along the ditch.

When the arrow tore into his shoulder he was almost expecting it. The impact made him stumble and then fall. Pain sheared toward his heart. The world began to dim.

I am not dead, he told himself as shadowy figures peeled

from the darkness like mist off a lake. That was important. If the Phage wanted him dead he would be dead.

Collapsing into the warm darkness, he felt Darra's arms around him and was at peace.

CHAPTER 35

For All Bluddsmen

Vaylo Bludd gave the order to Odwin Two Bear and Baldie Trangu. "Intercept them."

Neither man blinked as they stared at the small party of Bluddsmen closing on the roundhouse from the south.

"I remain here," Vaylo said. "Bring them to me."

They were standing on a small rise to the southwest of the Bluddhouse and south of the newly named Dog Camp. They had left the camp an hour earlier to exercise the horses. The sun was still rising in the east, dodging halfhearted scraps of cloud. Seven days had passed since Quarro had denied his father entry into the Bluddhouse, and Vaylo was discovering that fresh air could chafe.

He had never been a patient man. "Go," he told Odwin and Baldie. "Tell them the Dog Lord awaits."

The two swordsmen mounted their horses and rode down-slope on a course to intercept the return party. They were probably wondering why he, Vaylo, did not join them—three being a better showing of force than two—but how could they understand the loss of jaw involved in begging clansmen you had once ruled to "*Stop*"?

The Dog Lord took a final count of the return party—seven, two of those afoot—and then turned his back on the lot of them, including Odwin and Baldie. Some things a man was not built to stand.

Curious pity was one of them.

He whistled for the dogs and two of them came to him. The black-and-orange bitch was nose-down in some hole in the ground on the scent of gopher or mouse. She was getting bigger by the day. Some dog somewhere had had a good time at her expense. Vaylo swore she knew he was thinking about her, for her tail began to wag as she nose-dived the hole. It was a good thing there were whelps coming. The Dog Lord needed two new dogs. Wolf dog was gone and another had been lost that night, north of Dhoone, when he'd met Robbie's half-brother and thought him quite a young man.

As he scratched and cuffed the remaining dogs, Vaylo wondered when it would end, the loss of things he loved. Two men had died in the past seven days, both succumbing to injuries received at the Battle of the Deadwoods. Vaylo thanked the gods they died cleanly, without being claimed by the silky black smoke of the Unmade. One, young Rory Chaddo, had been in terrible pain. Vaylo had not possessed the medicine to ease him. An application dispatched to the Bluddhouse for the sole purpose of securing pain deadeners had been refused. Quarro had restated his offer to accept all of the party into the Bluddhouse, save the Dog Lord. Or none.

All medicines, he said, stayed at Bludd.

Vaylo would have liked to knock off his eldest son's head. With an ax.

Nan Culldayis, who was no one's fool, had spent the time

while everyone else was waiting on Quarro's response searching the stream banks for herbs. She had found some useful things, red clover and wild hops, and boiled them into a tea. It had been something. Rory Chaddo had died that night with Nan's tea inside his belly. Vaylo hoped the young man had found some relief.

It was getting harder and harder to not be inside the house. They were a party of thirty, twenty-eight of them men: hunting for game was not a problem. They had food and tents. The malt was gone but you could open the empty bottle and inhale. If you were not sick or injured there were worse places to be, but Vaylo could no longer stand it. His position was impossible.

He was a chief who was not a chief, living in a camp looking down on his old roundhouse. Quarro, who had always been his sneakiest, laziest son, had displayed a surprising talent for playing dog-in-a-manger. He was keeping tight hold on the Bluddhouse. Wait long enough in his fortress of stone and his crazy old father would succumb to some kind of blight; either an attack by Dhoone or the Unmade, or some kind of malady of the lungs brought on by the spring rains.

Vaylo knew what his eldest son was thinking: *Keep my head low and it will go away.*

Hearing the jingle of harnesses, Vaylo rose to see who, if anyone, Odwin and Baldie had brought with them on their return. He was aware of the figure he cut, in his tattered ground-length war cloak, surrounded by his dogs.

Three riders crested the rise. Vaylo recognized the third man instantly. He was the ax-and-hammer wielder Brisco Strager, who had fought with Hanro's company since Withy.

"Chief," Odwin hailed as they drew to a halt.

Brisco Strager did not speak that word. He nodded curtly, his gaze hard. He was an experienced campaigner, skilled in the use of all hatchets, and scarred by many battles. A bandage stained with blood was wound around his neck.

Odwin and Baldie dismounted. Brisco stayed ahorse.

So that's how it was. The Dog Lord could tell from looking at the man's face that he was not bringing good tidings. Vaylo saw no point in wasting words on greetings. "How goes it at Withy?"

Brisco glanced toward the Bluddhouse. "The messages did not arrive?"

It was simpler to say, "No."

Brisco stroked his horse's neck. Hammer blows to his hands had created the appearance of extra knuckles. He swallowed. "Withy is lost. Thrago is dead. Hanro is dead. Three hundred Bluddsmen gave their lives."

Vaylo felt a sharp pain in his chest. He put a hand to his rib cage and breathed. Thrago was his fifth son. Hanro his sixth. He had never imagined a world where both boys were not in it.

Odwin came toward him, but Vaylo shook him away with a fist. "What happened?"

"Dun Dhoone struck in the night while we were asleep. He broke in—we don't know how. Most of us were in our beds. We rallied but it was too late. Hanro called 'Yield' but in the confusion it was not heard. The Withyhouse is a warren. The battle was met in many halls. Hanro, Thrago and Gangaric were commanding separate forces in different sections. I was with Hanro when he fell. Dhoonish steel opened his throat. Thrago died holding the door so that the few who survived could flee."

Dear Gods. Vaylo had been in the Withyhouse. He could

imagine the hell of fighting in those closed, underground spaces. It would be dark and you would be cut off from other forces, and in many places the walls were so low and close that you would not be able to swing your hammer. Vaylo pushed the heel of his hand into his chest as he thought of it.

Robbie Dun Dhoone had done nothing but bring Bludd grief. The Dog Lord did not believe for one minute that Hanro's cry of "Yield" had gone unheard. Vaylo had looked into Dun Dhoone's cold blue eyes. He knew what was—and wasn't—there.

"What of Gangaric?" His third son, the one who had visited his father at the hillfort on his way to join his brothers at Withy. The one with Gullit's eyes.

Brisco shifted in his saddle. If he was regretting his decision to dismount for his old chief, it was too late for that. "Gangaric survives. He led the charge from the Withyhouse."

The words of war could be deceptive. Charge could more truthfully be called retreat. "Where is he?"

"Gone to join Pengo at Ganmiddich. I would be there with him but I bring wounded home."

You bring yourself. Vaylo could see the slow spread of blood on the bandage around Brisco's neck. Aware that such deceptions were necessary for a Bluddsman's dignity, the Dog Lord changed the subject. "Where goes Dun Dhoone after Withy?"

"Ganmiddich. He began the march south three days later."

Of course he would. Winning was like a bonfire: once it was burning you fed it more fuel. Vaylo made the calculation. Dun Dhoone would be there. Now. Today. Maybe sooner. Vaylo asked a question he already knew the answer to in the hope that a different, newer answer, might be supplied. "How many does Pengo command?"

"Two hundred and fifty."

The number of fighting men had not grown. The women and children were doubtless the same too . . . with the notable exception of one. Pengo's wife had given birth to a daughter at midwinter. Milkweed was the name the bairn was known by. Vaylo thought about her at night when he guarded the camp. That was his granddaughter there.

Damn his old chest. Why couldn't it stop hurting and just work? Vaylo forced himself to think. Dhoone would arrive from the north. Blackhail was camped at Bannen Field, which was to the northwest. The situation reminded Vaylo of something Ockish Bull had once told him about diamond mining in Trance Vor. "They heat the rockwall with fires," Ockish had said. "Heat it all day and all night until the rock begins to shimmer. And then they clear out—clear far out—and pump in the water. You can be standing ten leagues away and still feel the explosion. It's that big, that loud. And when the miners go in the next day the entire layout of the mine has changed."

That was what was happening at Ganmiddich. The rockwall was being primed. Dhoone, Blackhail and Bludd were converging, and the explosion when they touched would change the face of the clanholds. Old hatreds, new hatreds, ambition, possessiveness: it all came together at Ganmiddich. The question was: How would it go for Bludd?

It was a wonder that Pengo, his useless second son, had managed to defend the Crab Gate for this long. He'd probably done exactly as his older brother had done: ducked his head low, barricaded the door and held on. With women and children in the house, Vaylo could not fault him. Yet that door had broken once and it would break again. And two hundred and fifty Bluddsmen against the full might of Blackhail or Dhoone was not good odds. Vaylo would not bet on them.

He looked carefully at Brisco. "Has Quarro been applied to for reinforcements?"

Brisco looked down before he gave his answer and Vaylo could guess what he had to say. "Messages were dispatched a while back. Some may not have got through."

Gods stop my blood from boiling. Quarro had ignored Pengo's plea for aide. What kind of Bluddsman turned his back on fellow warriors in peril? Bludd was chosen by the Stone Gods— its purpose was to go to war.

At his side Vaylo was aware of Baldie Trangu blasting air at force through his nostrils. Odwin Two Bear was still; that boy knew how to keep his head.

Vaylo glanced at Brisco Strager. He felt almost sorry for him. The hammer-and-ax man was practicing so much self-deception it was a marvel he could stay on his horse. Vaylo decided to grant everyone present the mercy of not asking if Brisco was bearing yet another application for aid. They all knew it would arrive too late.

Whatever happened at Ganmiddich was out of their hands. Vaylo could imagine scenarios where Pengo and his house of Bluddsfolk came out unscathed. If Dhoone and Blackhail clashed before Ganmiddich they might happily cancel one another out. Stranger things had happened. Look how Pengo had possessed Ganmiddich in the first place. A city army had broken the Crab Gate with their new-fangled heavy machinery and then rode away and left it. Anything was possible after that.

He just wished it wasn't Mace Blackhail and Robbie Dun Dhoone leading the Hail and Dhoone armies. Mace Blackhail had slaughtered Bludd women and children in cold blood on the Bluddroad, and Dun Dhoone had killed all the Bluddsmen and Bluddswomen occupying the Dhoonehold the night he'd retaken it. Vaylo was alive only because of the quickness of his dogs and a few words dropped by Angus Lok concerning—of all things—a secret passage. Now to hear Brisco's story of Dun Dhoone conveniently not hearing the cry "Yield." What hope did Pengo have if Ganmiddich's walls were breached by either chief?

Realizing he was bending slightly at the waist, Vaylo straightened. The pain in his chest had eased a little. He breathed and then made an effort.

"Who are your wounded?" he asked.

Brisco gave him the names and conditions of the Bluddsmen in his party. It was a day of bad news.

"Go," Vaylo told the hammer-and-ax man when he was done. "Tell your men the Dog Lord does them honor and then go home with gods' speed."

Brisco nodded his large head gravely. "I will tell them," he said.

Vaylo, Odwin and Baldie watched as he rode downhill and joined his party. A cool wind had begun to blow, stirring the oat grass on the rise. Vaylo was set to turn and fetch his horse when one of Brisco's party raised an arm toward him. It was an acknowledgment, and Vaylo found himself absurdly grateful for it. He raised his own arm in answer, holding it out while the man rode by below him.

It was something to take with him on the journey back to Dog Camp.

Odwin and Baldie knew to keep their peace, and no words were exchanged as they rode across the fields. The dogs, sensing their master's mood, scuffed behind the horses, tails down.

It was a good time of year to be in the Bluddhouse. The sun started coming in through the back windows. There would be longhunts for migrating elk, and the maids would begin wearing their pretty dresses, the ones cut low without sleeves. Vaylo had imagined the doors would open for him. That Bluddsfolk, tired of Quarro and wanting their old chief back, would begin to mutiny, riding out to Dog Camp in defiance of Quarro and declaring themselves for the Dog Lord.

It had been his secret hope.

Now he realized that would not happen. Brisco Strager had greeted him without even a show of respect. Brisco was a decent, tough-minded warrior and at one time he would have rode to battle on Vaylo's word. Now he couldn't leave the seat of his horse. His opinions had been poisoned, and Vaylo knew he had his own seven sons to thank for that.

Five now. Five.

He had not been a good father, he knew that, but hadn't he always been a fair chief?

Approaching the camp, Vaylo dismounted. The bairns were playing with that damn bird, bickering over the right to hold its globe-shaped cage. "Take it," the Foebreaker had said to Vaylo ten days ago. "Sull needs Bludd. Bludd needs Sull."

"Granda!' Aaron cried, scrambling to his feet and running toward Vaylo. "Pasha said that *you* said I had to obey her all day." The boy was indignant and a little upset. His older sister bossed him without mercy.

Vaylo held out his arm and the boy came to him. He was a skinny thing, less than eight years old. He felt hot and weightless next to Vaylo's chest.

"There's only one time when you need to pay heed to your

sister," Vaylo told him, "and that's if the camp's attacked and you and Pasha are separated from me and Nan."

It was not the comfort the boy was expecting, but Vaylo had always found that if you gave children clear facts they respected them. Aaron nodded, wiping his nose on the back of his hand.

"Say it back to me."

"I only take heed of Pasha when the camp's attacked and you and Nan aren't there."

"Good." Vaylo laid his hand on the boy's head. What sort of grandfather was he to risk the lives of his grandchildren? Would he not serve them better by walking away one night, leaving the camp and allowing the bairns, Nan, Hammie and the rest to find safety in the Bluddhouse?

They were so exposed, that was the thing. Every night his grandchildren slept with only a thin sheet of canvas between them and forces which wished them harm. Today more than ever Vaylo felt it. What if Robbie Dun Dhoone won victory at Ganmiddich? What if he judged, correctly, that Bludd was badly hurting and that Quarro at the Bluddhouse was weak? Dun Dhoone had already struck Bludd once. He and his army had torched the sacred grove and knocked down the structure believed to have been built from the rubble of the Dhoonestone. It was a daring strike, bold as brass. And it had been undertaken with a fraction of the numbers Dun Dhoone now commanded.

Vaylo could imagine it. Bludd routed at Ganmiddich and Robbie Dun Dhoone puffed-up with victory asking himself: What next? He was a king now, you could not forget that. Kings and clan were a dangerous mix.

Nan had been roasting wild carrot and leek on little wood

splints over the fire. When she spotted Vaylo she removed them from the heat and rose to meet him. Without a word passing between them she ducked under his free arm, slid her hand around his waist and drew him toward their tent.

Vaylo was glad of her. As he walked between his lady and his grandson, uncertain as to who was supporting whom, he tried to still his thoughts. He felt old and loose.

Word spread through the camp quickly. Thrago dead, Hanro dead, hundreds of Bluddsmen slaughtered. Vaylo sat on the hard ground in front of his tent and watched his men grow restless. They would ride on the Bluddhouse tonight given the choice. Quarro's refusal to send forces to aid his brother offended them deeply as Bluddsmen. "We should break the Red Gate by dawn," he heard more than one man murmur.

Vaylo did not bother to point out the two problems with this. One, that Bluddsmen would be fighting Bluddsmen, shedding their own blood at a time when clan was already suffering. And two, with Nan, Pasha, Aaron and three wounded in the camp, they boasted a force of twenty-four. And anyone would be very much mistaken if they thought the Dog Lord would lead a strike on the Bluddhouse while leaving his grandchildren and wounded unguarded. That meant the true number was something under twenty.

Under twenty could not take a house.

Talk was unsettled around the fire that night. Men had taken themselves for long rides, away from camp and into the woods. Things had been killed. Someone had brought down a boar. Vaylo could smell it, though it had not yet been butchered, just split and drained. Talk was of Withy. Many in the camp had lost friends or kin. There was a sense of time running out. Great and terrible events were happening to

Bludd while they were camped on a bald hillside, biding time.

Vaylo took to his bed early. He, Nan and the bairns retired to their small canvas-and-deerskin shelter and snuggled for warmth. Pasha had unfastened her braids and Vaylo ended up with his granddaughter's thick black hair in his face. He had to stop himself from hugging her and Aaron tightly to his chest. This time last year he had boasted nineteen grandchildren. Now he was down to three.

He did not sleep. He feared he would dream of Thrago and Hanro and he feared those dreams would be filled with blame.

When Odwin Two Bear's cry came Vaylo rose to his knees and buckled his sword. "Stay here," he warned the people he loved most. To Aaron he said, "Remember what we spoke of earlier."

The boy nodded solemnly.

Vaylo left.

The rest of the warriors in the camp were ahead of him — including Wittish Owans, who was one of the wounded. It was not a good night to strike Bluddsmen. Tempers were hot and they were liberal with their swords. The Unmade were already engaged.

Vaylo saw the rippling blackness and smelled empty and frozen spaces. You could hardly believe the forms had weight until you saw the grass flatten beneath them. Vaylo counted four. Only two were shaped to wield swords. The front two were something *other*, loping monsters who carried weight and muscle mass on their backs. They screeched like gulls. Ancient cunning lived in their small dead eyes.

They were more dangerous than the forms that held *Kil Ji*.

They had to be isolated, then circled with swords. Someone had to risk entering the lethal space they commanded. Bluddsmen were up for it. Tonight, northwest of their round-house with the news of Bludd losses still unsettled in their heads, they were the beings who were possessed.

Bludd had always been the most fiercely terrible of all clans. Here, on open ground, they found their stride. Later, when Vaylo thought about it, he would use the word *calling*. There was as much beauty to be found in Bluddsmen's sword-blows this night as there was in Sull arrows piercing hearts.

They lost just one man, the swordsman Harkie Selmor, whose father owned a dairy farm east of the roundhouse. Vaylo took Harkie's life swiftly after the boy lost part of his gut.

Afterwards Bluddsmen cleaned their swords. They sat on the grass and rested. The stench of earth burning as the two voided steel swords sunk beneath the ground was overpowering. Looking north toward the Deadwoods, Vaylo spoke a two-word prayer.

No more.

He stayed awake all night repeating it, watching for men and creatures that should have been dead.

They had been lucky. Four against twenty-five, including Wittish: fair odds when it came to the Unmade.

As the sky began to lighten in the east, Vaylo found himself recalling Angus Lok. The ranger had said many things to him over the years, but one thing, spoken in the Tomb of the Dhoone Princes, was beginning to stand out. *Return to Bludd and marshal your forces and wait for the Long Night to come.*

It sounded, now Vaylo thought of it, about right.

We are Bludd. Chosen by the Stone Gods to guard their borders.

Vaylo rose as the first rays of sunlight streamed toward the camp. There had been more than beauty present in the Bluddsmen's Swordblows. Truth was there as well. He knew what he had to do.

For a wonder, the bairns were asleep in the tent. The leather cage with the bird inside it was lying next to Aaron's foot. Vaylo took it and walked east from the camp.

By scheming with the Surlord of Spire Vanis, he had already made one unholy alliance in his life. What was one more compared to that?

A man could not lose his soul twice.

He had to retake Bludd. Dangers were mounting and he, his men and his grandchildren needed to be safe in the Bludd-house. Everything else must taken second place.

Sull needs Bludd. Bludd needs Sull.

Reaching a level area of land below the camp, Vaylo snapped open the cage door and took out the bird. The tiny gray starling was alert in his hand. When it was free of the leather walls it began to chuff.

Vaylo threw it into the air and watched as it rose high in the silver sky, circling to find its bearings.

It was a powerful bird. It commanded an army.

Four hundred Sull appeared on the horizon the next day to help the Dog Lord regain his house.

CHAPTER 36

Schemes

They took Hoargate into the city of Spire Vanis. Mallin said the gate itself had been carved from the largest tree in the world. "A bloodwood from the southern Storm Margin. It took them ten days to chop it."

The gate was twenty feet wide, twenty-five feet tall and four feet thick. It was formed from a single piece of wood that had been relief-carved with the likeness of a giant bird of prey. Bram had never seen anything like it in his life. He wondered about the machinery that was so powerful it could raise it.

"It's never raised higher than ten feet," Mallin told him, his gaze as always less than a second behind Bram's. "Remember this is a city. Much of it exists for show."

Bram tried not to stare too much as they passed beneath the gate and entered Spire Vanis, a city built from pale gleaming limestone. The scale of it was hard to comprehend. A hundred Dhoonehouses could fit between its walls.

"Shall we take the tour?"

Bram nodded. Mallin seemed almost jaunty. Some of it was probably relief. The ranger had given Bram detailed instructions on what to say if either of them were stopped at the gate by red cloaks. They had not been stopped. Even so Bram had noticed that Mallin had been pretty happy ever since they'd left the Weasel camp at Blackhail. Sometimes the ranger let his prejudices show.

"Hoargate market," Mallin said as they passed into a large open square filled with wood-and-canvas stalls. "If it's live they'll kill it for you and if it's dead they'll try and raise it."

Bram smelled the mouthwatering fragrances of charred meat, grilled onions, yeasty bread and toasted spices. He saw girls. Many wore substantially less than clan maids. They looked at him boldly; Bram wondered if it was because of his horse. Gabbie was slightly crazy and inclined to eat blankets but you could not deny he was a fine-looking stallion.

Mallin stopped and bought food—charred steak cut into slices and rolled inside flatbread—and they ate in their saddles as they rode south through the city. Bram felt like a king.

The journey here had been hard but uneventful. Bram guessed that Mallin had chosen a route to steer clear of events unfolding at Ganmiddich and Bannen, and they had spent a lot of time in the dense evergreen forest south of Blackhail. They had not stopped at any clan, though Mallin had slipped into Duff's stovehouse for an hour one evening. Nights were spent camped in the open air, with only bedrolls and longfires for comfort. Bram fell into deep sleep every night beneath skies filled with spring stars.

It was hard to deny that he had found the events at Weasel camp thrilling. Not at first, not while they were happening, but later when he thought about them. The seamlessness. The cool hand of Hew Mallin. The small but vital part that he, Bram Cormac, had played.

They never spoke of it later. Or before for that matter. It

520 † J. V. JONES

was something created out of nearly nothing. Bram had simply been reacting to Hew Mallin, watching the ranger closely, following cues. If it was a test Bram hoped very much he had passed.

They had poisoned the well.

In the Scarpe chief's tent, before Yelma Scarpe had entered, Mallin had slipped him a small package wrapped with squirrel skin. Bram had been alert after that, though at the time he had not realized that Mallin had sprinkled something on the brazier that would make him cough. A current in the tent had sent the smoke from the doctored brazier straight toward him. Mallin noticed everything, used what he could. He had been waiting for either the Scarpe chief or her nephew to lose patience with the coughing boy. All the ranger had to do when Uriah Scarpe sent Bram from the tent was to add, "Get yourself some water from the well."

It had been enough for Bram to understand Mallin's purpose.

What Yelma Scarpe would never normally allow—strangers access to her well—had been achieved in a series of flawless moves.

It was child's play after that. Bram had accepted a dipper of water from a Scarpe girl, dropped it so that it spilled on her dress, and then slipped the contents of Mallin's package into the wellshaft while she and her friends were distracted with drying off the dress and cleaning the dipper.

Bram didn't know what was in the package but if he were to guess he would say it was something to make people sick, not kill them. Softening, it was called on the battlefield. Mallin, and therefore the Phage, had softened Scarpe for Raina Blackhail.

The night Bram had spent above the stables at Blackhail had been enough for him to know how things stood between the chief's wife and Scarpe. "Chief's should make a strike," one of the groomsmen had murmured. "Clan would be behind her if she did."

Bram would have liked to know what happened. Had Raina Blackhail struck the camp? And if she had, would she even realize that the Scarpe defense was not as vigorous as it should have been?

Probably not. Clan warriors did not post signs informing people they were sick.

"And this is Mask Fortress," Mallin said, interrupting Bram's thoughts. "Sadly you do not see it at its best. It lost its high tower last winter. Rotten foundation apparently. Brought the whole thing down."

Bram looked and saw a gray-white fortress with high walls and three towers which looked plenty tall to him. The north face of Mount Slain rose behind it; ice still holding fast in its crevasses and at its peak. "That was the tower that killed the Surlord?"

"He was in it when he died. Let's leave it at that."

Judging from the pointedness in Mallin's voice, Bram guessed that the old surlord, much like Yelma Scarpe, was someone Hew Mallin had not liked.

It made it easier, Bram had discovered, when you liked the people you advanced and disliked those you undermined. It had been satisfying to put the poison in the well. Yelma Scarpe was a conniving weasel who was trespassing on Blackhail land. Raina Blackhail was beautiful and strong: she had *deserved* the Phage's help.

Who are they to interfere in matters of clan? Bram dismissed the small voice in his head. He was *"They"* now. Bram Cormac was Phage.

He held his head high as he toured the city. He was part of a brotherhood that shaped the world.

"I'm tired of viewing the sights," Mallin said abruptly after they had passed the windowless ivory facade of the Bone Temple. "Let's find some rooms and rest."

Bram was just fine with that. He noticed the ranger headed back in the general direction of Hoargate. Bram made a note of the route. He liked to keep track of his location. The streets were busy and dirty. Men wheeled barrows heaped with bloody lamb carcasses, draymen drove carts stacked high with wooden cages containing live chickens and piglets, and children and dogs ran everywhere, chancing for scraps.

"This should do," Mallin said as they approached a shabby, three-storied inn not far from the western wall.

The inn did not have a legible sign for Bram to read, but he did notice that the stableman who came out to greet them as they dismounted appeared to be acquainted with Hew Mallin. There was something knowing in the old man's nod.

"Day, sirs," the man said, pulling two carrots from a pack strung at his waist and feeding one to each horse. "Will we be having the pleasure tonight?"

Mallin told him they would. Addressing Bram, the ranger said, "Go ahead. Take a room, order some supper. I'll be with you soon."

It was a dismissal. Bram unfastened his saddlebags, hefted them over his shoulder, and headed inside. Fearing it might be impolite to enter the inn by the side door, he took the more public-looking front door instead.

It led directly into a dim, cave-like room where men and

women were drinking with solemn focus. Everyone halted what they doing to look at him. All dicing, supping and talking was suspended as the patrons appraised the stranger. Bram swallowed. He tried to appear harmless. The patrons looked mean. Two were wearing blood-soaked aprons.

"You got the wrong place, son." A big man with blond hair and a full beard stepped forward. "We only cater to locals here."

Bram's instinct was to leave, but he fought it. "If I might have a word?" He had planned on adding "sir" to the end of his request but dropped it at the last moment. Mallin never called anyone sir.

The big man claimed the space directly in front of Bram. He was wearing an apron too, but it wasn't blood-soaked.

"I'm with Hew Mallin," Bram said quietly so no one else could hear. "We need a room and something to eat."

"That so?" The big man did not give an inch. "What's the color of his eyes?"

"Green." Bram hesitated. "No, yellow."

The big man nodded once. "It'll do. Follow me."

It occurred to Bram that this rundown smoky inn had better security than the city itself.

The inn was a warren of small rooms, tunnels, nooks and screened-off alcoves. One tunnel led belowground. Bram heard the low laughter of men rising from it. In a small sitting area near the back, four young women, all wearing little black aprons and caps, were sharing a platter of tripe. Bram tried not to color as he passed them. One of the women whispered, not too quietly, "That's a fine-looking boy."

Bram didn't know what to make of that. At Dhoone he had been told he was too small, and had the look of the wild clans.

When he was seated he ordered whatever food was hottest and best, and a couple of drams of malt. "Dreggs or Dhooneshine?" the big man asked. Bram went with Dreggs. He downed his own dram quickly when it arrived and seriously thought about Mallin's. This was an odd, hostile place and he wondered what he was doing here.

Mallin didn't join him for the better part of two hours.

Sliding along the bench, the ranger ignored the congealing sweetmeats in gravy and the basket of hardening bread and looked carefully at Bram. "Why don't you take out the blue cloak and put it on?"

Bram blinked.

Mallin didn't. "It's cold in here," he said, "and we may be in for a long wait."

They were sitting in a small, screened-off alcove at the very back of the inn. There were no windows. A single lamp hung from a brass hook on the wall. Its flame guard was shaped like a rib cage. Bram watched the banded light it created jitter against the table. He recalled the moment when he had looked down the well shaft at Weasel camp. Ledges had extended from the well wall, probably so that the original digger could climb from top to bottom when he was done. It struck Bram now that being in the Phage was like climbing into that well. You were going down, but there were stages, places to rest during the descent. Bram had descended part of the way but had not reached the bottom. Mallin's request meant another drop.

Bram glanced at the ranger. He was sitting with both hands resting on the table, looking back.

The cloak was at the very bottom of the second saddlebag. Even though it had been rolled tightly into a cylinder for many days, the creases fell away as Bram unfurled it; the wool was that fine. It had been dyed the rich heather-blue of Dhoone and its edges were bound with fisher fur. Bram had not worn it since his time at Castlemilk. He did not want to wear it now. Robbie had given it to him after the reclaiming of Dhoone, and Bram had so many strong feelings about it they could have mounted a fair-sized battle in his head.

He pulled it across his shoulders and fastened the copper thistle clasp, and resolutely did not think of his brother.

Mallin ordered fresh food and tankards of beer, and they did not speak as they ate and drank. Afterwards, Mallin slipped away for a while and returned looking brushed down and refreshed. He spoke casually with the big blond man, who Bram learned was the innkeeper Janus Shoulder. His inn was named the Butcher's Rest. Bram supposed that explained the bloody aprons.

He decided it must be close to midnight, yet the inn was still doing fair business. People came and left. Someone picked out a tune on a stringboard. Janus Shoulder sent a boy to replace the wick in the lamp. Mallin stretched into the corner and nodded off. Bram couldn't imagine resting. The cloak alone prevented sleep.

Another hour or so passed and the inn grew quieter. Bram could no longer hear the party of black-aproned girls. He would have liked some water but didn't want to ask. Mallin was snoring lightly, but instantly came awake when the hard rap of booted footsteps sounded in the corridor outside. Pulling himself upright, he winked at Bram.

"Here we go."

A man with a drawn sword, wearing a cloak of glazed red leather entered the alcove. "Weapons on the table," he said evenly.

Mallin detached his scabbard and knife holster, so Bram did the same. The red cloak collected the weapons, then did a little motion with his finger, indicating that Bram should pull back his cloak for inspection. Bram obliged. The red cloak was the kind of seasoned veteran that clansmen could understand.

"What's your name, boy?"

"Bram Cormac."

It meant nothing to the red cloak. "Wait here."

He left. Bram heard footsteps, about three pairs of them, and voices. Someone grunted and then a single pair of footsteps pounded toward the alcove.

Marafice Eye, the Surlord of Spire Vanis and Master of its Four Gates, stepped from behind the screen. Bram knew him straightaway. His size was legendary, as was the dead, exposed socket of his left eye. Bram couldn't help himself, he began to stand. This was the man who had broken the Crab Gate. In the clanholds he was known as the Spire King.

Marafice Eye swiped a fist as big as a dog toward him. "Dammit don't rise, boy. I swear I'm sick of the drafts." Easing himself onto the bench next to Bram, he said with some feeling, "Mallin."

The ranger replied "Eye." Neither man was smiling.

Janus Shoulder entered the alcove and deposited a bowl of food and a tin spoon before the Surlord. Immediately Marafice Eye began to eat, wolfing down what appeared to Bram to be ham and beans. He was the biggest man Bram had ever seen, seven feet tall and built like a block. He was dressed in something fancy beneath a plain black wool cloak. A large gold ring carved with the image of a Killhound rampant glittered on his middle finger, left hand. The Seal of Spire Vanis.

The innkeeper brought beer, three mugs of it, checked on his surlord's progress with the beans and then withdrew. Bram recalled that Marafice Eye was a butcher's son. That would explain his ease here.

"I hear they're setting for the mother of all dog fights in the clans." The surlord spoke between mouthfuls of food. "Mad bastards are all going to kill themselves."

Mallin said, "I wouldn't bet on it."

Marafice Eye looked up at that. "Is that right, eh? Has the Phage picked who it would like to win?"

The ranger held up his hands. "In God's, not mine."

Eye chuckled. He pushed away his bowl. "Clan?" he asked.

It took Bram a moment to realize the surlord was addressing him. He nodded.

"And why the pretty cloak?"

Bram opened his mouth to speak, but Mallin didn't allow him the chance.

"He's brother to Robbie Dun Dhoone."

The surlord swiveled on the bench to get a better look. "Is that right?"

Bram drew air through his teeth. He threw a glance at Mallin. The ranger calmly met his eye.

Marafice Eye didn't miss any of this. He spent a moment looking carefully at Bram, and then turned to his beer.

Pushing both palms against his beer mug, Bram tried to anchor himself. He was spinning. Stupidly he had imagined that Mallin had recruited him into the Phage because he knew how to handle himself in tricky situations, like with the Dog Lord and Skinner Dhoone. Now he was beginning to see things differently. There were plenty of boys in the clanholds who were smarter than he was, but none of them were brothers to the

Dhoone King. What if Marafice Eye were right? What if the Phage had picked a winner at Ganmiddich and that winner was Dhoone? How useful would it be to have the winner's brother in your pocket?

Bram took a drink of beer, studying Mallin through the foam. The ranger had just used Bram's kinship to his advantage, hauling it onto the table to give himself and this meeting more weight.

Bram thought about the well.

Two ledges down, not one.

Marafice Eye pushed his empty beer mug the way of the bowl. "So," he said to Mallin. "What do you want?"

"I want the four hostages you took at Ganmiddich."

The surlord did not bother to cover his surprise. The eyebrow above the dead eye went up. "The clansmen?"

"Yes. Two Hailsmen, two Crabmen."

Marafice Eye puffed air through his lips as he thought about this. "You're not the first to want them."

"Oh?"

"Yelma Scarpe tried to take them off my hands." Something unpleasant happened to the surlord's face as he thought about the Weasel chief. "I didn't let her have them."

"I'm not Yelma Scarpe."

The surlord did not appear convinced of that. "What do you want with them?"

Mallin shrugged. "A little bargaining power. Grease for the wheels. They'll be returned to the clanholds in the end."

"All of them?"

This seemed to Bram an especially penetrating question. He would be willing to bet on Mallin's answer being a lie.

"All. If Blackhail and its allies triumph at Ganmiddich they'll be used to sweeten relations."

"And if Blackhail and Ganmiddich lose?"

"They won't be sold to Dhoone."

Marafice Eye leaned back on the bench. Bram sensed that he was withdrawing his curiosity, that to probe any further would not serve the surlord if he wanted to strike a deal. You could almost tell what he was thinking. Two parties had negotiated for these men: what were they worth?

Despite everything, Bram felt his excitement rising. This was where he wanted to be, in places like this at times like this, where decisions were made and deals were struck that altered the world. The Phage might use him but look what they paid in return. Who else was sitting next to a surlord tonight? Who else was party to such a meeting?

The inn was very quiet. A timber ticked in the ceiling. Marafice Eye drew air deep into his chest and held it there like a thought.

Meeting gazes with Hew Mallin he exhaled slowly and said, "Kill Roland Stornoway for me."

Mallin did not hesitate. "Done."

For a moment the surlord looked abashed, like a dog that had been wrestling for something only to have its opponent release it unexpectedly. He said, "It must not appear to come from me."

"Of course."

"And it must be soon. That man has tried to kill me twice."

"Within ten days," Mallin promised.

Blood began to pump at force through Bram's head as he realized the implication of this statement.

The surlord stood. The table legs scraped across the floor. "Come see me when it's done."

The ranger rested his cool gaze on the surlord. "We will."

The surlord grunted and left. Several pairs of footsteps pounded along the corridor and then the inn lapsed into silence.

Bram stared at the table. He was aware that Mallin was waiting for him to look up, to confirm his readiness for the latest task, but he needed a moment to think.

We will.

We.

This wasn't two ledges down. This was cold-blooded assassination: it was a plunge to the bottom of the well.

Bram thought about his brother, thought about what Robbie would do if he were in Bram's place. Robbie stopped at nothing to get what he wanted: the end justified all means.

Bram Cormac met Hew Mallin's gaze across the table at the Butcher's Rest. He was Phage. The decision made itself.

Bram unclasped the Dhoone cloak and let the heavy fabric fall to the floor.

The next day he began his training. Mallin said there was currently a shortage of trained assassins in the North.

CHAPTER 37

The Night River

Ash Mountain Born was beginning to suspect some-thing and as Zaya and the Trenchlander pushed off the barge, she thought about what it would mean if it were true.

It would change everything.

Zaya Mistwalker clambered onto the barge as it moved from the shore. The Trenchlander pushed it farther, wading thigh-deep into the water until the current caught the craft. Ash felt the tug of it, felt the massive power of the tow. She experienced a moment of unease as she realized the raft was at the mercy of the current, and then the Trenchlander released his grip and the barge and its three occupants, two alive and one dead, moved smoothly downstream.

The Night River was two leagues wide here. Its sparkling black surface was alive with birds and insects. Herons claimed shallow banks in the river's center, and swans floated on slow currents close to its black shale shores. Geese and ducks ran ahead of the barge, racing into flight. Clouds of mayflies hung above the surface, and damselflies, dragonflies and blowflies flitted through the river-pushed air.

Ash reclined in the cushioned barge seat, feeling like a queen. Zaya was behind her, working the tiller, and *Mor Xana* was standing on the barge's front edge, silently watching the way ahead. Khal Blackdragon had commanded him to be her ghost. During the thirteen days she had been at the Heart Fires, *Mor Xana* had rarely left her side. Ash did not know who he guarded.

Just like a child queen, she was dangerous and in danger.

It was late afternoon and light left the river as they floated south. Other craft, boats and barges and sculls, had taken to the water. More were being launched from the shore. All carried lamps that burned with the pure white light of the Heart Fires. The Sull were creating their own moon this night.

"It is said it takes a thousand fires to make a moon," Zaya had told Ash earlier. "If we take to the water and our fires are reflected we pray the moon we make will be full."

Ash thought about that as the sky darkened and the silent, grave Sull lit the river with boats. She was not the only one here living in fear. It was a new moon tonight, which meant there was no moon. The Sull were warding against forces that moved in its absence.

The Unmade.

Hugging a pillow close to her belly, Ash floated through the Heart of Sull. Their fortresses were set amid icewoods at the river shore. They were unlit and Ash believed unused. The Sull preferred to live in tents or out in the open. Only winter storms sent them inside.

A horn note sounded, long and low to the water. Others followed and a solemn and sad music played, like the moan of human voices.

Ash turned to Zaya. "Why do they play?"

The young woman was crouching by the tiller. Her black hair fell unbound to her waist. She was dressed plainly in deerhide pants and tunic. A large white stone hung from a silver chain at her throat. "We mourn," she said.

"Who?"

"Our own who held themselves separate and now are dead."

Ash heard steel in the Sull's voice. "I don't understand."

Zaya pushed the tiller, guiding the barge into the slow water midriver where a gravel bank broke the shore. Other boats were slowing too and the music soared as the horn blowers gathered around the island.

As she steered, Zaya said, "My grandmother, the Longwalker, had a sister who was named Lea Night Heron. Night Heron stole my grandmother's mate and had a son and a daughter. The daughter was named Yiselle No Knife. Some might call her my aunt. I do not—*did* not. She is dead. And those that followed her are dead also. We mourn for a hundred this night."

Ash said quietly, "I am sorry."

Zaya gave her a heartbreakingly lovely smile. "It is difficult, for No Knife was Sull and she was loved and needed, but she was rival to my father and he did not agree with how she chose to arm her fight."

"What did she do?"

Zaya's eyes were the exact same color as the Night River. They were liquid and beautiful but the face surrounding them was stone. "She tried to claim something that was not and could never be Sull."

Hairs along Ash's spine, arms and neck rose. She fought to stop herself from shivering, hugging the cushion close. Zaya was watching her intently. Ash glanced at *Mor Xana*. The ghost was standing with his back to them, his paired swords forming an X.

Unable to help herself, Ash said, "How did they die?"

"This Sull will not speak of that."

Ash felt as if she had been warned. *Something that was and could never be Sull.* Had Zaya meant those words for her?

It was hard to enjoy the evening after that. Even when the Sull came together at the end of the island and roped their boats into a single, circular mass, she found it hard to enter the spirit of the ceremony.

As hundreds of boats floated as one on the Night River, creating a reflection of a moon that did not exist, Ash Mountain Born realized she was alone.

Later they walked the nine leagues back to the center of the camp. The forest was cool and alive with bats, and lines of mist smoked from the icewoods. Ash found herself positioned close to the head of the procession and wondered if an honor was intended. Possibly it meant nothing at all. She still did not know the Sull well enough to make that judgment.

When she arrived at her tent she was light-headed with weariness and hunger. Zaya, who had walked at her side most of the way, commanded water and food from one of the Trenchlander servants. Her concern appeared genuine. She took a bowl of warm water and a cloth and wetted Ash's brow as Ash lay resting. "This Sull feels foolish," Zaya said. "She should have told you to prepare for the long walk home."

Did everything have two meanings this night? Or was she being too sensitive?

Snuggling under blankets as light and warm as summer air,

Ash decided she was too tired to worry, closed her eyes and slept.

She awoke at some point in the night. She was alone. A single lamp burned on the tent floor. The food Zaya had brought—smoked salmon, flatbread soaked in honey, and dried cherries stuffed with nuts—lay on a wood platter in the center of the tent. Ash ate hungrily. The cherries were bitter and sweet. She finished everything and then drank water from the jug. Afterward she thought she'd better head to the latrine and pee before returning to sleep, so she pulled on her cloak and boots and left the tent.

Mor Xana was sitting outside on a carpet of silver tissue. He rose as she walked past him. His hand descended into the space his body had just occupied, pulling up the carpet as he left. Ash was no longer surprised by his presence, though she did wonder if he ever slept. Together they walked the short distance to the screened-off area where latrines had been dug to service the tents in Khal Blackdragon's tent circle.

Ash had brought the lamp and she set it on the floor as she relieved herself. *Mor Xana* waited on the other side of the screen. You could almost hear him listening.

To surprise him Ash decided to walk down to the water. It wasn't far and she was beginning to feel awake.

Sull were asleep in their tents. A few were at their fires, sitting on the ground in silence as they awaited dawn. Moths fluttered through the camp, winking in and out of the darkness like stars. Ash descended to the shore. The shale crunched beneath her feet, and she noted that although the ghost's footsteps were lighter than her own she could still hear them.

She suspected he had been instructed to slay her the moment she began to reach.

The fortress dome built from milkstone glowed against the blackness of the river and Ash headed toward it. She was still waiting on a summons from Khal Blackdragon. She had seen him several times since her arrival but never alone. He Who Leads had asked her a question at that first meeting and there was no doubt in her mind he required an answer. *Can the Reach control herself?* Was he giving her time to achieve that? Or was he simply watching her and judging for himself?

She didn't know. She thought perhaps she was safe until he called her into his presence for an accounting. Until then she had time to observe and learn about the Sull.

Zaya had been helpful, and had shown her many things. Yesterday they had crossed the river and ridden south along its east bank. They had passed several settlements, the bony ruins of the Moon Palace, and a giant bowl-like crater that had been excavated for meteor steel. In the far south she had seen the cinder cone of a defunct volcano so high it was still clad in snow. Zaya called it *Moll'a Orko*, Sleeping Bear, and said smoke rose from it once a year. The young Sull was prepared to answer questions, but there was usually a point where she closed down conversation, making it clear she no longer wished to speak. Was she holding secrets or simply being Sull? Ash wasn't sure.

She wished the Naysayer had not left. "I will return," he told her four days ago at dawn. "Hold yourself until then."

He had gone south to visit Ark Veinsplitter's birth camp. It was his duty and honor, he told her. Ark's father and sister still lived there and the Naysayer must be the one to bring news of their beloved's death. It was owed. Ark had been Mal Naysayer's brother-in-arms, his *hass*.

Not for the first time Ash wondered about the Naysayer's

instruction. *Hold yourself.* Would he have spoken those same words to anyone else?

As she skirted the base of the dome Ash startled a pair of nesting geese. As they honked at her indignantly, she saw they had eggs. The female spread its wings and began to chase her. Ash darted to the side, and the female who was indignant and raring for battle turned her attention to the ghost. She charged him. Ash grinned. Here was proof *Mor Xana* wasn't wholly dead.

Shale tumbled as softly as a key turning in a lock. A figure rounded the curve of the dome. Ash knew its identity straightaway. The shape of the shoulders, the bearing of the head. It was Lan Fallstar. The last time she had seen him was at the Fortress of the Hard Gate when he had directed two Sull to kill her and then fled.

There had been no moon that night either.

Muscles in Ash's arms jumped. She dropped the lamp.

Behind her the ghost drew his swords. *Snick. Snick.* Light reflecting off the blades ran ahead of him like ill intent. Ash thought, *I am dead.* She held on to her breath. Why didn't people realize how close everything was? Life, death, the forces of creation and destruction. Suddenly they were all there, inside of her.

Reach.

She had to. She had more to protect than just herself.

Ahead of her Lan Fallstar raised his hands. Ash froze. She didn't understand what was happening and why she wasn't dead. Fallstar's mouth opened and he spoke. She was so confused it took her a moment to translate the Sull.

"I mean no harm," he lied. "I am here paying respects to our dead."

He was speaking to her but she realized his words were meant for the ghost. She glanced over her shoulder.

Mor Xana was five feet behind her. He held both swords from his body at arm's length, cradling her in steel. He had moved to *protect*, not harm, her. If Lan Fallstar had taken another step he would be dead.

Lan Fallstar feared the ghost. She could see it in his eyes.

"Leave," she told him. She understood by now that ghosts did not speak. "Keep your distance from us. You will not be warned twice."

Lan Fallstar edged backward, his gaze upon the ghost. His hard, beautiful face seemed made out of edges; she noticed he had new scars on both cheeks. As he rounded the milky wall of the dome, he threw her a look filled with contempt.

How could she ever have found him attractive?

After he disappeared she counted to five and then sank to the ground. She was shaking and had forgotten to breathe. Where was her peace? She had thought that once she arrived at the Heart Fires the hounding would end. Now she was beginning to realize she would be hounded as long as she was perceived as weak.

I must be strong then.

Mor Xana's count was longer than her own and he stood there, forming a shield around her as she sat with her face in her hands and tried not to feel despair. The ghost could only protect her against so much. She did not think his blades would stop a concerted attack, or a lone arrow fired at distance. Lan Fallstar was an excellent shot.

Ash stood. There was nothing else to do. She could hardly stay on the bank for the rest of the night, and she knew she would be safer within Khal Blackdragon's tent circle.

Tomorrow she would need to show He Who Leads that Mountain Born was a force to be reckoned with. She needed a good night's sleep for that.

As she turned, she saw the ghost couch his weapons; two hands, two swords simultaneously. It was a remarkable sight.

She did not look *Mor Xana* in the eye as she passed him. Between the goose charge and the sudden appearance of Fallstar she wondered whether he had noticed her arm muscles jump.

As she returned to her tent the Sull were stirring. Heart Fires were being stoked and fed, horses saddled, water hauled from the river. She was surprised when some Sull greeted her with short but not unwelcoming nods. It was confusing.

She was confused. It was a relief to slip inside her tent. She tied down the tent flap so that anyone seeking casual entry would know she wanted peace, and then dropped onto the bed and slept. She dreamed of a future where she was no longer alone.

Half a day passed before she woke. She called for food and water, relieved herself, washed, and then ate a fine meal of roast hare, bastard celery and wine. She was clearheaded now and decisions were easy to make. With some care she prepared herself, brushing her silver-gold hair so it shone and rubbing wine into her lips to make them red. Someone had thought to bring her a hand mirror and she angled it to view her face and body. Her reflection confirmed she had changed.

The ghost was waiting when she exited the tent. He trailed her as she crossed to the tent circle's Heart Fire. One of He Who Leads' servants was loading fresh pieces of heartwood onto the coals. She spoke to him.

"Tell Blackdragon the Reach wants to see him."

Nodding quickly several times, the Trenchlander set down his fuel basket and ran to do her bidding. He almost dove into the rayskin tent.

Ash waited a moment and then followed him. Now she had set this in motion she was eager to have it done.

She had made mistakes. The first was waiting upon a summons from Blackdragon. He had asked a question and told her to answer it when she was ready. By leaving it so long she was practically handing him an answer. If she was sure she could control herself wouldn't she have told him before now? What had made her think he would call her into his presence?

The second mistake was in not answering straightaway.

The rayskin canvas switched from green to blue in the late day sunlight. Edges of the tent caught air, whumping softly as they pulled against their ropes. After less than a minute the Trenchlander emerged and muttered something. He would not look her in the eye. Deciding she had been granted permission to enter, Ash ducked under the tent flap. The ghost followed.

Inside all was cool and dim. Khal Blackdragon was standing with such stillness that she did not see him at first. Again there was the shock of his coloring: iron skin and amber eyes. He looked so far from human he might have dropped from another world. The space around him was empty of adornment, with only a lamp to light the interior and carpets to soften the hard ground: Nothing more.

He spoke no greeting, and although she had been prepared for this she felt her resolve waver on the simple fact of having to speak first.

She made an effort. "I am sorry for your dead."

Blackdragon looked at her a long time. His attention made

her feel small and young. It set her in her place. The Sull had existed long before Man. They had lost more, seen more, learned the names of the real things to fear. She was a tiny part of that history. The Sull would continue with or without her.

"You know the clansman, Raif Sevrance?"

As always when Khal Blackdragon spoke, Ash had difficulty translating the words. Nothing in his tone or manner aided his listener's comprehension. The fact he had asked about Raif was so surprising Ash doubted her own ears.

Blackdragon waited. He was tall and lean, dressed in simple black skins. His pride was fierce but not quite all-consuming. It left enough space for fear.

Ash nodded.

"What kind of man is he?"

She thought about Raif, about the first time she'd seen him outside of Vaingate when he'd sent arrows through the gate's grille and into men's hearts. Later when they were alone on the journey to the Cavern of Black Ice, he had done everything he could to keep her safe. She recalled the deep brown, almost purple, color of Raif's eyes. It would have been easy to stay and accept his unwavering protection.

"He's a good man," Ash said softly. "He's lonely."

Khal Blackdragon's shoulders bowed as if they were accepting weight. He closed his eyes. When he opened them again his shoulders were once more upright and straight. "This Sull wishes some things had not happened."

Ash didn't understand what he meant, but she heard the regret in his voice. It made her sad for both Raif and the Sull.

"Did you harm him?" She was surprised at the sharpness of her voice.

Blackdragon did not react. When he spoke it was as if

she wasn't there. "I did not intervene. That was this Sull's mistake."

"Is he hurt?"

"He is alive and on my land."

The amethyst lamp that was set on the floor near the tent's central pole buzzed as if something had been caught inside it.

Knowing she had to speak and sensing Blackdragon's distraction might be to her advantage, Ash cleared her throat. "Fourteen days ago you asked me a question. I am here to answer it."

Blackdragon turned the full force of his attention toward her, the amber eyes flickering to life.

So much for an advantage. Ash met his gaze. "You asked if the Reach can control herself and I'm here to tell you I can."

It was a lie, but it arrived with so much force behind it that it sounded like truth. She would almost have believed it herself if she hadn't begun to reach earlier today by the river. Ash was counting on the fact that Blackdragon and his ghost did not know about that, did not know that she had already come close to losing control.

She held her head level as he inspected her. She was filled with purpose, and she hoped that he sensed the strength of it but not its true cause.

Khal Blackdragon, the leader of the Sull, watched the Reach. Time passed. Sunlight ceased hitting the rayskin canvas and the tent darkened. Scents of woodsmoke and cookery drifted from outside.

Finally Blackdragon spoke. "The Sull accept your word, Ash Mountain Born. Do not fail us."

I will, she knew instantly. *I will fail the Sull.*

She acknowledged his words with a deep and formal bow.

As she rose upright she said, "Lan Fallstar surprised me at the river this morning. I would wish it not to happen again."

"He will be sent away."

Ash exhaled. That was a large part of what she wanted.

Khal Blackdragon said, "You will not be harmed by the Sull."

As long as you keep your word. Ash heard what went unsaid. She nodded. He was He Who Leads and he had to do what he had to do. She was Ash Mountain Born, and there was a child growing inside her, and she had to do what she had to do.

Perhaps for a while their purposes could be joined.

She left him, proud and deceived in the darkness. Any shame she felt fell away as she walked through the warm night air.

She was pregnant. Keeping herself and her unborn child safe were more important than any contract with the Sull.

CHAPTER 38

Stripping Outer Bark

Watcher had two rules. Only bring down what he could eat and stay away from the Sull. They were good rules. They simplified his actions and made it possible to live a peaceful life.

He hunted for small game: wild turkey, opossum, ground squirrel, hare. When he needed fat he fished for salmon in one of the streams that forked from the big river. He wasn't a good fisherman and could spend half a day catching nothing, but he was learning. He had time.

He built and tested fish traps, whittling wood and knotting strips of hide to form lattices. While he waited to see if the traps would work he gathered plants, tender new leaves of dock, fiddlehead and chicory. Most of the time he ate them raw, folding them into his mouth and letting the sweet greenness rest on his tongue before he chewed them. Food tasted good. On the rare occasions he lit a fire and roasted his game, he relished the tender juices and crispy skin.

Most nights he slept out in the open. He made beds of spruce, balsam and cedar and fell asleep drawing their rich and soothing fragrances into his lungs. When it rained he raised the simplest shelters, lean-tos and bivouacs. The nights were cool but not cold. Even this far north, the snows had passed.

He seldom camped in the same place more than two nights. He did not question whether it was restlessness or caution. It felt right to be moving. The forest was large and contained many things; some were worth seeing, some worth avoiding. He left it at that.

He knew he was in Sull territory but saw no reason to leave. He had earned a right to be here. They had made him who he was.

They had created what they feared.

Most days Watcher put effort into avoiding them—their fires, their horse tracks, the stone circles where they erected their tents, their heavily used trails—but he would not be gentle if they tried to take him.

He no longer feared them. It was not possible to fear a people after watching so many of them die.

Reaching a fork in the trail, Watcher turned north. He was heading along a deer path through a section of forest that looked as if it had been thinned. Elderberries and bearberries were in bloom and bumblebees buzzed from plant to plant. Sun touched Watcher's face. His pack was heavy with the remains of the turkey he had killed and smoked last night, and that meant he would not have to hunt for two days. This pleased him. Later, when he'd settled on a place to camp, he might work on another fish trap. He had some ideas about modifying the design. He was pretty sure his last one had caught, and then released, a trout. Scales left on one of the interior posts had been his clue.

He grinned at his own stupidity, and words from another life sounded in his head.

Us Sevrances were never made to fish.

Watcher's heart leapt.

He continued walking, and after a while holding himself separate from the familiar voice, the memory faded. It was for the best.

No good would come from remembering his dead.

He spent the rest of the morning moving north, more or less following the course of a swift-running creek. Boulders on the creekbed made the water froth. He didn't think it would be a good place to test traps. He had an idea he might might whittle a pole, fix the head from one of the queen's arrows to the tip, see if he could he could spear some frogs. When he arrived at a small spill pond fed by the stream he thought he might as well stop and do a few things. There was a strip of dry bank on its north shore that seemed as good a place as any to spend the night.

It was his habit to prepare the camp early and then spend the rest of the day doing as he pleased. Before he left the Sull camp he had stripped the queen and her den mates of some belongings, and he now possessed a fine Sull hand knife. He used it to cut-and-strip spruce and cedar needles from nearby trees to form a bed. The trick was to use only the soft tips of the branches. He had woken up the first few nights with sticks in his back. Now he knew what he was doing, he worked quickly, raising a mound of soft needles above the bank.

Afterward he cleaned the sticky resin from the knife with a scrap of hareskin and some fat he'd pressed from the liver of the last salmon he'd caught. He would have preferred to use tung oil but it would do.

Later he sat on the edge of the water and whittled hardwood. It was almost warm so he took off his cloak—also

Sull—and rolled up his shirtsleeves. Scars from his many fights made his arms look like maps. They were healing, the skin dry, the edges paling to white. Looking at them, he knew he would never speak of the fight circle to anyone. He hoped it would pass into the area of his mind where memories floated away.

Finished with shaping the oak sucker into a spear shaft, he went to find some twine. Earlier he'd spotted a basswood by the oak. Now he retraced his steps downstream. The inner bark of basswood made good cordage and he needed something to bind the arrowhead to the pole.

He would never understand how the girl slipped into the camp while he was away. He had thought himself vigilant. He was wrong. He had thought himself prepared to deal with anything that happened to him.

He was wrong about that too.

The work of removing the outer bark was hard but not unpleasant. Some bit of a song came to him and he hummed as he cut and stripped the tree. Deciding it was a good policy to have extra cordage on hand, he took more than was needed to bind the spear. Arms full of basswood bark, he returned to the camp.

The girl was standing waist-deep in the water, washing her hair and face. She turned her head at his approach, acknowledging him with a single look, then returned to her task. Her long dark hair glinted with oil in the sunlight. The fine linen shift she was wearing was soaked and pressed against her skin.

As Watcher walked through the camp he noted the sturdy little pony pulling dandelions from the shore. He saw the boots, dress and wool stockings the girl had discarded to enter the water. He spied two saddlebags in a nearby sumac bush and decided that they, and he, shared something in common. All three had been inexpertly hidden.

Because there was nothing else to do, Watcher set down the load of bark. Although he had not planned on a fire, he set about building one from unusable pieces of bark, stripped cedar branches and discarded oak suckers. He tried, unsuccessfully, not to watch the girl as he worked.

She seemed in no hurry to leave the water. Arms stretched out, she walked deeper into the pond. Her hair floated behind her, fanning out on the surface. Watcher was dimly aware of the calm, strong beats of her heart.

He shredded inner bark for kindling. Using the Sull queen's shortbow and one of her arrows with the head removed, he drilled into a piece of oak. The oak was damp and he had to work the bow hard to generate heat. He raised some smoke, but when he threw kindling on the hot spot it didn't catch. As he repositioned the bow and arrow for a second attempt at firelighting, the girl spoke up from the water.

"There's a flint and striker in one of my packs. They're in the bushes."

He looked at her and could not think.

"Do you know who I am?" she asked, wading toward him.

He did and did not. It was no kind of answer so he remained silent.

"Mallia Argola," she said, emerging from the water. "I've come a long way to find you."

She was the most lovely thing he had ever seen. Her skin was the color of raw honey and her eyes were deeply, greenly brown. The wet linen shift revealed her round high breasts and the dark down between between her legs. Watcher set down the bow and went to her. She waited for him, sure of her own worth.

She smelled of spicy ferns. Her lips were soft; they opened quickly when he kissed them. The pond water drying on her skin was a shocking coolness that had to be penetrated to reach her warmth. Her breasts and buttocks filled his hands. When she pulled off her shift and showed herself to him he wept.

She was that alive and that beautiful.

They lay down on the bank. She bit his shoulder as he entered her and called out a name he had left behind.

Afterward they dozed under a fading sun as dragonflies skimmed the water. She woke him by taking his hand. "Come on," she said, smiling as she pulled him up. "Let's swim."

They ran into the water. It made him catch his breath. Diving, he went under. She didn't follow him down but swam to him when he surfaced. Wrapping her legs around his waist, she kissed him and laughed. "I'm so happy," she said.

He pressed her hard against his chest, feeling her softness and vitality and half her weight. When they returned to the shore they made love again.

He cooked for her later and she ate with appetite and appreciation, grinning and asking for more. He was delighted. To sit opposite her across the fire and watch light from the flames shimmer across her skin seemed like a gift. When she shivered, he brought her his cloak to keep her warm.

"This is beautiful," she said, running her fingers across the soft midnight-blue hide. "Is it Sull?"

"Yes." It might have been the first word he spoke to her.

"And the knife and bow? They're Sull too?"

He did not understand why this mattered.

Perhaps something in his face warned her off, for she said, "It's not important. We're here. We found each other."

Watcher knew he had not found her so said nothing.

Rising, she went to tend the pony. He used the time to feed the fire and reshape the cedar bed so it was wide enough for two. The stars were out and there was no moon. Far, far in the distance he was aware of a moon snake winding north. He didn't pay it any heed. It had sensed him. It would keep away.

The girl returned to the fire and brushed out tangles from her hair. "It took a long time to get here. I lost track of the days."

Watcher remembered marks scraped on a cage and then a stone wall. Her words could have been his own.

"Do you know how I found you?"

He shook his head.

Smiling softly she looked him in the eye. "It was *khodo*, the magic of my homeland." She raised her fist to her mouth and mimed biting it. "Tooth and hand. Do you remember?"

He did not.

"I bit you. I struck a claim." She was watching him carefully. He had nothing to say in response but this did not appear to worry her. "In Hanatta when a woman wants a man she bites his left hand. If there is no prior claim, *khodo* may occur. And then when the man and woman are parted for the first time the woman will know where he is." She shrugged. "It doesn't work the other way. It's women's magic. Very strong."

He stood and took her to the cedar bed. He understood from her words that she wanted him and that was enough. She kissed his face in the starlight, covering every part of it with tiny little brushes of her lips. They fell asleep.

He awakened before she did, and he was happy to lie on

the cedars with her warm, fragrant body next to his. When she stirred they made love. He wanted to crush her and keep them both in this moment.

Already he knew she had come to bring him back.

Still, he could not help himself. As he washed in the pond, he made plans. He would need to hunt more. He could live on small, lean game but it would not do for the girl. He would bring her deer, fat with spring grasses. And he would use their hides to make a tent. The pony meant they could carry more, and he wondered if he should chop some logs. It occurred to him the girl might have a hand ax in her pack. He turned to call her.

She was standing by the small pile of his possessions. She had drawn Loss. When she realized he was looking at her, she hesitated, froze and then raised her chin defiantly. The sword was so heavy, she had to rest its tip on the ground. "I wanted to look."

"Put it back," he told her.

He watched as she struggled to return the blade to a sheath that had not been made for it. Leaving the water, he went to help her.

"I'm not sorry," she said when he took the sword from her grip. "Anyone would be curious. It's the one, isn't it? The sword from Red Ice?"

He sheathed the sword and closed his eyes. He wished there was a way to stop hearing what she said.

"What happened to Addie Gunn?"

Her heart was four feet away and there was nothing but clear space around it. He could destroy it in less than an instant, make it stop. Aware that his hand muscles were twitching and afraid he would do her harm, he laid the sword on the grass and walked away. Did she not understand that the words that hurt most in the world were all names?

As he passed the campfire he picked up the bow and arrow case. He could not recall the last time he had wanted to hunt large game.

He moved east, crossing the creek upstream and heading deep into the woods. It was spring and the days were growing longer. Animals were on the move. A lynx was padding through the trees on the scent of a newborn fawn. Pack wolves to the north were idly tagging a moose, and a fox was returning to her set with something still alive in her jaw for her kits. Watcher kept moving. He had perceived a powerful deer heart to the north and hoped it might be a stag.

It was. Watcher stalked it for hours through pine and hardwoods. The Sull bow did not have great range so he had to get close. For the final six hundred paces he was belly-down in the pine needles, bow parallel to the ground, drawn and ready. The stag was a tawny red color and its antlers formed an eight-foot spread. Its heart pumped blood around its body at a swift and elevated rate. It suspected the danger. Its head came up as Watcher angled the bow. It leapt into motion, but Watcher had anticipated the movement. He claimed the heart.

He ate part of the liver while it was still warm. While the carcass was draining he made a travois from spruce saplings, cutting and weaving the wood. It was good, hard work but he did not enjoy it. When the stag carcass was loaded and secure, he dragged it back to the camp.

It weighed twenty stone and took half a day.

Sweating and weary he approached the camp. The girl came tearing toward him, her face streaked with tears.

Dropping the poles of the travois, he waited for her to come. She was shaking as she fell into his arms, breathlessly murmuring his old name. "I was so frightened. I thought you'd gone."

He wondered what had happened to her magic. Had she said it worked only once?

She kissed his neck and he felt her tears against his skin. "I'm sorry I unsheathed the sword. Forgive me."

Taking her by both shoulders, he set her a foot away from him so he could look at her. Her eyes were red and her skin had the blotchy look of someone who had been crying for some time. A little hiccup made her entire body jerk.

"I love you," she told him.

He did not understand why. Because it was the only thing that was important, he said, "Why have you come?"

She was beautiful and clever and he was not sure he expected the truth from her.

"We need you. You can't just live in the woods and forget about us. You have to come back and help us fight." Watcher let her go and she stood, breathing hard in front of him. "You promised. You spoke an oath."

Watcher knew that oaths did not matter. They were words; they could not bind a life. He did not tell her because she was young and almost sincere, and the hard truths you learned for yourself.

He looked over her shoulder at the little camp. The bed, the fire, the trail already worn between the camp and the water. This was a life worth living, a quiet, self-reliant life. He wanted to see the woods in summer. He wanted to lie in long grass and bake in the sun. He did not want to use the sword, didn't want even to look at it.

Why didn't you drop it in the big river, then, let the current sweep it to sea?

Watcher had no answer to that beyond, *It's mine.*

He returned his attention to the girl and decided it did not matter if she came of her own free will or had been sent. He wished she had come sooner and said nothing, or later when he was . . . ready.

He smiled hard at that. Who would ever be ready to wield that sword for the purpose it was intended? Ready did not exist in such a world.

He did.

Do not forget who you are. Addie's final message, the one that had not been spoken, claimed space in Watcher's head. He heard love for himself and love for clan in it.

Watcher stood in the forest and listened to the cardinals call and forced himself not to wish for another life.

This one would do. He would reclaim it.

At dawn the next day they were on the move.

EPILOGUE
The Steps to God

You could not climb the Steps to God in a dog cart. The mountains men stubbornly called the Coastal Ranges were too high and treacherous for sleds. Glaciers and crevasses ate anything with two runners or four legs. And just because they could wait years for a meal didn't mean you should forget and tempt them with something tasty like nine dogs and a loaded sled. Fools had been dying that way for centuries, dragged down into great holes in the ice with all their possessions plummeting around them along with their own good sense.

Sadaluk No Ears, Listener of the Ice Trappers, wasn't about to fall into that trap. He and Nolo had gone north instead of east, along the great ice ledges of the continent, across the Bay of Auks, the wastes of the Wrecking Sea and the Bay of Whales. Others lived here, not Trappers, but men and women who had the old dark blood in their veins and knew how to exist in the bear days of winter when the sun barely cracked the horizon and the skies were so empty they robbed your breath, warmth and life in that order if you spent too long looking up.

Winter was done here, though, and the hare days of spring had begun. The sun spent hours in the southern sky, giving off a brilliant white light, but it melted only a small portion of the ice. Travel was harder because of it, for ice-melts were fickle things and if you thought you could predict their location, length and depth you were wrong. Nolo had good eyes but he still had much to learn. Sadaluk had little to learn but poor eyes. Together they managed. They spotted telltale slicks above the ice and the warning darkness of water below it. They sniffed for salt and the green scent of multiplying algae. Any Ice Trapper worth his sealskins knew it wasn't sufficient to look and smell, but Sadaluk's days of listening for weaknesses in the ice—cracks, whirrs, soft plops and even softer ticks— were gone and would never return.

Nolo listened, but it wasn't the same.

Sadaluk was glad when they reached the Lake of Lost Men and could turn east. The inland sea was shrouded in mist and the sun rarely touched it. Even if it had, the Listener did not think there was enough power in the heavens to melt these frozen waters. The ice was old here and it had sunk its taproots deep. It made its own weather and dictated the length of its own days. Sadaluk had gone on a journey once, traveling south and east to meet people who shared interests with the Ice Trappers and to see something of the world for himself. What struck him was people's misconceptions about frozen lakes. They thought them as smooth as glass, imagined that Sadaluk could climb onto his sled and skate into the sunset with barely a push from his dogs. "It is rock," he had told them impatiently. "Ice makes cliffs and boulders."

He did not think they believed him. Either that or his

language skills had not been up to the task. He would have liked to have shown them the Lake of Lost Men and said, "See. Here ice and land behave the same."

The lake was tough going and there were many days where he and Nolo had to carry the sled. You'd think the dogs would be grateful for the rest, yet they wasted their energy scrapping with one another with such fierce relentlessness that Sadaluk had to break up the fights. He was not gentle with his stick. You could not afford to be, this far north.

No one lived east of the Bay of Whales. The world was empty here. Two men and nine dogs did not fill even its smallest cracks.

It took them thirty days to traverse the lake. One night before they reached the eastern shore, Sadaluk had looked at the dogs and the remaining supply of frozen seal meat and perceived a shortfall. No Ice Trapper would keep a dog alive at a human's expense, yet Nolo had argued for only a partial culling. He bit off his gloves and held out four fingers and wagged his head toward the sled. *Who will pull it?*

Sadaluk had frowned until Nolo held out his thumb.

They had four dogs now. Nolo had modified the sled so that it wasn't much bigger than a child's toy. Both he and Sadaluk worked it each day, pushing or pulling as the frozen waste rose and fell.

Every day after they left the lake, Sadaluk woke in the morning and asked himself, *Am I in the Want?*

He had never entered the great white desert at the heart of the continent. He was an old man. What did he know?

The river they took east from the lake narrowed and branched and eventually failed. Nolo broke down the sled and used the runners to make stiff backpacks for himself,

Sadaluk and the remaining dogs. The dogs, not realizing their own luck, fought the packs, yanking their heads to bite at them, and dragging themselves belly-up along the ground. They were sled dogs, not carrier dogs. The Listener could not fault them.

Nolo slaughtered them and cached the meat. Sadaluk was not a man given to sadness, but the sight of Nolo building a pyramid of stone to mark the cache site gave him pause.

He did not think either of them would be coming back.

The Listener did not say anything—what good would be done?—but he did spare a thought for Nolo's young wife, Sila. He thought about all the people he himself had left behind. He recalled the time many years ago when a great ledge of ice had sheared from the sea and slammed into the village. No one had seen it coming. No one had imagined such a thing could happen.

Yet the ice had always been there in plain sight.

Sadaluk knew that from now on he must be the one to watch the ice. When it moved, when it broke open, he had to try and block it. The white bear had bound him to this task. Could one man do such a thing, halt a force of pure destruction?

The Listener did not know. But one man—*two* men—were better than none and that was why he had undertaken this journey.

Loading their possessions on their backs, they left the cache site and hiked through a land of frozen, mounded gravel and dwarf trees. The sun moved exactly as it was supposed to, keeping to the south, and they did not realize they had entered the Great Want until the stars went missing that night.

Sadaluk No Ears, son of Odo Many Fish, heard the sound

of extinction in their absence. He stayed awake, listening, and at dawn he got his answer.

Soon.

He woke Nolo and they headed Want-east.

extras

about the author

J. V. Jones was born in Liverpool in 1963. When she was twenty, she began working for a record label and was part of the Liverpool music scene of the early eighties. She later moved to San Diego, California, where she ran an export business for several years and was the marketing director for an interactive software company. Her interests include cooking, gardening, reading, playing RPGs, watching old black-and-white movies, and pottering around the house.

Find out more about J. V. Jones and other Orbit authors by registering for the free monthly newsletter at www.orbitbooks.net

CHAPTER ONE

Vérella

A small boy clambered from a cellar wall into an alley. He picked his way through the trash along the wall to a nearby street, walked quickly to the next turning, went left, then right. The street widened a little;

the people he passed wore warmer clothes. He ducked into an alcove and pulled off the ragged jacket that had concealed his own unpatched shirt and tunic, folded the ragged one into a tidy bundle, and tucked it under his arm. Now he moved at a steady jog into the wealthier part of the city, nearer the palace. Finally he turned in to a gap between buildings, found the trapdoor he sought, and went belowground again.

In the cellar of a tall house within a few minutes of the palace gates, he gave a coded knock. A hard-faced man with a spiked billet opened the door. "What d'you want, rat?" the man asked.

"For Duke Verrakai's hand only," the boy said. "From the Horned Chain."

"I'll take him," another man said, stepping out of looming shadows. He wore the red and black of Liart, and the horned chain was about his neck. "Come, boy."

Shaking with fear, the boy followed, up stairs and along a corridor, to a room where another man, in Verrakai blue and silver, sat writing at a table by a fire.

"I am Duke Verrakai. You have a message for me: give it."

The boy seemed to choke, and then, in a deep voice not his own, spoke the words Liart's priest had bade him say. "The man is free, and his companions; the paladin is ours. Without her aid, he can be taken. He must not reach Lyonya alive."

"He will not," Duke Verrakai said. "Is there more?" The boy dug into his tunic and pulled out a folded paper; Verrakai took it and read it. "Well," he said, with a glance at the man in red and black. "It seems we must return this boy with our answer." He wrote on the reverse of the message, folded it, and handed it to the boy. "Go the way you came, swiftly."

Less than a half-glass later, a man in Verrakai blue rode out the south gates of Vérella and turned east on the river road. Later, after the turn of night, Kieri Phelan, newly revealed king of Lyonya, also rode through the gates, with an escort of the Royal Guard.

Duke's Stronghold, North Marches, seven days later

Jandelir Arcolin, senior captain of Duke Phelan's Company, rested his forearms on the top of the stronghold walls, where he had the best view to the south. On one side of the road to Duke's East, Stammel was putting his own cohort through an intricate marching drill. On the other, the junior sergeant of the recruit cohort supervised a sword drill with wooden blades. Beyond, the trees along the stream showed the first soft golds and oranges of ripening buds, though it would be hands of days yet before the fruit trees bloomed. Old snow still lay knee-deep against the north wall.

He heard steps behind him, and turned. Cracolnya, captain of the mixed cohort, came up onto the walkway with him.

"Are you putting down roots up here?" he asked.

Arcolin shook his head. "Hoping for a courier. We should have heard something by now. At least the weather's lifted. Though not for long." He tipped his head to the northwest, where a line of dark clouds just showed over the hills.

"Your worry won't bring the Duke faster," Cracolnya said. He turned his back on the view south and leaned against the parapet. "I wonder what we'll do this year."

"I don't know." Arcolin glanced down at the courtyard below, to be sure their inquisitive visitors, merchant-agents from Vonja, weren't in earshot. "He said not to take any contracts until he got back; I suggested they go to Vérella and talk to him, but they were afraid of missing him on the way."

"What are they offering?"

"A one-cohort contract to protect farmlands and roads from brigands. I told them we'd need two for that—"

"At least. Better the whole Company, or you're without reliable archery. Or were they planning to assign their militia to help?"

"No. From what they said, they disbanded half the militia. Trade's down. But what do you think the Council will say? With the trouble this past winter, the Duke can't say it's entirely safe here. Yet—we have to do something. This land won't support so many soldiers year-round."

Cracolnya leaned over the parapet, watching the recruit cohort. "We've got to do something with those recruits, too. They signed up to fight, and all we've done with them is train . . . and he's taken their final oaths: they'll be due regular pay soon."

"He'll think of something." Arcolin looked again at the line of clouds along the western horizon. Buds or no buds, another winter storm was coming. "He always does. But if he doesn't come soon, we won't get the good quarters in Valdaire." He looked south again, sighing, then stiffened. "Someone's coming!"

A single horseman, carrying the Company pennant, moving fast on the road from Duke's East. Not the Duke, who would have an escort.

"Should I announce it, sir?" the sentry asked.

"No. It's just a messenger." Unfortunately. They needed the Duke. Arcolin turned and made his way down to the court-yard with Cracolnya at his heels.

"I'll tell the stable," Cracolnya said, turning away. Arcolin moved to the gate, where he could watch the messenger approach.

Whatever the message might be, it was urgent enough for the rider to keep his mount at a steady canter, trotting only the last few yards to the gate and then halting his mount to salute the sentry before riding in. Arcolin recognized Sef, a private in Dorrin's cohort.

"Captain," Sef said, after he dismounted and handed the reins to one of the recruits on stable duty. "I have urgent news."

"Into the barracks," Arcolin said. Through the opening to the Duke's courtyard, he could see the two merchants hurrying toward them, but merchants were not allowed in the barracks. He led the way, and turned in to the little room where the sergeants kept the cohort records and brewed sib on their own hearth. "What is it? Is the Duke coming? How far behind you is he?"

"No sir, he's not coming, and you won't believe—but I should give you this first." Sef took a message tube from his tunic and handed it over.

Arcolin glanced at the hearth. "See if there's any sib left, or brew yourself some; you've had a long ride. And if I know Stammel, he's got a roll hidden away somewhere."

"Thank you, sir." Sef turned to the hearth, stirred the fire, and dipped a can of water from the barrel, setting it to heat.

Arcolin unrolled the message. A smaller wrapped packet fell out; he put it aside. There, in the Duke's hand—with a postscript by Dorrin, he saw at a glance—he found what he had never imagined. Kieri Phelan revealed as the rightful king of Lyonya—Paksenarrion had discovered it, come to Tsaia to find him—Tammarion's sword had been his sword all along, elf-made for him, and it had declared him. Arcolin glanced at Sef, who was stirring roots and herbs into the can. "Did you see this yourself? Were you in Vérella with the Duke?"

"No, Captain. I was with the reserve troop. Captain Selfer come up from Vérella, him and the horse both near knackered, and said the best rider must go fast as could be to the stronghold." Sef swallowed. "He thought it would be only two days, maybe, but that fog came in. I couldn't go more than a foot pace, mostly leading the horse. It's taken me twice as long as it should have, three days and this morning."

"I'm not surprised," Arcolin said. "We had thick fog for days, up here; you did well, Sef." He read on, while Sef stirred the can of sib, struggling to make sense of what had happened. His mind snagged on Paksenarrion—once in his cohort. *I must go, and leave her in torment*, Kieri had written. *Otherwise her torment is meaningless. Yet it is a stain on my honor. You will rule in my stead until the Regency Council confirms a new lord. I recommended you, but do not know what they will do. This letter and my signet ring will prove your identity and authority.*

Arcolin unwrapped the smaller packet and found the Duke's ring. Not one of the copies he lent to his captains on occasion to do business for him, but the original, the one he himself wore.

Dorrin's postscript was brief. She was going with Kieri, on his orders; her cohort would follow. She feared more attacks on the Duke—scratched out to read *King*—on the road east. She did not know when she might return; it would depend upon his need.

Arcolin rolled the pages and slid them back into the tube.

"Well. You will have traveled ahead of any word of his passage to the east—" He tried to estimate where Kieri might be, where Dorrin might be, seven days on a road he himself had never traveled. Impossible.

"Right, Captain." Sef stirred the can again, sniffed it. "Want some sib, sir?"

"No thanks. Go ahead."

Sef took a mug down from the rack and poured one for himself as he talked. "Captain Selfer said Captain Dorrin expected his cohort to catch up with the Duke before the Lyonya border. Wish I was with them—" He took a swallow of hot sib.

"I'm—I must admit I'm shocked . . . amazed . . . I don't know what to think," Arcolin said. "Our Duke a king—all the rest—" Remembering Paks as a recruit, a novice . . . the steady, reliable soldier she'd become . . . why she left, and when . . . the rumors . . . and then her return. He squeezed his eyes hard against tears, at the thought of her in Liart's hands, shook his head, and looked again at Sef. "You've done very well, Sef. Go tell the cooks to give you a hot meal, and I'll get Stammel to find you a place to sleep undisturbed."

Sef saluted, then carefully rinsed the can and set it to dry before going out. Arcolin followed him, wondering if he'd have to explain to the Vonja agents before he found Stammel. Instead, Stammel met him at the gate. Arcolin smiled.

"Your good instincts again, Sergeant."

"My insatiable curiosity, Captain. News from the Duke could always be marching orders."

"It's strange news indeed, and I'm not sure what will happen now," Arcolin said. "The courier was Sef of Dorrin's cohort—he needs a quiet bed to sleep; he was three days in thick fog between here and the south border. I sent him to the mess hall."

"I'll see to it, Captain."

"I need to talk to the other captains before I spread the news," Arcolin said. "I can tell you this—nothing will be the same."

"It never is," Stammel said. "That's why we like it. Your leave, Captain."

"Go ahead," Arcolin said, thinking again how lucky he was to have Stammel as senior sergeant.

He found Cracolnya in the stables, talking fodder with the quartermaster.

"And I don't know where more hay's coming from, this time of year," the quartermaster said. "Nobody's got enough stored; it's not to be bought, not at any price, and I know the Duke wouldn't want us to take from the farmers' stock."

Arcolin made a motion with his head, and Cracolnya nodded. To the quartermaster he said, "A messenger's come from the Duke; maybe an order to move out—that would help."

"I hope so," the quartermaster said gloomily. He spat into a corner. "I can't be sure . . ."

Arcolin led the way down the aisle between rows of tie stalls to the box stalls at the end, empty now but for his and Cracolnya's mounts.

"What is it? You look—strange."

"I should. You must read it yourself." He handed over the message tube; Cracolnya opened it, unrolled the message, and started to read. Arcolin's roan ambler moved up to the front of the stall and nudged him; he rubbed the velvety muzzle absently while watching Cracolnya's face.

"I—I don't know what to think," Cracolnya said, when he'd finished. "He's a king? In Lyonya? How did that happen?"

"I don't know more than this."

"They have a king already," Cracolnya said. "What's he think about it?"

"You missed a bit," Arcolin said. "He stuck it in between lines. Their king died without an heir. Paks was there—that's where she went when she left here. She felt called to find the heir." He ran a hand over his head. "But—what do we do now? He wants troops out guarding the Pargunese border; he thinks they might use this as an excuse to attack."

"Scouts haven't said anything."

"No. And this about a contract. You know what he said before he went south; he expected to take the Company south. But only one cohort?" He shook his head. "You know the Vonjans. They'll want twice the work for half the pay."

"One cohort out, with pack mules, would ease the fodder situation," Cracolnya said. "Two would be better, if you can talk them into it."

"What about protection here, though?" Arcolin said. "He's worried about the Pargunese, and the south border. A cohort each way, plus mine in the south, will nearly empty the stronghold. And we'll have to use the recruits, until Dorrin comes back." However long that might be.

Cracolnya shrugged. "This recruit cohort's the best-trained we've ever had. They can garrison this; I can split mine between east and south. Or, the recruits can do their first real route march and take the southern end—we haven't had trouble with either of the neighboring domains, barring the odd thief, since Count Halar's father died."

"That's a good idea, about using the recruits to garrison

down there if needed," Arcolin said. "But first, I need to tell the Company about the Duke."

"Maybe we should wait until we hear from Chaya," Cracolnya said. "Just in case."

"In case—"

"He was attacked once. Suppose Verrakai raised a large force against him?"

"He's got Dorrin's cohort."

"He's got Dorrin's cohort on the way, but what if they don't get there in time? He could be killed. Something could go wrong in Lyonya."

"I don't—" Arcolin took two steps forward, turned, then took two steps back, avoiding the thought of Kieri Phelan dead. Instead, he said, "We have to tell the troops something—they have to know he's not coming back."

"He left it to you," Cracolnya said. "But if you want my advice—" Arcolin nodded. "Then," Cracolnya went on, "make us a contract, and tell the Company that, and then tell them what you've heard, that it's all we know."

"Ask the quartermaster how many beasts he can feed until spring grass," Arcolin said.

Cracolnya looked smug. "I already know. Twelve."

Arcolin looked down the rows of tie stalls, mostly full. "Better get moving, then." He left Cracolnya in the stable and headed back to the officers' quarters and offices.

The Vonja agents had retreated to the inner court, but came to meet him as he entered. "Have you heard from the Duke?" one began. Arcolin held up his hand.

"I have word from the Duke that I'm to make a one-cohort contract, subject to approval by the Council in Tsaia; he's reasonably sure they'll give it."

"But the Duke—is he coming?"

"He's . . . detained," Arcolin said. "But the messenger who arrived brought his word and seal."

"How soon can you leave? Today? Tomorrow?"

"Certainly not today. As the Duke himself is detained, I must visit the councils here, send couriers—" All at once the enormity of the changes ahead hit him, stunning him. Kieri Phelan had been the one constant in his life for years; he never thought that would end. He saw the concern on their faces, the uncertainty, and with his own uncertainty churning inside, it was too much. He bowed slightly. "Sirs, with this word from Duke Phelan, I have orders I must give; you must excuse me."

"Of course," the senior said. "I only meant, should we ourselves pack to ride today or tomorrow?"

"Not sooner than tomorrow, and probably the next day," Arcolin said. To his relief, he saw one of the house servants hovering in the doorway. To him, he called, "One less for meals; I'm riding to Duke's East and Duke's West; I'll eat there."

He felt like a fraud. As Kieri's senior captain, trusted and experienced, he knew how to do what he must do, but—he was not Kieri. He could not be Kieri. And to have this handed him, without being able to see Kieri, talk to him, ask questions, be sure . . . it was too much.

But Kieri trusted him. He had to do it.

Cracolnya was just coming from the stable as he neared it. "Well?"

"We'll split the recruit cohort tonight; I'm taking enough to fill out mine for a contract. I'll still have to get Regency Council approval, in Vérella. You'll command the remainder of the recruits and as many of your cohort as it takes to fill them out. You go east; Valichi will have to take the southern group until I can find him a junior captain—and you, too, for that matter."

"Val's not going to like campaign living," Cracolnya said, grinning. The recruit captain, oldest of them all, had talked of retirement all winter, and used the excuse of crowding in the stronghold to move into Duke's East after Midwinter Feast.

"He can have Kieri's tent," Arcolin said. "I'll take mine."

"Better take Kieri's yourself; you need to impress the Vonjans. All those southerners think bigger is better." Cracolnya, proponent of traveling light, had the smallest tent of any of the captains. "About supplies—"

"I can send back supplies from Vérella, after I've seen the bankers," Arcolin said. "You should have enough until then." He glanced at the sky, gauging the amount of daylight remaining. "I must go—I have to get to Duke's East—"

"Shall I tell Stammel?"

"My head! I need to do that first, of course. Thank you. Tell them to saddle the chestnut, will you?"

"Of course."

The tail end of his cohort was just entering the mess hall; Stammel, by the door, raised his brows at Arcolin, and Arcolin nodded. Stammel came to him.

"Captain?" Unasked questions danced in his tone.

"The Duke's not coming; we're going south. Usual route. One-cohort contract. We fill out with recruits. Captain Cracolnya will command here; he and Captain Valichi will patrol the east and south boundaries. I know you have more questions, but I must ride to Duke's East. We'll have a captains' conference tonight; join us then. How soon can we march?"

"Day after tomorrow, sir, if we get right to it. Unless it's an emergency, I'd like an extra day for balancing loads and the like. Road firm enough for wagons, do you think?"

"Talk to Sef. I'll be sending supplies back from Vérella, so if the road's good, we'll use them."

"Right, sir."

"Eat lunch first, Stammel."

"I always do, sir," Stammel said. It was an old jest; Arcolin felt better when he felt himself smiling again.

CHAPTER TWO

On the road to Duke's East, the chestnut pulled hard at first, but finally settled into a smooth canter that eased Arcolin's tension. It would be all right. He would do what the Duke wanted, even without the Duke there—he had done it before. He had the Duke's signet ring and the Duke's written permission to use his funds. Worry returned. What if the Crown didn't agree? What if they wanted to seize the Duke's property, land, and money?

What if the sky and land turned upside down and he fell off the road? He taunted himself, then slowed to an easy jog as he came into the town. Small children ran alongside, waving. He looked around, seeing Duke's East with a new eye.

Heribert Fontaine, the mayor, opened the door of his house as Arcolin rode up to it, and two boys stood ready to hold his horse. "News, I'll warrant—I saw the courier go by, not even stopping for a word."

"News indeed. I'll come in, if I may." Arcolin dismounted, tossing the reins to the boys. "Walk him around; don't let him just stand in this cold."

Fontaine held the door open and Arcolin came in. "There—left—the parlor."

It faced east; sun had left the windows, but the room still held a little of its warmth. A bowl of apples on the table scented the air. Arcolin pulled off his gloves and took a seat at the mayor's wave.

"You'd better read this," he said, handing over the Duke's message. "It's all I know."

Frowning, Fontaine read, his brow furrowed. Then he looked up. "The Duke . . . *our* Duke . . . is a king? Of . . . of Lyonya?"

"It would only surprise me more if it were Pargun," Arcolin said. "All I know is that he's taken Dorrin's cohort, and headed east on the river road."

"And the paladin? Paks?"

Arcolin shook his head. "I don't know any more than this. Nor did the courier. I would suppose she is dead; that must be what the Bloodlord priests intended."

"And he's told you to do whatever you think best. Gird's right arm! I know you're senior captain, but—does he mean take over the domain?"

"I don't know that, either. I've taken a one-cohort contract with the Vonjans. I know we're squeezing supplies up here."

"So you'll take . . . how many away?"

"One all the way to Aarenis, if the Crown approves; the other two in the domain but not here. One cohort, under Cracolnya, to patrol the Pargunese border; one south, under Valichi, in case any ambitious lordling tries to move in. And I'll be sending supplies from Vérella for the troops."

"That will ease things," Fontaine said. "And I don't think we'll have more trouble up here for a while. Have you told Valichi? And will you be sending out recruit teams this year? When are you leaving?"

Arcolin held up his hands. "No, I haven't told Val—he's here in town somewhere. I'd like you to send someone to him, tell him to come up to the stronghold today—we must have a captains' conference. As for recruiting—not until the domain itself is settled. As for leaving—as soon as we can. I hope as soon as day after tomorrow. And now I must leave; I need to get to Duke's West today as well."

"And you're in a hurry. Let me have m'wife fix you a stuffed roll for the ride, if you won't sit down to eat."

"I can't stay, but I'd thank you for a roll . . . anything . . ."

In a few minutes, Arcolin was mounted again; he set his horse's nose to the west breeze and eyed the rising dark cloud there with apprehension. His horse was willing now to canter quietly; Arcolin unwrapped the stuffed roll—hot fried ham, onions, and chopped winter greens—and took a bite. Lucky mayor, he thought as he finished, to have such a cook in the household. A second roll nestled in his tunic, in case of need.

The ride to Duke's West took most of the afternoon as the cold breeze stiffened and the cloud rose higher, soaking up all the light. Before he arrived, he saw the glow of light through windows brighter than the day outside. A sentry called challenge; Arcolin halted his horse.

"Captain Arcolin of the stronghold to speak to the mayor," he said. He dismounted, stiffer from the cold than he'd expected. "It's gone dark early this evening."

"Storm coming, Captain. Sorry to question you—"

"No, that's right, after the mess we had before. But I need to speak to the mayor; we've had word from the Duke."

"I can take your horse, Captain. We'll find a place out of this wind. You're staying the night—"

"No, I mustn't." Now others had come out in the cold, windy near-dark, some with torches, and Duke's West's mayor,

Alwyn Foretson, hurried over. Younger than Mayor Fontaine, he'd lost a hand on campaign.

"What's wrong, Captain? Attack?"

"No, not that. Word from the Duke. If we could go to your house—"

"Of course." Foretson led the way. Duke's West, newer than Duke's East, was a little smaller, but the mayor's house was just as comfortable. Rich cooking smells permeated the front rooms. "You'll eat with us," Foretson said, as if there were no doubt.

"Gladly," Arcolin said. "Do we have time to get the business over with?"

"Yes. I told Melyin to hold the dumplings when I left the house and that's another half-glass."

"Good. You should read this—it came from the Duke by courier this morning and I know nothing more."

Foretson raised an eyebrow, took the message, and went into the passage, coming back with a four-stick candleholder. "She put the dumplings in and she's keeping the children in the kitchen. Let's see now—" His brows went up his forehead as he read. Arcolin walked about, stretching after the ride. The room had a fireplace, but no fire had been laid; a blanket covered the opening. He grimaced; the stronghold had asked the villages for more wood only the week before. Foretson looked up at last. "King?"

"So it says," Arcolin said.

"I served under the man fifteen years until I lost my hand. I didn't know he was royal bred." Foretson sounded as if that were a personal insult.

"Nor I," said Arcolin, who had been with the Duke longer, as they both knew.

"Well-bred, certainly," Foretson went on. "But a king?"

Arcolin said nothing. The mayor's wife came to the door, looked in, shrugged, and went back to the kitchen.

"This is going to cause . . . problems."

"I think so," Arcolin said. "But I have no answers. I do have a one-cohort contract with Vonja, and as the Duke requested, I'm moving Cracolnya's cohort and the recruits to the east and south."

"Think the Crown will accept that?"

"I'll find out," Arcolin said, trying to sound cheerful. "I don't know who the Crown will transfer the domain to—"

"Oh, gods! I didn't think of that one. We could end up belonging to Verrakai or someone like that—" He gave Arcolin a searching glance. "They should give it to you."

"They won't," Arcolin said. "I'm not a native; I have no family behind me—"

Foretson cocked his head. "Do you want it?"

Did he? Arcolin thought for a long moment; the mayor said nothing. "I don't know," he said finally. "I never considered it . . . I never thought beyond . . ."

"Well, you'd best think now. There's lords enough will want it, want it enough to squabble over it. Verrakai and Marrakai both, I shouldn't wonder, and woe to us if Verrakai gets it. Marrakai wouldn't be so bad, except his own land's so far west. No overlap. We'd do better with you, Captain, though without an heir—"

"Aye. And no one's offered it yet, and I have a cohort to take south. And I must eat and go, I'm afraid."

"Is this to be kept secret? And if so, until when?"

"It can't be," Arcolin said. "People must know; they deserve to know. But they need to know even more: what's coming next, and that I can't tell them. I should learn more in Vérella, and when I do I'll send word."

"I hope he's safe in Lyonya," Foretson said. Then, shaking his head: "Royal-bred and half-elf, and I never saw it . . . what a fool I must be."

"If you, then all of us," Arcolin said. "Including himself, for that matter. He had more chance to figure it out than any of us."

Foretson laughed. "I suppose . . . but I'm not calling the Fox a fool, even with him this far away and not coming back."

Not coming back. Arcolin shivered, but supper was hot and tasty, and he mounted again determined to do his best for Phelan's land and people, whatever that might turn out to be.

He refused the mayor's offer of an escort back to the stronghold, and rode away in an icy drizzle that stung his face. It would be sleet or snow by morning; he hoped it would blow over before they marched away in it.

Halfway back to the stronghold, he met a squad with torches; Cracolnya had sent them. Soon enough he was safely inside, cold and wet but in a seat by the fire, upstairs in the Duke's study. Valichi was there, with his personal pack; he had even brought his armor. Stammel, waiting for Arcolin by the inner gate, had followed him in and up the stairs. Arcolin waved him to a seat as well.

"Fontaine told me," Valichi said. "Though I find it hard to believe."

"So do we all," Arcolin said, pulling off his wet boots. Servants had put dry clothes to warm by the fire; he stripped off his wet ones and dressed as they talked.

"How'd the village mayors take it?" Cracolnya asked.

"Stunned. Confused. Glad we're taking hungry mouths

away, but worried about the future. Who the Crown will give the land to."

"It could be you," Valichi said. "You were here from the beginning."

"I don't think so." But he could not help imagining it, seeing familiar things, familiar people, in a new way. He pushed that aside. "And anyway, I've got that contract to fulfill. I can't start off by breaking one."

"You need the Crown's consent, remember—if you don't get it, the merchants will understand."

"That doesn't produce gold or grain," Arcolin said. He yawned. "Believe me, I will argue hard if they refuse; I will not toss away what Kieri worked so many years to build. How's the preparation going, Sergeant?"

"On target, sir. All the farriery finished today. The smiths say they'll have the last of the weapons and repairs done by supper tomorrow. We'll be ready to march day after tomorrow, as far as the fighting troop's concerned. And Sef says the road's no worse than usual, this time of year."

"We split the recruits already," Cracolnya said. "Your cohort's up to the usual start-of-season strength. I didn't know what staff you'd want to take along for just one cohort—you'll want a smith, I'm sure, but will you want a quartermaster? Clerk? Teamsters and wagons?"

"Teamsters and wagons, yes," Arcolin said. "Most will come back here with replacement supplies. Kolya's still in Vérella; she can supervise that. A smith for certain, and one of the surgeons. Stammel, who in the cohort might make a quartermaster?"

"Devlin, sir, if he weren't my junior sergeant. Don't see how he could do both."

"Agreed," Arcolin said. "Others?"

Stammel shook his head. "No, sir."

"We need someone," Arcolin said. "One of the quartermaster's assistants, then; we need him here. Stammel, talk to the quartermaster— I'm inclined to think Maia, but leave it to him." Arcolin yawned, then stretched. "It's time we went to bed, captains. Tomorrow will be a full day."

They rose; Arcolin gathered up his wet things and carried them to the kitchen, to be dried by the cooking hearth. Back upstairs, he went into Kieri's office and looked around.

Kieri had asked for nothing from this office, from the stronghold. Things he had bought in Aarenis or Vérella: the striped rug Tammarion had chosen, a carved box with a running fox on its lid, a favorite whetstone always placed on the left of the great desk, a candleholder of translucent pink stone that glowed with light when the candle was lit, the chest in which—as Arcolin knew—Kieri's dead wife's armor and the children's daggers were wrapped in Tammarion's troth dress. Kieri had asked for none of these.

Not ever to return. Arcolin forced himself to take a deep breath and consider what records he might need, for either a contract or . . . that which he did not want to consider.

Tired as he was, he sat up late, making notes, packing away those records he would not take in the chest where they belonged, packing the ones he would need into waterproof bags. The room seemed emptier than it should, emptier than it ever had.

"I'm trying," he muttered to himself, then shook his head and went to bed.